Picture Me Rollin'

Picture Me Rollin'

BLACK ARTEMIS

NEW AMERICAN LIBRARY

New American Library
Published by New American Library, a division of Penguin Group (USA) Inc., 375 Hudson Street, New York, New York 10014, USA Penguin Group (Canada), 10 Alcorn Avenue, Toronto, Ontario M4V 3B2, Canada (a division of Pearson Penguin Canada Inc.) Penguin Books Ltd., 80 Strand, London WC2R 0RL, England Penguin Ireland, 25 St. Stephen's Green, Dublin 2, Ireland (a division of Penguin Books, Ltd.) Penguin Group (Australia), 250 Camberwell Road, Camberwell, Victoria 3124, Australia (a division of Pearson Australia Group Pty. Ltd.) Penguin Books India Pvt. Ltd., 11 Community Centre, Panchsheel Park, New Delhi - 110 017, India Penguin Group (NZ), cnr Airborne and Rosedale Roads, Albany, Auckland 1310, New Zealand (a division of Pearson New Zealand Ltd.) Penguin Books (South Africa) (Pty.) Ltd., 24 Sturdee Avenue, Rosebank, Johannesburg 2196, South Africa

Penguin Books Ltd., Registered Offices:
80 Strand, London WC2R 0RL, England

First published by New American Library,
a division of Penguin Group (USA) Inc.

First Printing, June 2005
10 9 8 7 6 5 4 3 2 1

LIBRARY OF CONGRESS CATALOGING-IN-PUBLICATION DATA:

Black Artemis.
Picture me rollin' / Black Artemis.
p. cm.
ISBN 0-451-21513-3 (trade pbk.)
1. Puerto Rican women—Fiction. 2. Bronx (New York, N.Y.)—Fiction. 3. Ex-convicts—Fiction. 4. Sisters—Fiction. I. Title.
PS3602.L24P53 2005
813'.6—dc22 2005000002

Set in Horley Old Style / Designed by Ginger Legato

Printed in the United States of America

To all Warrior Womyn,
Realized and Emerging,
Alive and Transcended,
Celebrated and Unsung
And the Men Fierce Enough to Love Them

Acknowledgments

Thanks to:

My family of origin for their unwavering support. As you realized, the first book was only the beginning of the blessed madness. Thank you for loving me through the ebbs and flows.

My second family, at Chica Luna—Auro, Sone Boogs, MariDiosa, Sonia, and especially E-Fierce. You got next, ma! Mad love and appreciation to the next generation of Chica Lunatics—Ana, Karly, Elvira, Jen, Natalie and Rafaela, and of course, baby girl Angelique. Thank you for all your gifts, especially the poetry. A.I.R.E. has arrived (as in breath of fresh so get it right!).

Alexander Ramirez, *porque su casa es mi refugio y lo aprecio muchisimo.*

Linda Nieves-Powell, Rosemary Rivera, Marilyn Torres and Aleeka Wade—so many times your own work or words helped me get through mine.

The Black Artemis Street Team—Kelvin Bonilla, David Ferreira, Jonathan Tirado and Giselle Martinez. You always represented me lovely. I hope to continue to be worthy.

Lillian Jimenez, Blanca Vasquez and Iris Morales for being the Maites of my life.

Joy of Resistance—especially Fran Luck—for continuing to fight the good feminist fight on the radio waves so that I could continue do the same on the page.

Gwendolyn Pough, for your time, insight and support even when attempting to complete and promote your own, important work.

Angie Pickett-Henderson. By the time this book hits the streets, I will owe you a thousand more thanks.

Shirley and Edgardo at SomosArte for your friendship and integrity.

Johanna Castillo, our partnership may have changed but the magic continues.

Toni Blackmon, Deepa Fernandes, Nakia Booth, Marcela Landres, Desi Moreno-Penson, Lisa Tolliver, Felicia Pride, Martha Diaz, Aurora Flores, Sandra Gúzman and Judith Escalona *y a todos mis hermanas* in this fascinating arena for having my back.

The Hispanic Association of the Arts, El Puente, the Caribbean Cultural Center, Imix Bookstore, the New York International Latino Film Festival, Llegamos, the Bronx Academy of Arts and Dance, and the Bronx Museum of the Arts and all the other institutions who never thought twice about supporting an Afro-Latina sister writing hip hop fiction.

Juan Caceres, Ka'aramuu Kush, Kenji Jasper, Gary Santana, Billy Wimsatt, Jeff Chang, Gary Phillips, Neil Porter, Karl Franklin, the Omicron chapter of Sigma Lambda Beta International. You are proof that indeed there are brothers for the sisters.

Cinque, Charlie, Bruce and all the Playahatas for setting the bar high for the rest of us in the hip hop zone.

To my African-American readers and reviewers who supported my first novel and will ride with me through this one especially the APOOO Book Club, the Rawsistaza Reviewers, the Mahogany Book and, of course Readincolor. You will never regret calling me sister.

Last but never least, my phenomenal team at the New American Library, especially Kara Cesare. As often as I tested your patience, never once did you lose confidence in me. I know I am a better writer because of it.

For anyone that time and memory may have caused me to overlook. You have my permission to reach out and say, "What's up with that?" I will be sure to respond with a sincere apology and overdue thanks.

IN MEMORIAM

Tupac Amaru Shakur

Prologue

Esperanza shuffled as she lugged the books over to the checkout desk. She lobbed them onto the counter, then bent over to inspect the dust at the hem of her orange jumpsuit. Isoke rose from her computer station behind the counter.

"Hey, Oshodi," said Esperanza. Most prison officials insisted on calling Isoke by her government name, Debra Cherise Glover. Ever since that Fourth of July incident, Esperanza addressed Isoke by her New Afrikan name to express solidarity with her cellie. Except for the hard rocks with something to prove and the new jills who had no idea who Isoke Oshodi was, all the other inmates soon followed Esperanza's lead.

"Sister Cepeda. Cleaning out the cell before you rejoin the so-called free world, are you?" Isoke said. With a weathered hand she brushed back her graying dreads, then pulled the returned books toward her. She opened the first book, picked up the computer wand, and swiped it across the bar code on the inside cover.

"You could say that."

Isoke placed the first book onto a cart behind her and opened the second one. She skimmed the title and sneered. "You actually read all these?"

Esperanza peeked at the title. "Yeah. Finished it, too," she said, pointing to Machiavelli's *The Prince*. "But I just wasn't feelin' it. Jesus and his boys be saying shit like that all the time, but they must've gotten it from watching *Scarface*. Them niggas are illiterate."

She said it to make Isoke laugh, but the reaction on her face warned of an impending lecture. "Esperanza, I have to tell you time and again . . ."

". . . that no matter how often young Blacks use them as terms of endearment today, the words *nigger, nigga,* and even *Negro* are laden with the white supremacist history of dehumanization."

Esperanza's recitation finally earned her a smile from her elder. "So you do listen to me from time to time." Then Isoke picked up and waved *The Art of War* at Esperanza before adding it to the cart. "Did you finish this, too?" Esperanza shook her head, confused as to whether she should be proud or embarrassed. "When you came in here a year ago, you couldn't wait to read this."

Esperanza shrugged. "I've changed."

"Have you?" asked Isoke, her voice loaded with daring.

Esperanza and Isoke had argued about this many times. After lights-out, in strained whispers, or during work detail, shouting over the hum of the sewing machines, they bantered almost every day about Esperanza's future. Having made a choice but not wanting to hurt Isoke's feelings, Esperanza played ignorant. "How does a person come to a place like this and not change?"

"But is your change for the better?" Isoke issued her challenge in her usual motherly tone, and her eyes narrowed as if to see through Esperanza's soul. "Are you going to be a thug, Esperanza, or a revolutionary?" she asked. "Because I'm afraid that brother Tupac was wrong. Thug life is not the new Black Power. It makes no sense to rage against the machine without purpose or principle. You cannot be both a gangsta and a soldier, Esperanza, so you must choose."

Esperanza sighed. *Neither, 'cause either way I'll end up back in this muthafucka, or dead.* "All I know is that I'm never coming back here."

Isoke looked over her shoulder at the prison librarian reordering books in the stacks several yards behind the counter. She picked up *The Art of War* and tossed it to the side. Then she reached below the counter and emerged with another stack of books.

She leaned forward and whispered, "Take these."

Esperanza shook her head. Those books again. "Maybe I shouldn't. I mean, I ain't got but a week. I'm not gonna read all that by then, so why . . . ?" Ever since Dulce's first visit, when she had brought Esperanza her Tupac books, Isoke had nagged her to read all this political stuff. *Tupac was the son of a Black Panther,* she argued. *He had a political analysis, a social vision. He read with the intention to liberate.* Esperanza promised Isoke she would read the books but never did, except for the biography of Afeni Shakur that Isoke's son managed to sneak into the prison in a care package.

As much as she appreciated Isoke's desire to take her under her wing, Esperanza felt the time when such words might have mattered had passed long before she entered Bedford Hills.

Isoke gave the books a decisive shove toward Esperanza. "Take 'em with you. Just promise to return them when you're done so another sister can benefit from the wisdom within those pages. Do it for an old lady who's never going home."

Esperanza read the cover of the first title, a glossy textbook called *Stenography in Thirty Days.* "Oh." Probably a donation from Isoke's political group in Bed-Stuy, which did everything from monitoring beat cops to prevent harassment and brutality to offering tutorial programs with a heavy dose of Black cultural and political history. "OK." Esperanza accepted the stack. No sense in insulting Isoke's pride seven days before going home, and certainly not after all the ways she had looked out for Esperanza over the past twelve months.

Isoke had become much more than her cellie, commanding Esperanza's respect from the start. Even though prison regulations stated that inmates over forty automatically received the bottom bunk, Isoke insisted that Esperanza take it. *I like the physical challenge of climbing in and out of that top bunk,* she said. *It reminds me that I'm still alive no matter what they do to me.* In those first critical weeks, how many jealous bitches left her alone out of deference to Isoke? How much harder Esperanza's time might have been had Isoke not reminded her of her rights. How much longer the year would have dragged without Isoke's preaching, debating, and storytelling. And as if Esperanza had so much to do, she had read only one of the books that Isoke had recommended. When she had told Isoke the circumstances of her arrest, she said, "Sounds like Afeni's story," and suggested that Esperanza read her autobiography. Similarities or no similarities, Esperanza might not have bothered had Isoke not told her that Afeni was Tupac's mother. As much as she ached to go home to Dulce's home cooking and even her nagging, it scared Esperanza how much she would miss Isoke.

She also felt guilty over her release, while Isoke faced another sham parole hearing. That first day when Isoke asked her what she was in for and how long, Esperanza had said, "Got caught out there with a gun, and they gave me twelve months. That's mandatory in New York. You?"

"Got caught out there with a conscience," said Isoke with a bittersweet smile. "And they gave me life. That's mandatory in the U.S."

Under the weight of the new books, Esperanza shuffled down the gloomy corridor past fellow inmates on their knees buffing the floors.

When she reached her empty cell, she yelled to the guard, "seven-two-five-seven-one-three."

The bars pulled open with a large buzz, and Esperanza stepped inside her cell. She watched as the bars buzzed again, then clanked shut behind her. Only a month into her stint she had learned to block out that sound. But today she watched and listened. In a week Esperanza would never have to hear this hellish noise again. Something about Isoke's words made her want to seal this sound in her memory lest she have to return to prison to remember it.

Esperanza laid the stack of books on the floor next to the cardboard box provided for her belongings. She reached into it for her notebook and pen, grabbed the textbook, and climbed into the bottom bunk. Esperanza paused to reminisce about the many nights she had lain awake thinking about her mother, Brenda, wondering if she was doing the same thing in California. To distract herself from the pang in her chest, she cracked open the crisp textbook cover. Flipping through the coarse pages, she discovered lines upon lines of text. No glossy illustrations, penmanship grids, or cursive fonts, as she had expected from a stenography text.

Esperanza turned back to the first page and began to read, and within seconds sat up with excitement. "You go, Isoke!" Over the past year she had read everything she could get about Pac, and now Isoke had slipped her the biography of his aunt Assata. Maybe not his biological aunt, but she mattered to Tupac, and so she mattered to Esperanza. She lay back on her bunk, propped her new treasure against her elevated knees, and began to read.

ONE

Troublesome

Tupac growled through the speakers, and the accompanying bass shook the portable stereo and threatened to hurl the jagged pile of books that sat on top of it.

Esperanza finished darkening her eyebrows into a sinister arch, then dropped her pencil to join Tupac in his defiant acceptance of judgment. *Or send me to hell 'cause I ain't beggin' for my life/Ain't nothing worse than this cursed-ass hopeless life/'Cause I'm troublesome.* From her memories of countless videos, Esperanza channeled Pac, lowering her voice into a masculine rumble and jabbing her fingers in the air in West Side formation. Just as she prepared to spew the next verse, the disk halted.

Esperanza turned to face her older sister, Dulce, standing there in her supermarket workshirt and carrying her polyester knapsack. Bad enough Dulce had trashed all her Tupac posters; was she going to ban her from listening to him too? Esperanza watched as Dulce's eyes traveled from her gelled sideburns to her glossy lipstick to her red spandex dress with the mandarin collar. "What? Why aren't you getting dressed? You seriously not going?"

"No, and you shouldn't be either."

She anticipated that Dulce might want to skip the party. Still, she hoped that Dulce might put aside her ill feelings toward Xavier to celebrate her release from prison. And Esperanza really did not want to face Jesus and the others by herself. But she would be damned if his crew and the wannabes partied in her name while she stayed home, especially when they owed her so much.

"C'mon, Dulce, when am I ever gonna get another release party?" Esperanza giggled. "Get it? A release party?" Dulce just stared at her, so Esperanza flipped the stereo back on and returned to the dresser mirror to check her makeup.

Dulce snapped off the stereo again. *"Me dijiste que ibas a dejar esta mierda. ¡Me lo juraste!"*

"And I meant it, Dulce," said Esperanza. "But I have to get my money. Otherwise, why'd I fuckin' spend twelve months on lockdown?"

"You've been home three days, and did you find a job or enroll in a program? No, you get all dressed up and run out the door to see Jesus. Have you forgotten what the parole letter said?"

How could Esperanza forget? When her public defender convinced her to cop a plea, he told her that once she did her year, she'd be truly free. "So long as you don't get in trouble while inside, you're done once they release you."

"You mean they won't put her on parole?" Dulce asked.

"Exactly."

But while Esperanza did her time, an election came and laws changed. Once she learned Esperanza's release date, Isoke began to prepare her, as she had many cell mates before her. As Esperanza sewed her final stitch on a slipcover, Isoke said, "Try to get your record expunged. And go to my organization. They have programs that will help you."

"Ma, I live in the South Bronx. I can't be going all the way to Bed-Stuy for some program. There's bound to be some where I live."

"At least call them. They might know of some that your parole officer doesn't."

"I'm not going to be on parole. My lawyer said that when my year's up, I'll be done. I don't have to report."

"Do you know how much a system can change in just one year?"

Sure enough, Esperanza went through a hearing and eventually came home to a letter from the New York State Department of Parole. Because of changes to the state penal code, she had to report to her assigned parole officer for one year. If she failed to follow this officer's rehabilitative program to the letter, he could violate her parole and send her back to prison.

"The letter didn't say I couldn't have a welcome-home party," Esperanza snapped. Dulce just shook her head, grabbed her knapsack, and began to leave the bedroom. "I hate when you do that!"

Her sister whirled around. "Do what, Espe? Just what is it that I do to you?"

Esperanza searched for the words, and Tupac provided them. "Look at me like I'm hopeless. I'm not. You'll see." Dulce scoffed and left the bedroom, slamming the door behind her.

Esperanza turned to her reflection in the mirror and found a dash of red lipstick on her cheek. She pulled a tissue from the box on the dresser and dabbed at it, when her eyes caught a photo of Dulce and herself wedged in the mirror's frame. She plucked it out and studied it.

They took the picture on a trip to Six Flags with Jesus and Xavier. Their three-year age difference never diminished the Cepeda sisters' resemblance to each other and their Puerto Rican father. The thick head of coffee curls that both routinely heated into straightened submission. Crescent eyes set deep between short yet plush eyelashes caked with charcoal mascara. Honeyed skin that emphasized an indigenous nose and African lips darkened around the edges in lipstick pencil. On that day Esperanza had worn her hair in a tight ponytail fastened high on her crown while Dulce had wrapped her head in a bandanna of the Puerto Rican flag. In the photo they stood back-to-back, arms tightly knit across their busts as they flicked a choice finger at Jesus's camera.

Esperanza's eyes flickered from the photo to her reflection, and she saw what Dulce had seen. The same manicured hair and hard makeup. Another dress from the ghetto-fabulous wardrobe bought one size too small now further straining to contain the additional curves furnished by prison fare. The look of an unrepentant moll.

She wedged the photo back into the frame and gave herself one last inspection in the mirror. Dulce may have decided she had neither the time nor money to waste on her appearance, but after a year of sloppy braids and chapped lips, Esperanza had no intention of leaving the house without hooking herself up. How could Dulce fault Esperanza for not having anything to wear but her old gear? She liked the way the collar of this dress hid her scar the way few sexy dresses did. And just because she had decided to go to the party that Jesus was throwing for her didn't mean she intended to get caught up with him again.

Esperanza clicked on the stereo and rejoined Tupac in his rebellious declaration. " 'I'm hopeless! I live a thug life, losing my focus, baby. I'm troublesome!' " She gave a short laugh but then grew stern with her reflection. "No, I'm not," she said to her reflection. Then Esperanza turned off the radio, grabbed her coat and purse, and sauntered out of the bedroom.

She entered the kitchen, where Dulce sat at the table, studying. Esperanza placed her purse on the table to put on her worn wool coat. "So you're not coming with me? Not even for a little while?" She smoothed her collar, picked at lint, and struggled with her zipper, just waiting for Dulce to speak. Esperanza welcomed anything—a plea, a protest, a warning—but nothing came. "C'mon, D, come with me, I don't plan to—"

"Don't call me D."

Esperanza snickered. "OK, Dool-say!" Her sister continued to read even when Esperanza snatched her purse off the table. In her best Tupac imitation she said, " 'Why niggas look mad? Y'all supposed to be happy I'm free. Y'all niggas look like y'all wanted me to stay in jail.' " She mimicked his boyish laugh, then left Dulce in the kitchen, seething.

Esperanza bounded past the busted intercom through the rickety lobby door and onto the walkway. The crisp February air forced her to nestle deeper into her coat. When Jesus gave her the money he owed her, she would break off Dulce with some cash, then buy herself a new one.

"Espe!"

She stopped, turned around, and looked up. Dulce hung out of their twelfth story window, the wind flattening her curls into lax spirals. Esperanza smiled, waiting for her sister to ask her to wait.

"Tupac's dead, Espe. He's not in Cuba with his *titi* or on any other goddamned island writing poetry or making records. He's fuckin' dead! Keep messin' with Jesus and see if you don't wind up dead, too." Then Dulce snapped her head back inside and slammed the window shut.

Esperanza looked for witnesses to Dulce's outburst. Two hefty women with shopping carts made their way home three buildings over, while several boys in the playground ahead of her attempted to coax a stray cat toward them with a sliver of beef jerky. Relieved that the gossipy trio of project girls who usually hung out in front of their building were nowhere in sight, she continued down the walkway toward the street. Esperanza flipped up her collar and buried her face in the neck of her jacket, now more from embarrassment than from the cold.

* * *

The muffled beat of Fat Joe's latest met Esperanza at the landing of Jesus's floor. As she walked toward his door, she remembered her last time in the apartment. He had woken up randy that morning, excited about the day's agenda. She had not slept all night, and when he heaved himself on top of her, she cringed in dry pain. Then Chuck and Xavier arrived an hour later, and they rehashed the plan while they waited for Feli. After her boss went to lunch, and she cleared the check cashing joint of any customers, Priscilla would signal Jesus on his walkie. As he, Chuck and Xavier cleaned out the place under Priscilla's guidance, Feli was supposed to wait across the street in the car. Meanwhile, Esperanza had to plant herself in front of the entrance to distract any customers that might happen upon them. When it became evident that Feli had bailed, Jesus had to revise the plan. Eager to have his back, Esperanza volunteered to drive. Xavier protested and almost convinced Jesus to allow him to drive instead, but eventually Jesus handed her the keys. Hours later Esperanza found herself handcuffed to a bench at the Fortieth Precinct.

Esperanza paused before Jesus's door and reconsidered her options. She needed money. She had given the little she had saved during her bid to her sister. Dulce refused it at first, but Esperanza insisted she accept it as an act of good faith. In addition to working at the supermarket and attending school at night, Dulce was battling with the New York City Housing Authority to keep Esperanza off its "not wanted" list, and this time she had refused any help from Jesus. Dulce used the little money Esperanza had made as evidence of her rehabilitation and intention to contribute positively to their household. But Esperanza knew that after a few utility bill payments, the money would be gone by the end of the week, and Dulce's patience soon would follow. She had no job leads, and doubted her *street skills* were the sales experience that Kmart and Old Navy sought. Esperanza needed her money. She had done a yearlong bid in Bedford Hills, the only one of the crew who got busted that day. Dulce told her to give up Jesus and the others, but she refused, and for that she deserved her cut and to walk away from them for good with no hassle. Esperanza wanted it all—the dough, the daps, and the deliverance she had earned with her silence and sacrifice.

Just as Esperanza poised to knock, the door swung open, accompanied by a waft of herb. A young couple stumbled over the threshold and past her. Esperanza entered the apartment, stuffed to the corners with bodies leaning, writhing, and grinding. In the corner under a banner that read

WELCOME HOME, ESPE!, a deejay spun records as the twins who usually hung out in front of her building admired his every move. At the opposite side of the room, guests swarmed by tables filled with tins of food—*arroz con gandules, tostones y maduros,* octopus salad, even collard greens, yams, and macaroni and cheese. As soon as she got her money, she would give a little face time, serve herself a heaping plate, fix one for Dulce, and then head straight home.

Esperanza eased her way into the crowd, searching the bobbing heads for a warm face. Even the familiar few were too engrossed in their macks and swerves to notice that she had arrived, let alone welcome her home. She spotted clockers working the crowd, slipping powder samples into eager hands yet refusing to accept payment. Esperanza chided herself for thinking that people attended a Jesus Lara party for any reason other than to fulfill their own needs. For Sus, throwing a party was little more than executing a marketing strategy, and with this welcome-home theme he had cast Esperanza as the pretty spokeswoman who kept heads from switching to another channel and buying the same product from his competitor. Just as she caught herself grudgingly admiring the bastard, the last guest Esperanza expected to greet her became the first.

"Espe!" Priscilla flung her arms around her in a crushing embrace. Over Priscilla's shoulder, Esperanza looked across the floor in time to catch Xavier closing the door to Jesus's bedroom. She smelled his Chrome on Priscilla's neck and pulled away from her. "Welcome home, girl!"

Esperanza filled with shame as Priscilla took in her dated outfit. As hard as Priscilla tried to dress older, her low-cut sweater against her buttercup breasts and tiny skirt over her skinny legs made the nineteen-year-old seem twelve. Her dark roots screamed from the top of her yellow hair, which curled around thrice-pierced earlobes. A slash of blue that matched Priscilla's sweater cut across her eyelids, and her lips jutted out with the matted pinkness of cotton candy. Yet next to her in last year's trends, Esperanza felt a decade past her twenty-four years, a never-been desperately trying to hang onto her youth and aging herself that much quicker for trying.

"*Mami,* it's so good to see you," said Priscilla. "You look as fly as ever. Just the other day—"

"Stop frontin', Priscilla," Esperanza said. "You don't think I know you've been fuckin' Jesus while I was upstate?" She shoved Priscilla aside and marched toward the bedroom.

Esperanza barged in and found Jesus splayed across the bed, laughing, the air around him filled with buddha and cologne. From the doorway she could see the pink lipstick Priscilla had branded on the strap of his undershirt. Jesus, too, had not changed over the past year. He still parted and swept his dark hair to the side over one eye, the other piercing through her like a green knife. Jesus's goatee remained a rectangular tuft that shadowed upward in fine trails of hair over his jaw into his sideburns. His eyes fixed on her like those of a cheetah on his prey, Jesus pulled himself onto his elbows, his biceps flexing under his golden skin. Esperanza had come to hold so many things against Jesus over the past year, but at that moment what she resented about him most was how goddamned sexy he remained.

None of them had changed. Dressed in black as always from his Rocawear sweatshirt to his Tims, Xavier gnawed at a toothpick and camped by the door like a hound before the gates of hell. Sitting on the floor by Jesus's feet while leaning against the bed, Feli scrunched his acne sprinkled baby face as he dragged on a thick blunt. In front of him on the floor sat the ever present Monopoly game. Feli passed the blunt to Chuck, where he leaned against the dresser still tittering from his last toke and wiping sweat off his bald head with a stubby hand.

"Here she is," said Feli as he rose to his feet. "What's up, ma? Welcome home." He put his arms around her, the first sincere embrace Esperanza had received since Dulce clung to her in the Bedford Hills parking lot. She pulled away only when she saw Jesus eye them with suspicion.

"Thanks, Feli. How's *la doña?*"

"Kickin' it hard still. You know how my *'buelita* be."

Chuck lined up for his turn. "Espe . . ." He hooked a stiff arm around her shoulder and then retreated. "A year on lockdown ain't change you a bit."

"You think so?" said Esperanza, pretending to appreciate the compliment. "You oughta try it sometime." Xavier cackled along with her, but when she turned to face him, he had returned to his usual scowl. "Long time no see, X."

"Word." Xavier removed the toothpick from his mouth, flashing the gap between his front teeth. As if he read Esperanza's mind, Xavier asked, "Where your sister at? She coming?"

For the first time Esperanza supported Dulce's decision to stay home. "If you gotta ask."

Jesus groaned and stretched to his feet. "OK, y'all need to clear out of here so my lady and I can get reacquainted." He opened the door and gazed at Esperanza as his lieutenants filed out of the bedroom. As soon as he closed and locked the door, Jesus advanced toward her. He drew her to him and kissed her in the way that had first made her love him. She pulled away from him, staring at her feet, and Jesus just laughed. "I have a welcome-home gift for you."

Esperanza released her smile. "You didn't."

"Of course I did." Jesus bounded to the dresser, picked up a rectangular jewelry box, and handed it to her.

Esperanza hesitated, knowing that accepting it would mean opening herself to him. Over the past year a gift for her birthday or Christmas meant a book from Dulce or a drawing from another inmate. After his first and last visit—he was on a mission to make sure she would not speak—she had not received so much as a card from Jesus. Perhaps he wanted to make up for it, and, like her cut of the robbery, Esperanza deserved it.

She removed the lid and tossed it on the bed. Along a bed of felted cardboard lay a herringbone necklace with a golden "2" pendant. Esperanza lifted it out of the box and dangled it in the air. Jesus pulled it out of her hand and motioned for her to face the mirror. As she did, he reached around to hang the necklace around her neck. "A two, huh? Took a year without me to get over your jealousy."

Jesus clasped the pendant and stepped back. "Jealous?" Before she could answer he yelled, "Fuck no. How'm I gonna be jealous of some dead nigga? Can't believe you still on that shit, Espe." Then as quickly as he blew, Jesus softened again. "That two's for me and you, ma."

He turned Esperanza around and kissed her again. She cringed as he tightened his grip on her waist and grazed his teeth against her neck. He pressed against her, pushing her back toward the bed. "I missed you so much," he said, his hot breath creeping down her spine like glue. They fell backward on the bed.

"C'mon, Jesus." Esperanza tossed her head in an effort to get away from his invasive lips. She had to resist those lips. "Slow your roll."

"Still got those sexy legs, I see." Jesus clamped his hand on her thigh and tried to hike up her dress. "Yo, Espe, it's been a year since I've seen you."

She repressed the urge to comment on Priscilla. Instead, Esperanza shoved his hand away and said, "That was on you." Jesus rolled off of her, and she sat up.

He leaned back on his elbows. "You know it was too risky."

"Ain't write neither," she continued as if he had said nothing. "Never seemed to be around when I called."

"You know what they say. Ain't no secrets in the penitentiary. Kept your commissary flowin', though."

"More like tricklin'."

"Oh, you still real funny," Jesus said. "You know they'd only let me put so much there. I put in the max, even though that was risky, too." He leaned in, kissing her neck and rubbing her thigh.

I woulda rather you come see me. Esperanza jerked away.

"What the fuck, Espe?"

"Everybody's outside and shit." She expected someone like Priscilla or Chuck to bang on the door at any second. Esperanza almost wished someone would. "Least you can do is talk to me some first."

"Talk to you about what?"

Priscilla's name jammed in her throat. "Like what you've been up to while I was away."

Jesus snickered. "What else am I gonna do? Hold it down. You know, for us."

"Oh, yeah? So what'd you do with my cut? Invest in Microsoft or something?" Esperanza laughed.

But he just glared at her. "So that's what all this is about? Fine." He reached under the bed and pulled out a cash box. Jesus opened it to reveal several envelopes. Esperanza's heart leaped when she recognized them as the letters she wrote to him from Bedford Hills. Jesus put the letters aside to reveal several packs of bills. He grabbed a stack of twenties and handed them to Esperanza, then walked over to the window and threw it open.

On sight, she knew it fell short. Without taking her eyes off of him, Esperanza took the stack. She snapped off the rubber band and quickly counted the money. "There's only twenty-five hundred here."

"I know what's there." Jesus lit a cigarette.

"The deal was ten apiece."

"Look, the guys stepped to me and said that since they took most of the risk—"

"Bullshit!" Esperanza jumped to her feet. "I'm the one who got sent up on that fuckin' gun charge."

Jesus dragged on his cigarette and tapped the ashes against the sill. "The cops weren't supposed to be checkin' for you, and—"

"I can't believe you let them do this to me. I want my money, Jesus!"

He took another drag. "Esperanza, calm down."

Esperanza got into his face. "I will not fuckin' calm down! I didn't spend a year on lockdown for you guys so you can fuck me over. And you—"

Jesus pounced on Esperanza, gripping her jaw with one hand and jabbing the cigarette inches from her nose with the other. "I said calm the fuck down. You did what you were supposed to do. Don't think 'cause you didn't roll over and got sent up for a year, shit done changed around here. I still call the shots and you still listen." The cigarette smoke crept up her nostrils and made her cough. Jesus lowered his cigarette but kept his grip on her face. "I don't keep those shiftless niggas in line just to let your bitch ass step out of it. Now sit the fuck down." Esperanza backed away from him. "I said sit down." Instead she stepped away from the bed and stood against the dresser. "So it's like that now. Prison done toughen you up, huh?"

"So much I ain't going back."

Jesus grinned and advanced toward her. "Of course not, baby." He dropped the cigarette on the floor and squashed it. Then he reached out to caress Esperanza's cheek. "You and me, we're gonna go someplace new and start fresh."

Esperanza relaxed. Jesus had never talked about leaving before. Not when he first brought her into the game. Not even when they planned to rob the check-cashing joint. Certainly not during his first and last visit to Bedford Hills. "Like where?"

"I'm thinking California."

Her mind leaped to perpetual sunshine, blue waters, and golden beaches. No Feli, Chuck, or Xavier. And depending where they settled, she could see Brenda regularly. "Really, *papi*? You mean it?"

"Hell, yeah, sweetheart," said Jesus, lobbing back the excitement in her voice. "We do one last job, and then we bounce."

Esperanza's heart crashed into her stomach. What made her think he was talking about leaving New York *and* the game? Only days out of the pen and she had fallen back into her naïveté. "Look, Jesus, you do what you gotta do. But between my sister and parole officer, I can't fuck with that."

"Espe, ma, I promise you this ain't some wild shit like the fuckup we pulled last year. This shit's solid, and I don't want to do it without you. Let me show you love for riding with me." Jesus put his hand on the back of her neck and pulled her face into his. "We need our queen bee, ma, and that's you. You think that after how things went down, we ain't wanna get the hell outta here? The fellas sure as hell did, but I wouldn't let 'em. I said, 'Any nigga try to run now is gonna get his cap peeled.' I wasn't going nowhere without you, Espe. Not after how you showed and proved. We've been waiting on you. I've been waiting for you."

Jesus locked his arms around her waist and smashed his lips against hers. Esperanza pressed her forearms against his chest and pulled back her head. "Don't you get it, Jesus? I can't—"

He forced another kiss on her so hard, he wrung tears from her eyes. He pulled Esperanza from the dresser to the bed and forced her down on it.

Experience taught Esperanza not to resist Jesus, and memory reminded her how many times she had fantasized about reuniting with him. Even when he never came back to visit her, evaded her telephone calls, and ignored all those letters she wrote, Esperanza lay in her bunk many nights, touching herself and reliving Jesus's every loving stroke. When squinting over a piece of fabric in her machine or staring at the curled wire on the fence around the prison yard, Esperanza cursed Jesus. At night, however, she craved him.

Jesus slipped her hands between her thighs and whispered in her ear, "And when it's all over, you and me, we're never gonna be apart again, ever. 'Cause you love me, and I love you."

A few moments later, Esperanza left the bedroom with her pocketbook tucked under her arm. She smoothed her hair and wiped her eyes, smearing mascara across her fingers. Keeping her head low, she inched her way through the crowd toward the bathroom. She found a line of partygoers, including Feli, Chuck, and Priscilla, but Esperanza just filed behind the last person and hoped no one would notice her.

"Ay, yo, Espe!" Feli said, waving her to the front. "Espe, come here." Esperanza pulled away from the wall and headed to the front of the line.

"Hey, no skippin'," said a female partygoer.

"Shut up!" snapped Feli. "She the guesta honor."

Esperanza broke a smile as Feli put his hand around her shoulder. She hooked her arm around his waist and eyed Priscilla. *That's right, bitch. The true queen bee is back.*

"Ma, I need you to school these muthafuckas. Tell 'em how you know Tupac's still alive."

"Nah, they don't want to hear all that right now."

"Aw, c'mon, Espe," said Chuck.

"Maybe later."

Then Priscilla said, "Check this out. In the first video that came out after Tupac got shot, he's wearing some kicks that weren't even out yet when he died." Everyone turned to her, and she started to gush. "And you know how he started to call himself Makaveli? If you change the letters around, you can spell out 'I'm alive.' Oh, and in the "Hail Mary" video, there's this gravestone, right? And it says Makaveli on it, but it's cracked with a big hole in front it."

A male guest said, "Like he rose from the dead."

Esperanza planted her hands on her hips as others in line leaned in to hear Priscilla.

"And you know on the album cover where Tupac's, like, crucified?" She looked to Esperanza for the title, but she just let Priscilla hang.

"*Seven Day Theory,*" said another male partygoer behind her in line.

"Yeah, that's it. So there's, like, five bullet holes in the picture, and remember? Pac was shot five times."

Now the crowd turned to Esperanza and awaited her expertise. She debated whether to bother. Chuck and Feli probably just called her to instigate a catfight between Priscilla and her. But Priscilla had all these people hanging on her every word when she had it all twisted. Esperanza was the guest of honor. Jesus made it clear that only one woman could rise in his organization on his arm, and that would be her. *She* was the neighborhood authority on all things Tupac. A year on lockdown had not changed that, and these people needed to recognize it.

"Who you think you are, studying videos? Roger Ebert and shit?" said Esperanza. Chuck, Feli, and the other guests laughed as Priscilla's pale cheeks flooded red. "Forget that shit. And forget the numerological, word-scramble shit, too." The guests hooted, and Esperanza felt a fire light in her belly. "All you have to look at are the facts. Fact: Pac never went anywhere without a vest except the night he got capped in Vegas. Fact: He changed his name to Makaveli 'cause in the book written by the real Machiavelli, he says, 'A prince who wishes to achieve great things must learn to deceive,' and that included staging his own death to fool his enemies." The fire exploded into a blaze that propelled Esperanza's hands into Priscilla's flushed face. "And if you're gonna look at what Pac left behind for clues, to hell with the music videos and album covers. He ain't control that shit. Look to what he created. Listen to his lyrics."

Esperanza stood back as if to summon Tupac. Dropping her voice to imitate his, she prepared to rhyme when she spotted Jesus making his way toward her.

"There you go," he said. "Come over here, ma."

She remained frozen, her hand in the air, ready to spit. Jesus hated it when she went on these bents. One time while riding the subway together, he became so furious with her rhyming along with Pac on her portable CD player, Jesus grabbed her stereo, opened the door leading to the next car, and tossed it onto the tracks. "I'm a fan of the nigga, too, but you're fuckin' obsessed." Not once had Jesus asked her to lower her voice or stop rhyming altogether before he destroyed her stereo, and she would have had he just asked. The next day he bought her a new and better Discman, but Esperanza left it in the plastic for weeks.

Jesus reached them and took Esperanza's hand. "C'mon out to the front. I got something else for you." As he led her away, he motioned to Chuck and Feli to follow.

Esperanza saw Priscilla's face, her forehead and chin now as ruby as her cheeks. Esperanza stopped and rhymed: *I heard rumors I died/in cold blood, traumatized pictures of me in my final states.* Jesus tugged her arm and squeezed her hand. "Espe, por favor, enough with that shit." He led Esperanza to the center of the living room and toward the deejay, who faded the current record and handed Jesus the mike. The crowd stopped and closed in on them. Behind Esperanza stood Feli, Chuck, and Xavier, grinning. "Yo, me and the fellas wanna dedicate this next jam to our first lady. Our Foxy Brown. Our queen bitch. Welcome home, boo."

The guests applauded, and Esperanza giggled. "Y'all niggas better not sing."

"Oh, we gonna sing. And you know we had to pick a song by your boy, so . . ." The deejay started the record, and at the sound of the Cameo sample the crowd roared and began to clap along with the song. Jesus joined his crew, and the foursome began their twisted serenade.

The crowd jumped into the chorus. *It's all about you!* Jesus pulled Esperanza to him and ground against her. She buried her face into his shoulder and hoped everyone would mistake her humiliation for shyness. As everyone continued to sing along with "All Bout U," Esperanza shoved herself away from Jesus, whose hands remained clasped around her waist. "'It's all about you,'" he sang. She forced herself to smile and tried to break away from his grip. "What? Where you going? Dance with me." He grabbed hold of her hand as she pulled away.

"I was tryin' to pee when you dragged me out here," Esperanza said. She wrangled her hand from his and bolted down the hallway toward the bathroom. Esperanza raced past the line of guests, pushed herself past the girl just leaving the bathroom, and closed the door on the curses of those waiting.

Esperanza threw down the toilet seat and dropped onto it, sobbing. She reached behind her for some tissues on the shelf and wiped at her eyes, leaving streaks of black and beige makeup across the whiteness. Esperanza stood up to look into the mirror. Dark smudges of mascara encircled her eyes, just as if Jesus had punched her in the face.

She turned on the water and pumped hand soap into her palms. After scrubbing her face clean, Esperanza yanked the towel off the shower rod and rubbed her face dry. She looked down at the towel and the smears of makeup she had left behind. Instead of tossing it into the hamper, she flipped it around and threw it back over the shower rod.

Esperanza looked at her reflection in the mirror, her face now bare and ashen from the antibacterial soap. When she noticed the few strands of her hair that poked out from her temple, she trickled water over her fingers and smoothed them back. Then her eyes landed on the "2" pendant around her neck. She grabbed the necklace and shoved it under her mandarin collar. Still, through her dress, she could feel the bottom of the pendant dangling over her scar and causing it to itch.

She opened the medicine cabinet. Right in front of her sat the tub of cocoa butter, where she had left it. Esperanza undid the buttons of her collar and slid her hand inside. She ran her fingertips along the raised skin on her chest where it ran from her clavicle to her breastbone. Opening the jar of cocoa butter, she dipped her fingers into the greasy cake, scooped up a thick dollop of butter, and lathered it across her scar. Did Jesus keep it for her or did he just forget about it? After all that had happened, Esperanza did not know what she wanted to believe. Jesus's voice echoed in her head. *That two's for me and you, ma. . . . I wasn't going nowhere without you, Espe. . . .'Cause you love me, and I love you.* That was what he wanted her to believe.

Maybe she was overacting about the song. Jesus sometimes had a twisted sense of humor that Xavier never missed a chance to encourage. And he had chosen a Tupac song, too, remembering how much Esperanza admired him. That had to count for something since Jesus usually had little patience for her love for Pac. And despite all the fucked up lyrics, the point of the song was ultimately, "It's all about you."

Esperanza yanked, ripping off the necklace and pulling it through the opening over her dress. Then she dangled it over the toilet. As the "2" spun and glistened in the harsh bathroom light, she realized a better use for it. Esperanza stashed the necklace into her purse and opened the bathroom door.

She peeked around the corner joining the hallway and the living room.

She scanned the crowd for Jesus and found him with a pouting Priscilla in a corner. Jesus reached out to stroke her hair. But when Priscilla swatted his hand away, Jesus grabbed her arm, dragged her across the floor into the bedroom, and slammed the door shut. Esperanza thought of her coat where she had left it on the floor. Checking over her shoulder for the other guys, she bustled toward the door, yanked a random leather jacket off the coatrack, and fled the apartment.

TWO

Queen Bitch

Praying that Dulce had not chained the door in a fit after she left, Esperanza slipped her key into the lock. She slowly opened the door, gently slicing the darkened hallway. After locking the door behind her, she tiptoed into the kitchen and flicked on the light. Only when she saw the large pots on the stove did Esperanza notice her hunger pangs, having not eaten a damned thing at that stupid party.

On the chair closest to the stove sat Dulce's battered knapsack, a polyester rag she probably got for twenty bucks from the Korean shop at the Hub. Whatever happened to Dulce's Timbuk2 messenger bag? Then Esperanza remembered that Xavier had given it to Dulce for Christmas a few years back, and now that she wanted nothing to do with him, the bag probably lay crushed in the corner of the closet. Esperanza just didn't get it. Xavier was a dick and all, but why should Dulce cart around that *trapo* instead because of that? Esperanza pulled the cash out of her purse. She counted twenty-five twenty-dollar bills for herself and stuffed the rest of the cash in the outer pocket of Dulce's knapsack.

Her stomach rumbled, and she headed toward the stove to see what Dulce had cooked. Esperanza pulled back the lid on the largest pot and found it filled with white rice. Because Dulce had learned how to cook just like their Dominican mother, Esperanza knew the rice could stand on its own. But just like Brenda, Dulce never cooked *arroz blanco pelado*. Sure enough Esperanza opened the refrigerator and discovered a pot of *carne guisado* with wedges of potatoes and carrots to pour over the rice. She fixed herself a heaping plate and heated it in the microwave.

Esperanza sat at the table to eat alone with nothing to keep her company but Dulce's knapsack in the seat across from her. She considered turning on the radio but decided against it. Even though they had argued earlier that evening, Dulce had still cooked a great meal for her. Esperanza did not want to disrespect her sister, risking awakening her when she had to get up early for work.

She ate a few spoonfuls in restless silence. Then Esperanza put down her fork and reached for Dulce's knapsack. She opened it, hoping to find something interesting to read while she ate. Although the gleam of the thick textbook cover signaled otherwise, Esperanza still pulled it out of the knapsack. The cover read *Accounting,* with an orange USED sticker pasted on the front. The damned thing still cost nearly a hundred dollars! Esperanza had seen sitcom kids hit their parents up for several hundred dollars for schoolbooks, but she never believed that they really were that expensive. No wonder Dulce always stressed about paying for school.

In Dulce's knapsack Esperanza also found an accompanying workbook, a quarter of its soft beige pages etched with numbers in her sister's curly print. Dulce had always had a head for that kind of thing. Once Jesus even considered putting her in charge of the crew's finances, but Xavier squashed that shit. Esperanza hated math, always struggled with it. If not for Dulce's tutoring, she might have never made it out of junior high school. To help Esperanza understand percentages, Dulce took her to the Hub and made her calculate discounts at the clothing boutiques. They had so much fun that afternoon. Papi was still around, so they had a little money to spend. They probably had had too much fun, because Esperanza got everything else wrong but the percent questions on the test the next day. She laughed at the memory. She sure failed in style with her fly new Rockports that were fifty percent off at Modell's because they were a season old.

The third and last book in Dulce's knapsack that Esperanza removed had a soft cover and was titled *Sister Outsider: Essays and Speeches,* by Audre Lorde. If this Audre Lorde made the kind of speeches important enough to collect into a book like Martin Luther King, Jr. or Malcolm X, why had Esperanza never heard of her? Maybe she was the latest Oprah Winfrey or Iyanla Vanzant to hit the scene during Esperanza's bid. In her cover photo, the middle-aged Black woman with her neat Afro, simple glasses and kinte scarf seemed at once sly and motherly. Like she knew something you didn't but would readily share if you asked in the right way. Esperanza opened the book to a random page and immediately stumbled over words that might as well have been in a foreign language. *Reformism. Polarities. Dialectic. What the hell is Dulce reading?* Frustrated that she couldn't understand the words, Esperanza dropped the book back into Dulce's knapsack and ate her dinner in silence.

After storing the leftovers in the refrigerator and washing her dishes, Esperanza tiptoed into the bathroom. Her face already scrubbed clean, she stripped off her dress and slipped into a T-shirt hanging behind the door. She headed into the living room and flicked on the television. Esperanza surfed through the channels until she found *Above the Rim* playing on Black STARZ!

Although it was not her favorite Tupac film—that would be *Poetic Justice*—she stopped to watch the scene when Pac as Birdie joins his brother Shep at their mother's grave. Esperanza always related to Birdie, because he entered the game to take care of their mother when Shep abandoned the family. The joy he eventually took in the perks of his "trade" never surpassed Birdie's love for his family nor his need for their love in return. No other scene in *Above the Rim* made his yearning more evident, and it always touched Esperanza like no other in any of Tupac's films.

She shared Tupac's joy when Birdie threw his arms around his older brother and says, "I knew you'd be back." She saw through the anger that masked his pain when Shep rejected his request to help him push weight. Pac had been cast as the villain, but Esperanza sympathized with him. Shep's obliviousness to Birdie's need for his brother to accept him infuriated her. How could he not hear past Birdie's angry words his begging for Shep to appreciate that he took care of their mother even if he disapproved of the way he did it?

But now Esperanza watched the scene with different eyes. Instead of watching Birdie while he ranted, she fixed her eyes on Leon's Shep as he knelt before their mother's tombstone. She wondered if her sister ever felt the same disgust parked on Shep's face as Birdie yelled, "You ain't the muthafuckin' man no more, I'm the one!" Esperanza had never gone off on Dulce that way; she had too much respect for her to go there. She had not done a damned thing to insist she was the woman. Game or no game, Dulce was the woman, and they both knew it.

She fell asleep and awoke on the sofa, her sweaty skin sticking to the upholstery. She peeled herself off and shuffled down the hallway and into the master bedroom. Then Esperanza slipped into the queen-size bed beside her sister.

"Did you eat?"

Happy that Dulce had waited up for her, she searched for words to make peace. "Yeah. It was real good. Just like Mami's." Although Dulce lay in the darkness with her back to her, Esperanza knew the compliment made her sister smile.

"How was the party?"

"No big thing. Same dogs, same birds. You ain't miss shit." Esperanza peeked over her shoulder, debating whether to say anything more. "X asked for you."

"Fuck X."

"Word."

Esperanza felt Dulce toss her chin over her shoulder. "Fuck Jesus, too!"

"No," Esperanza said as she sat halfway up in bed. Now she could make out the outline of Dulce's head against the pillow in the dark. "Fuck Jesus more!"

The bed creaked as they giggled. Esperanza sank back into her place, nestling her face in the nape of her big sister's neck like she did when she was little. Dulce exhaled, and soon both Cepeda sisters were asleep.

Esperanza awoke several hours later to beat Dulce to the kitchen. By the time her sister awoke, she had set the table, brewed the coffee, and chopped tomatoes, onions, and peppers for omelets. Dulce reached for an egg and cracked it against the mixing bowl. "Sit down!" ordered Esperanza. "I'm making breakfast for you." Dulce shrugged into a long stretch and then made her way to the refrigerator to pull out a carton of milk for her coffee.

As Esperanza whisked the egg yolks in the mixing bowl, she said, "D—I mean, Dulce—I was thinking. Maybe I can go to school with you one of these days. Sit in on one of your classes. Check it out."

Dulce perked up. "You have to come to my women's studies class. The professor's all that! We read books by these fierce women of color, and they be breaking shit down."

Women of color? School had Dulce talking like those bourgie suits on those Sunday-morning programs after the cartoons and before the old movies. Still Esperanza played along. "Like the books Oprah talks about?"

"No, these women are like . . . Think of them like the female Martin Luther Kings and Malcolm Xs, you know what I'm sayin'." Esperanza prided herself on having made that connection on her own last night but decided not to admit to going through Dulce's knapsack. "These sisters be calling shit out. And the cool thing about the professor is that she doesn't have us read the books and then spend the entire class time telling us what we just read."

"She? Your professor's a female?" Esperanza usually thought of professors as old white men with rings of gray hair around their balding heads, fat bellies hanging over their khakis, and itchy blazers with coffee stains. Even the young, hip professors on reruns like *Gilligan's Island* and *The Parkers* were men.

Dulce nodded. "Professor Daniels asks us how we think what we've read relates or doesn't relate to our lives, you know. Our discussions get mad deep, Espe. Sometimes we're there talking long after the class is supposed to end."

Esperanza had never taken a course she didn't want to flee two seconds after the bell rang. "So when's the next class?" She turned around to slide the vegetable bits off the chopping board and into the mixing bowl.

"We meet on Mondays from seven to nine."

"Monday? Oh, I can't go."

"Why?"

" 'Cause . . . Monday's Valentine's Day."

"And where are you going?" Before Esperanza could answer, Dulce grabbed her coffee mug and started out of the kitchen. "Never mind. Forget it."

Esperanza grabbed her arm. "No, sit. Eat. I'ma go with you to class on Monday." Dulce hesitated, then lowered herself into a seat. Esperanza returned to the counter and poured the eggs into the spitting skillet. Why shouldn't she go? It wasn't as if she had plans that night anyway.

Monday came and Esperanza puttered around the house looking for something to do. The last thing she needed was to turn on the television or radio and be bombarded with Valentine's Day bullshit. She searched for a major cleaning or reorganizing project, something that would make Dulce happy.

But between work and school, her sister managed to keep cleanliness and order in their one-bedroom apartment. When they had grown too big to share the room with their mother, Brenda let Dulce and Esperanza have it while she slept on the couch. Many a boyfriend hounded her to apply to NYCHA for a two-bedroom apartment, but Brenda always resisted. Her daughters knew what Brenda feared. One bedroom meant no man. No abuse for her girls to suffer. Less drama for them to witness. Then Brenda met *el cabezón*. He moved in and the apartment ceased to be a haven for any of them. Where was NYCHA and its fuckin' "not wanted" list then?

Esperanza walked over to the bedroom closet and opened the door. Although she had been gone for almost seven years, Brenda's clothes still dominated the closet. She immediately spotted the Timbuk2 messenger bag in a corner, picked it up, and put it aside. Boxes of shoes, yellowing reference books, hairpieces, and appliances were stacked haphazardly across the shelf in the closet, while a mound of shoes, fallen garments, and shopping bags lay all over the floor. Esperanza found the project she had been seeking.

She leaned into the closet and groped around until she found Brenda's old suitcase, a huge taupe Samsonite with a hard case and a broken lock. Esperanza dragged it out of the closet and heaped it onto the bed. She opened it and found several posters rolled up. Surprised, Esperanza removed the rubber band, and Tupac's face unfolded before her. In her favorite poster, he gazed soberly though his wire-rimmed glasses as the words THUG LIFE in a gothic font scrolled down the right side.

When she walked into the bedroom on her first night home, she had wondered what Dulce had done with her Pac posters. They had already fought about going to Jesus's party, so Esperanza held her tongue, seething at the thought of her sister yanking them off the walls, crumpling them up, and throwing them in the garbage.

Relieved to not have accused Dulce of doing something she had not done, Esperanza rolled up the poster, scooped up the others, and put them aside. Then she began to transfer the clothes hanging on the closet rod into the suitcase. A half hour into this task, the telephone rang. Esperanza opened the door to the bedroom so she could hear the answering machine in the kitchen.

"Espe. Yo, Espe, pick up. I know you there, so stop fuckin' around and pick up the phone," Jesus barked into the machine. "C'mon, ma, how you gonna dis me on today of all days? Look, I know you mad and whatnot, but don't front. You know you gonna forgive me, so why drag the shit out and spoil our Valentine's Day? Espe, you there?"

Esperanza marched into the kitchen and turned down the volume on the machine. She wanted to cut him off altogether, but then Jesus would know that she was home. He would rush over there and start some shit. In fact, what was to stop him from heading over that instant?

She had to get the hell out of there. Esperanza grabbed her jacket and pocketbook and bolted from the apartment. As she searched for her keys to lock the door, she found the pendant Jesus had given her at the party. She grinned to herself as she gave the knob one last twist and jogged down the staircase. Now her flight to the streets had a dual purpose.

* * *

She had passed Miss Madge's thousands of times on her shopping sprees along Third Avenue but had never glanced at the window, let alone walked inside. Esperanza could never imagine wanting to buy something from a pawnshop. Dulce told her that she had come here to hock all the things that Xavier ever gave her, accepting whatever Miss Madge offered.

A heavyset Black woman in her forties, Miss Madge sat behind the counter reading *Jet*. Esperanza opened her purse, grabbed the pendant, and slapped it on the glass case of abandoned watches and forfeited lighters. "How much for this?"

Miss Madge picked it up, placed it on a scale, then said in a Jamaican accent, "I give you sixty-five."

Esperanza had never pawned anything before, but she knew Miss Madge expected her to haggle, with no intention of offering an additional five, maybe ten bucks. Having overestimated the necklace's value, she felt a pang of disappointment. She considered keeping it. Despite Jesus's explanation of the number's symbolism, the "2" still meant something different and significant to Esperanza. *Probably why the bastard chose it.*

Perhaps that meaning alone gave it more value than Miss Madge could ever offer. And to think she almost flushed it down the toilet.

Then Esperanza remembered why she wanted to flush it and the reason she had stopped. She wanted to get some cash and get rid of Jesus's stupid gift. With Dulce's employee discount at the supermarket and her shopping savvy, sixty-five dollars would put some pork or chicken on their table for a few nights. Compared to the lint in her pocket, sixty-five dollars was a mint.

"I give you sixty-five," Miss Madge repeated.

Esperanza nodded. "Fine."

After pawning the necklace, Esperanza walked the streets of the Hub. She stopped at the window displays of urban gear she could not afford and fought the temptation to go inside the discount stores. If she did, browsing would turn into buying and all her money would be gone. Isoke had warned Esperanza about the impulse to squander the first check she earned. "I know after going so long without having anything nice, it's going to be very hard not to run out and buy new clothes and toys, but that's the trap. First you feel entitled to a few luxuries, and you rush out to get them. Soon you get bored with those things, and start to focus on what you don't have. Then you make foolish choices in an effort to get those things, and before you know it, you're in the hole again. Remember, Sister Esperanza, there are many prisons on the outside, too. The free world is not all that free." Esperanza had five hundred and sixty-five dollars to her name, but she could not risk spending it. She would need it for lunch and carfare when she enrolled in school and started a new job until the paychecks started. Hell, a single textbook might put her back one hundred bucks even if it were used, too, and she did not want to bum Dulce for any of the money.

Except to buy herself a pretzel and a soda from a street vendor, Esperanza clung tightly to the cash. She almost gave in to the urge to buy herself a gorgeous wool coat when she remembered how she "happened" on the leather jacket she was wearing. She imagined Jesus handling the scene the jacket's owner surely had made at the party. If the owner was a woman, he probably offered her the choice of any jacket he had in his bedroom closet, and if her man did not appreciate Jesus's offer, he had better keep it to himself. If the coat Esperanza had taken belonged to a man, Jesus would ask him how much it was worth, throw him double the amount in cash, and order him out of his crib. Regardless of sex, if the person rejected Jesus's amends, he would direct Xavier to remind the guest of all the great fare he or she had just enjoyed at his expense by imparting a terrifying lesson in gratitude.

She strolled by the basketball courts, reminiscing about the summer days when she had watched Jesus and his crew play. Esperanza would whistle at him as he pulled off his shirt. He would laugh and throw it at her, and she would wrap it around her waist. Looking sexy in her cutoffs and having no competition from the guys absorbed in their pickup game, Esperanza made crazy money on days like that. Rain or shine, she always had mad money because the male customers preferred her, but due to the longer days, idle time, and scarce clothing, every summer brought a spike in her sales.

"Is that Espe?" She looked up as Hector tossed the basketball to his friend and jogged over to the fence. Unlike some of her other customers, Hector knew how to flirt without overstepping his bounds, respecting that the only thing in Esperanza's jeans for sale sat in her front pocket.

"I finally get to see you."

"Yeah, pa, weren't you at my party?"

"When I showed up, they said you had already come and gone. Sus said that the whole thing was mad emotional for you. Comin' home to all that love and attention after being all caged up and shit."

"Yeah, he said that?"

"And you know I understand, Espe, 'cause I went through the same thing when I came home. All that good stuff you been missing comes at you *en un cantaso,* and it's mad overwhelming. And you like, Damn, what's wrong with me? I been living for this day to be reunited with all my family and friends, and all I want is for people to leave me the fuck alone." Hector spoke with a conviction that had no impact on her. Maybe it was a guy thing. She had yearned to be overwhelmed as he described. "Heads were like, 'Where's Espe at? I didn't get to speak to her. Yo, I didn't even see her.' Sus said he shoulda done something more, you know, intimate. *Mira, nena,* you haven't changed at all. You look amazing!"

"Ah, I gained a few pounds." Isoke had explained to her that while some prisons used the bad food to punish the inmates, others stuffed them with fare that made them sluggish and docile. *Some of the most notorious prison rebellions in U.S. history were sparked in part by food,* she said. *It's a means of control.* Esperanza dismissed it as another one of Isoke's conspiracy theories until she came home and could barely fit in any of her clothes. Then again, between sitting at that sewing machine, shooting the shit with Isoke, re-reading her Tupac books, daydreaming about her mother or Jesus or just life on the outside and shunning most inmate games to avoid the seemingly inevitable catfights, she did spend most of her time in Bedford Hills on her butt.

"In all the right places, but don't tell Shanette I said that."

"Oh, y'all are back together again? That's sweet."

"For now. You know how that is. We go back and forth. Today we're at back. Tomorrow we're on forth." Hector and Esperanza shared a laugh. "Next week, who fuckin' knows?"

"You're too funny. Hey, how's your little girl?"

"Little?" Hector hissed and lifted his hand to his rib cage. "Jewel's this big now."

"Wow, God bless her."

Hector reached into his jeans pocket and pulled out a square of bills. "*Mira,* I'm a little short, but can you hook me up with . . ."

Esperanza held up her hand. "Whoa, can't help you, pa."

"C'mon, *nena,* you know I'm good for it."

"Nah, it's not that. I turned a new leaf, you know. Not trying to go back to where I just came from, *¿m'entiendes?*"

"That's good." He shoved his money back in his pants and looked past Esperanza. "Good for you, ma."

"Thanks." Esperanza pulled away from the fence and started down the street. "You take care, pa," she called over her shoulder. Hector did not hear her, having already flagged down another cat who could give him what he wanted.

Esperanza crossed the street and hoped no one else recognized her. She should have thrown her own welcome-home party so she could reconnect with folks without Jesus's influence. The streets knew of Esperanza's sacrifice for him, and it should have afforded her some status whether or not she remained with him. If anything he had thrown the party to capitalize on that, but before she could benefit from it, Esperanza had let him chase her away. Five hundred dollars was not much, but with it she could buy some crates of beer, maybe hire a deejay. . . .

"All I know is that Jesus is my man, he's been my man for the past eleven months, and he's going to stay my man, so she needs to keep the fuck away from him." Esperanza turned in the direction of the voice, so lost in her thoughts she had not realized that she had wandered past Priscilla and three of her girlfriends as they stood outside of VIM, each carrying two large plastic bags of new clothes in each hand.

A closer look revealed that Priscilla had befriended the trio of girls who hung out in front of Esperanza's building, all of them about sixteen years old. The ringleader—a plump girl named Rosie who flaunted her voluptuous figure in low-cut sweaters and tight jeans—lived in the building. The other two were fraternal twins named Patricia and Paula from a building across the grounds, and they often reminded Esperanza of Dulce and herself at that age. Patty even seemed slightly older than Paula. Although she flat-ironed her shoulder-length hair and etched on her eyeliner and lipstick with precision, Patty dressed like a tomboy in black-and-white camouflage pants and gold work boots. She spoke at a vigorous pace and laughed loud, just like Dulce. Meanwhile, Paula sashayed around like a model for Lady Enyce with her patched jeans and pink nylon jacket, letting her gear do all the talking. Priscilla probably had Rosie and the twins spying on Esperanza and reporting back to her.

"Good if that bitch hears me." Emboldened by the company of her homegirls, Priscilla looked directly into Esperanza's eyes, daring her to respond. "I'm not fuckin' afraid of her 'cause she went to prison. Lemme catch her near Jesus again and see if I don't kick her ass."

Esperanza walked back to them. "If Jesus is your man, then why did he have a welcome-home party for me last week, Priscilla? Why was he fucking me while you stood outside his bedroom door crying? Why did he throw a few dollars your way to get you out the door so he can blow up my phone wondering where I'm at on Valentine's Day?" With every sentence, Esperanza inched closer to Priscilla until she towered over the small girl. "You had a year to lock that shit up, and you're still nothing but a trick looking for a treat, so don't get it twisted 'cause Sus threw you a bone. You heard the man. I'm the queen bee, and anytime I want to see Jesus, I will, and he'll welcome me with open arms and anything else I want. So why don't you and your little friends run on home and play dress-up before I show you what I learned in lockdown?"

In a brave attempt to stand her ground, Priscilla hesitated, and Esperanza respected that. Still, she saw the fear in her younger rival's eyes, and it gave her a sense of power she had not felt in a long time. Imagining the scenes that ran through Priscilla's head in that moment of hesitation excited her. Esperanza wilding out on a jailhouse gang and shanking every last one of its members. Spitting in a prison guard's eye and laughing during the ensuing beatdown. Busting out one-arm push-ups while in solitary confinement. In Priscilla's eyes, Esperanza saw a montage of every prison movie ever made, and she enjoyed the way it made the little girl quiver.

"C'mon, Priscilla," Rosie said with the slightest Dominican accent. "Let's just bounce. It's too cold for this shit."

Esperanza smirked as she watched Priscilla and her friends walk away. She never would have let Priscilla goad her into a fistfight on a crowded street. In a commercial strip like the Hub, po was never far, and Esperanza would never give Priscilla the satisfication of sending her back to prison. But it probably never occurred to Priscilla to even try to get her in trouble with the law, if she even had the guts to execute it. That was how they were different. That was how Esperanza was superior to Priscilla. That was a power Esperanza longed to recover.

With a lift in her step, Esperanza headed home. She had no time to finish cleaning out Brenda's closet, but she had to at least put everything back. Then she had to meet Dulce at her job so they could head to her women's studies class together.

When Esperanza arrived at the supermarket at six that night, she found Dulce standing by the storeroom holding a rose and talking to a tall and muscular man with tawny skin and a tidy mustache. Esperanza snickered at his pale yellow *guayabera* and carpenter jeans. A handsome dude, no doubt, but he had to be straight off the boat, wearing shit like that in the middle of February. He noticed Esperanza first.

"Mira quien viene," he said in a tenor steeped with friendly confidence. *"Tiene que ser tu hermana. No me digas que no."*

"Sí, es mi hermana, Esperanza." Then Dulce turned to her sister. "This is Chago. He owns the company that imports and distributes the Dominican produce to all the supermarkets 'round here."

Chago smiled at Esperanza and extended his hand. *"Encantado."*

Esperanza just waved to him. "What's up?" With Dulce eyeing her, they all became embarrassed until she took Chago's hand. It felt warm and smooth, the thickness of his palm over her delicate fingers the only evidence of masculinity. She smelled his cologne. Just like Jesus, Chago wore Chrome, except he had mastered the art of applying it with a much gentler hand. For that Esperanza offered him a tender smile. Then she turned to Dulce. "Ready?"

"Sorry, Chago, I gotta go now."

"*Que* sorry, *ni* sorry." In Spanish Dulce thanked Chago for the rose and wished him a good night. "Happy Balentine," he said.

Esperanza choked on a giggle, and Dulce slapped her arm. "Stop it."

"I didn't say anything." When they arrived outside, Dulce hung left. "Where you going?" Esperanza pointed toward the subway in the opposite direction.

"To the bus stop."

"You gonna stand out in the freakin' cold waiting for the bus when the train'll get us there in fifteen minutes?"

"That's why I asked you to meet me early." Dulce proceeded toward the bus stop.

Esperanza skipped behind her. "C'mon, Dulce . . ."

"You know I don't take the fuckin' train if I don't have to."

Esperanza dropped it. Wrapping her arms around her shivering torso, she followed her sister to the bus stop, and within minutes the bus arrived. Dulce dipped her Metrocard into the fare box and then passed it to Esperanza. As the bus chugged forward, they headed to the back and took their seats.

"So," said Esperanza, "Chago give you that rose?" Dulce's silence told her all she needed to know. "Chago and Dulce sitting in a tree, k-i-s-s—"

"Oh, grow up," Dulce said. "He likes me, yeah, but I'm not feelin' him like that." She took another whiff of her rose, but Esperanza fought the urge to finish her song. Dulce would never give Chago any play, but she liked that her sister had a rose for Valentine's Day. It almost made up for the fact that for the first time in years, Esperanza had received nothing. Even at Bedford Hills last year, some of the other inmates made her cards and shared their chocolates with her.

Then she remembered: Jesus had called, and she had dissed him. She had done the right thing and ignored him, but still he called. With a bittersweet pride, Esperanza leaned back in her seat and watched couples walking hand in hand down the street as the bus lurched by.

THREE

All About Love

"I'm just saying that some things you can't judge unless you've been there," the young woman said, raking jagged nails with chipped polish across the pages of her closed notebook. "I don't think the writer has experienced what she's talking about. If she had, she wouldn't have written what she did."

Esperanza felt little sympathy for her. A month into the semester, and this chick didn't know better than to argue with Dulce? She must have been cutting class or not paying attention.

"You don't know that," said Dulce. "And even if she didn't, so what? You have to go to hell to know it's hot there?" Even Professor Daniels chuckled at that, but she did not intervene, and that made Esperanza like her even more.

For the past hour they had been discussing a book called *All About Love* by some woman named bell hooks. When the professor asked the students for their impressions of the book, Dulce set it off. Even though hooks knocked everything she had been taught about love—that love was unconditional, something we felt beyond our control instead of something that we chose to do, an emotion so passionate that it demanded violence to be authentic—she loved it. "She's so on point," Dulce said. "All these Hallmark ideas we have about love are wrong, and that's why no matter how much we say, 'I love him,' or, 'He loves me,' we're not happy. All this love we supposedly have, but what do we do? We cheat or put up with cheating. We lie, get lied to . . . lie to ourselves! We get hit, and we hit our kids. . . ."

And then that woman—another Latina about Esperanza's age with curly auburn hair and a soft voice—interrupted Dulce to ask the professor if the writer had ever been married or had children. She sounded offended, and before the professor could answer, Dulce asked her why that mattered.

"Some things you can't judge unless you been there," her classmate responded. "When my son gets outta line, I swat him on the butt *pa' que lo sepa*. That's not abuse." With every word, she grew more defensive. "If anything, I spank him because I do love him. Nobody's going to tell me I don't love my son."

"Pero nadie te está diciendo eso," said Dulce. "No one's saying you don't love your son, mama."

"Look, I don't beat my son down like my father did me, but you know what? My father loved me, too. And maybe it wasn't the ideal love we see on TV, but considering what my father had been through, and how he got to be how he was, that was the best he could do. So I don't think this woman knows what she's talking about."

By the way the woman riffled through the pages of her notebook and jiggled her knee, Esperanza guessed that reading *All About Love* triggered something painful in her. This woman's body betrayed her as she defended this unnamed hurt. It reminded Esperanza of the way Brenda's healthy eye would twitch after *el cabezón* had punched the other shut as she lied to a neighbor about walking into a door or falling down the stairs. Now Esperanza did feel for this young woman, and she hoped Dulce would ease up on the tough love. Not everyone could take it the way Esperanza could.

As if she heard something in the woman's words that no one else did, Dulce said, "I know what you're talking about." She reached out and placed her hand on her classmate's hand. "I've been there. That's why I can tell you that what you're saying and what the author's saying isn't all that different. People can only give as good as they get. Can't give respect if you've never gotten it. Can't trust someone when no one has ever trusted you. And you can't love anyone—not just care about 'em but really love them—if you haven't been really loved. What she's saying is, yeah, we should feel for them—you should feel for your father, I should feel for my ex—but that doesn't mean we have to settle for whatever they got. Nor do we have to dish that out to anyone else." Then Dulce gave her the rose that Chago had given her.

Plenty of times Dulce had made Esperanza proud. Even on those occasions when she secretly swore she hated her older sister, she never felt ashamed of her. Not even when that whole thing had gone down with the girl on the subway. She never tripped when people in the 'hood referred to her as D's little sister. If Esperanza had to walk in her sister's shadow, best to have a sister like Dulce who could make you laugh just as easily as she could beat your ass. But in this classroom Dulce displayed an intelligence and compassion Esperanza had not seen in forever. She had never felt more proud—and even a little jealous that some other woman had evoked it.

On the bus ride back to the apartment, Esperanza asked Dulce, "What did that woman write that got that girl so upset?"

"That love and abuse cannot coexist." Dulce turned her head and looked out the bus window. "So many people believe love hurts and all that. You know, Espe, I don't think I know a single person who doesn't. Well, I don't anymore." Then Dulce gave a laugh as she pointed to a wiry teenage boy struggling to give his chubby girlfriend a piggyback ride.

Esperanza's eyes traveled from the laughing couple back to Dulce's smile. It fascinated her that Dulce could believe in such an unusual thing. That she could read these ideas in a book and find them to make sense, especially when the Cepedas had experienced the exact opposite.

Esperanza put her head on Dulce's shoulder. "Dulce?"

"What?"

"You gonna help me with my college application?"

"Of course, *negrita!*" Brenda used to call her that. Esperanza was *la negrita* and Dulce was *Dulcita*. She would say she had daughters like the best coffee—dark and sweet. "First thing tomorrow I want you to make an appointment with the admissions office. And I want you to draft your résumé, too. These motherfuckers in Albany have been cutting financial aid left and right, so you're gonna have to get a job. It sucks to have to work full-time while you're trying to get your learn on, but that's just the way it is."

"Even if it weren't . . ." Esperanza had to scratch her party idea, but at least she had something exciting in its stead. Not just because they would need money. She and Dulce never had discussed it, but they both understood that money would be tight for a while now that they were both out of the game. Even if employment were not a condition of her parole or they had money saved, after a year of sewing cushions for dormitory furniture shipped from Bedford Hills to upstate colleges for seventy-five cents per hour, Esperanza needed real work. "I gotta get a job regardless."

On the morning of her first appointment with the college admissions office, she met with an academic counselor named Ms. López. She put

Esperanza at ease, appreciating that she had arrived early and waited patiently while she handled a brief crisis via telephone. Even when Ms. López began to ask difficult questions, like how long it had been since Esperanza had attended school and if she had a job, she kept a gentle tone and nodded without judgment at Esperanza's answers.

Then fuckin' Ms. López locked her into a room and gave her a bunch of tests. For the first ten minutes Esperanza sat paralyzed. Dulce had not said anything about no fuckin' test! But Dulce had a high school diploma and probably did not have to take them. She slowly started to work and felt herself making good progress through the reading section. Then Esperanza reached the math section and froze again.

She had not even reached the writing section when Ms. López returned to say her time had run out. She smiled at Esperanza and said, "It's only an assessment, Esperanza, not an admissions exam." Esperanza had no clue what the difference might be, but she feared asking and further hurting her application. Seeming to have read her mind, Ms. López said, "I give this to all the students I counsel just to see where they are so I can recommend appropriate programs and courses."

"I didn't get to finish," said Esperanza. "I left whole sections blank."

Ms. López put her hand on Esperanza's shoulder as she slipped the exam off her desk. "It's only to help you, Esperanza. Not to judge you or otherwise hurt you, I promise. You probably just need an adult education course or two to bring you up to speed and prepare you for college-level coursework. I'll give you some material to read while I review your assessment. We'll meet again next week and determine what you need besides your GED to get you enrolled, OK?" She gave Esperanza a second appointment, and that relieved her.

The following week Esperanza headed back to the college. The closer the four train brought her to Bedford Park Boulevard, the more excited Esperanza became about going to college. No one had ever told her what college could be like. She always thought it would be just like high school except fewer classes, longer hours, and more homework. That instead of reading books and rewriting them into reports, she could actually have and share an opinion about what she read. That you didn't get a good grade by memorizing and repeating what the teacher told you was important but by understanding what you read and maybe even defending your views on it. Esperanza realized now what made college tough, and she craved the challenge. You had to think for yourself, present your thoughts, stand by them. Esperanza was down for all that. If someone had hipped her to the college vibe, she might've tolerated the bullshit at her high school long enough to get into one, any one. She would have gotten her GED while at Bedford Hills because she would have seen it as a means to something more meaningful rather than just an end in itself.

As Esperanza hunched over the course catalog, she drew asterisks next to the classes she might take. Whole departments devoted to learning about Blacks and Puerto Ricans! How could she fail? Maybe she would improve her Spanish or learn a new language altogether. Or take some kind of artistic class, like creative writing or basic drawing. A computer class in Web design or graphic arts though would enable her to find a decent job that actually might be fun. Would Dulce mind if they took a class together? Because Esperanza really wanted to take a women's studies course, too.

She was searching for classes taught by Professor Daniels in the catalog when Ms. López interrupted her. "Esperanza?" The admissions counselor peeked around the doorpost and summoned her to follow her. Dropping the catalog into the Timbuk2 messenger bag she had recovered from her closet-organizing project, Esperanza leaped from her seat in the reception area and followed Ms. López to her office. As she sat down opposite her desk, she noticed a photograph of a concrete path through a row of plush trees called *Life Is a Journey.* Esperanza leaned forward to read the inscription beneath the photo:

In the end, each of us will be judged by our standard of life, not by our standard of living; by our measure of giving, not by our measure of wealth; by our simple goodness, not by our seeming greatness.

Esperanza grinned. It reminded her of the kind of things Isoke would say. Esperanza would shake her head at the New Afrikan diva and her quotes, appreciating her intentions but never quite buying all her lines. But sitting in this office about to enroll in college when only a week earlier she had been another high school dropout behind bars, Esperanza wanted to believe. She needed to believe.

"Esperanza, my job as an academic adviser and admissions counselor isn't merely to guide you through the application process but to prepare you to become a student here at Lehman College."

Esperanza's nerves began to buzz. "I know. I don't even have my high school diploma," she said. "But I figured that I'd take a class, maybe two, while I study for the GED and put in my paperwork. By the time everything's processed, I'll be ready to become a student. At least part-time." But Ms. López seemed unimpressed by all the thought Esperanza had put into launching her academic career. "I mean, I know I got to do some remedial work. OK, probably a lot. But I'm ready to do it. You tell me which—what you call 'em again?—adult education courses. You tell me which courses to take, and I'll—"

"That's the problem, Esperanza," Ms. López said. "It's not just the fact that you don't have your GED. You can get your GED, but I'm afraid you'd still be way in over your head here."

"But I said I'd take the remedial classes."

The counselor exhaled. "We don't offer remedial classes at the college anymore. With all the budget cuts, we had to eliminate our Adult Learning Institute."

She might as well have punched Esperanza in the gut. "Are you saying I can never go to college here?" If a public college like Lehman would not take her, where was she supposed to go? *I'm good enough to make cushions for college students but not enough to be one.*

"No, I'm not saying that. But we can't give you what you need to succeed here. I don't want to set you up to fail." Ms. López jumped from her seat to pace, and Esperanza wondered why she had become so angry. "And it's not because you dropped out of high school either, Esperanza. Even if you had graduated, you probably would struggle here. The public high schools are so overwhelmed and underresourced, they make the college system seem like an academic paradise." Ms. López halted and folded her arms across her chest. Esperanza started to speak when her counselor rushed to a file cabinet and rifled through some papers. "We used to provide everything. Adult basic education. GED prep. Tutorials, assessments, follow-up. Everything!" Ms. López yanked a red folder from the file cabinet, opened it, and pulled out a brochure. Handing it to Esperanza she said, "Enroll in this program. It meets on Saturdays for twelve weeks. If you complete it and get your GED, I will see it to that you're admitted to Lehman or any college in the city university system. I can't say I know how, but I'll find a way. By the time you finish the program, I'll have it figured out."

"But what if I'm way in over my head?" She had taken only the first step and already felt besieged.

"We'll cross that bridge when we get to it."

Esperanza hesitated before accepting the pamphlet. A moment ago Ms.

López made college seem impossible. Now she offered her a guarantee. Still, Esperanza took the paper. "I'll call them first thing tomorrow."

For the first time in their meeting, Ms. López smiled. She reached across her desk for a business card and handed it to Esperanza. "I'll see you in twelve weeks."

Esperanza tucked both the card and brochure in the messenger bag and left. Maybe all the material she had collected would satisfy Officer Puente when she visited him later this week. In fact, she intended to ask the GED program that Ms. López recommended for a letter verifying her registration. She wanted to prove to her parole officer from the first visit that she had no intention of going back to prison.

FOUR

Wonda Why They Call U Bitch

"This stupid new law, multiplying my workload as if I'm not already overwhelmed and without hiking my salary, of course . . ." Esperanza stared at the nameplate on her parole officer's desk while he looked over the brochure for the GED program. Conrado Puente. In the last two years she had seen nameplates of all kinds—from the police precinct to the Legal Aid office to the courthouse to the prison.

Puente copied some information from the brochure and handed it back to Esperanza. "And what are you doing about employment?" She hesitated only a second too long. "Don't think because you're going to school, you don't have to work."

"I never thought that." Esperanza checked her tone even though she felt that was a stupid thing for Puente to say. Did this guy actually have parolees who could afford to go to school without holding a job? People with that kind of dough didn't do time in the first place. "I have to help my sister with bills and whatever. Besides, the program only meets on Saturdays. I'd go crazy sitting in that apartment all day by myself with nothing to do."

"That's the other reason why you'd better get a job," said Officer Puente. "I don't want you having too much time on your hands, and you know why."

Esperanza also knew he didn't know shit. If Puente knew the first thing, he'd know that she didn't take up with Jesus because she had too much time on her hands. None of her troubles—least of all those related to Jesus—had a damned thing to do with having too much of anything. First, her father left so Mami went on welfare and got that waitressing job. Then as if the Cepedas lived like royalty off five hundred dollars per month, Clinton and Giuliani made like rich daddies trying to retrain spoiled children and slashed welfare. Even though her boss paid Brenda under the table, between showing up with huge bruises on her face and being forced to report to workfare, Brenda eventually had to quit the diner. During that time, her family lost a hell of a lot more than the ability to buy trendy clothes and watch cable. Maybe she should become a parole officer, because she already understood thug life much better than he did. But with her felony record, she probably could forget about that shit.

"Even if I couldn't find a job—"

"I don't want to hear *if.* You can always find a job. I don't care what it is. I don't even care if you get paid. You find something to do with your time during the week besides hanging out with Jesus Lara or anyone in his crew."

"Like I was saying, I'm not trying to hang out with Jesus and them regardless."

"Then why did you go to that party at his apartment last weekend?"

Esperanza swallowed hard. For someone who resented the increase in his workload, he had gotten in her grille pretty deep, real fast. "No disrespect, Officer Puente, but can I ask you something?" He remained quiet, and she took that as permission to proceed. "Where'd you grow up?"

"In the Bronx, just like you." His voice assumed a number of excuses. Puente thought Esperanza expected him to say that he grew up in a nice neighborhood so she could complain how easy for him to say that she, too, could be a law-abiding civil servant like himself. "In Soundview," he continued, thumping his chest. "I grew up on Watson Avenue between Boynton and Elder."

"Mad rough over there," Esperanza conceded.

"Damn right, it is. And you know what?" Officer Puente tapped his desk with a pudgy index finger. "When I was growing up, it was a whole lot worse. During the eighties right in the middle of the crack epidemic. You wouldn't believe the shit I walked through every day on those two blocks to and from Monroe High School." He added that tidbit to tell Esperanza, *I went to a public high school, too, and now I got a good job with the city, so don't give me any shit about the school system failing you, either.*

"Then you know exactly what I'm going through," said Esperanza. "You know from experience that the worst thing you can do besides run with the wrong crowd is act like you're too good to run with them,'cause that's when they really fu—I mean, mess with you. You don't want to hang with them, but if you're not cool with them, they start feeling like they need to take you down a notch or two. So you say, 'What's up?' when you see 'em on the street. You parley with them on the stoop every once in a while. Offer them a cigarette or maybe even ask to cop one just so they won't think you're turning up your nose at them and decide to vic you."

She wanted to add that it was harder when you were girl. You had to thank muthafuckas who made nasty comments about your body when you walked by, like that was the deference you owed for walking on *their* streets. You had to regard dudes you played Spin the Bottle with when you were twelve like you actually fucked them last week, 'less they dirty your name for *not* giving them play. And sometimes it got so bad, you had to get with the baddest one of all, thinking he might keep the others at bay. That it'd be easier to deal with a single muthafucka behind closed doors than to manage a bunch of them on the street. That his initial sense of ownership might eventually grow into some kind of genuine love for you and yours for him, which might actually compel him to protect you against that shit, if not take you away from it altogether. Esperanza wanted to say all this to Officer Puente, but something told her that she would lose him if he could not—or more likely would not—sympathize with her circumstances.

Officer Puente gazed at Esperanza for a moment, then said, "I know it's hard to avoid your old crew because you live in the same neighborhood. So in addition to getting your diploma and finding a job, you seriously need to consider saving some money and moving the hell out of there. I can't hold it against you if you run into someone from time to time and have to make nice. But beyond that don't let me find out that you're fraternizing with Jesus Lara. Or with Xavier Bennett or Charles Whitley, for that matter, either." He would have mentioned Feli had he been there that day, but something had gone down with his grandmother, and he hadn't shown. Feli's unexpected absence was the first thing that went wrong that day.

Puente handed her a card with a reminder for their next appointment. Esperanza took it. "I don't want a damn thing to do with Jesus Lara, and wherever he goes, they go."

"Trust me, Esperanza. I know."

Esperanza scraped the *pegado* from the bottom of the pot while Dulce piled their dinner dishes into the sink. "Oh, stop it, Espe. You're not gonna be the only grown woman in the room. That's probably why Ms. López recommended that program in the first place," said Dulce as she sprayed water over the dishes to rinse away grains of rice. "There're gonna be, like, forty-year olds in the class who just got off a plane from Carajo Land last week. Some of 'em will barely know English. If they can do it you can do it."

A harsh bang against the apartment door startled them both and resonated throughout the tiny kitchen. "Espe!" Jesus yelled from the other side. "Espe, open up!" Dulce shot Esperanza a look that demanded a fast explanation. Jesus pounded on the door again. Esperanza put her finger to her lips and crept into the hallway closet. "Espe, I know you in there."

"*¿Y qué? ¿Me va tumbar la* fuckin' *puerta?*" Esperanza cracked open the closet door wide enough to see Dulce head to the front door. Within seconds Jesus entered her narrow line of sight, holding a bouquet of roses. "Espe's not here, OK?"

"So where is she then?"

"I don't know." Dulce appeared, stepped around Jesus, and then disappeared from Esperanza's view again.

"Yeah, you know."

"Don't tell me what I know."

"I know you ain't been giving her my messages."

"Don't blame me 'cause she doesn't want to speak to you." Jesus turned away from Dulce and looked directly toward the closet. Esperanza cowered behind the coats and held her breath to control the deep heaving of her chest. As if Dulce heard her telepathic plea for noise to drown out her breath, the kitchen faucet gushed and dishes clanked against one another.

Jesus placed the bouquet on the table, then moved toward the kitchen, out of Esperanza's sight. She heard the cabinet doors creak open and slam shut several times. Then something muffled the running water. "Get out my way," Dulce said. "I told you Espe wasn't here, so why don't you just get the fuck out of my apartment?"

The water ran at full force again, and Jesus reappeared with a filled vase in his hands. He placed the vase at the center of the kitchen table and dropped in the bouquet. Esperanza watched Jesus as he contemplated the roses. "Look, ma, I know why you can't forgive X," he said as he teased apart two entangled flowers, his voice as tender as the petals. "You like a sister to me, D, and truth be told, I haven't forgiven him either for what he did to you." Then Jesus pulled out a rose with a large bloom and extended it in Dulce's direction. "But you know I ain't never did Espe like X did you, so don't poison her against me."

"You never did Espe like X did me? Don't give me that shit. You must be rolling in your own blow again if your memory's that shot."

"Once, ma. I did that once, and if I hadn't, I never would've wilded out.

And Espe wasn't exactly innocent in all that, but no matter. I never did that shit again, 'cause I got mad love for your sister, and you, too. But fuck it. I don't need you to admit it to know you've got some for me, too. After all I've done for y'all? Yeah, you still got love for me."

Esperanza heard stillness. Then Dulce said, "You know what, Sus? You're right. I still do have something for you."

Dulce's feet shuffled in the kitchen. Esperanza saw Jesus grin as he lowered himself into a seat. "What you made for dinner tonight? Got any leftovers? A brother hungry." He pulled his chair toward the table and spotted the stack of Dulce's schoolbooks. He picked *Sister Outsider,* gave the cover a quick read, and then flung it across the table like a worthless lottery ticket.

Esperanza scowled in the dark. What the hell did Dulce suddenly have for Jesus? Why did she accept that rose from *her* bouquet? Was she going to fix him a plate and let him eat it right there while she sat there in the freakin' closet? Maybe Esperanza should jump out of the closet. Snatch her roses—all twelve of them—and bounce with Jesus.

Then Esperanza saw the Beretta pointed in Jesus's face. "A brother hungry?" said Dulce's voice from behind the poised arm. "Then he better get his ass down the street to the Chinese takeout." Esperanza forced back a gasp. She had forgotten all about that piece. Apparently Dulce had not seen fit to hock all of Xavier's gifts.

Jesus eased out of the chair and to his feet. "Girls shouldn't play with guns."

Dulce scoffed. "Damn, Jesus. Espe rolled with that gat so she can have your back, and that's how she ended up in the jump in the first place. Now it turns out you ain't the equal opportunity muthafucka I had you out to be after all. Think you know somebody." Dulce cocked the Beretta.

Jesus sneered at Dulce. "I got you, D. Frontin' like you all reformed and shit. But there you go." Esperanza knew his words stung Dulce. Jesus knew it, too, as he gently pushed his chair back against the table and headed toward the apartment door. The second he fell out of Esperanza's sight, Dulce stepped into her view, holding up the gun with one hand and the rose in her other.

From where he stood outside of Esperanza's vision, Jesus said, "Tell Esperanza I dropped by to apologize." Dulce threw the rose at him, and Esperanza braced herself to come to her sister's defense when Jesus tried to leap back into the scene. Instead she heard him unlock the door and quietly close it behind him.

The Cepeda sisters didn't dare to breathe until they were sure Jesus would not make a hasty return. Esperanza slipped out of the closet and stood in the hallway. Dulce remained in her place, the gun still raised in the air. Only Esperanza understood the nuances of Dulce's many faces of rage, and this one she had not seen since that unspeakable incident on the uptown two train in Brooklyn three years ago.

"D calm down, OK?"

"Don't call me D." Dulce uncocked the gun, fled into the kitchen, and threw it in a drawer under the microwave cart.

"Why are you yelling at me?"

"Look what you made me do." Dulce flailed her arms, and Esperanza noticed the dried droplet of blood on her finger where a thorn had pricked her. "You ain't been back a week, and you got me backsliding into this wannabe-gangsta bullshit."

"I didn't make you stick a gat in Jesus's face. Why you still have that shit in the first place?" Dulce turned back to the dishes without answering her. "Why'd you go do something stupid like that? You just made everything worse."

"You say that because you do want to go back with him. I knew it."

"The one who wants me to go back with him is you," yelled Esperanza. "No matter what I do, you're always talking shit about my going back to Jesus. You even said that shit when I was locked down and couldn't see him."

"'Cause I know damned well you tried to contact him."

"If you don't want me to live here, Dulce, just fuckin' say so."

"Don't put words in my mouth, Espe."

"Fuck this." Esperanza grabbed her jacket and her portable CD player. "Sorry I came back home and ruined your little reinvention, Dulce." Her sister hollered something at her back, but all she heard as she stormed out of the apartment was Pac's "Wonda Why They Call U Bitch." As Esperanza bypassed the elevator for the stairwell, she hit the program button on her player until the display flashed REPEAT ONE.

"Espe!"

Esperanza heard the shrill voice over the bass pounding through the headphones of her portable CD player. Sliding the headphones off her head, she turned around and saw a chubby shadow running toward her. Esperanza stepped under the streetlight and made out Rosie's face, pink with cold, as she drew closer.

"Hi."

"'Sup, Rosie."

"Listen, I just wanted you to know that I ain't got no beef with you.

What's between you and Priscilla is between y'all two. It's none of my business. . . ."

"You got that right." Esperanza found herself impressed with Rosie's command of English. She had left the Dominican Republic only several years ago, yet she barely had an accent and had the street lingo down-pat.

Rosie nudged her head toward the front of their building, where the twins bounced to stay warm while monitoring their conversation. "Anyway, Patty and Paula feel the same way. We just wanted you to know that no matter what Priscilla says or does, you cool with us. She speaks only for herself."

"Does Priscilla know that?"

"Hell, yeah, she knows. You know me, Espe; I ain't got no problem speaking my mind to friend or foe. Just 'cause I'm Priscilla's friend don't mean I gotta agree with everything she does. I told her, 'That's fucked up, you tryin' to move in on Espe's man while she's away. When she comes back, and he goes runnin' back to her, don't come cryin' to me.' I told her just like that. You can ask the twins."

Maybe the door had not been broken, but Rosie let Jesus in the building. "I appreciate that, ma, so I'ma give you a little bit of advice."

"All right."

"First thing Priscilla did when she saw me was front like we were girls, 'cause she thought I didn't know that she was messin' with Jesus while I was gone." Esperanza got her hands into it, relishing the part that Dulce usually got to play. "So watch your back, Rosie. Watch your back and your man, and you can tell Priscilla I fuckin' told you that."

"What? You think I don't know? For real, Espe, you know what they say. Keep your friends close and your enemies closer, word. That's what it's all about for me."

"All right, *mamita.* I gotta go catch up to my man. But good lookin' out."

Pleased to have earned Esperanza's appreciation, Rosie let her grin stretch from one pink cheek to the other. "No doubt, ma. Welcome home. It's good to have you back."

Esperanza watched Rosie run back to huddle with the twins and convey the good news—they remained on the right side of the queen bitch. Esperanza still did not trust those little girls. But she was mad flattered that they needed her approval.

* * *

Maybe Dulce was right. She did want to get back with Jesus. Or maybe her sister was wrong and Esperanza only went there to spite her. Maybe she wanted to get that apology she deserved, or see if he would tell her what Dulce did to him.

For whatever reason, Esperanza headed straight toward Jesus's building. Once there she found him sitting on the stoop with Priscilla, who held the same rose that Esperanza saw Jesus give Dulce. When her sister threw it at him on his way out of the apartment, he must have turned around and picked it up off the floor. Heat spread to her face as she remembered all the things she said to her in front of VIM. And now Priscilla cuddled up with Jesus, her head on his shoulder and her leg dangling over his knee, probably wearing a new outfit that he bought for her while Esperanza shivered in someone's else's leather jacket. From behind the lamppost, she spied them as Tupac thundered in her ears. *I love you like a sista, but you need to switch, and that's why they called u bitch, I betcha.* Priscilla brushed Dulce's rose from Esperanza's bouquet against Jesus's cheek. He jerked his head away and summoned one of his young clockers working the corner. Pushing Priscilla's leg off his, Jesus stood up to meet him. Priscilla sniffed the rose, but Esperanza could see that the pleasant aroma had lost the power to melt the bored frown off her face.

Tupac stopped mid-rhyme, and Esperanza glanced down at her player. The battery icon flashed several times before her player died. Might as well, because hell, no, she didn't love Priscilla like a sister. These days Esperanza had to reach deep to find love for her own blood, let alone that hoochie. Esperanza pulled the earphones down around her neck and walked down the block.

After wandering for over an hour, Esperanza returned to find the apartment dark. Wanting to avoid another one of Dulce's interrogations, she planted herself in the living room. She clicked on the television and flipped through the channels. It surprised her how much she missed in a year on lockdown. Esperanza recognized very few of the sitcom faces on UPN and the recording artists on MTV, and no one impressed her much. She much preferred to watch an old favorite like *Poetic Justice*. Janet Jackson sucked, but not enough to take away from Pac's sensitive portrayal of Lucky the mailman. After the night she had, she needed to see a brother be loyal. Gentle. Loving.

Esperanza stood up and walked over to her shelf of videocassettes. As inexpensive as DVD players had become, Dulce clung to their massive VCR for some unknown reason. All Esperanza knew was that Dulce had better not have tossed her Tupac collection, because they weren't where she always kept them.

Prepared to do battle, Esperanza marched into the bedroom and clicked on the light. "Dulce, where the hell . . . ?" Their bed remained empty and untouched. All this time she thought Dulce had called it another early night when she actually had bounced.

Fuming, she scanned the room. Although she had not finished cleaning out the closet, she knew that her videotapes were not there. Nor were they in her drawers. One thing she could say about Dulce: She didn't go through Esperanza's shit, which made her more determined to find her tapes. She spotted a stack of titles on Dulce's night table and walked around the bed, but no videotapes. Just more of her sister's schoolbooks, including the one they discussed when she visited her class—*All About Love: New Visions* by bell hooks.

Esperanza took the book and sat on the edge of the bed. She turned to the table of contents in search of the part that got Dulce and her classmate arguing, but the chapter title that caught her attention read "Honesty: Be True to Love." Leaning back and kicking her legs up on the bed, Esperanza flipped to page thirty-one. She skimmed the first page, quickly growing frustrated with the names of psychologists and their books.

But then bell got real, if not obvious. Of course people lied all the time in order to avoid conflict and hurt others' feelings. Wasn't that what good people were supposed to do? Sure, lots of people learned to lie when they were kids. In Esperanza's view, kids had a lot to lie about these days. They did dirt like adults, often because adults did dirt to them, from dragging them to R-rated movies they wanted to see or talking to them or touching them in nasty ways. Then bell wrote about the lying that men do:

> *Many men confess that they lie because they can get away with it; their lies are forgiven. To understand why male lying is more accepted in our lives we have to understand the way in which power and privilege are accorded men simply because they are males within a patriarchal culture. The very concept of "being a man" and a "real man" has always implied that when necessary men can take actions that break the rules, that is above the law. Patriarchy tells us daily through movies, television and magazines that men of power can do*

> *whatever they want, that it's this freedom that makes them men. The message given to men is that to be honest is to be "soft." The ability to be dishonest and indifferent to the consequences makes a male hard, separates the men from the boys.*

Esperanza cradled the book in her lap and contemplated bell's words. The words rang with some truth even though she did not know what the word *patriarchy* meant. She remembered the old dictionary among the old books she had found in the closet, but that was more work than Esperanza wanted to do right now.

Esperanza put the book back on the pile on Dulce's nightstand. She curled up on her sister's side of the bed and stared at the digital clock. Where was Dulce? Why wasn't she home yet? Didn't she have to work tomorrow?

She looked up at the bare spaces on the walls where her Tupac posters once hung. Then she closed her eyes and imagined walking on a beach in Cuba and finding him reading *All About Love.* Esperanza sat down next to him as if they met there all the time.

"You like it?"

Pac flashed her that impish grin and nodded. "Yeah, this sista's deep."

"Word," Esperanza said. Then she nudged him in the knee. "You ain't get mad when she wrote all that stuff about men lying just 'cause society lets them?"

"Why should I get mad when that shit's the muthafuckin' truth? I know you don't want to hear that, but it's for your own good. Peep game, girl."

"And you can say that 'cause you ain't one of them guys she's callin' out, right?"

She expected her teasing to make him laugh, but Tupac grew very sad. He massaged the cover of *All About Love* with his thumbs. "Tellin' the truth is how a nigga like me got here in the first place."

"Me, too." And because they had become cool like that, Esperanza finally asked him, "So when you said you didn't hurt that girl you met at Nell's . . ." She braced herself for Pac's vehement denial, but instead he stared out at the water as it lapped the sand just inches from their feet. " 'Cause you gotta understand why some people think that you did."

"Espe, we've been through this. I didn't do what that woman said I did. But I do own up to the fact that I didn't look out for her, either."

"It's just that you write all those cool songs for the sistas, you know, like "Keep Ya Head Up" and "Can U Get Away"; then outta nowhere it's like we're all bitches, tricks, and hos. . . ."

"You know I'm not talkin' about all women when I say that. I'm certainly not talkin' about you, Espe, and you know that. Why do you take it that way?"

"That's what alla y'all rappers say. That's some bullshit excuse I expect to hear from Snoop and 'em. You supposed to know better than that, Pac." He conceded with a slight nod. "I mean, if that's true, and y'all are only talking about certain women, then why's that the only kinda women we ever hear y'all talking about? Why you spend so much time writing rhymes about them of they're so bad, like those the only women you know? Like a sista never showed you love. I don't know, Pac. When I hear that shit, it still hurts me. It's like when you say that about one sista—even if it's true—you're sayin' that about alla us." Esperanza placed her hand on Tupac's knee. "Remember when you said to old folks that no matter what they think of you, you're still their child, and they just can't turn you off like that?"

"Yeah?"

"Well, no matter what you think of a woman, she's still your sister. Or your mama or wifey or whatever. Point is, you can't turn her off like that."

Pac placed his hand over hers, looked into her eyes, and said, "You're right, and I'm sorry."

Esperanza leaned into him, and he put his other arm around her shoulder. And as much as she didn't want to—she just couldn't help it—she cried and cried and cried. And Pac cried with her.

Human warmth pulled Esperanza from the sleep that overcame her during her fantasy. As Dulce slipped into the bed beside her, Esperanza lifted her head to turn over her tear-soaked pillow. She waited for Dulce to speak—mutter an apology for waking her up, or even demand to know if she went to see Jesus. Anything to end the silence between them. But Dulce only gave a single cough and fell into stillness.

Then Esperanza noticed the hint of Chrome hovering above Dulce's head. Did she go to see Jesus? No, she had to have been with that guy Chago. Now Esperanza yearned to know all the details of her sister's night, but since she had no intention of breaking the silence first, she lay awake for another hour wondering.

FIVE

Talking Back

"'Harry's Mazda gets sixty miles per gallon, and diesel fuel costs an average of $1.25 per gallon,'" the Ethopian woman read from the workbook. "'For summer vacation Harry drove his family fifteen hundred miles to Yellowstone National Park. How much did Harry pay for fuel?'"

"Thank you, Brihan," Mr. Hudlin said as he turned to the chalkboard. His deadpan tone made clear that no one else in the room could give less of a fuck than he did. "Let's start with the facts."

The fact is your ass is boring. Esperanza tuned Hudlin's voice out to concentrate on her drawing. She had only the slogan left. Although Pac's actual tattoo of Nefertiti consisted only of black ink and mahogany skin, she opted to color her crown and collar red to contrast against the lined white page. Esperanza recapped her red pen and reached again for her black one. She had finished etching beneath her red and black Egyptian queen 2.DIE.4 when a hard buzz boomed over the PA speaker to signal the end of class. As Esperanza collected her books she thought the sound appropriate. *A buzzer. Just like in fuckin' prison.*

Ms. "Not Miss" Rodriguez's class proved only slightly more interesting. Although a petite woman with gray streaks across her dark mane, Esperanza liked the way Ms. Rodriguez commanded the room and tried to pay attention to her. Then she launched a grammar review that would have driven Esperanza to the door had she not lost herself in her second drawing—Pac's tattoo of Christ's head burning over a cross. Esperanza wanted to bounce, but she didn't want to disrespect the language arts teacher. Unlike Hudlin's condescending rehash of basic addition and subtraction, Esperanza could tell that Ms. Rodriguez's detailed lecture on subject-verb agreement aimed only to increase the confidence of the many students for whom English was a new language.

"Be careful with certain nouns like the indefinite ones," she coached as she scrawled a list on the board. *Any. Each. None. Something.* "They may not refer to one specific thing, but that's exactly why you treat them like singular nouns."

A guy in the back of the room named Pete raised his hand, and Ms. Rodriguez acknowledged him. "But what about"—his finger pointed to a phrase in his textbook—"collective nouns?"

Esperanza chortled. *Fuckin' teacher's pet, asking questions just to get noticed.*

"Excellent question, Pete," said Ms. Rodriguez. She turned to write another list on the board. *Class. Family. Union. Team. Audience.* "These nouns refer to groups, but each group is a single whole. We are one class. One team. One community." Ms. Rodriguez spoke with the passion of a preacher. "Is that clear, Pete?"

"I think so," he said, dragging his pencil's end along his gelled hairline as if he wanted to erase the mole on his temple. "Can you gimme another example?" Esperanza rolled her eyes and colored the flames of Tupac's tattoo in her sketch.

Ms. Rodriguez moved to sentence corrections. Although she never raised her hand, Esperanza answered them all correctly in her head. She had to write to Isoke and give her daps for that. She had told her reading would not only pass the time and increase her knowledge but also improve her ability to speak and write. Esperanza remembered the books Isoke made her take home with her with the promise that she would read and return them. She had not cracked open a single one after she finished the autobiography of Pac's aunt Assata. Esperanza liked it enough—especially the poetry—but felt cheated when Assata skipped over how she escaped from prison. Why was that book contraband when the one thing inmates might want to know had been left out? Still she felt guilty that she had not finished reading Isoke's recommendations and had failed to return them. If her GED classes continued like this, she probably should bring them to class.

" 'I'm not always there when you call, but I'm always on time. . . .' " Esperanza looked up from her sketch and to the back of the room. A Black girl who had introduced herself as Kiki was imitating Ashanti. When that song hit the charts, Esperanza used to sing it to Jesus when he complained about not being able to track her down. " 'And I gave you my all. Now baby be mine,' " sang Kiki while teacher's pet Pete puckered his lips and plucked out the song's harmony.

The class laughed and, confused, Esperanza turned to face front. Ms. Rodriguez had scrawled on the board, *When our team work together, we are always on time.* "OK, how many of you say that the proper way to correct this question is, one, remove the comma after '*properly*'?" Half the students shot their hands in the air, a few hooting for good measure. "Now how many of you say the answer is five, No correction is necessary?" The other half raised their hands. Ms. Rodriguez turned to the chalkboard and circled the correct answer, and the entire class let out a good-natured groan. "The correct answer is three, change 'work' to 'works.' Remember 'team' is a collective noun. It may refer to a group of people, but it does so as one whole. There's only one team, so the verb has to be a singular verb."

Without raising her hand, Esperanza said, "The sentence is still wrong, though." Fuck it. Fun had broken out, and she almost missed it. She wanted in on it. The only thing worse than teachers like Hudlin who obviously thought himself above teaching dropouts and émigrés were those who tried too hard to be down. Esperanza liked Ms. Rodriguez as much as she could any person in authority, but she had to bring her down a few notches.

"I'm sorry"—Ms. Rodriguez referred to her seating chart—"Esperanza." Even though she usually spoke like a bona fide Nuyorican, she rolled her name in perfect Spanish. "Did you say the sentence is still wrong?"

"If what you just taught us is true, yeah. Even if you change it to 'If the team works together, we are always on time,' there's still something wrong with it."

"OK, please explain."

Ms. Rodriguez's sincerity unsettled Esperanza. "Nah, forget it."

"Esperanza, my job is to prepare you for this exam, and if you think that any other answer than the one on my key is correct, I have to know why. English is a tough language with many rules and just as many exceptions."

"Too freakin' many," said Pete.

"Maybe you came upon an exception I overlooked. You said that even if we change 'work' to 'works,' the sentence is still incorrect," Ms. Rodriguez said. "How is that?"

" 'Cause . . ." Esperanza did not know whether to respond in jest or present a serious argument. She knew the correct answer. She only wanted to mess with Ms. Rodriguez for a minute. Now she had gotten herself into some shit. Why did she always do that? "You said that most collective nouns need singular verbs because even though they refer to a bunch of people, those people make up a single group. So 'team . . .'" She searched for the proper term. "'Team' agrees with 'works,' right?"

"Yes, that's correct."

"Then it should be 'is.'"

"I don't understand." Ms. Rodriguez seemed genuinely sorry, holding up her nub of chalk like a defective magic wand.

"The correct sentence should be, 'If the team works together, we is always on time.'" The class burst into laughter, and Esperanza's face burned with anger. She had started this for kicks, but now muthafuckas were laughing at her instead of with her.

"That's enough. Let Esperanza make her case." But she had no fuckin' case to make, so now Ms. "not Miss" Rodriguez was teaching her a lesson. "So why do you think 'we are' should be 'we is'?"

"Because 'we' is a collective noun. I mean, a pronoun. Whatever. It refers to a group of people acting like a single group. So the verb that agrees isn't 'are'; it's 'is.' It should always be 'we is.'"

The class laughed again, and Ms. Rodriguez let them. Esperanza slammed her notebook shut. The clock read five minutes to the bell, but she wanted to get the hell out of there and never come back. Esperanza shot the teacher one last glare, but instead of a smug expression on Ms. Rodriguez's face, the teacher had a look of disgust aimed at all the other students.

"Let me know when you're finished laughing at Esperanza, because she's absolutely right."

The laughs turned into huffs. "You fuckin' kidding?" said Pete.

"Excuse me!"

"My bad."

"According to the rules of English grammar, we should say 'we is.' And when we refer to a single person instead of a group, sometimes it should be 'you is.' Just another one of those exceptions I was warning you about."

Pete said, "Yo, Ms. Rodriguez, you saying that sometimes Ebonics be more right than English?"

"It be."

This time Esperanza led her classmates in their laughter.

When the bell rang, Kiki stopped by Esperanza's desk. "You wanna come have lunch with us?"

She really wanted to join them, but to thaw the ice between Dulce and herself she had promised to go the neighborhood library after class and work on her résumé. Instead she grabbed a pizza and a soda and headed to the Melrose Branch on Morris Avenue at 162nd Street to make good on her promise.

As a little girl, Esperanza had loved the library for no other reason than that she felt it belonged to the entire neighborhood. Every other place belonged to someone else. The playgrounds belonged to the boys playing hoops and ball. The stoops belonged to the older heads who set wooden slats on crates to play dominoes or poker. And every other place—from St. Mary's Park to the track and field at South Bronx High School as well as every corner in between—belonged to the dealers. They even commanded the community center of Esperanza's housing project. In other neighborhoods a good parent sent her child to the center to keep him off the streets and away from the negative element. But the attentive mother on Espe's block told her kid, "If I ever catch you hanging out with those hoodlums at the center, I'll smack you into next week!"

When Esperanza was five Dulce had first brought her to the library when their parents got into a nasty fight over *Papi*'s mistress. Dulce read her picture books like *The Cat in the Hat* and *Busy, Busy Town*. Eventually Dulce set Esperanza up with a stack of picture books so she would be free to read her own books. That worked only for so long, as Esperanza wanted to read whatever Dulce had in her hands. So her sister read to her *Ramona the Pest* (substituting "Espe" for "Ramona," to Esperanza's delight) and then *Amy Moves In* and *Tales of a Fourth Grade Nothing*. Dulce registered for a library card and took books home for both of them, but soon Esperanza insisted on having her own card. Dulce taught Esperanza how to write her signature and instructed her to practice. On Esperanza's eighth birthday, Dulce took her to the library to get her own card. She filled out the application for her, but Esperanza signed her own name. Soon thereafter Dulce started junior high, and discovered boys. Then they made separate trips to the library as dictated by school assignments, until Dulce received her GED and Esperanza dropped out.

Esperanza lifted her head and pulled open the door with verve. Even though it had been years since she had been there, she wanted to roll in as if she visited every day. She headed straight for the main desk and asked the librarian where she could find a book on résumés. As the librarian led her to the employment resources section, she said, "You can sign up to use the computer for a half hour at a time. If you need to print, the first five pages are free; then it's five cents per page after that. Or you can bring your own paper. And you always have to bring your own diskettes." The librarian handed her a clipboard. "Sign here and take number four."

"Thank you." Esperanza randomly grabbed three résumé books and parked herself in front of the computer. She stared at the screen dotted with little graphics she did not recognize. Except to play solitaire on Jesus's old computer or read celebrity gossip on the Internet, she never used one. Even those times Jesus set up everything for her. She would say, "Sus, can I play with your computer?" or "Put me on *Star* magazine, *papi.*" Jesus would walk over to the computer, hit the keys, and click the mouse to make electronic cards fan across the monitor, or a picture of J. Lo in an evening gown with her latest boyfriend pop onto the screen.

Once Esperanza said to him, "You gotta teach me how to do this for myself so I don't have to keep bothering you."

"No worries, ma. I got you." And she had thought him so chivalrous.

Now she sat in front of computer number four feeling lost and inadequate. If it would have benefited Jesus in some way for Esperanza to learn how to use the computer, he would have ordered her to learn and paid for her tuition at a computer school. Jesus had sent her to driving school and drove her to the parking lot at Orchard Beach to practice. Although he never allowed Esperanza to keep a gun of her own, Jesus had taught her how to shoot one long before he decided they would rob the check-cashing joint. When Esperanza told him she wanted to learn karate or kung fu, Jesus initially agreed. "That'd be hot for you to know how to get down like that," he said. "And any niggas who try to run up on me won't be expectin' it." But two weeks into her classes, Dulce and Xavier went mano a mano, and Jesus canceled Esperanza's membership at Tiger Schulman's. "I'm all the protection you need," he had said, even when Esperanza's self-defense did not motivate him to pay for her classes.

"Espe?" She jumped in her seat. Feli stood behind her with a cart of books. Instead of his usual baggy jeans and sweatshirt, he wore crisp khakis and a polo shirt. He noticed Esperanza staring at his unusual attire and said, "Yeah, my boss, Miss Henson, wanted me to dress more professional. I throw my street gear in a bag and change clothes before I leave."

"You work here?"

"Part-time," Feli said. "It's a front for my *abuelita.* You know how she can be."

Looking at most fifty of her sixty-two years, and with twice the energy of women half her age, Feli's grandmother, Doña Milagros, did not play. A recommitted Catholic who went to mass every morning and made *pasteles* for her neighbors during the holidays, Doña Mili also brought wreck to the streets without warning, fear, or apology. One summer Jesus sent Esperanza to Feli's to get him. Doña Mili took one look at her crop top and lowriders and slammed the door in her face. She reopened it seconds later to throw a sweater into Esperanza's face. "*¡Vístate!*" she yelled, and then slammed the door again. Once, after finding a stash of weed in Feli's room, Doña Mili ambushed Jesus on the street corner, calling him the devil's spawn, tossing holy water from a Poland Spring bottle in his face, and telling him to stay away from her grandson. She managed to knock him twice in the head with the plastic bottle before an embarrassed Feli dragged her away. Jesus had just laughed as he wiped his face with his T-shirt. "Another reason why you can't shit where you eat." The incident inspired Jesus to step up his game, and he soon got off the streets and moved with his moms to an apartment on the Concourse. The move led to promotions for Esperanza, Dulce, Chuck, Xavier, and of course, Feli, and they became Jesus's inner circle. Xavier wanted Dulce off the streets so Jesus had her tracking all the inputs and outflows, and Esperanza went from being a shorty executing hand-to-hands in St. Mary's park to assisting Jesus with everything besides trafficking and enforcement. Until Esperanza's arrest, that pretty much meant keeping Jesus's bed warm, running the occasional errand and getting out of his face when he did not want her around. Priscilla probably did all those things now or at least tried to.

"So you work here just for show?" The crew understood that if Doña Mili knew Feli still hung out with Jesus, let alone worked for him, she would put him out on the street. "Why not just quit—you know—your other job? Or move out?" she asked.

"Don't let my grandmother fool you, Espe. She may be all young-looking and vibrant and shit, but that don't make her any younger than she actually is. Somebody gotta take her to the doctor and make sure she takes her medication and all that. And it ain't like Social Security and Medicare cover everything she needs either." Feli glanced across the room to check for his boss. He grabbed the chair from the computer next to Esperanza and pulled it up next to her. "Where would I go anyway? Chuck lives with his baby's mother and their three kids in that two-bedroom apartment. Xavier is . . ." They scoffed together. It astounded everyone that Xavier could stand his damned self.

"Move in with Sus." Years ago Jesus had sent his mother to Florida. Once Esperanza asked to move in with him, but Jesus joked that he needed a break from having estrogen in his crib. She laughed it off, never letting him know how much that hurt her. Eventually Esperanza convinced herself that he meant nothing by it. Jesus's moms had been a piece of work, and in time he would ask her to move in if she didn't cling to him the way his mother had. But Jesus never did.

"C'mon now, Espe. That'd be like taking my work home or living with Miss Henson over there," Feli said, smiling as he motioned toward the librarian who had assisted Esperanza. "Besides, it's not like Jesus—" He suddenly rose to his feet and returned his chair to the adjacent computer station. "Anyway, I'd better get back to work."

Esperanza understood. Just because Jesus lived alone didn't mean he was ever alone. Even though she and Jesus were done, she appreciated that Feli thought enough of her feelings not to throw Jesus's other women in her face. "Before you go, could you set me up here? I've never done this before."

Feli glanced at her résumé books. "Sure." Esperanza watched him carefully as he leaned forward and grabbed the mouse. "I guess you need the word-processing program." He moved the arrow on the screen until it pointed to a tiny notepad, then clicked a button. The screen turned white, with thin bars of words and pictures scrolled across the top. "For now just type in your information."

"But how do I get it to look nice, like the one in the book?"

"No worries, ma. I'll come back later and show you how to hook it up."

"Gracias, Feli." Esperanza waited until he rolled his cart out of sight, then turned back to the blank screen. She flipped through the résumé book and found a model that she liked. She quickly tapped her name, address, and telephone number across the screen. Esperanza had received a rare A in high school in typing, and it pleased her that the skill remained with her after all these years. Next she had to enter her education, starting with the school she had most recently attended. Esperanza typed the name of her high school followed by the year she began, but unlike the model in her book, she had no graduation date or diploma.

Esperanza had accumulated barely enough credits to qualify as a junior when she dropped out of high school. On the last day of classes before Columbus Day weekend, she walked out the school to find Jesus pacing in front of the Navigator he drove back then. Parked in the Navigator behind him sat Chuck, his girlfriend Deziree, and their three kids in a rare family moment. "Yo, ma, great news!" Jesus said when he spotted Esperanza in the crowd. "No-No invited us to spend the weekend at his summer home in the Poconos."

"Papi, don't play with me like that," Esperanza said, sharing in his excitement. Everyone wanted to be down with the legendary No-No, who had entered and rose in the game in unorthodox ways. Although he grew up poor in Red Hook, Wesley LeMar Knowles had stayed clear of the streets and kept his nose clean. He excelled in school, ran track, and volunteered for his church's after-school tutoring program. They said that he got the nickname No-No because he could not be tempted into any kind of wrongdoing. No-No never smoked or drank, let alone sold rock. His excellent grades earned him a scholarship to a prestigious boarding school somewhere in Massachusetts. No-No returned from that place a changed man. The streets offered many wild stories as to what exactly happened, but only the result was certain. Spending four years with white people born with crazy loot had planted a bitter seed in No-No that would eventually mushroom to put a stronghold on a sizable portion of Red Hook's underworld. True to his steelo, however, No-No did not graduate from that snobby New England boarding school to run the streets of Brooklyn. He considered himself too smart to enter the game at street level and rise up the ranks like most heads aspired to do. Instead No-No finished college at Princeton and earned an MBA at Harvard. After two years as an account representative at a global investment bank in New York's financial district, he approached a Mexican cartel and offered his expertise in depositing their narcotic proceeds in banks around the world and hiding the money's ownership from law enforcement authorities. They had all heard the rumors about No-No's desire to make moves in the Bronx. He had his lieutenants scouting homegrown talent, and everyone dreamed that his crew would be tapped for "collaboration." The invitation to his Poconos home on Columbus Day weekend meant that he was giving them serious consideration. "For real we're going to the Poconos this weekend?"

"Swear on my mother." Jesus ran to the driver's side of his SUV. "C'mon, we gotta go now. I don't want to get caught in traffic so we can beat everybody else there."

"I can't go like this," said Esperanza as she pointed to her velour set and boots. She climbed into the passenger seat. "I gotta go home and pack some nice things to wear to make a good impression."

Jesus started the SUV and sped toward the Major Deegan, with Chuck closely tailing him in his Navigator. "No time, ma. Everything you need I'll buy you when you get there. You want new clothes for a special occasion like this, right?"

"Yeah, but it'll only take a minute for me to run upstairs and throw some things in a bag when we go to pick up my sister."

"Dulce's not going. I can't take her and not take Xavier, and I don't wanna bring that nigga."

"Sus, how can I go to the Poconos without—"

"Espe, keep fuckin' arguing with me and I'm dropping you off right here. This is mad important, and I can't risk Xavier acting the fool 'cause he thinks some dude is making eyes at your sister." Jesus pulled onto the Major Deegan and quickly shifted into the fast lane. "Besides, she should probably stay home with your moms."

Although Esperanza did not appreciate his using Brenda's situation to justify leaving Dulce behind, she would be damned if Jesus went to the Poconos without her so some hoochie could sink her claws into him. If anything, she had to be pleased that Jesus thought to take her. Still, Esperanza gave him the silent treatment until they stopped at an outlet mall in New Jersey so Jesus could buy her some new clothes, as he promised. She could hardly stay angry with him after that.

When they arrived at No-No's place they were shown to their own room, which was stocked with crab legs and champagne. After they showered and changed, Jesus and Esperanza joined the two dozen other guests at the pool. That first night Jesus let go as he had not in a long time. While Chuck stuffed his face, Jesus played *Jaws* with his kids in the pool. He salsaed with Esperanza for over an hour, crushed her lobster for her and fed its meat to her, sneaked her off to the greenhouse to make love to her amidst the aroma of wildflowers, then carried her back to the pool to dance some more. Lost in the smorgasbord of food, music, and liquor, No-No's guests took an entire day to notice his prolonged absence, and his people offered no explanation. Feeling less pressured to mind her Ps and Qs, Esperanza reveled in the party.

But Jesus grew anxious. "This is a setup. Some kind of fuckin' test to see if we fit into their bourg-jack set. Instead of being here himself and grilling us on our shit like a true OG, No-No's boys are reporting to him on shit like who's eating their salad with the right fork and knows the difference between Chablis and chardonnay."

"Papi, don't be so paranoid."

"What if someone saw us fucking in the greenhouse? No-No gonna think we're a spic operation full of *locos* who can't control ourselves. Know what? Fuck 'im then. I'm sick of muthafuckas tryin' to mix thug life with white bread. That shit ain't gangsta."

Jesus brooded for the rest of the weekend and chastised Esperanza if she laughed too loud, ate too much, or otherwise had a good time. Before they left that Monday evening, he made a show of thanking No-No's lieutenants for the hospitality and offering to make a contribution to offset the expense of the party. Instead of dropping her off at her apartment, Esperanza insisted that she go home with him. As his woman, she felt obligated to believe in him and soothe his ego, and she could not do that by leaving him alone to fester in his insecurities. So Esperanza skipped school that Tuesday, assisting him with his business and satisfying his every need. Tuesday became Wednesday, and then it made no sense to return to school for two days. Esperanza never went back to school at all, and Jesus finally allowed her to work for him.

With only five thin black lines across the top of the résumé, Esperanza grew desperate to fill the white page. But she had nothing to write. What was the point of including her high school "experience" when the only thing that seemed to matter—the diploma—she failed to obtain? And other than working for Jesus, she had had only two jobs in her life, but neither lasted more than two months. In junior high school, she worked for a *bodeguero* who kept trying to corner her in the storeroom and making nasty suggestions about what she could do for him behind the counter. After a year of going to school, hanging out, and going to school *to* hang out, she responded to a sign in the window of a clothing store on Third Avenue to work for a store manager who nagged Esperanza to spy on every Black girl who entered the store. Both employers paid her scraps under the table to work ten-hour days for six days a week. In each case, she spent several weeks completing menial tasks, collected her pay, and left the store, never to return.

Esperanza backspaced over all she had written and started another project.

Dear Isokey (did I spell that right?),

You warned me that it would be very hard to get my life together when I got back outside, and while I certainly believed you, I thought you were exaggerating. Well, I could never lie to you, so I won't start now. It's MUCH HARDER than I thought. I can hardly use this computer, so I don't know how I'm going to find a job.

I went to register for college like you and my sister always said I should. I even went with Dulce to this class that I really liked. You would've liked it, too. No, I take that back: You could've TAUGHT it!

But the college no longer has the prep classes I need so they wouldn't take me. Isokey, you always used to tell me I was so smart. I would tell you no, I'm not. Now you know who was right. For once!

But just so you know that I'm not just complaining or making excuses, I did get into a GED program. It's just so boring and irrelevent, Isokey. Nothing they're teaching has anything to do with real life. I sit in that classroom with lint in the pocket of my busted jeans being talked down to by these teachers. Except for my language arts teacher, Ms. Rodriguez. She's OK. Still dudes out there are stacking their paper and taking shit from no one. I feel like the poodle in the house that sits and begs for a little pat on the head while the pit bulls run the streets hunting their own food and commanding respect. I don't know how I'm going to stand this program for eleven more weeks, but between my sister and my parole officer, I guess I don't have a choice, right?

Oh, by the way, I'm sorry I haven't returned the books. I haven't read them yet, but as you can see I've had a lot of things on my mind. Let me know if you want me to send them back anyway.

Anyway, my time is almost up on this computer, so let me say good-bye. Just wanted to write you and let you know that I'm not out here living it up. Even when I'm wondering what the hell for, I'm doing the right thing. It'd be easier if you were here. Believe it or not, I probably miss you a whole lot more than you miss me (smile).

Love always,
Espe C.

"So how'd your first day of classes go?" Dulce asked as she served Esperanza a plate of *arroz con gandules* with *chuletas.*

Esperanza shrugged. "It's just like high school except everyone's older, just like you said." By telling Dulce she had been right, she hoped to satisfy her curiosity and then change the subject.

"And did you go the library to work on your résumé, like I asked?" Esperanza put down her fork and reached for her glass of water. "Espe, what's wrong?"

"What's wrong is I don't have any education or skills to put on a fuckin' résumé." Without taking a sip she placed her glass back down on the table with a hard clap. "What's wrong is that I spent the last year in jail doing nothing someone's going to hire me for. What's wrong is that I'm stupid and . . ." Before Esperanza knew it, she started to cry.

"You are not stupid!" Esperanza swiped her wrist under each eye and waited for another tough-love lecture about how she was just lazy and impatient. Instead Dulce handed her a few tissues to wipe her nose and said, "*I'm* stupid, thinking that what I'm learning in my business courses applies to your situation. Drink some water." Esperanza did as Dulce told her. "You don't need a résumé to find a job just yet, and you can find one, Espe, 'cause you're mad smart. You pick up things really fast. And you're good with people, too, and that's not something you can learn in any class. You either are or you aren't."

Esperanza never thought of herself as good with people. If remaining nice toward everyone even when she suspected their motives for being nice toward her meant she was good with people, then maybe Dulce was right.

"So how am I going to get a legitimate job without a résumé?" Esperanza asked.

"You're going to have to hit the pavement, kid." Esperanza groaned, and Dulce laughed. "Go to the boutiques, fast food joints, the drugstores and ninety-nine cent shops, everywhere. Walk in and ask if they have anything. Fill out the application wherever they have one. No matter what they say, leave them with your name and telephone number. Ol' school."

"Every teenybopper out here does that."

"Yeah, but you got something that they don't, and that's life experience."

"That code for rap sheet? That's what they teaching you in business class?"

"What I'm saying is that these employers are gonna see that you're a little older than the folks that usually come through, and they're gonna consider you because of that. When they start asking you questions, that's when you put your people skills to use. Make 'em think, 'I'd be smart to hire her.' And before you go to some chain like Burger King or Foot Locker, it helps if you do a little research on the company. Most of them muthafuckas running those places don't know the first thing about the corporations they work for. They'll hire you just to cover their ass." Esperanza's sniffles turned into chuckles. "Let me tell you, Espe. Whether in the boardroom or the backroom, some business strategies are universal."

SIX

Womyn Is as Womyn Does

The following morning Esperanza bought every tabloid and returned to the apartment. When Dulce came home from work that day, not only would she want to relax with the Sunday paper, she would look for some sign that Esperanza had searched for work. As she sat at the kitchen table with her red pen in hand, she willed herself to ignore the entertainment supplements and turned straight to the classifieds.

AUTO
$20.60 to start, medical/dental, paid vacation, no weekends.
Must have at least three years of experience as mechanic.

BATHROOM ATTENDANT PT/FT
For upscale Manhattan restaurants and clubs. English a must.

DRIVERS/OWNER-OPERATORS NEEDED
Drive your car or lease ours. Must have TLC license. High pay w/benefits. Signing Bonu$$$. Busy base, great earning potential.

FREE JOB TRAINING AND PLACEMENT
Cust Svc, Medical Billing, Computer Repair.
Food Stamp Recipients Accepted.
Public Assistance Recipients NOT Accepted. Call for appointment.

MODELS & TALENT
Models, actors, and singers wanted. Make up to $2,000 per day!
All ages, types, and sizes. Many jobs, no fee.

The legitimate offerings—often in construction or mechanics—were beyond Esperanza's ability. Meanwhile, not a single one demanded a high school diploma or GED. If someone told her she could make twenty bucks per hour doing body repair, she would have checked it out and maybe graduated from high school to boot.

The only other remote possibilities for employment smacked of scams or slavery. Many people had told Esperanza she was pretty enough to model. Whenever he flipped through the "sticky pages" in *Don Diva*, Jesus always told his boys, "None of these skeezers comes close to my Espe." Despite the flattery, she never got it twisted. She knew damned well that "all ages, types, and sizes" did not pull down two Gs per day. To a bona fide modeling agency in Manhattan, 'hood pretty didn't count. She remembered another inmate at Bedford Hills—a gorgeous but plump girl named Ruthie—who had spent over seven hundred dollars on photographs, classes, and an "agenting fee" that never led to a single assignment. She went back to demand her money and walked out in handcuffs charged with assault. When Ruthie told this story, she joked, "Hey, I finally got my picture in the paper."

Before she left for work, Dulce warned Esperanza about other scams. "If you call about a job in an ad and get a school, just hang up. They gonna promise to teach you all these things and find you a job. Next thing you know, the school goes out of business, and you owe the state thousands of dollars in student loans!"

"Could I even get a student loan, you know, with my record?"

"Yeah, *negrita.* If you had been convicted on a drug-related charge, you couldn't. At least not until you completed a year of random drug testing or a rehab program. But it don't matter, 'cause that's not what you got sent up for, thank God."

Dulce would know. In a few years welfare would show her the door, so she had little time to put herself in a better position to live beyond survival and support Esperanza while she went legitimate. She convinced her manager at the supermarket to pay her off the books so she could remain on Section 8, keep Medicaid, and go to school at night. To go legitimate herself, Dulce still had to hustle, and she hustled without regret or apology. "There are educational programs out there that won't take me unless I'm on welfare, when welfare wants me picking up garbage in St. Mary's Park instead of learning something that's gonna get me off welfare in the first place. Everything's a hustle, Espe. You just gotta choose wisely which ones you're gonna be down with."

Esperanza doubted that any of these "opportunities" in the newspaper would be good choices. Still, she was circling several ads for messengers and the like when the telephone rang. "C'mon, Dulce," she mumbled as she pushed aside the *Daily News* and reached for the *Post*. "Stop sweatin' me."

The machine answered the phone. "Espe," said Jesus. "C'mon, ma. If you're there, pick up." His voice sang as if he knew she stood only inches from the telephone. "All right, I'ma try you again later. Yo, D, stop fuckin' around and give Espe my messages, 'cause I'ma keep tryin' until I reach her." The telephone clicked.

Esperanza rose to her feet and walked over to the telephone. Jesus could help her find a legitimate job. A good job, too. Jesus knew everybody. People owed him, and he owed her. She could call him back and ask him to hook her up. Of course, he'd try to get her to come back to work for him, reminding Esperanza that she had insisted he put her on in the first place. Or maybe Jesus would tell her that he'd take care of her so long as she came back to him—and Dulce, too, if she insisted.

But Dulce wouldn't have it. Esperanza would have to sneak around like Feli. That itself would be a job.

Esperanza reached over and deleted Jesus's message.

On Monday morning Esperanza hit the streets. Before resorting to the places she had circled in the tabloids, she hoped to score something closer to home. After all, she lived only a short walk from the Hub, one of the Bronx's most popular shopping districts. Esperanza would save time and money if she did not have to commute into Manhattan.

She wanted to work at a small boutique where she might get an employee discount. Bad enough it'd be a minute before she could afford to get her hair or nails done, but at least a year on lockdown taught her how to live without that. After wearing variations of that orange bag and coming home to a closet of ill-fitting and outdated clothes, however, Esperanza yearned for new gear. Even if she could not rock the name-brand fashions she had grown accustomed to, at least she could avoid the no-frills shit from the ten-dollar store.

So she strolled into a shop with a HELP WANTED sign in the window. *se necesita hablar español.* Esperanza walked past the racks of embroidered jeans and party dresses to the counter and asked for the manager. He took one look at her worn black jeans and her old sneakers and said, "We already found somebody."

"I speak Spanish. And I'm real good with people."

"I'm sorry. I don't have anything."

"Then why you got the sign up in the window?"

"I forgot to take it down."

"Yeah, right."

After an hour of similar luck wherever she went, she walked in to McDonald's to eat. As she waited for the cashier, whose name tag read Tenille, to bag her order, Esperanza looked down at the counter. WE ARE CURRENTLY ACCEPTING APPLICATIONS FOR ALL SHIFTS. She did not want to work there. No one wanted to fuckin' work there. People worked there because they had to. And after walking up and down Third Avenue going into novelty shops, beauty salons, and jewelry stores, whether they had HELP WANTED signs in the window or not, with nothing to show for it, Esperanza had to.

When Tenille gave Esperanza her bag and her change, Esperanza said, "Can I have an application, too?"

Esperanza drained the last of her soda as she completed the application; then she came to the question she dreaded. Isoke had warned her about this moment and how it would make her feel. Still, no warning could have prepared her for it.

Have you ever been convicted of a felony or first-degree misdemeanor?

Esperanza poised her pen over the check boxes for YES and NO. If she checked the first, she also had to provide an explanation in the space that followed. She had asked Isoke if she should lie. "I can't tell you that," Isoke said. "You have to decide that for yourself."

"Damn, ma. I figured you'd just say I shouldn't 'cause it might come back to haunt me."

"Only you can determine what's the right thing for you to do in any given situation."

"You say you wanna mentor me and whatnot, Soke, but then you never give me any straight answers. What's up with that?"

"Your life is not mine to run. My job is to teach you how to know yourself and encourage you to be true to whoever that is. That way no matter what happens, you can live with the consequences of your choices, whatever they might be."

What were the consequences of her choices in this situation? If Esperanza told the truth, she might lose the job before she ever had it. But if she lied to get it, what were the chances that the truth would come out later? At least if Esperanza lied, she had a chance of getting the job and proving herself. And if she succeeded, if and when the truth got out, Esperanza stood a chance of convincing her boss not to fire her for lying on her application.

If the truth got out. How would it get out? Esperanza imagined PO Puente, strolling up to the counter, flashing his badge, and asking to see her. As her pen hovered over the checkbox marked NO, she realized that he didn't even have to do that to blow up her spot. All Puente had to do was place a call to her boss, something he undoubtedly would do immediately after her next visit to confirm that Esperanza truly had this job she claimed to have found.

Esperanza checked YES but kept the space for the explanation blank. Fuck it. If this fast-food restaurant manager wanted to know all her business, he would have to call her and ask her straight-out his damned self.

She bused her tray and took her application back to Tenille. "The manager can look at this right now and speak to you," she said. "Wait right here while I get him." Before Esperanza could answer, she whirled around and disappeared past the grills and into an office.

Esperanza had not planned on speaking to anyone. She had not even intended to apply for a position at McDonald's. Esperanza surveyed her outfit. Her clean but faded jeans now seemed too snug, and she had dropped a gob of mayonnaise on the worn leather jacket she had "borrowed" from Jesus's faceless guest. Esperanza rushed to the condiment counter, grabbed several napkins, and wiped furiously at the stain, which only grew bigger. She looked up and past the counter down the same path Tenille had disappeared. Just as the office door opened, Esperanza dumped the napkins in the trash and ran out of McDonald's.

Esperanza called the places she had circled in the newspaper, and only a "school" had returned her call. Like Dulce had coached her, she asked about their job placement record, complete enrollment costs and refund policy. The so-called admissions counselor ignored Esperanza's questions, pressuring her to come down to his Manhattan office so he could give her a proper assessment and walk her through the process of applying for financial aid. *You ain't no Ms. Lopez.* She hung up on him in the middle of his pitch. Her GED program might have been boring, but at least it was legitimate.

* * *

Ms. Rodriguez entered the classroom and placed a portable radio on top of her desk. "I wanted to start today's class by thanking Esperanza for her contribution the last time we met," she said as she untangled the cord and plugged it into the wall. Things are going to be very different in this classroom for the rest of this program."

Esperanza sank in her seat under the weight of the eyes upon her. The woman had taken an entire week to plot her revenge and intended to target the entire class. Esperanza should have taken Kiki up on her lunch invitation, because after whatever Ms. Rodriguez had planned, she would never make a friend in this class. She might even have to quit the program. It was one thing to quit on her own out of boredom, as she had high school, but quite another to be driven out by the hatred of her peers.

Ms. Rodriguez hit Play on the portable, and the sound of congas filled the classroom. Over the beats sailed the raspy voice of a woman reciting a poem. She sounded young and street. Esperanza picked up the twang of her Puerto Rican accent from the very first verse.

They say raise your daughters and love your son
But unloved daughters can raise no one
When all they've learned about love is wrong
Love is not a slow song on the quiet storm,
Roses without thorns, a Hallmark poem
Love is what one does

If womyn is as womyn does
Then womyn who fight is womyn who love . . .

They say love conquers all, they say love at first sight
But we conquer love, so it's love at first fight
A fist in the air, a lock of our hair
The struggle within us, the struggle we share

If womyn is as womyn does
Then womyn who fight is womyn who love

We birth the nations, we nurture our kin
We shadow our fears, we hold it within

Love equals fury and fury to flame,
The fight of our passions, the fight for our name
There is no red roses, there is no white dress,
There's only the fervor they try to suppress.
We fight for our people, we fight in the light,
We fight in the darkness, we fight with no sight.

If womyn is as womyn does
Then womyn who fight is womyn who love

They say a woman's place feeds the whole world,
They say sons should be strapping, no fight for our girls
They say love is a kiss, they say love is sweet,
But if love is elation, if love is complete
Then why are the womyn the ones who get beat?
Dragged in the trenches, thrown in the dust
According to them, love's only Lust
Obsession, Addiction, a drug to a fiend
Control over others, a lust that demeans

But if womyn is as womyn does
Then womyn who fight is womyn who love

And I choose to fight, as a woman should
I chose to fight, as I knew I could
Fight for my blood, fight for my land
Fight for my power I hold in my hand
I fight and I struggle, therefore I love
A passion within me, a fist raised above

If womyn is as womyn does
Then womyn who fight is womyn who love

I fight and I struggle, therefore I love
A passion within me, a fist raised above

If womyn is as womyn does
Then womyn who fight is womyn who love

By the end of the piece, Esperanza led the entire class in reciting the refrain along with the fiery poet on the scratchy audiotape.

Womyn is as womyn does
And womyn who fight is womyn who love

The teacher stopped the tape and Esperanza yelled, "Who's that MC, Ms. Rodriguez? She's phat!"

"That's that Puerto Rican girl on Def Poetry Jam," Kiki said.

"No, it ain't," Pete said. "And she's not an MC either. But she could be."

"That's me back in 1965," said Ms. Rodriguez. "I was nineteen years old."

The class gasped in surprise, and Esperanza began to applaud.

"Damn, Ms. Rodriguez, that makes you, like, almost sixty-years old," said Pete.

"Shut up, Pete!"

"I'm sayin' she looks good though!"

Ms. Rodriguez attempted to quiet down the students, but they continued to bombard her with questions. Did she write that poem? Where did she tape it? Did she still write and recite poetry? Was she almost famous? Why did she become a teacher when she clearly had the talent to become a star?

"I began writing my own poetry after I joined a study group of other women in college. We created the group not to reinforce what we were learning in class but to study what we *weren't* learning. Our own history. Women's history. The histories of Black and Latino people not just in this country but the nations from which our ancestors came." The immigrants in the room nodded their heads as Ms. Rodriguez spoke. "And we didn't just read history. We watched films and listened to music. We read literature and poetry. And when I discovered the poetry of Audre Lorde, she inspired me to write my own."

Esperanza popped in her seat at that name. She knew that name. That was the name of the woman on Dulce's book. "She wrote *Sister Outsider*."

"That's right, Esperanza." Ms. Rodriguez looked at Esperanza with the same pride she felt. She started to ask Esperanza but stopped herself. Instead she clapped her hands and said, "We should get back to today's lesson." When the class groaned she added, "Don't worry. No more boring lectures and drills. Thanks to Esperanza, our last grammar review reminded me of this poem, and I wanted to share it with you."

"But where do we get a copy of that tape?" asked Esperanza. Her classmates hooted in agreement. They had no intention of allowing the teacher to continue unless she gave them a satisfactory answer.

"OK!" Ms. Rodriguez waved the class into a murmur. "Here's the deal. I will give a copy of the tape to anyone who receives his or her GED on the next battery of tests. How's that?" The students cheered the incentive, and Esperanza led them in another round of applause. Bet Mr. Hudlin didn't have anything cool like that to offer.

Esperanza rushed home, eager to tell Dulce about Ms. Rodriguez's incentive. Dulce would like to have something like that. She would make a copy for her so she could take it to her women's studies class. Why didn't they teach classes like that or have study groups like Ms. Rodriguez described in high schools?

A fender bender delayed Esperanza's bus ride home, and she arrived at the empty apartment a half-hour later than usual. Too excited to study, Esperanza decided to surprise Dulce with dinner. Preferring to hang out in the streets than to be cooped up in the kitchen, she never learned to replicate any of Brenda's specialties but she made a decent spaghetti sauce. Esperanza filled a large pot with water and set it to boil while she assembled the other ingredients. Just as she finished chopping up the vegetables, the telephone rang.

"Hi, Espe. How was school?"

"School was so dope, Dulce. My language arts teacher Ms. Rodriguez brought in this tape, right? These drums start playing and then . . ."

"I can't stay on long, *negrita*. I just wanted to let you know that I'm not coming home for dinner tonight, and that you got . . ."

"Why? Where are you going?"

"Chago's taking me out."

"Thought you said you weren't feelin' him."

"I'm not."

"He's kinda old for you."

"I know." Dulce sighed as if she wanted to be convinced. "He's been married. Has two kids."

"And he's such a *jibaro*."

"Don't be a bitch, Espe. Chago's really nice. It isn't gonna kill me to go out with him once . . ." Dulce stopped to say a few words to someone behind her in the employee room. "Look, I gotta go. I just called to tell you don't wait up, and that's there's a message for you on the machine. When I tried calling you earlier, I found a message from the manager at McDonald's. John something. Anyway, call him back right away 'cause I think he wants to interview you. OK, I really gotta go now. Love you."

"Love you, too." Esperanza clicked the receiver and then hit play on the answering machine.

One saved message received today at two thirteen PM.

"Hello, this is John Luciano calling for Esperanza Cepeda. You submitted an application last week at the McDonald's at the Hub? I'd like you to come in for an interview this coming Monday sometime after four PM if that's possible."

He left a number. Esperanza raced to her messenger bag for her notebook and pen and replayed it. On the same page where she sketched her Tupac tattoos, she scribbled the number. She immediately called, but the employee who answered told her Mr. Luciano had the day off. "OK, just tell him that Esperanza Cepeda called, and that I'll definitely see him on Monday after four o'clock."

When she hung up the phone, Esperanza pranced around the kitchen. She didn't have the job yet, but she told the truth on her application and still managed to score an interview. Esperanza wanted to call Dulce with the good news but thought better of it. Not only did her supervisor frown on personal calls at work, Dulce had already heard the message herself. She considered heading over to the supermarket, but by the time she finished eating dinner, Dulce would be gone with Chago on their date.

The stovetop hissed as boiling water overflowed into the blue flame. Esperanza leaped to turn down the fire. She grabbed a handful of uncooked spaghetti, broke them in half and dropped them into the pot. Needing less pasta than she had planned, she replaced the rest of the spaghetti into the box.

About twenty minutes later, Esperanza settled at the kitchen table with her bowl of spaghetti and her GED prep book.

SEVEN

The Killing of Tupac Shakur

On Monday morning after Dulce left for work, Esperanza called the library when it opened. "Hello, is Felix Nazario scheduled to work today?"

An older female who she guessed was Ms. Henson sighed in frustration. Girls probably called looking for Feli all the time. While nowhere near as fine as Jesus, Feli was kind of cute in his own way, and Catholic schoolgirls—not the poseurs trying to prevent getting shipped to boarding school or to their Caribbean relatives but the genuine achievers who wanted to believe they were as tough as their surroundings—went for his shy goofiness. Feli had worked for Jesus since he was fifteen, and he remained as sweet as ever although he had one annoying habit. When he went overboard with his efforts to imitate or impress Jesus, Xavier referred to him as "the devout Christian."

"Felix won't be in until one," said Ms. Henson. Then without asking if Esperanza wanted to leave a message, she hung up on her.

While she felt relieved that Feli would be there, it unnerved Esperanza to have less than three hours to prepare for her McDonald's interview. The worry made her math homework even harder to do. If Esperanza couldn't get a job at a fuckin' McDonald's, what the hell was she going to do for money?

Hoping its serenity might help her concentrate, Esperanza packed her books and headed to the library anyway. However, the silence only seemed to make the numbers resound in her head like marbles in a pinball game. She thought she might tear out her hair when Feli appeared.

"Hey, Espe." Feli smiled as as he approached her with his cart. "Man, you're not playing around. You know, we have programs on the computer that can help you get ready for the GED."

"For real?"

"Yeah, you want me to show you?"

"Sure!" Then Esperanza remembered her primary reason for wanting to see him. "But not today 'cause I need you to help me with something else."

"No doubt."

"Can you get on the Internet from these computers?"

"Hell yeah," laughed Feli. "C'mon, Espe, you weren't gone that long."

"Whatever. I don't want to get on for the hell of it. I gotta find some information."

Sitting in the lobby waiting for Mr. Luciano, Esperanza reviewed her notes and munched on an apple pie. Once she looked up and saw Tenille bussing trays and wiping soda rings and stray fries off the tables. At one point Tenille looked Esperanza's way and caught her eye. She recognized Esperanza and smiled at her. Esperanza liked her smile. It was sincere. If Luciano hired her, maybe Tenille and she would become friends. Maybe she would become friends with other employees. Customers, too.

Tenille made her way to the table beside Esperanza. "Hi."

"Hi."

Tenille knelt to pick up a straw off the floor. Before rising again, she looked around and whispered to Esperanza. "Don't let Luciano get you all riled up. He likes to do that to female applicants. Claims he wants to see if they can handle rude customers, but the truth is he's an asshole. If you can't get on the register, ask to be put on the grill. Or even fries. The last thing place you want to get stuck in is the lobby."

"Thanks." She wondered why last week Tenille was behind the register yet now was doing the very job she loathed. "Weren't you . . . ?"

"Esperanza Cepeda?" Wearing slacks and a tie with the Golden Arches sewn on it, Luciano crossed the lobby, holding her application in one hand and extending the other toward her. "I'm John Luciano." He crushed her fingers under his palm. She hated muthafuckas who shook hands like that. How could a man not know he was squeezing a woman's hand too damned hard? Esperanza swallowed the pain and squeezed back as hard as she could. Luciano gestured for her to follow him, and he led her to an office behind the kitchen.

Without waiting for an invitation, Esperanza sat down across from his desk. Luciano peered at her application as he took his seat. He cleared his throat and spoke in a slow drawl that reminded Esperanza of Agent Smith in *The Matrix*. "People are under the impression that just because there's a McDonald's on every corner . . ."

"And a Burger King, a Popeye's . . ." He scowled at Esperanza, and she shut up.

"You think that working in a place like this isn't really work, don't you?" Her application trembled in his hand. "That you don't need any education or experience to be employed here?" Guilt pulsed in Esperanza's chest. She believed exactly that. But who didn't? Then guilt became disgust. And they believed that shit for a reason. "Maybe this isn't Sony or Merrill Lynch, but the McDonald's Corporation happens to be a Fortune 500, blue chip company with thirty thousand restaurants in over one hundred twenty countries . . ."

". . . Generating revenues in excess of eleven billion dollars every year," said Esperanza, reciting the Internet research she had just done upon Dulce's suggestion and with Feli's help at the library.

Luciano squinted at her application and pointed to the felony conviction question. "The career counseling upstate gets better all the time."

Oh, fuck you, Mace Windu. "I wish that were true." How did he know Esperanza had done time upstate? Nowhere on the application did it ask that question, and even if it had, she would not have answered it. If Luciano denied her the job, she would demand a reason. Isoke taught Esperanza her rights, and the state's human rights law said she was entitled to a reason. She wanted anything and everything she was entitled to even if it didn't add to much.

"Getting a job's one thing. Keeping it is another. Despite what you think, you need skills to work here."

"I got mad skills," Esperanza said. She barely stopped herself from calling Luciano *son*. "They're just no place for them on a resume."

"I'll bet."

"Look, Mr. Luciano, I could've lied. You know that." Esperanza pulled her seat slightly closer to Luciano's desk. "I didn't 'cause I know I can do this job. I be where I say I'm gonna be, and I get along with all kinds of people."

"I suppose where you spent the last year you had to be." As much as she wanted to send Luciano to hell, the hard drive, the Jedi Council or wherever he was spawned, she had to ignore him. If Tenille was right and he just called her for an interview for sport, Esperanza would be damned if this robot got the best of her. "What kind of position did you have in mind?"

Esperanza recalled Tenille's advice. "Register. I'm real good at math." The lie was safe since the electronic register handled all calculations. She would not even have to memorize what anything cost. All she had to know was how to count money so she could give the customer the correct change according to what the register said.

"Cashier, huh?" Luciano zeroed in on the felony question on her application for the umpteenth time. "You didn't indicate here what you were convicted of."

"Nothing that's got anything to do with working here." Isoke said she could not be denied employment because of her conviction unless there was a direct relationship between her offense and the job in question. If Luciano did not have the balls to ask straight out, Esperanza refused to volunteer shit. He probably already knew just like he happened to know she did her bid upstate. It was public information that Luciano had a week to uncover on his own which he obviously did.

"So then tell me."

Esperanza leaned back in her seat and folded her arms across her chest. "Possession of a firearm."

"Excuse me, I could not hear you."

"Po-session of a firearm."

"Nothing else? You had a gun just to have it. You weren't planning on doing anything with it, like, rob someplace."

Esperanza leaned forward and tapped her application at the address line. "You see where I live, right?" She laughed, but he just gave her a cold stare. "C'mon, Mr. Luciano, do you really think they would've given me just a year for anything more than that?" She laughed again, but Luciano continued to glare at her. "Call my PO if you don't believe me." A gun charge in New York State carried a mandatory minimum sentence of one year so even as a first-time offender, the judge could not give her any less than that. Hell, the fuckin' prosecutor pushed for three because Esperanza refused to cooperate with the police. Jesus had covered the fellas' tracks well, and without her the po had nothing but suspicions. And for that the muthafucka didn't break off a single bill to hire decent representation for her. Had he even peeled a few off her own roll, she might have beat the case altogether, but fuckin' Jesus . . .

The room grew too hot for Esperanza. She wanted out and rose to leave. "If you don't want to hire me because of my record, so be it," she told Luciano. "But dis me because of what's *on* the record. Don't be speculating about things that aren't there looking for an excuse not to hire me."

Esperanza had turned the doorknob when Luciano said, "Guess there's no risk in giving you a trial period." He spun in his chair and consulted a calendar on a clipboard hanging from the wall. "Be here Saturday at eight-thirty."

Fuck. "I can't work on Saturdays until after two. My GED program meets on Saturdays from nine to one. But other than that, I can work whenever."

Luciano gave Esperanza a slight raise of his eyebrow with a matching one-sided sneer. "OK, come back on Monday." He checked the calendar again. "At noon. You can start on the floor."

Esperanza wanted to ask if by floor he meant lobby but thought better of it. Even if they were one and the same, she had no intention of complaining. She didn't want to risk her new job seconds after landing it.

On her first day of work, Luciano gave Esperanza a stack of forms to complete, a hideous uniform to wear and an employee manual to read. Then he sat her in the employee room and made her watch a boring videotape on the appropriate way to clean a McDonald's lobby. In her school notebook, Esperanza pretended to take notes when she actually finished another Tupac tattoo. By the time the tape ended, she had just colored the bullet over the letter I in THUG LIFE. Esperanza rewound the videotape and took it to Luciano's office. He noticed her shoes.

"Esperanza, those boots are inappropriate," he said of her black booties. They were one of the few things she owned that fit right and did not look ridiculously outdated. "The McDonald's Corporation requires its employees to wear soft-soled shoes. Not only is it more uniformed and professional, it's for your own safety. These tiled floors can get very slippery when wet. Just go to Payless, and buy a pair like nurses wear. But no tennis shoes or sneakers of any kind."

Y'all gonna reimburse me for that? "OK, Mr. Luciano."

Esperanza spent the next four hours bussing trays, emptying garbage bins and cleaning the floors. During a particularly slow period, she mopped the already pristine lobby until her back ached just to have something to do. When Esperanza found an abandoned newspaper in a booth, instead of throwing it away, she snuck into the employee bathroom for an unauthorized break.

Reading on the sly became a habit of survival until Tenille caught her. Esperanza rushed to throw away the newspaper. "I just found that in here so . . ."

Tenille just grinned. "Girl, when I do lobby, I bring in a little paperback, and stick it in my waistband under this ugly shirt. When things are slow, you can only mop the floor so many times."

"Wish my uniform was baggier," said Esperanza smiling. "Then I could stick my homework down my pants. Get my study on."

"But then it'd be uglier than ever."

"True."

They both laughed, and Esperanza returned to the lobby. As she leaned from her aching waist to wipe a table, she tried to coach herself to take pride in her work. *The McDonald's Corporation was a Fortune 500, blue chip company,* she said to herself. *Thirty thousand restaurants in over one hundred twenty countries. Eleven billion plus every year.* She watched a homeboy at the next table devour his Big Mac in three bites, grab his soda and bop out of the restaurant, leaving his tray on the table. Esperanza snatched it and walked it to the garbage can. As she peeled the ketchup-soaked liner, her thoughts shifted. *¡Bruto!* Was it so fuckin' hard to pick up the tray and throw out his trash? If he spotted her on the street, this same idiot would be trying to holler at her. But he saw Esperanza there in this polyester eyesore and thought he could treat her like a damned maid.

She spotted a smashed French fry under the table and lowered herself to scrape it off the floor. But when Esperanza reached the rust colored tiles, she kneeled back on her haunches and sighed. Feeling the ache in her side give slightly, she leaned against the seat for a break. People stooped to jobs like these not only to survive, she figured, but to prove to themselves and everyone else that they were contributing members of society and whatnot. Now that she had spent two weeks here, Esperanza did not understand how that could be. If she did not show up tomorrow, no one would miss her. Another girl—maybe a newly arrived *mejicana* or *dominicana* lucky enough to get the right papers—would take it to help her family. At least that girl had some purpose. At least she would matter, her life had some meaning. For Esperanza this job did nothing to make her feel self-sufficient and law-abiding. It only reminded her each day of how little consequence she was. Instead of beeping her awake in the morning, her alarm clock might as well yell *Get up, bitch, 'cause you ain't shit.* That would kill her much faster than the monotony if Luciano did not move her to something better soon. For this shit Esperanza could have stayed in prison.

When Esperanza received her first paycheck, she treated Dulce to dinner at the Red Lobster in Co-op City. At first Dulce protested knowing that the meal probably would eat up most of her sister's pay, but Esperanza insisted. As they waited for the server to bring their meal, Esperanza examined her pay stub one more time.

"They take out so much money for what?"

"Schools. Sanitation. The po."

"Shit. You'd never know it. Schools are all fucked up, streets be dirty . . ."

Dulce nodded. "I never would've minded paying all those taxes if I got what I paid for. All my hard-earned money going to shit I'm not down with. I don't want to send some kid from around here across the world to bomb some poor village full of people that didn't do shit to me." She grabbed a cheese biscuit and tore into it. "On the back of the W-2s should be a survey where we could vote where our money can and cannot go. That's what I call a democracy."

Esperanza grabbed her knife like a pen and pretended to complete a survey on her placemat. "Colleges, yes. Hospitals, yes. Prisons, fuck no."

Dulce laughed. "Thanks for not cracking that stupid joke."

"What stupid joke?"

"Who the hell is FICA, and why is she taking all my money?"

Esperanza heard that one a few times on television sit-coms and never got it until now. "That's so played out." She took a sip of her water. "But who the hell *is* FICA?"

The Cepeda sisters giggled. "Social security. Don't know why they're still taking that shit out. Supposedly, by the time we're supposed to be old enough to get it, all that money will be gone."

"Where?"

Dulce shrugged then lifted her glass. "Welcome to the ranks of the working poor as Professor Daniels calls us."

That Esperanza needed no explanation to understand. "You know what's really jacked up, Dulce? If they did let us vote about how to use our taxes, I couldn't. 'Cause I'm a . . . you know. They can tax the shit outta me, and I'll never even have a say which muthafucka gets to decide what to do with my money."

Esperanza waited for Dulce to remind her that she never voted in her life, and she loved her sister just that much more when she did not. Instead she shrugged and said, "You ain't missing anything."

"I guess I should feel lucky that I have a job with my record and all."

After dinner they walked to the Barnes & Noble's. Dulce wanted to find other books by bell hooks on Professor Daniel's recommended reading list. As her sister browsed the women's studies shelves, Esperanza browsed the study aids and selected a GED prep book to supplement her studies. Then she slipped into the music section to look for any new books about Tupac that might have been published while she did her time.

Esperanza found a few that were much too expensive for her. *Tupac: Resurrection* cost almost thirty dollars and the bookstore did not have any softcover editions. If she had that kind of money, she would buy the DVD of the movie, but then again, she did not have a DVD player or the money to buy one. She skimmed through the other hard covers of old photographs and poetry written in Pac's sharp print, her fingers caressing the smooth pages and longing to take his words and images home with her. Dulce appeared at the end of the aisle cradling a stack of books in her arm. "Knew I'd find you here." Esperanza quickly returned the book in her hands back to the shelf. "I'ma go pay for these."

"I'm right behind you." Dulce disappeared and Esperanza gave the shelf one last gaze. Her eyes fell on a slim red volume she had seen many times but never bought or even borrowed from the library. *The Killing of Tupac Shakur* by Cathy Scott. The cover featured the picture of Tupac sitting next to Suge Knight in his car minutes before someone rolled up on them in a white Cadillac and opened fire. The back cover demanded to know, "Who did it and why?" and boasted "exclusive photo evidence."

As much as she adored Pac, some books and videos Esperanza had to pass by. She refused to get ensnared in the long-winded obituaries and conspiracy theories about Tupac's "murder," and the title alone gave her enough reasons to ignore it. Nigga was brilliant. Got the sharpest heads caught up in the ruse of his demise. Not her. She listened closely to him, and therefore, understood his plan. Esperanza learned quickly how futile were her attempts to convert the faithless. And perhaps that was just how Tupac wanted it because it kept him safe.

"Espe!"

She jumped as Dulce appeared behind her. "Damn, D, you fuckin' startled me!"

"Look, I'm not trying to be a bitch, but for real, I gotta get home. I need to do some reading and then go to bed."

"OK, I'm comin'."

Dulce bounded around the corner. Esperanza reached for *The Killing of Tupac Shakur* and flipped it over. The back cover boasted pictures including an autopsy photograph. It had to be a fake. Pac lived no matter what people like Dulce or Jesus or this Cathy Scott said. If they really got him, they would know that he had no choice but to hide from the haters in Cuba with his *titi* Assata who protected him. When new drama erupted in the world, she was the one who had to convince Tupac to bite his tongue for his own safety. How hard that must be for Assata. How hard that must be for Pac.

"Espe, I'm leaving!"

Esperanza grabbed the book and rushed behind Dulce as she rushed to the register. Like Tenille suggested, she would slip it into the waistband of her uniform pants and poke holes all over Miss Cathy's theories. The only thing Esperanza was scared of was Dulce's reaction when she saw that she bought yet another Tupac book.

She got on line behind Dulce. "What are you getting?" she asked. Esperanza made a defiant pout as she held the book in the air, silently daring her to criticize her selection.

Dulce read the title to herself. "Oh."

"What?"

"Nothing." Dulce turned around to face forward. "Your money."

The image of an icy and silent bus ride back to the South Bronx tempered Esperanza who caught herself before spitting out *That's right.* Instead she peeked over sister's shoulder. "What'd you get?"

"I haven't decided." Dulce held up her two options—*Sisters of the Yam* in one hand and *Talking Back* in the other. "Which one you think I should get?"

By answering Esperanza's question and asking her opinion, her sister had offered to maintain the peace. She took both books from Dulce's hand and placed them on top of *The Killing of Tupac Shakur* and her GED book. "Both."

EIGHT

Yearning

No matter how often she did it, Esperanza's heart always sank when she unlocked the apartment door to stillness. She wanted to be happy that Dulce met Chago, and when Esperanza opened the door to find Dulce cooking dinner or studying at the kitchen table, happiness came easily. Over a home-cooked meal, she loved hearing her sister's stories about attempting to translate for Chago in her broken Spanish what she read for class or heard on HOT 97. "It bugs me out sometimes, Espe," Dulce once said. "*Mami*'s Dominican and she raised us, but we're still, like, mad Boricua. I guess it's because we grew up around here instead of Washington Heights or Corona. Remember how we used to front like *Mami* was Puerto Rican?"

"We didn't front," said Esperanza. "Some people just assumed she was Puerto Rican, and we didn't correct them. People were dissing Dominicans, even the Puerto Ricans. Like being born here made them white or something."

"Anyway, I like that Chago gets me in touch with that part of who I am."

On Sunday mornings when Dulce had not spent the previous night at Chago's, Esperanza made breakfast for her sister and jockeyed with her over the entertainment section of the newspaper. Her favorite moments involved nothing more than sitting with Dulce at the kitchen table in silence, each absorbed in her own studies with nothing between them but textbooks, soda cans, and a bowl of Cheez-Its, Brenda's and now her daughters' favorite snack food.

When Chago first entered the scene, Dulce became a joy to live with.

She still got on Esperanza's case about eating too much junk and watching too much television, but now the tough love stressed more *love* and less *tough*. But now that Chago's charm had softened Dulce up, he kept her all to himself. Some days she saw Dulce for only the half hour she came home to primp for her dates.

At times Esperanza curled up on the living room sofa with her workbooks, only to be distracted by an eerie yet familiar feeling. Her eyes would roam the living room as if for the first time, inspecting it for something out of place. Everything from the dusty photographs to the homemade dolls in their yellowing skirts sat where they always did, but Esperanza could not shake the feeling that something was not right. One night she realized that the problem was not what was missing or misplaced, but what had infiltrated her home that did not belong there. Despite sitting on the couch in her favorite sweatpants and fuzzy socks and surrounded by her schoolbooks and loose-leafs, Esperanza tensed with loneliness so distracting, she felt as if she were back in her prison cell once again when Isoke was not there.

Esperanza made herself a peanut-butter-and-jelly sandwich for dinner and sifted through the mail Dulce had left on the table on her way out the door. "I'm Resident, and you're Occupant," her sister once said, trying to make Esperanza laugh. Brenda had just been transferred to California, and she could not stop crying.

"Who opens it if it's for *Mami*?"

"Nobody," said Dulce without missing a beat. She never missed a beat, not with Esperanza. Not at times like that. "We save it for her 'cause she's gonna win her appeal, and she's gonna be home soon. You know *Mami* doesn't care how old we are. She'll give us *pow-pow* if she finds out we went through her stuff."

Finally Esperanza laughed at the thought of Brenda spanking them even though they were grown women. Brenda rarely raised her hand to them, but she had her limits and made her daughters respect them. But she was far from the calculating murderess the prosecutor made her out to be. The jury had convicted her one month shy of Esperanza's eighteenth birthday.

Although Esperanza had been dating Jesus for almost two years, Dulce was the one who solicited his help in keeping their apartment. After the verdict Dulce and Jesus had carried a hysterical Esperanza out of the Bronx courtroom and ushered her into the backseat of Xavier's car. The second Jesus closed the door behind them, she slumped her head against the window and overheard Dulce say to him, "First thing NYCHA's gonna try to do is kick us out." It dawned on Esperanza that as much as Dulce had assured her that the jury would never convict Brenda, she herself had been anticipating a guilty verdict all along. Dulce preached optimism to Esperanza, allowing her to live hopefully while she herself made contingency plans based on the grimmest scenario. "You know I wouldn't ask. . . ."

"No worries, ma," said Jesus. "I got your back." He made telephone calls and sent Chuck to visit unnamed people. Within days the letter came placing the apartment in Dulce's name.

As Esperanza sifted through the shopping bulletins, subscription pitches, and charitable solicitations still addressed to Occupant after all these years, she missed Dulce more than ever. And Brenda, too. On a whim she knelt and found the cardboard box under the kitchen table where Dulce stacked the recyclable paper. Sure enough, Esperanza found a stack of letters for Resident.

Then she came across a small envelope with nothing but *Espe* scrawled across the front. It had no return address, and when she held it to the light, she saw a sheet of yellow legal paper with more handwriting. Someone must have hand-delivered this letter and stuck it into their mailbox. Maybe Dulce had missed it and accidentally thrown it into the recycling box. Esperanza turned the envelope around—it had been torn open. When she pulled the legal sheet from the envelope and smelled Chrome, she immediately knew that Dulce had not made a mistake at all.

Dear Espe,

I had to write you this letter (and you know I hate to write!) because your sister won't let me see you when I come by your place, and I know she's erasing my telephone messages, too. Any other guy would have given up by now, but I'm not going to give up, Espe, because I love you. And I'm going to keep coming by and blowing up your phone and writing you letters even though I'm a terrible writer. Still, I want you to know I love you so much. More than any other woman I have known. Don't sweat Priscilla, because she's a girl, not a woman. You're a woman, Espe. All woman, all the time. Only the love of a real woman like you brings out the best in a man like me, that's why I need you in my life. You know there's only two ways out this game, ma, but without you in my life, I got nothing else to live for.

Anyway, I want to make things up to you, but I can't do that if you don't give me a chance. (And you need to stop frontin', because you know you want to ha, ha, ha.) Like Boy George says in that song, you miss me blind. I see you sometimes going to work with your uniform or carrying your schoolbooks, and even though I miss you, too, I be mad proud. But it breaks my heart, too, because you're a queen, and a queen is not supposed to work so hard for so little. When you're sitting in that classroom or wiping down those tables, do you think of me?

I'm going to stop right here because some things are better said in person, and I hate to fuckin' write, but I've got no problem telling you in writing or over the phone or whatever that I love you. I just hope I have another chance to say it to your pretty face.

Love always and forever,
Jesus

She read the letter over and over again until she heard the apartment door slam. Esperanza jammed the letter in her front pocket. Dulce stormed into the kitchen, ripped off her jacket, and flung it across a chair.

"What's wrong, Dulce? You get into a fight with Chago or something?"

"Yeah. No." Dulce opened the refrigerator door and pulled out a bottle of soda. She walked over to the dish rack and grabbed a glass. "Chago drove me home and walked me to the door. You know those girls who be in front of the building sometimes? He sees them out there and says, 'American youth are so spoiled.' Starts going on and on about how we get everything for nothing."

"Funny thing is Rosie just got off the boat from DR herself. You tell Chago that?"

Dulce poured her soda and swallowed half the glass in several deep gulps. "Then he really pissed me off with, 'And the girls here. Bad enough they want to be just like men; they try to be equal to men by imitating all their vices." Dulce uncapped the soda again and poured herself another glass.

"Take it easy on the soda or you're gonna be up all night."

"There's nothing fuckin' wrong with women wanting to be equal to men. I wanted to ask him, 'What you mean by vices? Getting paid? Enjoying sex? Speaking their mind and not taking shit from anybody? So all of a sudden those are vices 'cause girls wanna piece of the action?' No one's gotta problem with any of those things when a man does it, and it ain't just an American thing either."

"Word."

"And who's Chago to judge Rosie and them? He doesn't know them or what they've been through. 'Cause they're chilling in front of their building, automatically they gotta be bad girls?" Dulce got up and took her glass to the kitchen sink. Esperanza watched her as she washed it with soap, dried it thoroughly, and placed it in the cupboard. Esperanza said nothing waiting for her sister to reveal the true source of her angst. Dulce shut off the water and turned to face Esperanza. "If Chago finds out the truth about me, it's over."

Dulce meant that Chago might find out somehow that his straitlaced supermarket cashier who attended college at night once ran the streets with the boys and sometimes outdid them in their vices. But knowing Dulce as she did, Esperanza understood that what bothered her much more than that was that she actually gave a damn what Chago thought. Her sister cared what this divorced *jíbaro* in his late thirties who probably believed women belonged in only one of two places—behind "her" man or beneath him—thought of her.

"The only way Chago will know is if you tell him, and what reason would you have to do that?" said Esperanza. She tucked her hands into her front pockets and felt Jesus's letter wedged beneath her fingertips. "You're not that girl anymore."

Esperanza yawned as Hudlin read from his teacher's guide and wrote across the chalkboard about the kinds of numbers and their various properties. "An irrational number is any number that cannot be expressed as a fraction," he said, writing the very same thing on the board that he was reading from the book. Did he think that if he repeated it often enough, the students suddenly might understand what the hell he was saying? Talk about irrational.

She turned to the back of her notebook, where she had tucked Jesus's letter within the fold of the back cover. Only days in her possession and the envelope was already wrinkled from being removed, reread and resealed over and over again. Afraid to leave it in the apartment lest Dulce find it, Esperanza took it to work and read it on both official and unauthorized breaks. When Dulce finished studying and went to sleep, Esperanza read it once or twice before putting herself to bed. Today she read it again on the bus ride to school. And now Esperanza pulled it out again as Hudlin droned on about the associative property of addition.

Every time she reread his letter, Esperanza tried to read between the lines, interpret what he left unsaid, and compose responses in her head. When Jesus called her *all woman, all the time*, was he talking just about sex or did he mean something more important? How did he plan to make up things to her? Did he really believe the only way out the game was death or prison or could she get him to go legit? What exactly did he mean by *a man like him*?

Jesus's letter flew from Esperanza's hands into the air. " 'Dear Espe, I had to write you this letter, and you know I hate to write, because your sister won't let me see you when I come by your place . . .' " Hudlin read. Several of her younger classmates snickered and pointed at Esperanza, while the older students either smirked with righteousness or shook their heads in sympathy. Fueled by the laughter, Hudlin switched from reading to performing, adopting a thug grumble and bopping in place as he exposed her. " 'Any other guy would have given up by now, but I'm not going to give up, Espe, because I love you.' "

Esperanza leaped to her feet and snatched the letter out of his hand. "What the fuck you doing?"

"Don't you curse in my classroom."

"Don't be invading my fuckin' privacy then!" Although Hudlin towered over her by a foot, Esperanza jabbed her finger in his face. He stepped back to distance himself from her angry gesture, and Esperanza jammed the letter back into its envelope.

"If you had been paying attention to the lesson like you're supposed to, I wouldn't have had to embarrass you."

"If I had been doing what I was supposed to?" Esperanza tucked the envelope back in the flap of her notebook cover. "Muthafucka, I would've been doing what I was supposed to had you been doing what you were supposed to. Instead of reading straight out the book like we're a bunch of goddamn morons, why don't you teach?" Esperanza slammed her book shut and smashed the textbook on top it. "I'm not here because I can't fuckin' read. *¡Eso, si, yo puedo 'cer!*" She grabbed her books and jacket, slung her messenger bag over her shoulder and stormed toward the front of the classroom.

"Oh, so now you're going to run?" Hudlin said. Despite his sarcastic tone, Esperanza saw the panic in his eyes. Dulce had schooled her on this. The government or some charity probably gave this program a certain amount of money for every person who enrolled and succeeded. He didn't give a shit about her. He didn't give a shit about any of them. All Hudlin cared about was that they stay in the program and maintain his livelihood and sense of superiority. "Just remember if you go back to prison, Esperanza, it's no one's fault but your own." Several classmates gasped and others began to mumble under their breaths. As harsh whispers of words like *criminal* and *prison* scattered in the air, tears of embarrassment burned her eyes.

Esperanza marched over to his desk, grabbed Hudlin's teacher's guide, and flung it at him. "How dare you put me on blast like that, you son of a bitch! It's not my fault that you can't teach worth a shit." She turned around and punched the blackboard. "And it's not my fault that this boring shit that you can't teach is not relevant to my fuckin' life!" Then Esperanza ran out the door.

She raced down the empty corridor and into the stairwell. Gasping for air, she dropped onto a bottom step. Esperanza buried her face into the jacket in her hands and cursed Hudlin for humiliating her. She cursed her classmates for believing he thought any better of any of them and not having her back. Then Esperanza cursed herself. She shouldn't have given Hudlin the satisfaction of losing her cool. She shouldn't have been reading that stupid letter in class. She shouldn't have been reading Jesus's fuckin' letter at all. And reading it over and over again like it really meant a damned thing.

Esperanza looked at her watch. In less than fifteen minutes her social studies class would begin, followed by her science class an hour later. Her language arts class would not meet for another two hours. After the scene she caused in Hudlin's class, no doubt they would throw her out of the program. She imagined security barging in, in the middle of Ms. Rodriguez's lesson, and escorting her out of the building. Esperanza decided to save them the trouble and spare herself more humiliation.

After an hour of trekking up and down Third Avenue, Esperanza grew frustrated with window-shopping. Even if she could afford the clothes that beckoned to her from the boutique racks and window displays, she had no one to wear them for, and no place to wear them to in search of that person. Worst of all, these facts did nothing to abate Esperanza's desires for the sexy dresses and pretty shoes for which she had no use. On the contrary, they only made her yearn for them even more.

She tore herself away from the burgundy gown in the window of Revolutions and walked down the block and around the corner toward Willis

Avenue. In front of Chucho's bodega, Hector and several other guys shot dice against the tenement wall, each conjuring his own good luck when not cursing one another. Esperanza headed toward them for a closer view of the action.

"'Sup, y'all."

"Hey, pretty lady," said Hector. "How're you doing?"

"I'm good. *¿Y tú?*"

Hector scoffed. "*Nena,* do me a favor. Go in there and talk to Shanette. Otherwise we gonna be headed for 'forth' real soon, know what I'm sayin'?"

Esperanza laughed. "Yeah, I'd love to see her." She walked into the bodega. Behind the counter, Chucho sliced a loaf of spiced ham into wax paper for a Black woman Esperanza's age holding a toddler in one hand and several food stamps in the other. "Hey, Chucho, long time, no see."

"Esperanza! They told me you were back."

"Not so thin, Chucho," warned the woman.

"You handle your business, pa. I'll come back later to catch up with you," said Esperanza. She pointed to the door that led to the back room, where Chucho kept a pool table, a jukebox, and a slot machine. Even though he installed those things to make extra money, only certain people were allowed to hang out back there. Because of Jesus, she used to be one of them. "Is it OK if I . . . ?"

"*¿Como no?*"

"Thanks, Chucho."

Esperanza pushed open the door. Ja Rule barked through the jukebox speakers: "I got a hundred guns, a hundred clips, and I'm from New Yawk, New Yawk." Shanette leaned over the pool table, her long, dark hair grazing the green felt as she racked up the balls. "Netty!" Esperanza sang.

Shanette looked up and threw her hands to her mouth. "Espe!" She ran to Esperanza, and they embraced. "It's so good to see you. Hector wasn't kidding. You haven't changed a bit."

"Why does everybody keep saying that?" Esperanza giggled.

"'Cause it's true, bitch. You gotta problem with that? Jail made you sick of being gorgeous?" They hugged again. "Play with me."

"OK." Esperanza grabbed a cue stick from where they hung on the wall and rubbed the cube of chalk over its tip.

Shanette positioned the cue ball behind the headstring. "How's your sister?"

"D's good. Working hard. Going to school." *Falling in love.* "So . . . how're things with you and Hector?"

Shanette sucked her teeth. "Do not get me started on that nigga."

"What he do?"

"It's what he doesn't do, Espe. Fuckin' Madeline calls the apartment. . . ."

"Who's that?"

Shanette slipped her cue between her fingers. After a few preliminary slides she struck the cue into the ball. The white ball shot forward into the triangle, and colored balls scattered across the table. "You know that ho Madeline."

"Nah, ma, I don't. She just moved here or something?"

"Girl, that bitch moved in here, and now she's trying to move in on my man. Talking about how there's no ring on my finger. After all I been through with that nigga, she best believe he's mine, ring or no ring." Shanette walked around the table and aimed her cue. She tapped the white ball, knocking it into the orange ball, which stopped a few inches short of the middle pocket. "Shit."

Esperanza suppressed her grin as she prowled around the table for a shot. Shanette still could not play worth a damn, but her gossip remained hot. They never played for the competiton, always for the *bochinche,* and the more personal the juicier. "I feel you, ma." She spotted an opportunity with the yellow ball in the corner pocket. She leaned over and slid the cue between her fingers. "So Madeline calls the apartment . . ." Esperanza hauled back, then rammed the cue ball into the yellow ball. The target richocheted against one side of the table to the other and finally settled far from any pocket. "Damn, *lo metí con demasio fuerza.*"

"No, you didn't, ma. You hit it with perfect force. You just have to aim the cue at the right angle so it'll go in the direction you choose." Esperanza shot up and looked toward the door. Jesus leaned against the door frame in the shearling coat she had bought him last Christmas. "It's all physics. You master that, you can never miss." He shrugged off the shearling and draped it across a stool, revealing a ribbed V-neck sweater that clung to his chest and arms.

Esperanza stared at him as he sauntered toward her, those green eyes boring into her. "That's not exactly what they're teaching me in school."

Jesus licked his lips and smiled. "Then I'll show you."

She offered him her cue, but instead of taking it Jesus walked behind her and placed his hand on the small of her back. "Red ball, corner pocket."

He pressed his palm against her back, gesturing for Esperanza to bend over the table. She leaned forward, and Jesus followed, folding his taut body over hers and laying his hands over hers as she gripped the cue.

Pressing his head against Esperanza's temple, Jesus said, "You see how you have the cue pointed at the center of the ball?" His cologne wrapped itself around her head, and heat radiated from every point in his body and sank into her own. With every word Jesus spoke, his warm breath draped over her earlobe, then coasted down her neck. Jesus's chest leaned into her back as his broad shoulders sat upon hers. "If you were to hit it now, it'd go that way. But you want it to go over there." As Jesus nodded his head, his firm hips pressed against Esperanza's bottom, and she caught her breath. "So angle it like this." He guided her hands to shift the cue behind the white ball. She drew back and tapped the ball. With a decisive clack, it hit the red ball, which obediently fell into the corner pocket.

"Let's try it again." Esperanza never should have let him so close, but she had no will to pull away. She wished Shanette would leave, but she needed her to stay. Her man was outside, so why didn't she fuckin' go be with him? Hector probably called Jesus to tell him that Esperanza had shown up at Chucho's, anyway. But Shanette could not leave her alone with Jesus.

"OK. Let's see if we can sink the blue ball into this pocket right here." And as if he read Esperanza's conflicted mind, Jesus said, "Shanette, Hector's looking for you." Grinning, Shanette hung up her cue, grabbed her jacket, and left the room. "Those two are a trip, aren't they?"

"Yeah."

He waited for Esperanza to position herself to take the next shot. "They should cut all that bullshit, get married, and have more babies." Jesus spooned her again and shifted her cue. "Holding it like this will make it go like that. Try it."

Esperanza took the shot, and the blue ball sailed toward its goal but lost steam at the very edge. She straightened up and slammed the cue onto the pool table. "Damn."

Jesus placed his hand on Esperanza's arm and turned her around to face him. "Hey, you did good, ma. *Un poquito más fuerza,* and it would've rolled right in." He inched forward, pressing Esperanza between himself and the pool table. Before she could respond, Jesus lifted her up, set her on the table, then stepped between her thighs. "Remember the last time we made love on this table?"

Esperanza's mind had beaten his words to that memory. "X was banging on the door yelling, 'Rent a room, you fuckin' freaks!'" At first Esperanza had been embarrassed at the thought of all of Jesus's boys pressing their ears against the door.

"They're ruining everything," she had said. "Tell them to fuckin' go away, Sus."

Jesus continued to thrust into her. "Get the fuck away from that door!"

Esperanza heard the guys cackling behind the door. Then they started to chant. "Rent a room! Rent a room! Rent a room!" They might as well have been in the room, too, surrounding the pool table, pounding their fists, and cheering Jesus on as he fucked her in front of them.

She wanted Jesus to stop, fling open the door, and tell them to go away—bust some heads if he had to. But the audience only made him hotter, and he pounded into her until her thighs began to burn from rubbing against the green felt. Then Jesus did something to Esperanza he rarely did during sex no matter how much she told him it pleased her.

Jesus spread her thighs farther apart and dropped to his knees. Her attention shifted from the burn in the back of her thighs to the tension between them. Esperanza looked down at him, his green eyes peering over her hairy mound. "Let them hear you cum," he said, and then his eyes disappeared.

Now Jesus laughed at the memory as he ran his hands along her thighs. "I promise you no one's behind the door now." He reached for the button of her jeans. "But let's see if this time we can make them hear you on the street."

"No." Esperanza grabbed his hand. "Not here."

Jesus stepped back, and she jumped off the table. "Tell you what—we won't even go to my crib." He rushed to the stool and picked up their coats. Jesus put his on, then held up Esperanza's borrowed leather jacket. As she eased into the sleeves, he said, "I'll drive you to a fancy hotel downtown with the works. That's the first thing I shoulda done when you came home. The party could've waited."

Jesus grabbed Esperanza's hand, opened the door, and led her through the store and onto the street. "Wait here while I tie up some loose ends."

"OK."

She watched Jesus as he bounded over to Hector and his dice-shooting cronies while digging through his pocket. He withdrew his hand and offered it to Hector. Esperanza caught a glimpse of the cash in Jesus's palm before it disappeared in their handshake. She smiled at the thought of Jesus loving her so much he'd offer rewards to cats in the street who played matchmaker for him. Her eyes roamed the sidewalk as she wondered how many of these dudes had their eyes on her for Jesus's sake. Then Esperanza spotted the car.

Jesus taught her long ago how to spot an unmarked police car. They were always American cars, usually a four-door sedan stripped of all luxuries yet equipped with extra antennas and additional lights behind the grill and on the dashboard. The navy Crown Victoria with spot lights on the driver side sat across the street from Chucho's bodega. The smoke from the exhaust suggested that the driver remained warm inside, but the tinted windows kept him from view.

Puente? Did parole officers drive unmarked cars? Had Hudlin called Puente to tell him what had happened that morning? How long had he been following her around?

"C'mon, ma, my ride's right around the corner." Having finished his business with Hector, Jesus reappeared at her side and threw his arm around her waist.

She wriggled away from him. "No, I can't go with you."

"What? What's wrong? Why not?"

"'Cause I'm not supposed to."

Jesus grabbed her by the wrists. "Don't fuckin' play with me, Espe. What the fuck you come around here for then? You know these are my streets."

As she tried to pull away from him, Esperanza watched the navy Crown Victoria. If Puente was in that car, why didn't he help her? Maybe he knew that she had made him and believed that her protest was nothing but an act. She had decided to do the right thing at the wrong time. Hell, the right thing would have been never to roll through there at all. Now Puente was going to sit long enough to watch Esperanza hang herself.

To make matters worse, a crowd started to form around them. "You need to leave me alone, Sus."

"*Nena,* don't do him like that," said Hector as Shanette hung on him.

"Yeah, Espe," she said. "You know Jesus loves you."

"Jesus is gonna get me locked up again!"

"How you figure, ma?" Jesus reached for her, and she backed away. "I wanna make all that up to you and then some. Did you get my letter? I thought you got my letter, and that's why you came over here."

Esperanza wrangled herself free from his grip. "I got your fuckin' letter, all right." She busted through the crowd and down the street, praying that the navy Crown Victoria would not pull out after her.

Esperanza ran nonstop until she arrived at her McDonald's. She dropped into a booth where she could see through the window yet remain invisible from the street. Her head pounded as she concocted a story. If Puente walked in here right now, she would tell him that she stopped into the bodega for a *cubano* on her way to work, and Jesus happened to be there. But what if Puente asked her why she was on her way to work when she was supposed to be in school? Should she come clean about what had happened in Hudlin's class? No, the chances were that he did not know. But then how would she explain why . . .

"Esperanza?" Luciano hovered over her. "Tenille told me she thought she saw you sitting over here. I thought you couldn't work Saturdays."

"I told you just the mornings." Since Esperanza had first told Luciano that, he never scheduled her to work on Saturdays at all. Not even in the afternoons when she was free as if he wanted to punish her for not being at his beck and call. She walked out of the restaurant every Friday night singing good-bye to let Luciano know that he had done her a favor by keeping her Saturdays free. Never mind that she usually spent her weekend nights studying, watching TV and her videos, or just staring out her window at the people hanging out in front of the building like, *la gordita* and her twin friends. Luciano didn't know Esperanza had nothing much else to do on a Saturday night, and he didn't need to.

"By any chance, you free now? I could really use you. As you can see, the place is a zoo."

Too involved in her own drama, Esperanza had not noticed. She looked around and saw everything that Tenille loathed about working Saturdays. According to Tenille, as people traveled from all over the Bronx to the Hub to shop, Mickey D's remained packed from opening to closing. Besides the employees from the retail shops and nonprofit organizations along Third Avenue and 149th Street, the restaurant overflowed with their weekend patrons: mothers pushing their children in strollers, teenagers looking to squander their cash on sneakers and CDs, street hustlers hawking their bootlegs, young singles (as well some singles not so young, or the young ones who were not so single) filing into the salons to get ready for a night of macking, politicians shouting slogans through megaphones atop rented vans, evangelicals selling salvation in pamphlets—all in full effect, handling whatever business they could not handle during the week.

"This is the one day that never has a slow period, and you've walked right into the peak," said a flustered Luciano. "Can you help me out?"

Already drained from her eventful morning, Esperanza hardly wanted to spend her afternoon emptying garbage and wiping spills, least of all on the busiest day of the week. But if Puente was lurking outside, she needed a cover. For whatever it was worth, she had to do something good to counter the mistakes she had made earlier in the day.

"You got an extra uniform I can borrow?"

As Esperanza made her way through the lobby with a garbage bag in tow, an irate toddler hurled his fruit drink across the table. "My God, Jason. What's wrong with you today?" The child responded with a wail while his teenage mother leaped to fetch napkins to absorb his mess.

Esperanza ran to the supply closet, grabbed a mop and pail, and headed back into the lobby. She found Jason's mother on her knees holding a batch of soggy napkins drenched in red. Her son's drink dripped from her hands onto her jeans as she fought back tears.

"Let me get it," said Esperanza. She motioned for her to step back and then slapped the mop onto the spill.

"I'm so sorry. He's usually not like this."

Yeah, right. An eerie calm had overcome Jason as he watched his mother climb to her feet and wring her hands. *Little demon.* Almost as if he realized that Esperanza saw right through his angelic expression, he began to screech again. "It's OK. It happens," said Esperanza. "Everyone makes a mess sometimes, and it doesn't make us bad. Right, Jason?" At the sound of his name, the toddler stopped and gave her a quizzical look. "We all make mistakes, right, papa?" she cooed at him as she continued to mop the floor. "It was just a mistake. You didn't mean it."

"Say sorry, Jason."

"I sorry."

"That's all right, sweetie."

"Thank you," said Jason's mother as she picked up her tray.

Esperanza reached for it. "I can take that."

"Thank you." She picked up her purse and grabbed her son's stroller by the handle. "Thank you." Her gratitude seemed to cover much more than wiping up her son's spill or busing her tray—more than Esperanza could ever know.

"No problem." She surprised herself with her own sudden sincerity. "Come again soon. 'Bye, Jason."

" 'Byyyeee."

When Esperanza returned the mop to the closet, she found Luciano waiting for her. "What's up, John?"

"I want you to stop by my office before you leave for the day."

"OK. What do you want to talk to me about?"

"I don't want to discuss that here and now. It's inappropriate." Without another glance at her, Luciano headed back to his office. "Just see me after you lock up."

At eleven o'clock Esperanza let the last customer out and locked the restaurant door behind her. Her back and heels ached from spending the last six hours on her feet. Saturdays offered no chance to sneak into the ladies' room for a quick read, even if Esperanza had had a fun book with her. At least the constant work made the hours fly, leaving her with only the soreness in the muscles of her lower body to remind her how she passed the time. She even forgot about Hudlin, Jesus, and Puente at times, but her pending conversation with Luciano weighed on her mind.

Esperanza knocked, then opened Luciano's door. "Your keys." She placed them on his desk. "If it's OK with you, I'm just going to go home with the uniform on and bring it back tomorrow. Or I can even wash it first if you want." It was late to have to pull her aching limbs out of this baggy costume and into her street clothes, only to have to strip them off again when she got home. She felt too exhausted to care if anyone laughed and pointed at her as she walked home. Let them. At least she put in an honest day's work.

"OK, just bring it back whenever you wash it," Luciano said.

Esperanza smiled. He stuck to the rules of operation as if he were running one of Donald Trump's hotels. His permission suggested that he appreciated her work today. Maybe what he had to say to her would not be so horrible. Even if it were, she preferred to get it over with. "What'd you want to talk to me about?"

"How would you like to move to the register?"

More than anything Esperanza wanted to work the register. If she had to be on her feet all day, she preferred the variety of juggling orders than the monotony of dumping trash. She wanted the challenge of ringing up sales and making people smile. Esperanza rather joke and gripe with coworkers behind the counter than remain invisible to the customers in the dining area until a soda cup fell or the ketchup dispenser was emptied.

A moment of doubt hit her as the Hudlin incident flashed across her mind. What if being a cashier got her in over her head? *Nah, man, fuck Hudlin*! Just because he couldn't teach math didn't mean she couldn't learn it.

"I'd really like that. I've been dying to learn how to work the register, 'cause like I told you, I'm mad good at math." Esperanza remembered what Dulce had said about her. "And I'm good with people, too."

"I can see that. Come in about an hour earlier tomorrow," said Luciano. "I'll show you the training video and give you some time to practice on the register."

"Thanks, John. Have a good night."

"You get home safe, Espe."

"I will."

Esperanza skipped out the door and toward the employee lockers. Already in her street clothes, Tenille shoved her polyster cap into her knapsack. "Did John promote you?"

"Yeah." This was one conversation Esperanza did not want to have. Not now, not ever. She liked Tenille and did not want her own good fortune to hurt her feelings.

"Fries?"

"Register."

"Wow." Tenille forced a smile and heaved her knapsack over her shoulder. "Congratulations, Espe. You deserve it."

"So do you. I mean, you deserve it more. Why does he keep busting you back and forth between lobby and register?"

"This time? Because I let a customer pass me a fake twenty."

"How the hell were you supposed to tell?"

"All the cashiers have these special pens; you'll see. Anyway, if you suspect that a bill is counterfeit, you're supposed to use it. But Luciano wants us to suspect every Black guy who comes in here wearing jeans and a hoodie. Meanwhile, if I did do that shit, he'd probably complain that I was taking too long to complete each order."

"Never mind that. You do that, you're just asking for drama. And I don't mean from Luciano."

"His biggest problem with me, though, is that I don't like to upsell."

"What's that?"

Tenille grabbed the doorknob and winked at Esperanza. "You'll learn soon enough. See ya tomorrow. And congratulations again."

"Thanks, T." Other than her sister, Esperanza had never met another woman who could smile upon her good luck. After losing Jesus to Esperanza without her even pursuing him, Dulce just laughed and said, "Story of my love life." Other chicks were so catty, even when she had or accomplished something they did not even want. "You be careful on the way home, OK?"

Esperanza opened her locker and bent down to pick up her messenger bag, and for once the soreness in her back actually felt good. She remembered what Isoke would say before climbing into the top bunk: *No matter what they do to me, I'm still alive.*

As she neared the apartment door, Esperanza heard the television in the living room. For the first time in days she hurried to unlock the door and push her way into the apartment. She raced down the hallway and into the living room. "Dulce, guess what?" She found her sister on the couch cuddled up against Chago. She had only stumbled on them watching an action flick, yet all three of them grew awkward. "Oh, sorry. I didn't know you weren't alone."

"Hola, Espe."

" 'S up, Chago."

"Where you've been, *negrita*?" For once Dulce sounded more relieved than suspicious. "It's mad late."

"I went by the restaurant after school, and Luciano gave me some extra hours."

Dulce chuckled. "The restaurant?" She looked up at Chago and explained the joke in Spanish. *"Para ella McDonalds es un restaurante. ¿Qué chiste, no?"*

Chago shrugged politely. *"Pues los restaurantes sirven comida."*

"Awww." Dulce put her arm around his neck and pecked him on the cheek. "You're so nice." Esperanza started to leave the living room. "Espe, hey!"

"What?"

"What were you saying?"

"Nothing."

"When you came in, you were like, 'Dulce, guess what?' What happened?"

"Forget it. Didn't mean to interrupt you guys."

"*Que* sorry, *ni* sorry," said Dulce. The more time Dulce spent with Chago, the more she spoke like him, using his expressions and adopting his Dominican accent. "Talking like this isn't your home. So what were you saying?"

With that welcoming acknowledgment, Esperanza stepped back into the living room. "Luciano's gonna put me on the register starting tomorrow."

Dulce sprang to her feet as if Esperanza had just announced that her number hit. "Espe, that's fantastic!" She ran to her sister and threw her arms around her. "I'm so proud of you." Dulce pulled away from Esperanza to translate her good news to Chago.

"Ay, pues, mañana les llevo a un restaurante bien chévere para celebrar," he said. "No McDonald's."

"Chago, you don't have to do that," said Esperanza.

"I inseest."

Still unsure about Chago's intentions, Esperanza had mixed feelings about his offer. He sounded sincere, but so could any deceitful man thoroughly committed to his agenda. She had learned that the hard way. Then again, Esperanza deserved a little recognition for her achievement, especially before Dulce learned about her expulsion from the GED program. No one had treated Esperanza to a nice dinner in a long time. For the past several weeks she had not even been lucky enough to serve as the fifth wheel on one of Dulce and Chago's dates.

"So come straight home from work tomorrow," said Dulce. She shimmied her hips and did a salsa step. "We'll dress real nice, get all made up, maybe go dancing."

That sealed the deal for Esperanza. "Cool." She kissed Dulce on the cheek and headed for the bedroom, looking forward to a deep sleep and exciting dreams. "Night, Chago. *Te veo mañana."*

"Buenas noches, joven."

Just as Esperanza began to close the bedroom door, Dulce called her name. "Ms. Rodriguez called."

Esperanza's stomach flipped. "What'd she say?"

"She just left her number and said to call her back. Who is she?"

"She's my language arts teacher."

"Oh. I left the number for you on the refrigerator."

"OK. Thanks."

She heard Dulce and Chago laugh at something on the TV and sighed with relief. Ms. Rodriguez had no reason to call besides what had happened in math class. But why did she call instead of Hudlin or the program director? Esperanza glanced at the clock. It was ten to midnight; the answer to her question had to wait until the next day. Esperanza peeled off her borrowed uniform, stuffed it in the hamper, and crawled into bed. So much for a night of deep sleep and exciting dreams.

NINE

Sister Outsider

Esperanza awoke the next morning to find Dulce snoozing beside her. She eased out of the bed so as not to wake her and stole into the kitchen. Pegged to the refrigerator door under a coqui magnet, she found a scrap of paper with Ms. Rodriguez's name and telephone number in Dulce's bubbly script. Esperanza slid the paper off the refrigerator and lifted the cordless telephone off its base. As she dialed Ms. Rodriguez's number and the line rang, she slipped into the living room.

"Hello?"

"Hi, can I speak to Ms. Rodriguez?"

"You may, and you are," she said. "Is this Esperanza Cepeda?"

"Yeah. I mean, yes."

"How are you this morning?"

"Fine. And you?"

"I'm well, thank you. I was a bit disappointed yesterday, however, not to see you in my class."

"Didn't they tell you? I got kicked out of the program."

"Actually, all I heard was that you had a confrontation with Mr. Hudlin during math class."

"He caught me reading something personal in class, and he started reading it out loud to everybody, so I told him off." Her anger flooded back, and Esperanza readied herself to break off a piece of it to serve to Ms. Rodriguez if she went there. She was a nice lady and a good teacher, but she had better not have made Esperanza call her on a Sunday morning to dog her about something she could not undo. "I don't know what the *chismosos* told you, but the worst thing I did was curse at him a little and throw a book at him. Not that it got anywhere near him. I'm not, like, Mariano Rivera or anything."

Esperanza thought she heard Ms. Rodriguez laugh. "All I want to know is what made you think that what occurred in Mr. Hudlin's class gave you permission to cut mine?"

"I just figured they would expel me from the program after that."

"I understand why you assumed the worst, Esperanza, so I want you to understand me. I don't care what happens between you and any other teacher. I don't care what happens between you and your sister, your boyfriend, or anyone else. I expect you to attend my class unless and until I tell you that you're no longer welcome. Do I make myself clear?"

Almost breathless with gratitude, Esperanza said, "Yes, Ms. Rodriguez." She had had teachers nag her about attending their classes many times before today, but this felt so much different. Like Ms. Rodriguez wanted her in class for something other than attendance's sake. "I really like your class, Ms. Rodriguez, and I wanted to go. But after embarrassing myself in Mr. Hudlin's class, I didn't want security bustin' into your classroom looking to haul me out, you know."

"My classroom is your classroom. In fact, I had called you to give you the assignment you missed. Read pages twenty-three to twenty-seven in your workbook, and complete the exercises on pages twenty-eight through thirty."

"OK." Esperanza rushed back into the kitchen, where Dulce always left her schoolbooks and supplies neatly stacked in front of her seat at the table. She scribbed the page numbers across the slip of paper with Ms. Rodriguez's telephone number. "That it?"

"Of course not. Before you can return to my classroom, you have to complete an additional assignment as well." *Always a fuckin' catch.* "I'm preparing a lesson on similes and metaphors, and I want you to e-mail me some rap lyrics that contain examples of each. If you have any questions about the material or the assignments, call me at home. Don't be shy about it; just do so before nine."

"Sure! I don't have an e-mail address, but I got a friend at the library who can hook me up with one. When do you need the lyrics, Ms. Rodriguez?"

"I'd say no later than Thursday night, so I have time to review them and prepare for Saturday morning. You have my telephone number, so now take down my e-mail address."

"Go."

"It's M-A-I-T-E at people-dash-link-dot-org, as in organization. Got it?"

"Yes, Ms. Rodriguez."

"One more thing, Espe. Outside of class, please call me Maite."

"OK, Maite. I'll see you next Saturday. And I'll e-mail you those lyrics by Thursday, too."

Esperanza hung up the phone and bounced up and down on the sofa like a kid on her birthday. For some kind of punishment, this assignment sounded like mad fun, and if she had any problems with it, she had permission to call her teacher at home for help. In high school she rarely learned a teacher's first name, let alone where to reach them outside of school hours. Not that she had ever wanted to.

She wanted to begin her assignment right away, but most of her favorite CDs were in the bedroom, where Dulce kept the portable stereo after pawning the phat entertainment system Xavier bought her in an attempt to win her back after Dulce broke up with him for the umpteenth time. When Dulce woke up, Esperanza would take her CDs and place them in her bag. On her lunch break she would transcribe a few songs into her notebook. Then after work on Wednesday, when the library stayed open late, she would ask Feli to help her get a free e-mail account, search for some more lyrics on the Internet, and send them to Maite. If Esperanza had time, she'd look up what the name Maite meant, too.

But for now she had to be at work an hour earlier than usual to train for her new job as a cashier. Then after work she had dinner with Dulce and Chago. If Esperanza didn't know better, she'd think God had rewarded her for standing up to Mr. Hudlin. Or maybe this was His way of apologizing not for what had happened in math class—because Esperanza really should've just ripped up the letter once she knew it came from Jesus—but for everything. Or maybe just like Esperanza, God hated math, too.

Esperanza never thought she would be nervous about having dinner with her sister and her new boyfriend. Yet the longer she stood in front of her dresser mirror, the more uneasy she became. Dulce had come home with a new dress for Esperanza to wear that she had bought during her lunch hour. "I know you haven't had the money to get yourself some new clothes, and I thought since this was a special occasion, it wouldn't hurt to treat you to something pretty."

At the time Dulce gave it to her, Esperanza loved the turquoise dress. It had a racer-back bodice and four ruffles in the skirt, each an increasingly darker yet still vibrant shade of blue. It not only skimmed her curves but flattered the extra pounds she had gained in the pen.

Then Dulce showed Esperanza the dress she had bought for herself—a sexy fuchsia dress with a wraparound waist and halter top. Her sister noticed Esperanza's worried expression. "Don't you like it?"

"You kidding me? It's gorgeous. It's just . . ."

"What?"

"Two new dresses?"

"Oh, don't worry about it. Chago bought them for me." Dulce took her bathrobe off the back of the bedroom door and hung her dress in its place. "I mean, he gave me enough money to buy a dress and get my hair done and all that," she said as she pulled off her sweater and undid her jeans. "I decided to do my own hair this time."

Esperanza pulled her dress against her body. "I don't think Chago would like you spending money on me that he meant for you."

"He doesn't mind," Dulce said, throwing on her robe and unclasping the barrette from her curly ponytail. "And even if he did, too bad. You know how I feel about dudes giving me money, then telling me what I can and can't do with it." Before Esperanza could thank her for the dress, Dulce had taken her own new dress off the hook and left to shower.

As Dulce readied for dinner in the bathroom, Esperanza dressed in their bedroom and stressed over her sister's words. Xavier used to give Dulce money to buy clothes and visit the salon, too. Over time Dulce began to question his generosity, suspecting that a desire to control her lurked behind every chivalrous thing he did. Now Chago did the same, but Dulce thought nothing of it. She had pegged Xavier right, so now why not suspect the same of Chago? Because he was older? *Dominicano? Jíbaro*? If anything, shouldn't those qualities make Dulce more suspicious of him than she ever had been of Xavier?

Esperanza loved the dress but felt compelled to change into something more conservative. But with Chago due any moment, she would only trigger one of Dulce's interrogations, and Dulce's interrogations always led to fights. Instead she went into the kitchen and used dishwashing liquid to scrub her face clean of makeup. Then Esperanza returned to the bedroom to braid her hair and roll it into a bun.

She had jabbed one last bobby pin into the knot on her head when Dulce finally emerged from the bathroom. Dulce looked so beautiful in her fuchsia dress and gentle makeup. At once she seemed both much younger yet more sophisticated than her twenty-six years. Dulce's hair surprised Esperanza the most. For years she and her sister had subdued their natural ringlets with hair dryers and flatirons, resorting to baseball caps and bandannas when time or money wrung too tight to straighten their hair. Right before Esperanza went upstate, Dulce began to pull her hair into ponytails and braids, no longer subjecting it to long bouts of electronic heat, yet unwilling to let it free. Now she stood before Esperanza beneath a dark halo of thick curls much like those photographs of the Virgin Mary and her golden aura. "Stop staring at me, will you?" Dulce laughed.

"Your hair."

"What about it?"

"It's so pretty."

"Thanks."

"Not that it's not when it's straight. It's cute like that, too. I just can't remember the last time you wore it curly."

"Probably, like, in the sixth grade." Dulce walked over to Esperanza before the mirror and scrunched her curls. "I didn't remember having *complejos* about my hair before junior high school."

"Chago likes it like that, huh?"

Dulce paused to stare at Esperanza's reflection. "That's not why I'm wearing it like this."

"So why don't you blow it out anymore? You go to one of the *dominicanas* on Westchester Avenue, like, on a Monday, and they do it for you really cheap. Or on the weekends you can do it yourself."

Dulce huffed. "I told you. I don't have those *pelo-bueno-pelo-malo complejos* anymore. The only bad hair is mistreated hair, and when I stopped tugging and burning the hell out of it, I finally realized how pretty it could be like this."

Esperanza grinned at her. "But Chago doesn't care either way, right?"

Dulce bumped her with her hip. "I'm not saying he doesn't like it this way, 'cause he does. I'm just saying that it wouldn't matter if he did. *I* like it this way. Who knows? Maybe that's exactly the reason why he likes it like this, too."

"Girl, that man would like you bald."

"I don't know about all that!" Dulce turned away from the mirror toward Esperanza. "If it looks good on me like this, maybe you should try it. We've got the same kind of hair and face shape. And you're much prettier than I am."

"No!"

"At least take it down. Here you are in this supermodel dress with a schoolteacher hairdo. What's up with that?" Esperanza dodged as Dulce reached for her bun. "I thought you had already put your makeup on."

"I put on too much, so I washed it off."

"No wonder you look so dry and pale. What'd you use? Comet?"

"Stop sweatin' me."

"Chago's gonna be here any minute, and you're not ready."

"What do you mean, I'm not ready? I'm dressed, right?"

"You know what I mean." Dulce picked up a cosmetic pencil off the bureau. "At least put on some eyeliner and lip gloss." She advanced toward her sister. "Close your eyes."

Esperanza grabbed the pencil from Dulce and slammed it back down on the bureau. "Stop it!"

"Why are you getting mad at me?"

"Maybe I don't have any more *complejos,* either, about going out without all this makeup on and looking like a clown."

Dulce stared at her, stunned and hurt. "I wasn't trying to say you needed makeup. I just thought, since it's been a long time since you've been able to get dressed up and go out . . . you know. Since your homecoming party, anyway." Dulce waited for her to answer even after the intercom buzzed, but Esperanza barely looked into her face. "And you never looked like a clown, Espe. Curly hair, straight hair, makeup, no makeup, you're beautiful. You always have been and always will be." Dulce picked up her pocketbook and jacket off the bed and left the room to buzz Chago into their building.

He took them to a local but classy restaurant on Westchester Avenue, where Esperanza recognized the bartender, although she could not remember his name or where she had met him. He clearly remembered her and Dulce though, because he kept staring at them as they settled at their table. Trying to place him in her memory, Esperanza zoned out much of the dinner conversation as Dulce and Chago chatted in Spanish. Then she heard Chago mention Marin County.

"Marin County?" Esperanza returned her attention to the table to find Dulce laughing hard, with tears welling in her eyes. Grinning, Chago offered her his glass of water, but Dulce refused it. "What's so funny about Marin County?"

"Haven't you been listening?"

"I was trying to figure out where I've seen the bartender, 'cause he looks mad familiar." Dulce looked toward the bar, but he had disappeared. "Maybe he went into the back."

Dulce shrugged and wiped away her tears of hysteria. Then she turned to Chago and said, *"Explique otra vez para ella."*

Chago turned in his seat to face Esperanza. "My ex-wife? She get tired of New York. Say she want to live someplace else. *Pues yo le dije que se mudara a Miami porque ahí hay muchos dominicanos."* He switched into an impression of his ex-wife, who apparently could be very snooty. " '*¡Ay, no! Pa' que carajo me voy a* fuckin' *mudar a Miami. Para eso me quedo aquí e* fuckin' *Nueva York.'* "

Captivated by his amusing delivery, Esperanza said, "I guess she's had it with big-city living."

"*¡Pín-pún!*" said Chago, happy to have won her encouragement to proceed with his tale. "So I say to her, Then where you go? Where you taking my kids? *Y ella me dice que se va pa' San Rafael.* I say you kidding, right? You go back to Dominican Republic? She say to me, No, no, no! *Que hay una ciudad que se llama San Rafael en California donde viven un chorro de dominicanos.* I say, Really! *Porque yo nunca he oído de eso.* I know *que hay dominicanos en Nueva York y en Miami y también he oído que hay una comunidad dominicana pequeñisima en . . . en . . . ¿como se llame?"* He looked to Dulce for help, but apparently the name of the place slipped her mind, too. *"Providencia!"*

"Rhode Island?" said Esperanza. "There Dominicans in Rhode Island now?"

Dulce laughed. "That's what I said!"

"So I tell my ex-wife, 'If you sure, OK. Move *pa' San Rafael."* Chago threw his hands in the air as if to surrender. "I go to California to visit my children, *y no veo ningún dominicano* beside my own family." He counted off on his fingers. *"Hay blancos, hay negros, hay indios, hay mexicanos. Ahí tienen chinos, filipinos, koreanos, japonéses. . . ."*

"*¿No hay otros Latinos?"* Esperanza asked. "Besides the Mexicans, *¿no hay caribeños?"*

"A few Puerto Ricans, a few Cubans," said Dulce.

"Very few," added Chago. "I ask Susie—"

"That's his daughter Susana. She's eleven."

"I ask Susie *¿A dónde viven los dominicanos de San Rafael?* You know where my daughter take me?" Dulce tripped into a second fit of laughter at the coming punch line. "To the university."

"She took you to a college? You just said she's only eleven."

Dulce and Chago roared at Esperanza's confusion. "The Dominicans in San Rafael, California aren't from DR. They're, like, nuns and brothers and whatever."

"Frailes," said Chago.

"Yeah, friars. They have a Catholic university over there and everything. You know, like Fordham or St. John's here in New York."

"Oh, my God, that's hilarious!" Esperanza began to appreciate Chago's charisma. He hardly sounded like a divorced man pushing forty with two kids, and when he was telling a story, Chago's accent became downright endearing. "And embarrassing!"

"*Mira,* Espe, let me tell you something. My ex-wife, Gloria? She good woman, *y es una buena madre. ¡Buenísima, buenísima, buenísima! Pero* she no like your sister. She no very smart." Chago reached over and clasped his hand over Dulce's.

"But what's all this have to do with Marin County?" asked Esperanza, diverting her eyes from Dulce's and Chago's hands on the table as if they were doing something extremely intimate. "You mentioned Marin. What about Marin?"

Dulce smirked and explained to Chago, "She's a Tupac fanatic, and at one point he lived there."

"*¿Tupac el rapero?*" asked Chago. "You know where he get that name?"

"It's African."

"Que africano, ni africano."

"He's not asking you where his name came from. He's asking you if you know who Tupac is named after. Chago knows."

"Oh." Once Esperanza learned that Jesus could find out which Web sites she had surfed while on his computer, she didn't dare look up Tupac and spark one of his tantrums. But from her books, she knew that Tupac was born Lesane Parish Crooks even though his mother's government name was Walker and his father's Garland. That while he was still young, Alice became Afeni and changed her son's name to Tupac Amaru. She doubted Chago knew any of these things, let alone the meaning of Tupac's names. "I know that Tupac Amaru means 'shining serpent' and Shakur means 'thankful to God.'"

Chago said, "*Sí, pero Tupac Amaru no era africano. No conozco na' de Shakur, pero Tupac el rapero,* his name is from Inca chief. You know the Incas?"

Esperanza remembered learning about Incas, Mayans, and Aztecs in school long ago. Other than that they were the native Indians of Latin America who built amazing empires before the Europeans came and annihilated them, she had forgotten everything about them. Nor did her GED social studies class revisit this history, she realized. Her teacher focused on U.S. history, saying it accounted for 40 percent of the examination. "So what about them?"

"Habían dos Tupac Amarus."

"There were two Tupacs?"

"El primer Tupac Amaru, he was last Inca chief to fight *los consquistadores.* Even his enemies say he very intelligent. *Y eloquente también.* The people love him."

"*¡Como el rapero!* So what happened to Tupac the chief?"

"The Spanish capture him. They kill him. Cut off his head." Esperanza bristled. She did not want to know more, but Chago continued. "Thousand of Indians come to his execution, and he die with dignity after he give great speech."

Dulce caressed Chago's forearm. "And what about the second Tupac?"

"His real name was José Gabriel Condorcanquí. He come two hundred years later. He the representative of *los índios* to the Spanish who now control the empire. José Gabriel change his name. He take the name Tupac Amaru, and he lead the El Segundo against the Spanish *en Perú, en Bolivia, en Argentina . . ."*

"Yo, D!"

Esperanza, Dulce, and Chago all lurched back in their seats. As Xavier bopped over to their table, the swish of his oversize corduroys grated the air. Dulce dropped her head into her hands. "Oh, my God, please. This is not happening."

"¿Y quién es ese tipo?"

Xavier arrived at their table. "What's up, D? Espe." Neither of the Cepeda sisters responded. Not that Xavier waited for a reply before he turned to Chago. "I'm Xavier." Although he shoved his hand into Chago's face for a handshake, his eyes blazed with nothing resembling brotherhood. "Who you?"

Chago rose to his feet and accepted Xavier's hand. "Fernando Santiago." By the look on his face, Esperanza knew he had no intention of adding, *But my friends call me Chago.*

"Fernando," Xavier said.

Esperanza asked what she knew Dulce wanted to know. "What are you doing here, Xavier?"

Xavier looked down at Dulce, who avoided his gaze. "Brotha's handling his business, that's all." Esperanza looked toward the bar. The bartender had returned and fixed his eyes on their table. Although she still could not place him, Esperanza suspected that soon after their arrival he had made a call to Xavier, who dropped everything to corner Dulce and investigate her new man.

"You businessman?" said Chago. "I businessman, too."

"Yeah, well, business has been so good to me, I said I'ma skip McDonald's tonight." Xavier reached into the breadbasket on their table, grabbed a piece of bread, and sank his gapped teeth into it. "Treat myself to some good Spanish food, seeing I don't have me a fine Latina sister to make it for me no more." He stared at Dulce, who kept her eyes fixed on her place mat. "For now anyway."

"The food here is very excellent," said Chago. "I hope you enjoy your meal." Then he retook his seat, signaling his disinterest in further conversation with Xavier.

Esperanza had to fight her grin. When it had become evident to her that Chago knew who Xavier was and what he was trying to pull, she worried that he would either let Xavier goad him into a violent scene or attempt to prove his superiority by inviting Xavier to join them for dinner when no one wanted him there. You didn't do that with a muthafucka like Xavier. He would pull up a chair and eventually provoke you into that very scene you hoped to avoid by inviting his ass to join you in the first place. *Go, Chago,* she thought.

"You should order the paella," Esperanza said to Xavier. "It's divine. Enough for two." Then she drew her hand to her lips, pretending to gasp at her "faux-pas."

Xavier sneered at her, then turned to Dulce. He placed his hand on the back of her chair, leaned down, and kissed her on the cheek before she jerked away. "Nice seeing you, D." He walked a few paces, then called over his shoulder, "Pretty hairdo." Esperanza and Chago watched as he bopped past the bar, tossed his chin at the bartender, and left the restaurant without even a book of matches.

Esperanza looked at Dulce. Even as she propped her head against her temple, her face hung in shame. Esperanza searched for the words to comfort her but none came. So she turned to Chago. "Bravo, Chago, bravo."

Chago gave her a halfhearted smile, then turned to Dulce. He reached out to lift her chin with his fingertips until their eyes met. "*¿Y qué tu vas comer?*"

"Let's share the paella," Esperanza volunteered. The last thing Dulce probably wanted to do was eat, but the last thing Chago probably wanted to do was discuss what had just happened. Esperanza hoped Dulce caught her drift and followed her lead. "There should be enough for three." She reached over the table to nudge Chago in the shoulder.

Ignoring Esperanza, Chago whispered to Dulce, "San Francisco."

Finally Dulce smiled. Happy to see her sister relaxed yet eager to be part of the closeness, Esperanza asked, "What about San Francisco?" Her eyes bounced back to Chago, and she readied herself for another funny tale about his silly ex-wife, Gloria.

Chago said, "I think I move very soon to California to be close with my children again." And by the way he gazed at Dulce, he did not need to say another word.

"Slow your roll, Chago," Esperanza yelled. "Y'all just met."

"Espe . . ." Dulce started.

"I mean, what about your wife?"

"His ex-wife."

"Isn't she in California?"

"It's like you go deaf whenever it suits you. His ex is in San Rafael. Chago wants to move to San Francisco."

"And how close is that to where your ex is at?"

"Twenty minute, half hour."

"That's a little too close, if you ask me. Ouch, Dulce! Don't be kicking me."

"Stop it, Espe. Just stop it."

"You and your ex-wife, y'all get along?"

"*¿Y cómo no?*" Dulce fumed, but Chago remained cool, even relieved, as if he had been expecting this interrogation and wanted to get past it. "Gloria is good mother to my kids, bad wife for me. Now she no more my wife, we have no problem."

"And he left her, OK?" said Dulce. "Like five years ago."

"That's what he tells you."

"I'm about to reach across this table—"

"You gonna slap me now? For what? Looking out for you?" Esperanza felt her heart tear. "Forget it."

"Damn right, let's forget it."

With a slight wave of his finger Chago signaled disapproval of Dulce's tone.

She propped up her menu to block Esperanza's face, as if the sight of her sister might spoil her appetite. "I'm not in the mood for paella tonight."

"Pues yo, sí, quiero paella," said Chago. "Espe, you share with me?"

Esperanza shook her head. She no longer wanted to eat, least of all from the same dish as this dude trying to whisk her sister way across the country. "Order me whatever."

Chago drove them back to their apartment building. Holding the leftover paella he insisted that she take, Esperanza climbed out of the backseat of his car. She waited on the curb for Dulce to say her good-byes. The Cepeda sisters had a big fight ahead of them, and Esperanza did not care if they picked up where they left off in the restaurant upstairs or started fresh right there in the middle of the street. She just wanted her chance to convince Dulce that traipsing across the country with this stranger with more baggage than Samsonite was a stupid thing to do. Especially after all that Dulce had been through and built up in the past few years. And if the shoes were switched, Dulce would tell Esperanza the same thing.

But when she looked over her shoulder, Dulce remained seated in Chago's passenger seat with no intention of following Esperanza upstairs. Before they got down with Jesus, Dulce always made her current boyfriend take Esperanza home and accompany her upstairs before proceeding with him to his place for the night. Then Xavier came, but Dulce still made him drive and insisted that they wait until Esperanza got into the apartment and waved to them from the window. The plan was that if Esperanza took too long, Dulce would send Xavier into the building after her to be sure that some thug didn't intercept her on the way to the apartment.

Now Dulce sat in Chago's car waiting for Esperanza to get upstairs and signal her from the widow. After that she would drive off with Chago to spend the night with him. She cared more about fucking her *jíbaro* boyfriend than fighting with her only sister for giving him some legitimate hell.

"Fine, Dulce. Be like that." Esperanza ran inside the building

Once upstairs she slammed the apartment door behind her and slid the security chain across it. She tore off the turquoise dress that Dulce had bought her with Chago's money and stuffed it in the trash can. Then she proceeded to the bathroom, where she plugged the tub and blasted the water.

Just as Esperanza dipped her toe into the tub, she heard the apartment door clank, a violent push thwarted by the metal chain. She grabbed a towel, wrapped it around herself and ran into the hallway. From where she stood, she saw Dulce's face wedged between the chained door and its frame. "Espe, take off the damned chain."

Esperanza moved toward the door and did as ordered. Dulce brushed past her and down the hallway. She gave in to the temptation to follow her sister and found Dulce in the bathroom throwing her toothbrush, makeup remover, and other toiletries into her pocketbook. As many times as Dulce had spent the night at Chago's, she must have had everything she needed already there, so this had to be an excuse to come upstairs and talk after all.

But Dulce spun around Esperanza as if she were not there and moved into the bedroom. She found the drawstring bag from the boutique where she had bought their dresses.

Fighting the urge to swallow her pride and jump-start the argument they needed to have, Esperanza just watched as Dulce yanked open drawers and threw random articles of clothing into the bag. Less than a minute later, her sister pulled the strings apart to seal the bag and breezed past Esperanza on her way out of the apartment.

Just as Dulce opened the door Esperanza said, "I only have one question." Her sister stopped and faced her. Esperanza read in Dulce's expression a longing for reconciliation, but Dulce had hurt her too much for that now. "Do you know if Chago has his papers?"

"What?"

"Don't play dumb, Dulce. You know what I mean."

Dulce took several steps toward her. "Are you trying to say that the only reason he wants me is because he's trying to get me to marry him so he can stay in the fuckin' country?" Esperanza wished she could take it back, but it was too late. "You're jealous. That's why you were all nervous before he came. You didn't think I fuckin' noticed? You thought Chago wanted to take you out to dinner 'cause now that he's met you, you're the one he wants, and he's only been spending time with me to get to you. Who wants Dulce, right? She's all right, but Espe's the beautiful one. You were all nervous wondering, When's he gonna step to me? When's he gonna make a move on me? When I'm gonna have to tell Dulce that her man made a pass at me? And then he never did, and you couldn't handle that. Instead of being relieved that he's not another fuckin' Xavier, instead of being happy for me, you're jealous 'cause for once some guy wants me over you. And he's a nice guy. Chago's nice to me. It's because he wants me, Espe, that he's nice to you. Still, you make fun of him. Calling him old, saying he's a *jíbaro,* talking about his so-called baggage. Maybe all that's true, but you know what else is true, Espe? The first time either of us has ever met a good man—hardworking, honest, affectionate—and he's falling in love with me instead of you."

Dulce made her way back to the apartment door. Esperanza tightened the towel around herself. *I am happy for you,* she wanted to yell, but the words never came out. Not because they were not true, but because Esperanza felt much more sorry for herself than she felt happy for Dulce. *I'm not fuckin' jealous,* she wanted to scream, but she was. But not for any of the reasons Dulce gave. She did want a man like Chago, but not her sister's man. Esperanza wasn't jealous of Dulce over Chago. She was jealous of Chago over Dulce.

For such a nice guy, why was he rebuilding his family by poaching hers? If he were such a nice guy, why didn't he just say at dinner that Esperanza could come live with them in San Francisco, too? A nice guy wouldn't be trying to take Dulce away from Esperanza when she needed her most. The only problem Esperanza had with Chago's loving Dulce was his thinking he could ever love her more than her own sister.

"When are you coming back?"

Dulce answered Esperanza's question by slamming the front door. She stood in the hallway, shivering in her towel and listening to the faucet drip into her bathwater. Then another question came into Esperanza's mind.

Why had not Jesus come with Xavier to the restaurant?

TEN

Wounds of Passion

Esperanza flipped through one television show after another. Some she had peeped on occasion in the Bedford Hills rec room; others were new to her. Before prison she couldn't get enough of those reality shows. They provided many of the rare moments when she bonded with Jesus and the other guys. Sometimes a situation would arise on a show that would cause them to fight, but those fights were different. They never got out of hand. They were filled with love.

Like when Xavier loved that Jamaican girl on *America's Next Top Model* and defended her passionately when she tried to sabotage the girl who eventually won the competition by suggesting to Tyra Banks that the woman had an eating disorder.

"Yo, D, how you gonna side with that skinny white girl over the sista?" Xavier had barked when Dulce cheered after Tyra and the other judges sent Camille home.

" 'Cause she shady with two Es," said Dulce.

Xavier crawled over to Dulce and put his head on her lap. "Don't worry," he said with a Jamaican accent, "me love some Dulce."

Esperanza laughed but sided with her sister. Although Camille was one of the most stunning competitors, she disliked her from jump. The judges soon kicked off her favorite, Jenascia, on some bullshit about being only five-seven, so Esperanza shifted her loyalty to Mercedes, the perky biracial chick from Cali who looked like a hundred Latinas from around the way. " 'Bout time Tyra sent Camille and her weave back to Long Island," she said, and everyone—even Xavier—roared.

After a year in prison, Esperanza no longer cared for any of those stupid shows. Being on lockdown while people with all these options chose to act the fool in front of millions of strangers put shit into perspective. Soon after entering Bedford Hills, Esperanza quickly kicked her reality TV show habit. *Send them all to fuckin' prison for a year, and see how much they appreciate what they have then.*

Lost in her thoughts before the blur of images on the screen, Esperanza heard the answering machine click before she even realized the telephone had rung. Hoping to hear from Dulce, she pulled herself off the couch and shuffled into the kitchen.

"Essssspeeeee," sang Jesus. "Come out and plaaaaay. Nah, I'm just playin'. You lucky I'm mad forgiving after how you wild out on me in the street. You owe me an explanation, and you know I always get what's owed to me."

Esperanza grabbed the phone. "Why you sweatin' me now? What's the matter? Priscilla busy?"

"Hey . . ." She had caught him off guard. Each waited for the other to speak until Jesus finally said, "So you got my letter."

"No."

"You said you did."

"I lied."

"Espe—"

Esperanza hung up the phone. She unplugged it from the wall and took cover in the bedroom. Still, in her head she heard Jesus ring the telephone and speak into the machine. Esperanza locked the bedroom door, flung herself onto the bed, and buried her head under the pillow. She never should have answered the telephone. Jesus was an inch-into-miles muthafucka who could not be given any kind of leeway. She gave in to her loneliness and had encouraged him, cracking open a door that should have stayed locked. Now Jesus would press, and Esperanza had to brace herself to resist, now more than ever without Dulce's tough love to keep her in check.

Esperanza removed the pillow from over her head and sat up in bed. She glanced at the stack of books on Dulce's night table. She had finished these and left them behind, probably hoping that Esperanza might pick up one of them. Instead she reached over her side of the bed to the bottom drawer of her own night table. There she had stashed *The Killing of Tupac Shakur* under a box of tissues. Esperanza really had no desire to read, but the photo of Pac on the cover of the book reminded her of something else to do.

She went back to the closet and dug up her posters. If Dulce wanted to live with Chago, she lost any say in decorating their apartment. Esperanza found some tape and unrolled a random poster. POWER. RESPECT. JUICE. HOW FAR WILL YOU GO TO GET IT? Esperanza climbed on the bureau and taped the film poster above the mirror. She lowered herself off the dresser and stepped back to review her work. As his character Bishop, Tupac sported his hoodie and brandished his revolver as he eyed his friends with suspicion. "Perfect." When she woke up in the morning, this would be the first thing she would see. Esperanza set about hanging the rest of her Tupac collection. She placed the poster of him as Lucky from *Poetic Justice* with his porcelain smile and White Sox cap above the bed. On the closet door she hung the one of Tupac standing somber and shirtless, the band of his teal Karl Kani boxers peaking through his belted khakis. Esperanza taped the black-and-white photo of Tupac in a leather vest and matching pants with the slogan ONLY GOD CAN JUDGE ME behind the bedroom door. She even owned posters that had never made the walls to save room for Dulce's favorites, like the one Xavier gave her of Muhammad Ali towering over Sonny Liston, and small prints of the Bronx Botanical Gardens. But she put those up, too, including one Jesus had given her of Tupac holding up both middle fingers above his name and 1971–1996 that Esperanza had never liked but hung on the inside of the closet door. A half hour later she had papered her bedroom with twelve images of Pac in a variety of poses, clothes, and expressions. Yet when she stood in the middle of the room turning around to survey the results, all her defiance had faded, and Esperanza found herself missing Dulce more than ever.

She went back to the closet and dragged out the box of keepsakes. With Dulce away Esperanza had all the time and privacy she needed to give the mementos the attention they deserved. Maybe she would find something that would compel her to call Dulce at Chago's to say, "D, you'll never guess what I found?" and they could become a family again.

Esperanza first found a stack of old report cards from elementary school bunched together by a rubber band. To her surprise, Esperanza's third-grade teacher had rated her satisfactory in almost everything, even in math. She earned five "excellents," mostly in language arts. *Expresses ideas clearly orally. Reads for meaning. Reads for pleasure.* The remaining two "excellents" she received were under social skills—*shows concern for others* and *socializes appropriately with peers.* However, Esperanza also had five Is in areas in which the teacher thought she needed improvement. With respect to study skills, the teacher indicated that Esperanza needed to increase her ability to stay focused, but otherwise she participated in activities, followed direction, organized materials, and used her time as efficiently as any eight-year-old should be expected. Esperanza's teacher showed most concern with her other social skills, feeling that Esperanza had difficulty demonstrating responsibility, accepting the consequences of her actions, and accepting the consequences of her decisions. In the comment section of the report card, she wrote:

> *Esperanza is extremely bright and loves to learn. Her ability to exceed in all academic areas is limited by her need to please her peers. While this is normal for a girl her age, please encourage her to do things on her own for her own sake.*

As she wrapped the rubber band around the report cards, Esperanza wondered what her third-grade teacher would think of her now.

Then she found several green-and-white envelopes of film processed at the drugstore. Esperanza grabbed one at random, pulled back the flap, and found photos of a Halloween party that Jesus threw a few years back. Xavier had nagged Dulce to dress sexy, only to bitch about all the men staring at her when she came dressed as Janet Jackson in her *It's All for You* video. Esperanza smirked at the photo of herself in costume and remembered that no one knew who she was supposed to be. Did she have to shave off all her hair and arrive topless with fake tattoos drawn all over her torso? The bandanna knotted across her forehead—even if it were pink instead of blue—the fake mustache and "2" pendant of gold foil hanging around her neck should have been enough clues.

When Esperanza reached into the box for another batch of pictures, she came across a photo that had strayed from the rest in its set. In this one her mother, Brenda, sat on a wooden picnic table, with her daughters on either side. Jesus had asked Esperanza what she wanted for her twenty-first birthday, and she had told him, "I want to see my mother." Not only did Jesus buy her a ticket; he bought one for Dulce as well. They flew into Sacramento, rented a car and drove for two and a half hours to see Brenda.

Prison had aged Brenda the way no man's mistreatment had. Still she talked excitedly about the support group she created with other inmates convicted of the same charge. Dulce seemed so proud, and Esperanza suspected that visiting Brenda got her sister thinking about leaving Xavier once and for all. Esperanza wanted to be proud of her mother, too, but the more she heard about the other women's stories, the more she feared for Brenda. All that crusading was going to help not hurt her when she came up for parole.

Having no more heart for photographs of any kind, Esperanza grabbed all the other processing envelopes and lay them to the side. She reached for a stack of manila envelopes, the contents of each written across the front in black marker: *Mami's Case. Bills. Taxes. School.* Esperanza opened one that read *Hospital,* and from the first invoice discovered that Dulce still owed over a thousand dollars to Lincoln Hospital. No wonder she worried about money all the time. Everyday bills and stress ran high enough without Dulce receiving a monthly reminder of Xavier and the debt and pain he caused her. Esperanza replaced the invoice into the *Hospital* folder and resealed it.

Then she opened one labeled *CDC.* Esperanza found all the paperwork they had to file in order to visit her mother in Chowchilla. She had to complete a questionnaire, and about a month later the sergeant in the visiting office approved it. Once Dulce and Esperanza had been added to Brenda's visitors' list, she had to send them a packet filled with rules and regulations outlining what they could and could not bring or do. Years later Esperanza would experience the pecularities of New York State from the other side to place Dulce and Jesus on her own visitors list. Esperanza placed the California Department of Corrections forms back into their manila envelope.

She sifted through the remaining envelopes looking for one with court papers for her case, but found none. That cut and dry, huh? Instead she came across one that read *LaVern.* Confused, Esperanza undid the clasp and reached inside the envelope. She pulled out a half dozen newspaper clippings that were beginning to yellow at the edges. Removing the paper clip that bound them, Esperanza relived that wretched day as she reread the earliest and longest article, dated August 2002.

GIRL ATTACKED, LEFT FOR DEAD IN SUBWAY
By Sharon Nicoletti and Rob Warner
Daily News Staff Writers

A nursing student is fighting for her life after being beaten into a coma by two unidentified women in a Brooklyn subway station yesterday afternoon.

According to her friend, LaVern Bell, a 20-year old student at Long Island University, was followed by her alleged attackers when she got off the No. 2 train at Nevins Street.

"I can't believe they almost killed

> her," Renee Perez, 20, told the Daily News yesterday while keeping a tearful vigil at Brooklyn Hospital Center, where Bell lies in a coma after sustaining severe injuries to the head. "All because of a stupid comment."
>
> According to police, Bell and Perez boarded the southbound train yesterday at Fulton Street. The two suspects who were already on the train apparently overheard Bell when she made a disparaging comment about them to Perez.
>
> "The bigger girl was talking so loudly, and all LaVern said was that she wished she would tone it down."

"No!" yelled Esperanza. "That's not what she said. She said, 'Why doesn't that bitch shut the fuck up already,' that's what she said." Not that what LaVern said justified what Dulce did next, and she knew her sister would agree. Even though she knew the details of her sister's crime as well as she knew her own, Esperanza continued to read.

> When Bell got off at the Nevins station, the suspects followed her and apparently attacked her in the passageway where riders transfer between IRT and BMT lines.
>
> There were no witnesses to the assault, but soon after the start of rush hour, Bell was found unconscious and bleeding profusely from the head.
>
> "According to the emergency room doctor who treated her, Bell's injuries suggest that whoever attacked her struck her in the face several times with a blunt object until she knocked her down," said Frances Heismann, spokesperson for Brooklyn Hospital Center. "Once Bell fell, her attacker proceeded to bang her head repeatedly against the concrete until she lost consciousness."

When asked whether Bell would survive the attack, Heismann said, "She could go either way. She lost a great deal of blood. And if she does survive, she may have sustained irreparable brain damage."

Perez said that when the women followed Bell off the train, she suspected her friend was in danger. "I was banging on the glass and yelling at her to watch her back, but she didn't understand me. She thought I was playing around [with her.]"

Concerned over her friend's safety, Perez got off the train at the first opportunity to double back to Nevins Street. She arrived in time to find the paramedics tending to Bell as a crowd of straphangers watched.

"I had such a bad feeling about them," Perez said. "They looked like gangbangers."

Police say they are looking for two Black or Hispanic women in their early twenties, one approximately five-nine and 130 lbs. wearing camouflage pants and a black T-shirt, the other about five-seven and 110 lbs. in dark blue jeans and a white tank top.

"How can you almost kill someone over a few words?" said Perez.

Esperanza flipped through the other articles, most variations of the same story from other papers. In none of them did Renee tell the truth about what LaVern had said. Nor did anyone consider that perhaps Dulce never meant to hurt her so badly. None of the articles reported whether LaVern had survived the attack. Although she had witnessed the drastic transformation her sister underwent since that time, Esperanza had no idea that Dulce remained haunted to this day by her extreme act of violence against a stranger her own age. Why did she keep these reminders of the girl she most wanted to forget? She imagined her sister sifting through those articles whenever she felt tempted to go back to Xavier or the game.

Esperanza wanted off this dark road down memory lane. She opened the box, looking for evidence of better times. Things from the past that promised a future without poverty, violence, or confinement. The letter from the housing authority announcing that, due to Brenda's conviction, they had been placed on the "not wanted" list and had to vacate the apartment. A notice from the Human Resources Administration outlining the new laws that would end their benefits in five years and demanding that Brenda report to her nearest welfare-to-work center to get a "job" picking up trash along the Major Deegan Expressway. Dozens of cards in a variety of sizes that came either from the drugstore or attached to a bouquet of flowers, each with an apology from *el cabezón* scrawled across it. All Esperanza found were the legacies of abuse. Abuse by individuals and abuses by systems. The abuse the Cepeda women visited upon others and directed toward themselves. When Esperanza finally found a box of old birthday cards, Christmas photos, and classroom drawings, even they were dampened by the letters from Brenda from Chowchilla and her own to Dulce from Bedford Hills.

ELEVEN

When I Dare to Be Powerful

My Dear Sister Esperanza,

Thank you for your wonderful letter. I honestly doubted I would hear from you again when you left here. Nor would I have blamed you for losing touch. Yes, you have much more important things to contend with than an old woman who is likely to die behind these bars. Your letter lifted my spirits more than words can ever express.

Esperanza, who keeps telling you that you are not smart? The next time someone makes you feel like you are less than a living mirror to all that is wonderful in this world so filled with hate and injustice, ask yourself why. Ask yourself, What does this person gain by making me feel like I am less intelligent or beautiful than I truly am? What does he have to lose if I am as powerful as I know I can be?

And I do think you know just how powerful you truly are, my sister. You know and you are afraid. That's right. Afraid. And this is understandable. You have witnessed what happens to the powerful when they decide to use their power, whatever it may be, to free themselves or liberate others.

So I leave with you the words of Audre Lorde, who once said, "When I dare to be powerful—to use my strength in the service of my vision—then it becomes less and less important whether I am afraid."

Dare to be powerful, Esperanza, and you will cease to be afraid.

Much peace and progress,
Isoke Oshodi
Free the Land!

Isoke's letter gave Esperanza the courage to return to the GED program the following week. She even took her letter with her and left it on her desk in plain sight. If Hudlin wanted to "welcome back" Esperanza by reading her personal correspondence to the class again, she had something for his ass. *What does this person gain by making me feel like I am less intelligent or beautiful than I truly am?* But Hudlin conducted class in his usual boring way, without so much as a glance toward Esperanza, and she felt just fine with that.

Esperanza had e-mailed the rap lyrics to Ms. Rodriguez as she promised, and she actually used them in her lesson on similes and metaphors. Esperanza had thought she might not because of the curses and the N-word and things like that, but Esperanza sent her so many choices, Ms. Rodriguez found her way around the problematic words. Her classmates loved the lesson and in no time got the difference between similes and metaphor on lock.

When Ms. Rodriguez asked them to provide their own examples, Pete shot his hand in the air. Before she could even call on him, he called out, "I got one, Ms. Rodriguez. Check it. This is a 'xample of a simile." Pete pulled himself to his feet and said: *Cats front leave them leaning like Smirnoff.*

"Lean back, lean back, lean back," chanted Kiki, pounding her fist on her binder.

Ms. Rodriguez laughed and said, "Leaving them leaning like Smirnoff? I don't get it, but that's absolutely a simile. Who is that?"

As always Pete took the opportunity to tease the teacher. "Ah, Ms. Rodriguez, that's Mase from Harlem World. Isn't that where you're from?" Esperanza shook her head at that revelation. She had apparently missed a lot in last week's class. "You should know that."

"My bad," said Ms. Rodriguez, and everyone laughed.

As the other students filed out of the classroom, Ms. Rodriguez called Esperanza to her desk. "Is this a good time to talk or do you have to be somewhere else now?"

"No, I've got time." Ms. Rodriguez probably wanted to thank her for completing the extra assignment, maybe even praise her, since the class got so much out of it. Esperanza even hoped for another special assignment. She leaned her hip against the desk and waited for Ms. Rodriguez to ask.

"I very much appreciated the research you did for me. Thank you."

"Anytime, Ms. Rodriguez. I mean, Maite."

"I did have one question for you about the lyrics you selected."

"I'm sorry about all the nasty words. I didn't mean no—I mean, any—disrespect, but it's just mad hard to find rap lyrics without them, you know. Next time I'll take them out before I send them to you, if you want." *Why didn't I think of doing that in the first place?*

"That's fine, Esperanza, but my question is, why did you only send me Tupac lyrics?"

"Oh. Well, when I got the assignment the library was closed, and I wanted to start right away, so I gave you what I already knew. I wrote 'em out, typed them up, and then e-mailed them to you when I got to the library. I didn't have a whole lotta time to find you anything else."

Esperanza waited for Maite to pass judgment, but she only nodded. "You're a big fan of Tupac?"

"The biggest! I have all his movies and albums—well, I might have missed one or two 'cause he's always putting stuff out." *Not to mention being locked up for a minute.* "Got most of his books."

"So you read a lot about him, too."

"I love everything Tupac. Whatever I can get my hands on. You know, what I can afford."

"The documentaries, too?"

"No doubt!" Esperanza had never met an older person who wanted to talk about Tupac. None of her friends were as into him as she was either. "You've seen them."

"I sure have, and it surprised me how academic a few of them are." If by *academic* Maite meant all those old heads waxing philosophical about Pac, Esperanza usually pressed fast forward until a celebrity she recognized appeared. Somehow she felt as if Maite did not blame her for that. "What else do you read? Because I'm sure I don't have to tell you, Tupac was a voracious reader. He never graduated high school yet always had a book with him."

"Yeah, I know. Like I read *The Prince* while I . . ." Esperanza stopped herself. Maite had to know she had done time, so there was no need to mention it.

"You mean *The Little Prince* by Antoine de Saint-Exupéry?"

"I'm sorry?"

"The fable about a pilot whose plane gets stranded in a desert, where he then meets a little boy who's traveling from planet to planet."

Esperanza shook her head with confusion. "I might've read that when I was a kid," she said, even though she was pretty sure she had not. "*The Prince* I'm talking about is by Makaveli."

Maite's eyes widened. "Really? You read Machiavelli's *The Prince*. So what did you think of it?"

Esperanza hesitated. Who wanted to know what she thought of *The Prince*? Cool Maite who wrote poetry in the sixties, or Ms. Rodriguez the GED language arts teacher? Esperanza decided she liked them both, so she told the truth. "It was a'ight."

Maite smiled warmly at her. "Sounds like you weren't impressed with it."

Frankly, Esperanza thought the man was an asshole. Without having ever heard of his book, people in the 'hood already lived by it, and that made life hell for everyone, including those who wanted nothing to do with warfare. Drive-bys, gangbangs, catfights, an eye for an eye leaves the whole world blind, and all that. Not knowing how Maite felt about the book, however, Esperanza changed the subject. "I read Aferi Shakur's biography. Assata's, too."

"Did you?" Esperanza no longer knew if she should be flattered or offended by Maite's constant surprise. "How did you discover those books?"

Esperanza grew protective of her jailhouse mentor. Maite might be cool but perhaps she should not say too much about Isoke. "I'm such a 'Pac fan, one thing led to another." Not a total lie.

Maite kept quiet for moment as she took in Esperanza's response. Then she said, "In addition to working here on Saturdays, I teach a course at Barnard College. I need a teaching assistant to help me find material to supplement my class lectures. And some administrative things, too, like photocopying and filing. Would you be interested?" Before the offer registered with Esperanza, Maite said, "Now the position requires you do quite a bit of reading. You have to read everything I assign to my students, and you have to sit in on my classes."

Esperanza's heart raced. Maite thought enough of her to hire her as her assistant. She believed that Esperanza could handle books meant for college students, and even wanted her to take the class along with them. She pictured herself in a class like Dulce's, reading books that mattered and discussing them with others. If Maite could bring to life a class of self-conscious high school dropouts and vulnerable immigrants who felt they had few other options, imagine how she might teach a course for people who chose to be there? This might be the kind of job that might help Ms. Lopez to convince the powers that be at Lehman College to make an exception and admit her. Or better yet, Esperanza could just enroll in the college where Maite taught. And Maite had to pay at least as well as paltry McDonald's. Then again, she didn't say whether this was full-time work. If not Esperanza would have to keep her current job, too. Unless it paid as well or better. Then she could say good-bye to Luciano for good.

But could Esperanza do the job? She had managed to get her footing in this GED class, but had completed some high school and, like her third-grade teacher said, she always read for meaning and pleasure. But could she really be a teaching assistant to a college professor? She remembered how she struggled with parts of that *Sister Outsider* book that Dulce had to read for her class. Would Esperanza have the time, let alone the mind, to handle all that college-level reading? How could she help Maite teach a group of students who had not only finished high school, but did well enough there to get themselves into a four-year college?

"Thanks, Ms. Rodriguez—"

"Please. Maite."

"Thank you, Maite, for thinking so much of me and everything, but I can't do it."

"Can't or won't?"

"I've already got a job, and between that and school, I've got a lot on my plate."

"Where do you work?"

"I work at the McDonald's at the Hub."

"Full-time?"

"No, but I just got promoted so I think if I ask my boss for more hours, he'll give them to me."

She wanted to help Dulce with that Lincoln Hospital bill. And what if her sister did move with Chago across the country? Esperanza imagined asking NYCHA to put the apartment in her name only for it to seize the opportunity to put her on its "not wanted" list and evict her once and for all. "And I need to make as much money as I can."

"I understand. This is only a part-time job. But once you're in the university's system, you can find another job on campus and even take free courses."

"That sounds great and all, but I just can't."

Maite seemed as disappointed as Esperanza felt. "Would it be too much to ask if you'd help me prepare another assignment for this class?"

"No, not at all."

"Are you sure? Because—"

"No, I want to do it. Whatever. Anytime."

"Do you think by next week you can find me some poetry? In particular, I need a few poems that have examples of symbolism and personification. Do you know what each is and the difference between the two?"

Esperanza did. She spent so much time alone that when she grew bored with television, she sometimes read ahead in her language arts workbook. "Symbolism is, like, when one thing represents another. Like the way a flag stands for a particular country or people. And personification . . . I think that's when something that's not human acts like a person." She searched for an example. "Like if Mr. Hudlin scratches his nails across the board, and I write, 'The board squealed in pain.' "

Maite herself cringed. "He actually does that?"

"Sometimes." When we get too rowdy. And sometimes when we're too quiet . . . to get our attention."

Maite groaned, and Esperanza giggled. She never witnessed one teacher expressing disgust toward another. All her high school teachers had put on a united front as if every student in the building—whether on the honor roll or in special ed—had banded together and declared open season on them. She felt like she and Maite were girlfriends at a slumber party. "Yes, Esperanza, you've got it right. So please find me a few poems that have examples of each for next week's class."

Esperanza grabbed her books and bounded toward the door. "OK, Maite."

"Oh, one more thing."

"Yes?"

"I know Tupac was a poet, but would you do me a favor? Mix it up a bit. It's OK to bring in one poem by him, but could you also bring me some work by other people? Find me a few poems by women." Maite winked at her.

Esperanza grinned. "Women of color?"

"Exactly."

"OK. I'm headed to the library right now."

* * *

Now that Feli had shown Esperanza how to search for books in the electronic catalog and to locate them on the shelves, she couldn't shake him. She liked Feli and appreciated the way he took his job seriously and respected Miss Henson. Esperanza just wanted him to stop with the gossip about Jesus's crew and the questions about why she never hung out with them anymore.

"Oh, man, Espe, it was so fuckin' funny. You know how Chucky be sometimes. He the clown of the crew," Feli said as he hung by her arm.

Esperanza found Ashanti's *Foolish/Unfoolish* and added it to the stack of books in the crook of her arm, checking it off her list. "Yo, Feli, do you have say in which books the library gets?" She genuinely wanted to know as much as she wanted to change the subject.

"Every once in a while Miss Henson asks me for my opinion, you know," he said. "What young heads are into and whatnot."

"I ask 'cause they got some good shit in here. Somebody has to be keeping them up on it. I figured it had to be you."

"Know what Miss Henson told me the other day? She says, 'Felix, I listen to you more than anyone else here because only books you suggest are the ones that get stolen.' That's some funny shit, right?"

"That's mad funny."

"Miss Henson don't care if the book's about hip-hop or thug life. So long as young heads are reading books and passing them on to others. Vicki Stringer and Shannon Holmes today, maybe Toni Morrison and James Baldwin tomorrow, she says." Feli shrugged. "Not that I know who any of them people are, but I compromise for Miss Henson. I recommend to her stuff like that," he said, pointing to Ashanti's book. "It ain't Shakespeare, but it ain't gangsta either."

"Glad I copped this before someone jacked it."

"Word." Feli laughed. "Yo, Espe, how come you don't hang out with us at Chucho's bodega or Jesus's crib anymore?"

Esperanza sighed. "Feli, I can't. First of all, why should I? I'm not with Sus anymore. He's with fuckin' Priscilla now. What kinda pathetic female would I be, rolling with my old boyfriend and his new girlfriend?" Esperanza waited for Feli to say that Priscilla didn't mean shit to Jesus, but he just looked down at his feet. "Anyway, if I so much as said hi to any of 'em, my parole officer would have my ass in Bedford Hills in a blink. He's not playin', and neither am I." Esperanza scored two more books, including T-Boz's *Thoughts* and *Tears for Water* by Alicia Keys, and headed back to her table.

Feli followed her. "Yeah, but you come here and hang out with me."

I don't come here to hang out with you. "That's different, Feli. This is a public place, and you happen to work here. My PO can't tell me I can't go to the library 'cause you be here sometimes, and when you're not here, you run with Jesus."

"Look, Espe, I wanna tell you something."

"You better make it quick, 'cause I think your boss is headed this way." Ms. Henson had disappeared into her office long ago, but Esperanza wanted Feli to leave her alone.

"OK, I just wanted to say I feel real bad about everything. I mean, I told Jesus that they should give you your cut and then some 'cause you went up for them and everything. But X, you know how he be. He said I ain't have no vote because I'm a fuckin' mama's boy who wasn't even there and . . ." His voice trailed as his cheeks reddened. "Anyway, I was like, 'No matter, son. I didn't ride, but Espe did, and now she's in the jump. And if she had rolled on y'all, she could've walked just like that.'" Feli snapped his fingers. "'But she didn't, and what's right is right,' I said. And just so you know, Chuck agreed with me, too, 'cause I told him I was gonna bring it up, and he said that he'd have my back. But you know how he be, too. When I did bring it up, and X got all upset, he said, 'I think Feli's right, but I'ma go with whatever Sus says. If Sus is with it, I'm with it. If he not, I'm not.' *Y ahí se quedó.*"

So Jesus had voted against her. As the leader who was supposed to set and enforce the code, as the man she sacrificed her freedom to protect, and as the member with the deciding vote in the crew's lopsided democracy, he had betrayed her at every turn. He even lied to her about it, telling her that the guys stepped to him, wanting to divvy up most of her share among themselves. Esperanza did not know what felt worse—that she was not surprised or that she still cared. She cracked open Ashanti's book and said, "And then you wanna know why I don't run with y'all no more."

Esperanza hoped that ended the discussion, but Feli just pulled his chair closer to hers. "I can pay you back if you want."

"What?"

"I wanna make it up to you, Espe,'cause that shit just ain't right. I can't give you all the money, but at least I could give you my share of what they jacked from you."

"Feli, you never had a share 'cause you never showed."

"Still, I'm part of the crew, and that's how we're supposed to get down."

"I appreciate the offer, but I don't want your money. Besides, that shit ain't correct. You shouldn't have to pay what those muthafuckas owe me."

"Espe—"

"Look, I'm not trying to be rude, but I've got a lotta work to do here. The best thing you can for me right now is let me get back to it. That's how you can have my back right now."

Esperanza expected Feli to throw a bit of a tantrum. Not that she gave a shit if he did. Of course, he felt guilty. Had he shown up that day, she never would have been driving. The time to have her back had passed. Or for all Esperanza knew, if she took the money, Feli might brag to someone about his noble deed and when it got back to Jesus . . . How could that be? As much as Feli lobbied Jesus on her behalf, to this day he still remained—as Xavier called him—a devout Christian. Then why would he put Jesus on blast, telling Esperanza that he ultimately made the decision to short-change her? Unless Jesus put him up to making the offer in the first place.

As she watched Feli disappear down an aisle, her anger melted into guilt. She truly hoped his offer was not sincere. Of course Jesus put him up to it. Crush or no crush, Feli was not trying to maintain Espe behind his idol's back. And if his offer was sincere, Esperanza wished Feli would eventually understand that she could not accept his money to prove her appreciation no matter how much she could use it. Better for both of them that she not. Besides, Doña Mili needed it more.

Dear Isoke, (I got it right this time!)

A lot of good things have happened since I last wrote you.

Number one, I got promoted to the register at the restaurant. Didn't have to pay dues making french fries and apple pies first either! Not only is it better pay (just a little bit, but still), but the day goes much quicker because it's always busy at that Mickey D's, since it's in this big shopping area.

Number two, I even got offered another job. My language arts teacher asked me if I wanted to be her teaching assistant (she teaches a class at some college called Bernard or something like that). I couldn't do it, though, since I already got a job, but it was nice that Ms. Rodriguez asked. Outside of class she even lets me call her by her first name, which is Maite, like Prince's wife.

Things would be perfect now if my sister and I were getting along. She practically lives with her new boyfriend, so I almost never see her. He's a good guy, but I worry about her, since she just met him and he has an ex-wife and kids and all that. I mean, if it were me in her shoes, she'd be concerned, too, right? Anyway, Dulce calls or drops by a few times a week, but we don't talk like we used to. She pretends that she needs to pick up clothes or get the mail, but I know she just wants to check in on me. So I'm like, "If you miss me, come back home." Not that I say that to her. I guess we're both like my mother in that way. We both got a lot of pride.

I think this guy likes me. Thing is, he's a friend of my ex. In fact, he's still part of that whole set that I'm not trying to mess with. He's nice to me, and I'm nice to him, but that's it. And it's cool to have someone feel like that about me, even though I don't feel the same way. Not that I could do anything about if I did. Like I said, he's a friend of Jesus.

Speaking of which, Jesus be blowing up my phone, but I don't give him any real play. Don't worry, Isoke. I know he's just trying to get me caught up in some of his bullshit, and I'm not even trying to go there (or back to Bedford Hills).

Anyway, Ma, I just wanted to let you know that things are better, and that I hope you're proud of me. How are the others? Tell them I said hi!

Love,
Espe C.
P.S. You never told me what you wanted me to do with the books I borrowed.
P.P.S. Isoke, you mad gangsta. Here you are on lockdown because of your political stuff and you still sign your letter with "Free the Land." You know they be reading our letters, but no matter what, you represent! Remind me what you mean by "Free the Land" again.
P.P.P.S. THUG LIFE! (smile)

Every lunch hour the restaurant became an asylum, but because the mayor had instituted a tax-free weekend, things were even more hectic. Esperanza thrived on the challenge. Ever since Luciano gave her daps for working quickly and courteously, she pushed herself every day to do better. She had no interest in competing with the other cashiers, which was why they still liked her. She kept to herself her mission to outdo her personal best. Meanwhile, during lunch breaks, she cracked them up with her Luciano impressions and the nicknames she came up with for him. And if another cashier struggled, she helped out.

With an extra rush of shoppers, Esperanza knew she could top her own high today. Luciano told her that her only problem was that she sometimes sacrificed accuracy for speed which, of course, he called "inappropriate." He did not make an issue of it the two times her register come up short a few dollars, but Esperanza wanted to check herself to maintain Luciano's confidence in her. With the stink he made over her conviction during the interview, she did not want him to start wondering if she were dipping into the register. She once caught herself imagining herself as a manager and then quickly laughed at that thought. Esperanza Cepeda, convicted felon turned career woman with the McDonald's Corporation.

She had found a nice rhythm and grinned every time she glanced at the clock and saw how much time had zipped by. The bustle of the restaurant kept Esperanza's mind off her feet, but she knew once her shift ended she'd feel the ache in her arches. These ugly shoes Luciano regulated offered great traction but provided no support. She planned to stop at the drugstore on her way home, buy some bubble bath, and treat herself to a long, hot soak in the tub for once. She actually looked forward to going home and being alone.

"Thank you and come again soon," Esperanza said as she handed a man his bag. Before he stepped aside, she began her greeting to the customer behind him. "Welcome to McDonald's, may I . . ."

There stood Jesus with his arm around Priscilla, who was cracking her gum and batting her catty eyes at Esperanza. "Hey, girl, how you've been?"

All the momentum Esperanza had built dissipated. She gripped the side of the register. "I'm fine."

"You look good." Priscilla snickered at Esperanza's brown polyester uniform. Jesus chortled and nudged her. "Just order already."

"Lemme get a number two." She emphasized the word *two* and held up two fingers with one hand while tightening her grip around Jesus's waist with the other.

"What kind of soda?" She would treat this like any other transaction—quick and courteous. Get them the fuck out of here. She didn't know what the hell Jesus was doing here. Was he trying to make her jealous or was he trying to embarrass her over her job? Either way, Esperanza refused to let him get the best of her.

"Gimme a diet Coke. Gotta watch the figure."

First you gotta get one, you bony-assed bitch. Esperanza turned to Jesus. "And you?"

"I'll just have a Sprite, and . . . yo, give me an apple pie."

She punched the keys on the register and headed to the fountain.

"Espe, no ice!" Priscilla ordered.

As Esperanza filled Jesus's cups, Tenille waited for a new batch of cheeseburgers to wrap in yellow paper. "You know them?" she asked. They looked up and caught Luciano staring at them as he hovered over the grillers. He likely overheard Priscilla call out Esperanza's name and now intended to eyeball this transaction to its conclusion.

"My ex and his next."

"No wonder you were all smiles until they showed up." Esperanza's chest flushed. She thought she had played it so cool. "You want me to finish their order?"

"Thanks, but I gotta handle my business, you know."

"I feel you, but know I got your back."

Esperanza filled Priscilla's soda cup. "Thanks, T." Tenille's loyalty created the smile she needed to bring back to the register. "Your diet Coke." Feeling Luciano's eyes on her back, she widened her grin as she offered Priscilla her drink.

Priscilla took the cup and said, "Don't forget J's pie. Can I get a straw?"

"Say please," Jesus said. "Just 'cause Espe's serving you don't mean you gotta be rude and shit."

Priscilla gave him an annoyed look. "Can I get a straw, please?"

"The straws, napkins, and everything are over there," Esperanza said as she pointed to a station opposite the cashier lines. Serving her? That bitch didn't sign her check. At least Jesus told her to be polite.

Then Jesus said, "I'll get it, baby."

Esperanza left the register to complete their order. What kind of game was Jesus playing? Not only did he bring that trick in here, he had the nerve to get in Esperanza's line. One moment he was laughing at her, and then the next he was defending her. She bagged their food and returned to the register. "That'll be seven twenty-eight."

"Damn, this shit may be fast, but it ain't cheap," Priscilla said, before taking another sip of her soda.

"Stop complaining when you ain't paying." Jesus handed Esperanza a ten-dollar bill. "Keep the change."

"This is fuckin' McDonald's. You're not supposed to tip her."

"You know, Priscilla, one thing that I always appreciated about Espe when we were together? She never, ever counted my money."

"Maybe that's why you got more of it now."

"You funny."

The register drawer popped open, and Esperanza whisked out two singles, two quarters, two dimes, and two pennies. At first she held out the money to him, but when Jesus reached for it, she placed it on the counter and slid it toward him. On top of everything, she was not going to let him touch her, not even for a second. "Your change is two seventy-two."

Jesus glanced down at the money, took Priscilla by the hand, and led her into the dining area. The next customer approached the counter. "Lemme get a Big Mac Value Meal. . . ."

"Excuse me, sir, just a second." Esperanza turned around and found Luciano assisting Tenille as he placed numbered tags behind the various rows of sandwiches. "John, I need a break."

"OK." Luciano motioned over the new fry girl.

"I want Tenille."

"Excuse me?"

"I'd rather Tenille take over my register." She turned to the fry girl. "No offense."

Luciano motioned for the fry girl to proceed. "She doesn't have a problem upselling." Eager for some time away from the percolating bin of grease, the fry girl brushed past Tenille toward Esperanza's register.

Esperanza rushed into the ladies' room. She checked under the stalls. Her privacy assured, she kicked a stall door and slammed her fist against the towel dispenser. Then she just leaned against a sink and rocked back and forth. She would do anything before she shed any more tears over that bastard. A moment later Tenille entered the bathroom.

"You handled that so well, Espe. Had that been me . . ."

It felt good to hear Tenille say that. Esperanza could not imagine having done anything better. Yet she might not have believed that if someone else had not said it.

"You doing anything tonight?" Tenille asked.

"Why?"

"My cousin was supposed to go with me to the movies, but she flaked out on me, and I really don't want to go alone. My treat! I'll spring for dinner, too."

"You don't have to do all that."

"So you wanna have another damned Filet-O-Fish for dinner, is that it?"

Esperanza finally laughed.

* * *

She assumed that Tenille wanted to see a movie at the multiplex off the Grand Concourse. Instead she put them on a downtown train to TriBeCa. They reached the street and headed toward a small theater near the entrance to the Lincoln Tunnel.

Esperanza read the marquee in the distance. "The Screening Room? What's playing there?"

"You ever seen the movie *Girlfight?*"

"No." Esperanza had never even heard of it. She liked it already.

"OK, you know Michelle Rodriguez?"

"Yeah, the girl from *The Fast and the Furious* and *S.W.A.T.*" Esperanza liked her a lot, and not just because she was both Puerto Rican and Dominican, just like herself. "She's mad cool."

"*Girlfight*'s the first movie she ever made. She plays a girl who's learning to box behind her father's back. I have it on DVD, but I wanted to see it on a big screen." The closer they got to the theater, the faster Tenille spoke. Esperanza smiled at the difference in her energy, as Tenille was always so quiet at work. "The Screening Room's having a retrospective this week. . . ."

"What's that?"

"That's when they show a bunch of old movies that have something in common. Like maybe they're by the same director. They call this one Women Warriors, because all the movies this month are about women who kick butt." Tenille paused to laugh and then continued, "They're showing *Aliens, Terminator 2 . . .*"

"All the hot shit," said Esperanza. "How come we gotta come all the way down here? Guess they never have retrospectives at the theater on the Concourse?"

Tenille shrugged. They walked a few paces in silence. Suddenly Tenille stopped. "You know what, Espe?"

"What?"

"You don't need a retrospective to see five movies about guys who kick butt at the Concourse."

"What?" Esperanza agreed. "You can see that shit every freakin' weekend."

Afterward Tenille took Esperanza to an Indian restaurant, and they bonded over the movie.

"And when she whupped her father's ass, I was like, That's right. *¡Pa'* *que lo sepa!* I didn't feel the least bit sorry for that . . ." Esperanza caught herself before the N-word slipped. She had never heard Tenille say it and did not want to offend her. "That bastard got what he had coming to him after all those years, and it was only right that Diana brought it."

"I never get tired of that movie," said Tenille as she spiked a cube of lamb with her fork. "Especially the ending. It's so dope the way she doesn't throw the fight to keep Adrian."

"Word, I liked that, too," Esperanza said. "But the fact that they got back together? That's the one thing I didn't buy."

Tenille's hand flew to her heart. "I loved that!"

"Don't get me wrong," she said as she claimed another piece of nan from the breadbasket. "It's cute and all, but it's so unrealistic. In real life, not only would Adrian have never talked to Diana again, he would've gone straight back to that *flaquita*."

"Somebody's cynical." Esperanza didn't mind Tenille's teasing her for not being a romantic. Shanette or even "Dee" would have called her a hater because of what had happened that afternoon with Jesus and Priscilla. "Yeah, it's a fairy tale, but you know what? If it can happen in a movie, maybe it can happen in real life. Like Diana's beating her father's ass, right? A lot of people I know said, 'That could never happen.' Myself included." Tenille picked up the teakettle and refilled their cups. "I can believe it now, 'cause I wish I could've done the same thing when I was in a similar situation.' "

Esperanza put down the nan. "Your father used to beat on you and your moms?"

"No, nothing like that. My dad's dope. When my parents broke up for good and he moved down South, he always paid support and stayed in touch with me. But later my mother got with this guy who slapped her around."

"He used to hit you, too?"

"No. Not that he didn't want to. I think he knew if he put a hand on me, my father would fly to New York and tear into that behind! Anyway, I would spend every summer in Atlanta with my dad, and when I was fifteen I took up with this guy over there. One night I came home with this nasty bruise on my arm, and my father just grilled me until I admitted what happened. I mean, I just broke down and told him everything. What my boyfriend did to me, what my mother's boyfriend was doing to her . . ."

"And what'd your father do?"

"He moved back to New York and sued my mother for custody. That's how I ended up living with him. He wouldn't give her visitation until she dumped that guy. She threatened to take it to court, but c'mon. If my mother went to court, she'd have to expose her man and get him in trouble, right? She wasn't trying to do that. Eventually she got rid of him, and everything's cool now."

"Wow," Esperanza said. "When my parents broke up, my father picked up and moved to Florida with his new woman and never looked back. You and me, we got a lot in common. My mom went out with a guy who beat her up."

"What happened?"

Esperanza hesitated to answer. Although this aspect of her past initially created problems for her in the 'hood, it eventually gave her some status. At first people felt sorry for the Cepedas. Everyone knew that muthafucka beat her, and no one did a damn thing except stare at the welts on Brenda's face and whisper sympathies under their breath as she walked Dulce and Esperanza to school. When news of the stabbing hit the streets, no one doubted Brenda did it in self-defense. The rare person who believed she deserved the time she received kept it to themselves out of fear that Dulce or Esperanza might be just like their mother. Over time, however, Brenda's murder conviction became a badge of honor, especially when it became clear that neither Dulce nor Esperanza demonstrated their mother's gumption to stand up to her man's abuse. At least not until Dulce decided to quit the crew, and Xavier wilded out, thinking she would take it as she always had for so long.

But Tenille had revealed so much of herself. Esperanza suspected that Tenille knew about her own conviction, but she never asked, teased, or shamed her about it. "My mother killed him."

Even when on lockdown, Esperanza told few people, because she had come to hate how people reacted. They either shut down or asked a million questions. Neither response ever came from a place of understanding. Disgust, curiosity, maybe sympathy even, but never understanding. But Tenille just nodded her head and went back to her lamb curry as if whatever happened was supposed to have happened, and something about that made Esperanza smile. After all these months, she had finally met a bona fide homegirl.

TWELVE

Killing Rage

On the last day of the GED program, Maite handed out the results of the practice test she gave a week earlier and threw a party for the students. Although everyone passed, she reminded them of the incentive they had established at the start of the program. "I promised to give you a copy of my spoken word tape to every student who passes all her GED tests before the end of the year."

Pete groaned. "Aw, c'mon, Ms. Rodriguez. How 'bout just giving it to us for passing the language arts stuff? Why you 'specting more than that?"

"Because I know you can do it." If folks disagreed, they didn't argue with her. Esperanza helped cut and serve the cake Ms. Rodriguez had brought for them.

Kiki had taken a collection from the class and used the money to make Maite a gift basket. When she presented it to her, she said, "This is to give you a jump start on your next GED class." The class had given Kiki enough money to buy Maite several things, and she made great choices. She bought a copy of the *Hip Hoptionary,* several volumes of the Source's *Hip-Hop Hits* and the DVD of the movie *Wild Style.* "I don't know how you're gonna use the movie in class," said Kiki, "but you'll figure it out."

"Or maybe it'll teach me things I need to know about hip-hop so I can use all the other things effectively."

Esperanza stayed behind the party to help Maite clean up the classroom. Holding the garbage pail, she traveled from desk to desk collecting abandoned plates of half-eaten cake and empty paper cups.

"Esperanza, you look so sad," said Maite, as she moved desks and chairs back into their rows.

She tried to smile. "You know what's funny? I used to have to do this at my job, and I always hated it. Yet I volunteered to do it now."

"You're going to miss your classmates."

"Not really. Not to be cold, Maite, I just didn't really get close to anyone in class. Anyway, we all exchanged numbers and e-mails so it's no biggie . . . ." Esperanza really doubted that any of them would stay in touch now that they no longer had Ms. Rodriguez's magic to bond them.

Maite walked over to Esperanza, removed the pail from her hand, and set it on the floor. "And you still have my number and e-mail, right?"

Too touched to speak, Esperanza threw her arms around Maite and hugged her. *"Ay, Esperanza,"* Maite said as she stroked her hair. *"Claro que sí que su nombre es Esperanza."*

"Things are cool at my job. I'm full-time now that I'm done with school. Gotta admit that I'm mad nervous about my tests."

"And when are the dates of your exams?" Puente asked. He flipped through her file until he found a computer-generated calendar, and readied his pen to mark the dates.

"I have a test every second Saturday, starting with the social studies test on June eleventh and ending with the reading exam on October eighth," she answered. "Why do they spread them out like that? You'd think they'd understand that people just want to get them all over with." Dulce had taken hers over two consecutive days.

"You would think." The way Puente looked at her, Esperanza thought that maybe he had actually come to like her. Then he said, "When the board of education raised the standards, the bleeding hearts raised hell until they convinced them to spread out the exams. For the sake of working people and new arrivals and what have you. Look, if my parents can do it . . ." *Everything's a hustle.* Puente circled the dates and scribbled *GED* by each of them. "When's the last time you saw Jesus Lara?"

Son of a bitch. Long ago she had stopped worrying that Puente had spied on her from that navy Crown Victoria. Esperanza figured that if he had seen her with Jesus and wanted to violate her parole, he would have done so by now. Ever since that day at Chucho's she had managed to stay away from there through sheer will. Now Esperanza had spent the last fifteen minutes recounting all the positive turns in her life, and Puente only cared about trying to trick her into admitting she had been socializing with Jesus. "You tell me."

"Don't be a smart-ass."

"I haven't seen Jesus Lara." If he rolled up in her restaurant during her shift, Esperanza had no control over that. Not that she had seen him since that day with Priscilla. Although he probably saw her all the time like he wrote in that letter.

"And what about the others? Are you fraternizing with them?"

She thought of Feli and grew angry. The guy worked at the library. A public place. A positive place. She did not go to hang out with Feli, but she would not stay away just to avoid him either. "No, I don't hang out with any of them. I don't look for them. I don't even talk about them. But if I bump into one of them from time to time, what can I do? They live in my neighborhood. Like I said to you before, it's bound to happen."

Puente flipped her file closed and glared at her with steel eyes. "And like I said to you before, move."

On the morning of her first GED exam, Esperanza awoke to the smell of bacon sizzling. She leaped out of bed and ran into the kitchen. Dulce scraped the bacon from the pan onto a plate already filled with scrambled eggs.

"What are you doing here?"

"Isn't today your first test?"

"Yeah."

"You shouldn't take a test without having a good breakfast." Then Dulce looked at the plate and started to laugh. "Like this is all that different from what you can get at work."

"It is different," said Esperanza. "You made it." She hugged Dulce then she carried her plate to the table.

Dulce poured them each a glass of juice and sat down before her own plate. "Do they still score 'em the same way? When I took it, you could score from a 200 to 800, but you had to get no less than a 410 on each test."

"Yup, and your total score for all tests has to be at least 2250 in order to get your diploma."

"So they didn't change that. Nervous?"

"A little. But it's the social studies test. I think I'ma be all right."

"I know you're gonna be all right. So where's the test?"

"South Bronx." They giggled at the irony of Esperanza returning to the same school she had dropped out of to take her GED exam.

"Chago lent me his car. You want me to give you a ride? It's good to get there early, you know."

"OK." Esperanza had planned to walk. It was sunny and warm, and she thought the exercise might ease her nervousness. But she wanted Dulce to herself for as long as she could have her.

> *Mark is a local elected official in Georgetown where he has recently been accused of a felony. Because Mark also lives in Georgetown and is popular among his constituents, the prosecutor does not want to try his case against Mark in Georgetown. Which amendment can Mark's defense attorney evoke to keep his case in Georgetown?*
>
> *(1) Amendment IV*
> *(2) Amendment VI*
> *(3) Amendment XIX*
> *(4) Amendment XXIV*
> *(5) Amendment XVI*

Without a second thought, Esperanza circled number two, then paused. What if this Mark guy got convicted? He could run for office and probably win, all without ever being able to vote for himself. She snickered, and the exam proctor raised an eyebrow at her. Esperanza hunched over her exam booklet and colored in her response. She had this test on lock.

Inspired by her social studies exam, Esperanza sprang for a cab and headed over to the library. She found Feli and flagged him over. "What's up?"

"Listen, can you use the Internet to find, like, old newspaper articles?"

"Maybe. It depends what you're looking for. You doing just general research on a topic or are you trying to find something real specific?"

"Kinda both." The idea had just hit Esperanza during the test, when she had to read an excerpt of a newspaper article. She had not thought it through, since she did not know if what she wanted was even possible. "I don't even know if the article I'm looking for exists."

Feli's face lit with possibility. "You know what you could do? A lotta newspapers have electronic databases now where they archive old issues. You just plug in the words you're looking for and all the articles with those words come up."

"And I can do that on the Internet?"

"Yeah, but you gotta pay. With credit card."

"Fuck."

"But that's for heads who need it all the time. If you go to the main library on Forty-second Street, you can get that shit for free. Any and all the articles you want; you only have to pay if you wanna print them."

Esperanza grew excited. "OK, teach me everything. How to get there, where I go once I'm there . . ."

"I'll take you there, ma."

"But I gotta go now, 'cause I promised my boss that I'd work all day on Saturdays except for when I have my tests. If this doesn't work out, I gotta figure out something else, and I don't have a lot of time."

Feli looked over his shoulder, dug into his pocket for some change, and handed it to Esperanza. "Look, go outside to the pay phone and call the library. Pretend you my grandmother with an emergency. I'll meet you at the corner and take you to the library downtown and help you."

"I don't want to risk getting you in trouble, Fel."

"Ma, no worries. Now that it's warm out and folks are going to the beach and whatnot, it be kinda slow in here. You be doing me a favor."

Esperanza suspected that he also wanted to spend some time with her. She even wondered about Puente's all-knowing eye. Jesus's, too. But she really wanted to do this and needed Feli's help. "OK." She took the quarters. "Just give me some time, 'cause you know it's hard to find a pay phone around here that works."

"Word, I'd give you my cell, but then my number will show up on the caller ID!" Feli said as he rolled his cart down the aisle. "And make it good. You know how *'buelita* be."

"Do I?" she said, and sneaked out of the library before Ms. Henson could ever realize that she had been there.

Feli clicked on a graphic and a box popped onto the computer screen. "You want to search a particular newspaper?"

"Do they have the *New York Daily News* or maybe the *Post* on there?"

Feli clicked and Xs appeared in boxes next to the names of the papers Esperanza had chosen. "I'ma check the *New York Times,* too." Esperanza shrugged. She doubted what she was looking for would be in a bourgie paper like that. "Oh, damn."

"What's wrong?"

"I just realized something."

"What?"

"How far back you wanna search? 'Cause if you wanna go back far, they may not have that on computer. You may have to get microfiche."

"Micro¿ *que?*"

"It's a pain in the ass, but maybe you don't need it. How far back you wanna go?"

"I'm just thinking a couple of years."

Feli laughed with relief. "Oh, I thought you wanted to, like, go way back. We cool." He pulled away from the keyboard and motioned for Esperanza to take his place. "Just type in what you're looking for and click Enter." When Esperanza hesitated, he asked, "What's the matter?"

At the time of the fight, Dulce swore her to secrecy, and Esperanza had never betrayed her. Not even on some I-once-heard-about-this-girl or any shit like that. In their neighborhood, you told one person something, you might as well have shouted it through a bullhorn on the corner of 149th Street and Third Avenue like the street evangelists. Soon the po, some thug, or your ex's next was standing in your doorway. "This is kinda private."

Feli looked hurt, but he rolled away from Esperanza's monitor. "OK."

"I'm sorry. Don't think I'm not grateful, 'cause I really am."

"S'right."

"You sure?"

"Yeah, do your thing."

"When I'm finished, we'll go get something to eat. My treat."

That did the trick. Like a kid rushing to bed because the next day was Christmas, Feli stuck his face into the next cubicle. "I'ma be right here checking to see if I missed any important J. Lo news."

Esperanza giggled. "Yeah, maybe when you blinked, she divorced Marc Anthony." Then she turned back to her own monitor and typed in her search words.

When they finished at the library, Esperanza and Feli strolled west along 42nd Street. Esperanza hugged her printout close to her chest while Feli babbled about something. She just grinned and nodded at him like a bobblehead doll. Feli probably believed he had captivated her with his story, when she was just ecstatic to find exactly what she had hoped to at the library. Even better than she had hoped. So even though she had no love for sports, when Esperanza saw Feli's face light at the sight of the ESPN Zone sign, she said, "Let's eat there."

The hostess told them they had to wait a half hour for a table and handed them a pager. Feli grabbed Esperanza's hand and said, "Since you're buying me lunch, at least let me treat you to a few games." He led her to the Sports Arena on the third floor stocked with old-fashioned games like air hockey and Ms. Pac Man to modern simulations of extreme sports, complete with dirt bikes and Jet Skis with names like Downhill Biker and Wave Runner. Feli bought two five-dollar game cards and handed one to Esperanza. "What you wanna play first?"

She looked around the dimly lit arcade at all the prepubescent boys slapping the consoles and bouncing on the equipment as if their lives depended on their final scores. "I don't know." Esperanza turned back to Feli and looked at his outfit. Next to his crew in their baggy hip-hop gear, Jesus looked like the millionaire playboy in his fitted dress shirts hanging open over regular-fit jeans. The same designer clothes swam on Feli's lanky frame, making him seem no different from the other teenage boys swarming the game room while their aspiring girlfriends pouted behind them. "I don't care."

Oblivious to her sudden disinterest, Feli said, "C'mon, I'll race you." He bounded over to a row of empty race cars under a flashing sign that said NASCAR 50 while she dragged behind him. "I like this red one," Feli said as he jumped behind the wheel. Esperanza eased into a white car next to him. "Stick the card in there."

As she did, three boys about fourteen years of age ran over. "Mind if we race with you?" one asked Feli.

"Someone's gotta eat my dust," he said.

The kids whooped at Feli's challenge and jumped into the remaining race cars. Esperanza wanted to bail. She was too grown for this shit, and Feli, too, for that matter. But before she could quit, Feli smacked the start button and slammed his foot against the gas. "Go!" The other boys hollered over the roar of their simulated engines.

Esperanza looked at the screen before her and saw that all the other cars except hers had torn out of the starting gate. "Muthafuckas!" She clamped her hands on the steering wheel and jammed her foot against the gas. She quickly overtook a yellow car that had spun out and found herself on the bumpers of the blue and green ones. As she tried to rev her way between them, the blue racer purposefully swerved toward her. "Hey!" She regained control of her white car and glanced down the row at the snot in the blue racer at the end. When he cackled at her, she said, "So it's like that, huh?" She glanced at Feli, who ignored them all, peering at the monitor and gripping his steering wheel even though he held the lead.

Esperanza regained control of her car and sped up to her blue competitor. "I'ma get you, you little *cabrón*." The blue and green cars remained neck and neck, but when she tried to steer around them, the green racer veered right and jammed into her. Her car spun out and banged into the wall. "You bastard!" Esperanza eased off the gas and pawed at the wheel in her attempt to recover. Although Feli maintained a comfortable lead, the blue racer had closed the gap between them, and the green driver remained on his heels. Had he left Esperanza alone, he would have been head-to-head with the blue car, but obviously he thought it more strategic to run her off the road than to run his own race.

Esperanza sped up to the blue and green cars. Both drivers fell aside, giving her an opportunity to slip in between them. With their intentions clear in her mind, Esperanza pumped the gas enough just to dip in between them as they started a turn. When the blue racer swerved in for the crash, she tapped her brake. Her white car snapped back and the blue car collided into the green one. Both drivers cursed as their cars careened into the wall, and Esperanza ricocheted forward. On the monitor she saw Feli's red bumper and gunned for it like a bull at a matador's cape.

Feli noticed her in his shadow. "Nah, ma, don't even think about it." He leaned into his gas pedal with a vengeance.

"I'm not thinking 'bout it, bro. I'ma do it." Esperanza pulled her white race car up to his. She floored the gas, but that gave her only enough juice to parallel her front left wheel with his back right.

The finish line loomed in the distance, and Feli pumped a fist in the air with impending victory. "It's over, ma! Forget it!"

"It ain't over."

"I said it's over."

"I said it ain't." Esperanza threw her steering wheel to the left, crashing her racer into his. Feli's car spun out of control.

"Oh, shit!" Feli grabbed the steering wheel with both hands much too late. His car tumbled into a row of pylons as Esperanza zipped across the finish line. The other boys heckled Feli for letting Esperanza beat him. "I ain't let her beat me. She straight out whooped my ass."

His sportsmanship made Esperanza feel guilty. "I only did what I had to do."

"I ain't mad at you. You gotta do you. Don't get mad when I gotta do me, though."

"What's that supposed to mean?"

"It means I'ma order the most expensive thing on the menu."

* * *

Feli actually ordered a cheeseburger with all the trimmings, while Esperanza asked for a grilled chicken sandwich. The waitress left and they sipped their respective sodas in silence, occasionally glancing at the three dozen screens along the wall broadcasting an array of sporting events around the world. Then Esperanza asked, "I know why you do what you do, Feli, and you know I ain't one to judge. But I was wondering. You ever think about quitting?"

"Every day." Feli's ready answer surprised Esperanza. At most, she expected him to say *yes* or *sometimes.* "If I didn't have my grandmother, maybe I wouldn't. But I gotta see her face every day, wondering and worrying about me. So every day I think about getting out."

" 'Cause if she catches you, you're out."

"For real, Espe, I don't think she really would put me out. Sometimes I think she knows and pretends not to. I think about quitting 'cause I imagine what might happen to her if I got arrested or . . ." Feli looked away to a television screen replaying a botched Yankee play. "Damn, I told X they never should've let go Cairo!"

It then occurred to Esperanza that Feli lived with his grandmother because he needed his *abuelita* as much as, if not more than, she needed him. Doña Mili probably ignored Feli's street life less for her own sake than for his. She threatened to throw him out if she caught him slangin' so he would have no doubts that she loved him and thought better of him than he did himself. But Doña Mili knew that if Feli had no other place to go, the streets would eat him alive. Looking the other way and praying he came to his senses before it was too late—making the occasional scene to push him along—was the best the old lady could do.

Esperanza wondered about the rest of the guys. Did they have anyone in their lives who wanted them out of the game? While she rarely socialized with the crew, Chuck's girlfriend, Deziree, seemed to have no problem with the way he made ends meet. Their kids always flossed the latest gear, and Esperanza never saw her without her hair pressed and her nails airbrushed. She always brought the kids to Jesus's Fourth of July barbecue, but other than to make strained chitchat with Esperanza and any girlfriends *du jour,* Deziree minded her children and stuck to her own friends. When the couples' dominoes tournament started, she refused to play, and Chuck always had to team up with someone else. Except to bring her a single plate of food and a can of soda when she arrived, Chuck spent no time with Deziree, although he did play with his kids. While helping

Chuck dismantle and clean Jesus's grill after the party, Esperanza asked him, "Why doesn't Dezi hang out with all of us more often?"

" 'Cause she gotta watch all 'em kids," he said matter-of-factly.

Esperanza decided not to press, but later she recounted the exchange to Jesus while they were in bed. "I mean, they don't act like they're in love," she said.

"Why you say that?" he replied. " 'Cause they're not under each other all the time? Not everybody's like us, Espe." At the time, Jesus's answer satisfied her and even turned her on.

As for Xavier, he never mentioned any relatives besides his mother, whom he despised. He spoke rarely of her, and then only to call her names and to wish her dead. He never specified why. All Xavier revealed in bits and pieces to Dulce was that she had a string of boyfriends whose idea of fathering Xavier meant subjecting him to all kinds of terror in the name of discipline. Once Dulce pressed him for details, hoping that he would open up to her. "What did they do to you, Xavier? Did they call you names?"

"Of course they called me names. What you think?"

"Did any of them hit you?"

"No, I got sent to bed without my supper and shit. What you think? Look, I don't want to fuckin' talk about this shit no more."

Dulce feasted on the morsels he revealed, seeking an opportunity to know him better and bring them closer. Those opportunities were rare, and Dulce kept his confidences unless she absolutely had to divulge them. Like when they went to Six Flags that summer, and everyone but Xavier wanted to get on the Free Fall, which would lift them thirteen stories then drop them at fifty-five miles per hour. "It's hot as hell out here, and y'all wanna go on that bullshit ride?" he said, leaving them in line. "I'm going to Hurricane Harbor. Get my waterslide on."

Dulce started to follow him, but Jesus called out, "C'mon, X. We'll go on this one, and then we'll all head to the water park together."

"Yeah, X," said Esperanza. "Don't be skeered."

But when Xavier kept walking, Jesus said, "Fuck you, nigga. Don't be around when I'm ready to leave, and see if I don't leave your ass here."

Then Dulce ran back to them. "Chill out, Jesus! If your mother's boyfriend dangled you outta window when you were five years old, you'd be scared of that shit, too. How could you forget some shit like that?"

"Forget? He never told me anything like that." Jesus pulled Esperanza out of the line and started after Xavier. "Yo, X, wait up!"

"Please don't tell him I told you," Dulce said. "I thought you knew."

"I won't, ma." And he didn't. In fact, Jesus let Xavier have his way the rest of the afternoon, and that enabled them all to salvage their good time. Xavier met them half way, insisting on paying for all their snacks and drinks for the rest of the afternoon. The hot dogs cost four dollars each, and untrue to his cranky nature, X never complained. Esperanza felt bad about calling him scared. Yeah, she meant to fuck with his manhood a little, but she never realized how bad she had.

After he dropped off Dulce and Xavier at Xavier's building, Jesus admitted to Esperanza that it bothered him that Xavier never confided such things to him. "I mean, there's shit I tell you that I wouldn't tell any of 'em 'cause you my woman. I understand him confiding in D and all. But even though we didn't come up together, me and X go back. I just think that if we're boys, there's some shit I should know."

His words moved Esperanza. Jesus's desire to know even the most horrid details of Xavier's past seemed motivated less by the need as his boss to control his psychology and more as his friend to understand his pain.

"Do you talk to him about your mother?" she asked him.

Jesus scoffed and switched on the car radio, ending the very conversation that Esperanza had hoped to start.

"So you gonna go, right?" asked Feli, interrupting her train of thought.

"Go where?"

"To Jesus's barbecue."

"Oh." When did he slip in that invitation? Esperanza understood that Feli had a crush on her or wanted them all to reunite like some happy family or whatever. But he had to get it—she could not "fraternize" with them. And Esperanza was tired of telling him so. "Nah."

"This year the grand prize is two tickets to the Bahamas."

"Felix, stop already. I can't go, all right?"

His face twisted with rejection, Feli threw up his hands in surrender. "My bad."

"Don't be mad at me, Feli. It's not that I don't want to hang out with you. I had mad fun today, more fun than I've had in a long time." And she meant it. Esperanza liked Tenille, but she could be such a goody-goody. If Feli ever cut loose from Jesus and his crew, she would consider going out with him, at least once or twice. Give him a chance the way Dulce had Chago. But if Feli insisted on rolling with them, she couldn't give him any play. Besides Esperanza was Jesus's ex. *Jesus's* ex. If a woman was gonna mess with a man in the game, you didn't get down with a Feli if you could land a Jesus. And Priscilla or no Priscilla, Esperanza could have Jesus if she wanted him. "It's not you. It's the whole parole thing. If not for that I would go."

How much she wanted to go.

A week before Dulce's twenty-seventh birthday, Esperanza put Chago on notice. She found his cell phone number on the refrigerator from when Dulce tacked it under a Dominican flag magnet in case of an emergency and let him know. "Look, I know you probably have something really nice planned for Dulce's birthday, but I want her to have dinner at home. I'm going to cook her something special, and I want it to be only us. You can do whatever you want for her before and after dinner, but from six to eight, it's just her and me." Then she repeated it in Spanish so that there would be no misunderstanding. Not only did Esperanza want Dulce to herself for a few hours, but the gift she had for her required that no one else be present. Dulce could bitch and moan all she wanted about Esperanza icing Chago, but once she saw her present, she would be happy that Esperanza had not invited him.

"*Yo no tengo problema con eso,*" said Chago. "You make her dinner, I take her dancing. S'OK for you, s'OK for me."

"Bet."

"You want to surprise Dulce? Because I no say nothing to her. I pick her up from work, I bring her home to get dressed for dancing, you have dinner ready. *¿Qué crees?*"

"That's perfect, Chago. You the man."

"You go dancing with us?"

Moved by his invitation, Esperanza almost accepted it. But Chago had met her halfway, so she would show her appreciation by not bogarding their romantic evening. Esperanza figured it would be another birthday gift for her sister, although nothing as good as her original plan.

Dulce loved her surprise dinner, even if Esperanza had overcooked the chicken. How the hell did that happen when she had followed the cookbook to the letter? It really didn't matter, since the rice seemed fine and, of course, the salad was perfect. Dulce ate everything, so Esperanza knew she told the truth when she brought out the flan from her favorite bakery and Dulce said she couldn't possibly eat another bite.

"So take it with you."

"The whole thing? No, I can't do that."

"But it's for you. And Chago likes flan, doesn't he?"

"OK, how 'bout I take half with me tonight, and we keep the rest here."

Esperanza grinned so hard, she thought her face might crack. Dulce still thought of their apartment as her home. "Now for your present." Esperanza ran into the bedroom to get it.

"Present? I thought dinner was my present. Espe, you're too much!"

Esperanza returned with the white letter-sized envelope. "Let me say something first. . . ."

"You better not make me cry."

"If you cry, that's your problem." Esperanza cleared her throat, and Dulce rolled her eyes at her theatrics. "You know that I don't have a lot of money. . . ."

"Espe, you know I don't care about that—"

"I know, I know! That's my point. Will you stop interrupting me? Damn."

"OK, sorry."

"It's been almost five months since I came home, and this is, like, the first special occasion we've had together. So I wanted to get you something that . . . Well, Dulce, sometimes I don't think you realize how good you are. I mean, really good. You're only three years older than me, and you've been like my mom, and way before *Mami* went away. I only realized that when you weren't around as much. I got to thinking, 'Espe, she's tough on you sometimes because she believes in you. Dulce believes more in you than you do yourself. She believes more in you than she does herself.' You didn't have to let me come home. You didn't have to visit me every chance you could and take my calls in between. . . ."

"Of course I did. You're my baby sister. I love you."

"But if you had written me off when I went inside over the bullshit I did, you wouldn't have been wrong. Your life would be so much easier, and I wouldn't have been mad at you. But you forgave me and let me come home. So I figured if you're so good that you can forgive me, maybe I could find a way to show you that you're good enough to forgive yourself." When Esperanza said this to Dulce, she realized that she hoped that her sister would forgive her, too, for not stopping her on that day in August.

When the two train had pulled into the Nevins Street station and La-Vern bade good-bye to her friend Renee, Dulce had motioned for Esperanza to follow her.

Excited about the impending catfight, Esperanza had asked, "What you gonna do, D?"

Dulce unbuckled her belt and slid it out of the loops of her pants.

"I'ma teach her a lesson, that's all." She wrapped the belt buckle around her palm so that the faux-diamond DEE buckle that Xavier gave her sat on top of her fist.

"Yeah, she needs to mind her own business."

LaVern turned into the tunnel leading to the green lines, and Dulce struck. She raced down the corridor, knocked LaVern down to the concrete, and punched her in the face with the DEE belt buckle. "Who you calling a bitch?" she yelled as she slammed her fist into LaVern's head. "Who you telling to shut the fuck up?"

"That's right." Esperanza bounced excitedly as she looked out for other pedestrians. "OK, D, that's enough. We gotta bounce before someone comes." But Dulce became crazed. She grabbed LaVern by the head and started to bang it onto the ground. "All right, D, stop it; she's had enough. Oh, my God, Dulce, she's blacking out!"

In the distance, Esperanza heard a train rumbling toward the station. She lunged on Dulce's back and pulled her off the unconscious LaVern.

"Oh, my God, Espe. I killed her." Instead of distancing herself from the girl's lifeless body, Dulce crawled over to her and stroked her face. "I'm so sorry. I didn't mean to hurt you." She dropped her head onto LaVern's bloody chest and began to sob. "I'm sorry, I'm sorry, I'm sorry."

"Dulce, we gotta go." Esperanza dragged her sister to her feet. "A train's coming, and there's gonna be mad people here." A five train pulled into the station, and somehow Esperanza got Dulce on it. The three passengers scattered about the car remained in their own world as Esperanza led Dulce to the back of the car and forced her into a seat. Because her sister was too hysterical to protect herself, Esperanza took custody of Dulce. She unwrapped the bloody belt buckle from her sister's fist and shoved it into her pocketbook. Then Esperanza unknotted the sweater that hung around her waist to shield her from the subway's excessive air-conditioning. Like a mother dressing a child, Esperanza whipped the sweater around Dulce's shoulders, then knelt before her to button it, concealing the bloodstains on her T-shirt. As she did this, Dulce's red eyes caught Esperanza's and she said, "The other day I asked Xavier why he never calls me Dulce. He says, 'It's a stupid name.' I tell him, 'No, it's not. That's Spanish for candy. Dulce means sweet.' And you know what Xavier does, Espe? He smacks me in the head and goes, 'Shut the fuck up, bitch.'"

"Don't you think about that, Dulce," said Esperanza. "Don't you say a word to anyone, and don't worry about a thing. I'm gonna take care of everything."

The next time Jesus took her to City Island for a seafood dinner, she asked him for a few quarters so she could look through one of the telescopes for tourists to see the Throg's Neck Bridge, Stepping Stones Lighthouse, and other sights. When she reached the telescope, however, she checked around her, took the DEE belt buckle from her pocketbook, and tossed it into the Long Island Sound.

Now Esperanza handed her confused sister the envelope. Dulce ripped it open and pulled out a laminated sheet. Esperanza had found an article published in the *New York Daily News* in 2003 that she hoped would give her sister the peace of mind that had been evading her since that ugly day.

A year after the attack, the journalists followed up on LaVern Bell. After spending three months in a coma, not only had the former nursing student fully recovered, she moved south to study at Spelman College. The article concluded:

> With time Bell has come to forgive her attacker who has never been apprehended. "I'm not saying what she did was justified at all, just that I wasn't exactly innocent back then either," says the women's studies major.
>
> "I guess we were two messed-up girls who crossed paths and took out our pain on each other. It just turned out that she had a lot more pain to deal with than I did.
>
> "Anyway, I'm in a much better place now," said Bell, "And I pray that she is, too."

Dulce stared at the laminated article in silence, and Esperanza wondered if she had made a mistake. Had she opened the very wound she meant only to heal? Then Dulce began to heave with sobs mixed with relief and gratitude. Esperanza wrapped her arms around Dulce, who clung to her and sobbed into her belly.

When her cries ebbed, Dulce pulled away and looked up at her younger sister. "It wasn't just about LaVern, you know. When you got arrested, I kept telling myself, 'It's that Tupac shit. She's obsessed with him. She wants to be like him in all the wrong ways.'" And then the first time I visited you in that place . . ." She let out another sob and struggled to find her voice. "I was coming home on that bus, and I just started crying and crying. I just couldn't stop crying because I realized it was me. It was my fault."

"Dulce, how could you say that? You had no idea what I was planning to do. You had no idea because you had quit the crew." Guilt overpowered Esperanza, and she dropped to her knees and began to cry herself. "I didn't want to quit, remember? You wanted me to quit the crew, too, and that meant leaving Jesus, and I didn't want to do it."

"But I got you in the crew in the first place, *negrita*. If I hadn't gotten involved, you probably wouldn't have either. I'm your big sister, and my job is to protect you. I got you in that life, and I tried to change for your sake, but then it was too late. I should've—"

"*Que* should've, *ni* should've."

Dulce burst out in laughter. She pressed her head against Esperanza's and found her breath. "I'm sorry, Espe. I'm sorry for everything. Even for the things that might not be my fault, I'm so sorry."

"I'm sorry, too."

Dulce lifted her head, pulled back Esperanza's face, and planted a loud kiss on her forehead. "That was the best present anyone has given me, ever."

"Better than Chago's?"

"Yes, smart-ass. Better than Chago's. And he's taking me to DR for the Fourth of July!"

Esperanza forced herself to smile. "You must be excited." She figured Chago would plan something for the holiday weekend. She had assumed it would be something local, like a trip to the beach, and hoped he would invite her to join them.

"I wish I could share your gift with him. But like you said, the past is the past, and I've changed. Still, it would've been nice if I could show this to him and explain why it means so much." Dulce handed the article to Esperanza. "Will you put it away for me in a safe place?"

Esperanza took it from her. "Sure." She would place it in the LaVern envelope after throwing the other articles away.

"Lemme get ready. Chago's gonna be here soon. You coming with us?"

"No, you guys go and have a good time."

Dulce kissed Esperanza on the forehead again. "I love you, Espe."

"I love you, too, D."

As Esperanza cleared the table, she listened to Dulce singing "Happy Birthday" to herself in the shower. She almost gave into the temptation to pound on the door and tell Dulce to hurry up so she could get ready, too. Instead Esperanza washed the dishes and studied for her GED science exam.

THIRTEEN

Amerikaz Most Wanted

"We actually have a lot more fun than we do at Christmas, if you can believe that," Tenille said as Esperanza walked her to the bus stop after work. "My father and his brothers, they compete over everything. Who makes the best burger. Who plays the best music. Who mixes the best drinks.

"They're hilarious when they start drinking and talking politics. My uncle Jimmy? Straight-up Republican, but don't call him that." Esperanza laughed as Tenille imitated her uncle's posture. "'I'm a conservative. There's a difference. But seeing how these damned Democrats take the Black vote for granted, shyeet, maybe I should become a Republican.' Then my uncle Vince is like, 'They all the same. Fuck the Democrats, fuck the Republicans, they all the same. Until there's another choice, and it actually means shit, I'm not voting any goddamned more.' Then my father gets started, 'cause he's in the middle of the two extremes. 'They are the same,' he says, 'but how you not gonna vote when people gave their lives so we could? So what it don't mean shit today. Still gotta do it outta respect for those who died when it meant something.' Then everyone tips their forties for Dr. King and Medgar Evers and Fannie Lou Hamer. You know how people like to say, 'I'm sick and tired of being sick and tired?' That all started with Fannie Lou."

Esperanza loved to listen to Tenille, even when she babbled. She liked that she brought out this lively side to her friend. Tenille would never be Shanette, but Esperanza believed that her friendship brought out the girl's colors. In return, Tenille allowed her to be still without being alone, and sometimes even to learn without admitting her ignorance. "Nobody better ever drop a match in your backyard."

"Girl, you crazy! What are you doing for the Fourth of July weekend?"

"My sister's boyfriend is taking her to the Dominican Republic as a birthday present," Esperanza said. "So I'm gonna have the apartment all to myself."

As much as she tried to make her situation sound desirable, Tenille looked concerned. "Didn't you spend the last Fourth of July . . . apart from your family?"

"Big-time." Esperanza had spent her last Fourth of July in segregation, the only time she ever rebelled while locked up. The COs already had thrown Isoke in solitary because she refused to leave her cell for the staff-inmate party. "C'mon, Debra," Esperanza had pleaded as she attempted to pull Isoke onto her feet.

"I refuse to acknowledge this hypocritical holiday, and I do not answer to that slave name."

"Fuck the holiday." Esperanza could not bring herself to call her Isoke. She felt silly doing so, especially in front of the guards, who continued to refer to her by her birth name or inmate number. "Come out with me to get some sun."

The CO ripped Esperanza's hands off Isoke's wrist, grabbed the older woman by the biceps and yanked her to her feet. "If Glover doesn't want to come out into the yard to celebrate Independence Day, she can spend it in the hole."

Although she had never been in solitary confinement, Esperanza imagined Isoke sitting in the corner of a dark and smelly cell. As she watched the other inmates and guards put up the volleyball net, she felt Isoke's defiance seeping into her. Esperanza never gave politics a first thought, but this shit just didn't sit right with her. By that time she had completed half her sentence and had heard most of Isoke's story. The more she thought about it, the more it pissed Esperanza off to no end that this woman who was everything that America was supposed to celebrate—hardworking, community-oriented, educated by self and system—got twenty-five plus for practicing her right to free speech. And Isoke did everything for the other women that the so-called correctional system was supposed to do. She counseled them about anything and everything when the waiting list to see a trained professional was months long. While people on the outside complained over every little bone tossed the inmates' way, Isoke had her political organization in Brooklyn secure them used computers, books, and suits so inmates might be able to improve their slim odds of employment when released. Isoke lost good days and commissary privileges defending *other* inmates' rights. She once spent a week in seg just for telling Ruthie she could challenge a citation. The way Esperanza saw it, Isoke was the most bona fide American in the place, and that was precisely why the COs kept fucking with her.

So when Patsy—an older white woman doing seven for embezzlement—suggested they pledge allegiance to the flag before the staff-inmate touch football game, Esperanza remained seated on the bench.

"C'mon, Esperanza, you have to stand."

Esperanza felt a fleeting pang of guilt, because she actually liked Patsy and hoped that she would not take her refusal personally. "No." Once she said it, it no longer seemed so difficult, and Patsy's feelings carried less importance. "No." Again she pictured Isoke in the corner of her cell, hugging her knees in the darkness and humming one of those freedom songs she liked so much. "Fuck no. I'm not saying the Pledge of Allegiance."

CO Lynch overheard her, and it was on. She kept her cool through most of his patriotic tirade, then pulled an Isoke herself when she calmly stated that she had a right to *not* say the pledge as much as he had the right to recite it. At one point Lynch changed his tone and politely asked, "Will you at least tell me why you don't want to say it, Cepeda?" No matter what Esperanza said, they would take it out on Isoke, because it would give them more pleasure to persecute Isoke than to punish Esperanza. They would insist that Isoke put her up to it, especially because they were cell mates. So just as kindly as Lynch asked her, Esperanza pleaded the Fifth, even though she didn't believe anything she did would actually incriminate herself.

Lynch lost his cool. "Oh, now you want to plead the Fifth." He summoned the other COs over to them and said, "This inmate, this convicted felon, this transgressor against society wants to evoke her her right to plead the Fifth fuckin' Amendment?" Lynch flicked the collar of Esperanza's jumpsuit and spit in her face. "If you were in any other country in this world, I guarantee you, number seven-two-five-seven-one-three, you wouldn't be treated so humanely, if you were even allowed to live."

To that Esperanza just laughed and laughed and laughed. Apparently she could not have done anything worse than that. She spent a week in her own darkened box that reeked of feces and urine, with her only source of light a sliver of a window and the occasional flash when a faceless guard tossed her a tray of stale bread, tepid water, and a bruised apple. Halfway through her time, it occurred to her that Isoke might still be in solitary confinement, too.

"Debra? Debra, holla if you hear me."

"Shut up, Cepeda!" yelled the guard on duty. "You're not in the 'hood."

"Oh, gee, I forgot." Esperanza sank her chin back into her hands. Then she picked up her head once more. "Isoke!"

"Free the land!"

"Thug life!"

"Shut up, the both of you!"

Esperanza smiled, knowing that even though Isoke did not care much for Tupac's philosophies, she was smiling in her cell, too.

Tenille asked, "And what'd you do the year before?"

"Went to my ex's barbecue." Every year on the rooftop of his tenement, Jesus threw a party for the entire neighborhood. The crew papered the neighborhood with fliers. *ADMISSION FREE. FREE RAFFLE. GREAT PRIZES. CHILDREN OF ALL AGES WELCOMED.* Jesus hired several women in his building to cook as well as bartenders from the neighborhood lounges to serve. Although he demanded clean music, deejays vied to play his party and slipped him mixtapes throughout the year because the gig always led to future weddings and *quinceñeras*. Esperanza had tried to encourage him to bankroll a local talent's burgeoning record label, but Jesus dismissed the idea, saying the feds were all over hip-hop labels like stink to shit. Although he banned herb, the lusty potheads never missed it with that sexpot Natalia rolling gourmet cigars. The party ended with the raffle, and the prizes were so great, sometimes heads tried to bribe Chuck for extra tickets. Each year Jesus gave away hundreds of dollars in gift certificates to beauty salons and clothing stores No-No owned in Brooklyn, and the grand prize was always the year's latest gadget. The year before last Jesus gave away a rhinestone-studded iPod worth two grand. "But obviously that's not an option."

Tenille's bus appeared in the distance. "So come by my place. If you want."

Elated at the invitation, Esperanza said, "Should I bring anything?" In the past, Jesus sometimes had asked her to bring candy or a game like Twister for the kids at the barbecue, and Dulce always made a massive bowl of her famous sangria. Before Dulce left for her trip, Esperanza would ask her how to make it, and then she would find a way to lace it with a unique flavor.

"Just yourself," said Tenille right before the driver closed the bus door and pulled away from the curb.

My dearest sister Esperanza,

Yes, I am very proud of you! I congratulate you not only on your promotion but on the clarity it represents. I understand how difficult it is to trade the seductively easy money of the underground trade for the minimal wages of "legitimate" work. It seems that either way you somehow do injustice's bidding, but the difference is this: You have chosen to forsake the lifestyle that requires you to victimize your people. With the social and economic pressure that I have no doubt you are facing, that takes more courage than any hustle. Now that, my sister, is gangsta!

When I say or write, "Free the land!" I give voice to an important principle and objective of my people. We New Afrikans believe that, as Malcolm X once said, we live under terrible conditions because we do not control any land. Many enslaved Africans and their ancestors have lived, worked, fought, bled and died on the land that your history teacher would call the states of South Carolina, Georgia, Alabama, Mississippi, and Louisiana. We call this land mass New Afrika, and one day we hope to control it.

Imagine if your people owned all the places they have ever lived or worked. The islands of Boriken and Quisqueya, the Lower East Side, East Harlem, Bushwick, Williamsburg, Washington Heights, dozens of neighborhoods in your Bronx? Just imagine, Esperanza! A people who control their land control their destiny. So "Free the land!" is our battle cry, because we aim to control that land to which we have such a long relationship, and as a result, our own destiny.

Since you have left, I have tried very hard to broaden my understanding of thug life. I've had my son bring me books about Tupac and make me tapes of his music. As a former Black Panther, some of it actually makes sense to me. We never turned our backs on the people of the street. In fact, some of us were those very people. We saw the "thugs" as victims of their circumstances who rejected their victimization, and this, ironically, sometimes meant that the most forgotten and least desirable segments of our society possessed the most revolutionary potential. Now I understand that Brother Tupac wanted not only to give voice to the most marginialized and oppressed members of our society among his generation but also to inspire them to organize themselves into some kind of movement to change the very conditions that gave rise to thug life. I see now that he meant to humanize these brothers and sisters and not promote their way of life.

But the more I learn, the more questions I have. Where did he go wrong? When did elevation become glorification? What was Tupac's vision for a world after "thug life," and did he really understand the magnitude of the work that would entail? I realize now that in my desire to mentor you, I never stopped to learn from you, Esperanza. There are so many things I want to ask you, and I regret that I did not start on this particular quest while you were here. I feel remorse for the opportunity I lost due to my arrogance, and I miss you very much. At the same time, I am happy that you are not *here (smile).*

Please tell me more about Ms. Maite Rodriguez. Is she a small woman with a big presence? Before my incarceration I knew of a Maite Rodriguez whom my comrades and I lovingly called La Pitirre. Ask your Maite, and if she is the same one I had the pleasure to know, you would do well to ask your new mentor to tell you her history and to share your own with her as well.

Without ever calling it by name, you write so much of love, or at least what you perceive to be a lack of it in your life. The hardest thing you will ever learn in your life, Esperanza, is to love yourself the way you want others to love you. That truly should be your highest priority. If you achieve that, all your other goals will manifest. Most important, you will see the love that already exists all around you. Your sister's love. Your mother's love. The love of your truest friends. And when you love yourself the way you want others to love you, my sister, those who cannot or will not love you simply will disappear.

And just so there is no doubt, I love you (smile).

Much peace and progress,
Isoke Oshodi
Free the Land!

"A complete meal has four components," Esperanza said, imitating Luciano's Agent Smith drawl during a slow period. "The sandwich, the beverage, the French fries and the dessert. If I order a Big Mac and a Coke, what are you supposed to say, Tenille?"

Happy to finally have another shot at the register, Tenille took her teasing in stride. "Would you like fries with that?"

"And?"

"What about an apple pie or a sundae?"

"Customers frequently add the missing component to their order when you suggest it. You're not just a cashier, Tenille, you're a salesperson. Stop being so timid and sell the product. Upsell, upsell, upsell!" Esperanza jabbed her finger in the air to punctuate the unusual word, and Tenille giggled.

"Frequently my behind," Tenille said. "For the most part people know what they want and freakin' order it. I worked at Mickey D's one summer in Atlanta, and I didn't mind upselling there. But people around here get, like, offended when you suggest what they should eat. Do you know how many times some smart-ass has told me, 'If I wanted fries, I would've asked for them'?"

Esperanza did know. "And the attitude's not even necessary. A simple 'No, thank you' will do."

Tenille laughed and turned to her customer, a tall boy of about seventeen with a sneer on his face. "Yes, how may I help you?"

"Yo, this shake you sold me is spoiled."

She seemed flustered at the accusation. "Are you sure?"

"What you mean, am I sure?" He slammed the cup onto the counter.

Esperanza said, "That's the first batch of the day. I put it in myself." Tenille still looked panicked, so she added, "But I'll go check, 'cause maybe . . ."

As Esperanza walked to the shake machine, Tenille told her customer, "We're going to check it for you right now, sir." The guy sucked his teeth and mumbled something under his breath. Tenille joined Esperanza just as she had poured some milk shake into a cup and tasted it.

"There's nothing wrong with this, T. Taste it yourself."

Tenille refused Esperanza's cup. "Well, he says there's something wrong with it."

"He's just trying to get over. Go check his cup. I bet he drank most of that shit."

They both went back to their respective registers. Although she had a customer to serve, Esperanza kept her eyes on Tenille. The guy yelled,

"That shit you sold me is spoiled, and I want my money back." Tenille took his cup, removed the straw and lid, and took a sniff. "What the fuck you smelling it for?"

From where Esperanza stood she could see that the milk shake cup was two-thirds empty, as she suspected. For something that was so rotten, muthafucka sure had to drink a whole lot of it to notice. Esperanza greeted her customer, keeping one ear on her order and the other on Tenille's situation. *Good for you,* she thought when Tenille finally found the courage to taste the milk shake herself.

Tenille placed it back on the counter and said, "I'm sorry, sir, but there's nothing wrong with that shake."

"Bitch, what?"

Esperanza waited for Tenille to rip him a second asshole. Instead she said, "Even so, if you had brought it back somewhat full, I would've been happy to replace it for you." Esperanza rushed to finish her current customer, who herself seemed eager to get out of the restaurant.

The guy leaned across the counter and stuck his finger in Tenille's face. "I'm telling you, y'all sold me a spoiled milk shake, and I want my fuckin' money back now."

Tenille placed the cup on the counter. She took a deep breath and said, "This shake is just fine, sir."

"You think so?" He picked up the cup and tossed the remainder of the milk shake into Tenille's face. "Try that shit again." And then, as if nothing happened, he turned around and bopped toward the exit.

Esperanza gasped as Tenille stood frozen, vanilla milk shake streaming down her ebony face and dribbling onto her collar. Several coworkers rushed to her with napkins, and the girl on fries ran to the back to get Luciano. Tenille whimpered with humiliation as customers shook their heads and pointed their fingers.

Esperanza bolted over the counter and raced through the dining area. When within arm's reach of Tenille's attacker, she reached out and shoved him, tackling him to the floor. He hit the tile so hard his head banged the floor and his baseball cap sailed under a table. Esperanza pummeled him in the head until she felt a pair of masculine arms hook her into the air.

As Luciano dragged her away, she screamed, "The customer ain't always right so who you callin' a bitch?"

* * *

"Espe?" She turned away from her computer monitor to see Feli ambling toward her with his cart of books to reshelve. "What you doing here so early on a Saturday?" He pulled up a seat next to her and stared at her uniform. "Why aren't you at work?"

"What work?"

"You got fired?" She nodded. "And they let you keep that?" he asked of the uniform.

"Not exactly." When Luciano had dragged her into his office, he called her impulsive and irresponsible. The bastard said she had absolutely no excuse for becoming violent. "Your behavior was entirely inappropriate!"

Knowing she had nothing to lose after beating down that nasty kid, Esperanza let him have it. She called Luciano stupid and spineless and asked him how come his definition of violence did not include being called a bitch and having something hurled into your face. What kind of manager was he to not have Tenille's back? What kind of man was he? What kind of human being? How dare he call anyone inappropriate! Luciano fired her, and Esperanza stormed out of McDonald's, uniform and all.

"Wanna talk about it?" Feli asked. Esperanza hesitated, and it seemed as if he immediately understood. "I won't say nothing to nobody. I swear on my grandmother."

"Don't be swearing on your grandmother, Feli. Why dudes always be swearing on their mothers and grandmothers and shit? That way if they are lying, some poor ol' lady pays for it."

"OK, calm down." He sat for a moment in thought, then said, "We swear on mothers 'cause that's who loves us and takes care of us. Even if they don't do a good job, at least they're there. Who else we gonna swear on? Our fathers? Niggas ain't around."

"Swear on your damned selves then."

Feli made the sign of the cross, kissing his pinkie and raising it to the sky. "I swear on my life, I won't tell nobody what you tell me."

"I got fired for wilding out on a customer who threw a milk shake in my friend's face."

"Why'd he do something fucked up like that to her?"

"Don't you get it, Feli?" Esperanza said as if it were too obvious to mention. " 'Cause he could." She grabbed her things and stormed out of the library.

* * *

Except for Feli, they were all at the basketball courts. Jesus and his boys played skins as they ran up and down the full length of the court. On the other side, Priscilla and the women danced around coolers of drinks and food, cheering on the guys and exchanging gossip with one another. Everyone sported shorts and tanks, and somebody's ride pumped the summer's hip-hop anthem.

Esperanza hung back, sitting on a bench underneath a tree as she watched people enjoy their summer. No nine-to-fives. No exams. No polyester. She pulled the collar of her uniform off her sticky neck. She had to stick it out a few more hours. Dulce had taken the day off to finish packing for her trip to the Dominican Republic with Chago. No way did Esperanza want to send her off with the news that she had gotten fired.

The game broke, and all the guys headed toward the women. Like obedient molls, they jumped up to fetch beverages and sandwiches for them. She watched as Priscilla grabbed some ice cubes and rubbed them down Jesus's bare chest. He must have told her that he liked that, because Esperanza used to do it for him. The crowd teased them, and Jesus pulled away, embarrassed. Then he turned and spotted Esperanza. Although he already had a beer in his hand, he grabbed a bottle of iced tea and made his way toward her. Priscilla grabbed at him, but he shook her off and barked orders at her.

Leave. But Esperanza remained riveted to the park bench. When Jesus drew near, he offered her the bottle of iced tea. She accepted it, and he sat down next to her.

"You're out of work early."

"I'm out of work permanently."

"Why?" He listened attentively to her story. "Damn, that's gangsta." He laughed.

"It's stupid is what it was."

"Stupid to stand up for your homegirl? I know you don't really believe that. Even if you do, 'cause of what happened, I'm proud of you regardless. You handled your business." Jesus took a swig of beer. "Espe, let me ask you something."

"What?"

"Tell me the truth now."

"Sus, talk!"

"How long would you love me if I left the game?"

"Jesus—"

"For real, Espe. I'ma break it down for you, 'cause you keep frontin'. If you wanted a nine-to-five nigga, you would've got yourself one. You're a woman. A beautiful woman. Life is cake for you, ma, 'cause if you want a thug, you can get a thug. You wanna Wall Street cat? You can get yourself a Wall Street cat. A lawyer, a janitor, a baller, whatever. You think you need college to get a college muthafucka? You pretty, you got good conversation, and you're good in bed. Niggas are simple. That's all we need."

"If y'all are so simple, then why all the drama?"

Jesus laughed. "All I'm sayin' is I don't want some woman growing to love me. You do, or you don't. And the truth is, a woman always knows from jump if she can ever love a man. Like she can ride with him through whatever or she can just refuse to do that shit. I've seen y'all do it. I envy y'all that. I can't do it. Don't you think I'd stop loving you if I could?"

"Yo, Sus," Xavier called. "Let's finish executin' this beatdown." Their opponents groaned, and the shirts and skins began to talk shit.

Jesus stood up and offered Esperanza his hand. "C'mon."

"I can't go over there."

"I done told you. Don't sweat Priscilla. She—"

"It's not that. I don't wanna go over there in this corny gear. Besides, I need to shower and change."

"Will you come back?"

Esperanza hesitated. "Nah, Sus. My sister's leaving for vacation, and I want to spend some time with her before she goes."

"So I'll see you at my barbecue then."

"I got other plans."

"Oh."

"Not plans like that. My friend from work, the one who got dissed. Her family's having a little somethin'-somethin', and I promised I'd swing by."

"Too bad. I miss Dulce's sangria." Jesus reached into the pocket of his shorts and pulled out a wad of bills. He peeled off a few hundreds and extended them toward her. "Go get yourself some new gear."

"I can't take that."

"Yes, you can. At least buy yourself something so you can change out of that thing. You're beautiful in anything, ma, but that's just not your steelo." Jesus shook his head, and Esperanza had to laugh. "You're unemployed now, too."

"With Dulce's job, we'll manage until I find something else."

Jesus sneered and said, "Yeah, Pathmark makes all the difference." He offered her the money again. "Take it before Xavier comes over here and makes a scene."

Had she not been fired, it would have been easier to resist. But Esperanza had no idea when she might find another job. Even though Dulce spent most nights each week at Chago's, she still managed their household and paid her share. How would it look if Esperanza told her sister that she did not have her end of the bills?

She would buy herself just a few things while Dulce was in DR and put the rest away. And she would still look for a legitimate job, of course. The cash could tide her over until she did, and if she found one quickly enough, maybe Esperanza could start a nest egg for future emergencies. Especially if Dulce did move in with Chago. Or worse—away with him. "Thanks."

"No doubt." He placed his hands on her cheeks and kissed her sweaty forehead. Then he ran back to his basketball game as she watched, and Esperanza wished she could go with him.

Esperanza returned home and found Dulce zipping around the apartment packing for her trip to the Dominican Republic.

"You're home a little early." She folded a sundress and placed it a suitcase.

"I wasn't feeling well, so . . ."

Dulce paused and looked at her with concern. "You OK?"

"I think the place is starting to get to me," said Esperanza as she pushed aside Dulce's pile of rejected outfits and climbed onto the bed. The last thing she wanted to do was recount the story again. Even though Jesus and Feli had been sympathetic, she still could not shake the feeling that she had done something ridiculous and had gotten just what she deserved. She also didn't want to spoil Dulce's mood, especially if doing so meant making her sister angry with her. Esperanza would tell her about McDonald's when she found another job, and Jesus's money bought her some time. "I'm sick of the look, the smell, just everything."

"I feel like that about the supermarket sometimes," said Dulce. "Sometimes I think, 'I'm too good for this shit. Why am I standing on my feet all day? I should be doing something with my mind.' And then I see Richie stocking the shelves or mopping up a spill, and I start to feel guilty. He left his entire family behind in Mexico to come here and do the shit I think I'm too good to do. I'm not better than him. Just thinking I'm better than him makes me not as good as he is." Dulce tucked a few rolls of tube socks into her suitcase. "Then a girl with her baby comes in with her food stamps, and I start going back and forth. I start thinking 'She's probably got Medicaid just like that, but I had to lie to keep it.' But I remember what it's like when people feel they got some right to assume things and judge you because you're on welfare. I was that girl with the food stamps, and I had the cashier stare at my nails like I stole something from her. She doesn't know that my boyfriend paid for the manicure or bought me the gold chain I'm wearing. She doesn't know that because he buys me those nails or that chain, he feels he has the right to slap me upside the head whenever he feels like it. She doesn't know how it feels to have people think that just because you're poor you should be unclean, but then if you are unclean everyone says, 'That's why you deserve to be poor.' Can't fuckin' win. So I look at the girl with the baby and the food stamps, and I feel lucky to have this bullshit job that jacks up my back but doesn't give me any benefits so I can to go to the doctor to check it out without scamming Medicaid."

Esperanza rolled over to look at her sister. Here Dulce was packing for a trip to the Dominican Republic, and she seemed so sad. Then again, she had decided to take all of Brenda's old clothes to give away to Chago's relatives. "I'm glad Chago's taking you on this trip, Dulce. You need a vacation, and you deserve to have some fun."

Dulce smiled. "I'm real nervous about my Spanish."

"Girl, please. You and Chago be yakking away. Kwah, kwah, kwah, kwah, kwah." The rarely functioning intercom buzzed, and the Cepeda sisters looked at each other with anticipation. "Chago coming to get you?"

"No, he had some last-minute things to do at the warehouse, so I'm just going to take a cab to his place. You expecting anybody?"

"No." Esperanza rose from the bed and walked into the kitchen. She hesitated before the intercom, and it buzzed again. She hoped Jesus knew better than to follow her home. Or Feli. Curiosity got the best of her. "Who?"

"Is Espe there?" a female voice crackled over the speaker.

"Tenille?"

"Yeah, hi!"

Heartened by the sound of her voice, Esperanza quickly buzzed her in. Then panic set in when Dulce lugged her suitcase into the kitchen. Without meaning to cause Esperanza any trouble, Tenille was about to blow up her spot.

"Who was that?"

"My friend Tenille. From work."

"That's so nice, her checking up on you. I haven't met any of your friends from work. Or school either, for that matter."

Tenille knocked on the door, and Esperanza rushed past Dulce to answer it. She flung open the door and blocked Dulce's line of sight. "Hey, T, what're you doing here?" she said, hoping that by the expression on her face, Tenille would catch her hint. If she did, Tenille gave her no indication.

"Espe, let the girl in."

Esperanza stepped aside, and Tenille entered the apartment. "Tenille, this is my sister, Dulce. Dulce, this is Tenille. She works with me at McDonald's."

Tenille's face registered, and Esperanza's stomach settled. Tenille waved to Dulce. "Hi, Espe's told me so much about you."

"Yeah, the bitch from hell. That's me."

"I never said anything like that, did I, T?"

"No, she only says wonderful things about you."

"Then she's a liar." Dulce grabbed the suitcase with Brenda's clothes and dragged it toward the front door. "I'm the bitch; she's the liar."

"Very funny, Dulce."

Tenille reached for the suitcase. "You need help with that?"

"No, I'll be fine, thanks. So what are you guys doing tonight?"

Tenille looked at Esperanza and said, "I was thinking a movie."

"OK, but I'm not really up to going downtown or over to the Concourse," said Esperanza. She wanted very much to hang out with Tenille, but after all that had happened that day she felt undeserving of an outing. "I got a bunch of videos here we can watch."

Dulce groaned and opened the apartment door. "Run while you can, Tenille. She's got nothing but Tupac movies in there."

Tenille laughed and said, "I think I'll live."

"OK. Espe, come lock the door," Dulce said.

"Did you leave me your sangria recipe?" She explained to Tenille, "My sister makes a slammin' sangria, and I want to make it for your barbecue."

"Goody."

"It's on the fridge," said Dulce. "I'll be back later for my stuff." She blew Esperanza a kiss and closed the apartment door behind her. Esperanza locked the door and turned to Tenille.

"I'm really, really sorry about what happened."

"Why you sorry? It's not your fault."

"But you got fired defending me. I feel so bad."

"I shouldn't have gone so far," Esperanza said. She realized the significance of her confession. "I let that guy win, because I paid for what he did to you." Esperanza filled with shame and she could no longer look Tenille in the eye. She pulled away from the door and went into the living room.

Tenille followed. "You did what I wanted to do." Surprised to hear this,

Esperanza faced her again. "When he threw that shake at me, I wanted to go off on him. I stood there hating him, wanting to hurt him so bad for what he did to me. And then I saw him leaving, like nothing happened. Everyone talking about how terrible, how vicious, how wrong, but no one had the guts to check him. Not even me, who he had just humiliated in front of all these people. Then I couldn't move because I went from hating him to hating myself for just standing there while he walked away. Sometimes I'm so angry, Espe, and I've got no way to let it out. People like that guy, they get mad, and they let it out. I have all this anger inside, and I can't let it out. It's like my anger got into you somehow, and you let it all out for me. I guess I came by to thank you for that."

Esperanza didn't know what to say. As much as she appreciated Tenille's gratitude and apology, she felt like a fraud. She didn't know if that jerk had picked on another cashier besides Tenille whether she would have gone to the same extreme, let alone done anything at all. What Esperanza did know was that much of the rage that fueled her attack was not just empathy for Tenille's humiliation or loyalty to her friend. Most of that anger she unleashed was all her own.

"You want to watch videos?"

"Sure, what you got?"

Esperanza popped in the videocassette *Tupac VS.* As many times as she had seen this documentary, she remained riveted to it as if for the first time. Ordinarily she paid little attention to the professors and activists when she watched her "Pacumentaries," as she liked to call them. When ol' heads talked about him, they made him sound dead and buried, when they did not sound as if they spoke a foreign language. Esperanza would tune out or fast-forward to a rap star or Pac himself. They spoke in her language, and even when they used the past tense, they talked about Tupac in ways that proved he remained alive. Thinking of Isoke's last letter, she realized that she had to mind her elders, and when she watched *Tupac VS* this time, it surprised her that when Professor Dyson said things like, "Pac's thug life is the critique of the revolutionary impulse that couldn't pay the bills" or "Tupac at once represented the expression of that evil that needed to be resisted and the need to resist that evil," she understood his every word. Esperanza could no longer accuse him of dissecting Pac's psyche, because now she saw how his long words painted her own life in vivid colors. The professor got Pac, and therefore, he got her. They were at once exactly the same and completely different. Esperanza always cried when she watched these documentaries, but she did so now for a reason other than heartache.

She glanced at Tenille, herself quiet with reflection. But when Esperanza pulled the cassette out of the VCR and stuck it into the rewinder, Tenille said, "He was so full of it."

"The professor?"

"No, Tupac. You can't be a thug and a revolutionary at once, and he damned well knew it. He was working whatever angle kept him from going broke. I've seen other movies about him, and the man contradicts himself left and right. In one interview, it's 'Don't come to jail. It's not the spot. But if you gotta be a thug, at least give back to the community you're raping.' Which itself is stupid. Then in the next interview he's like, 'I'ma smoke blunts and drive a Benz and carry a gat, 'cause that's what niggas do.' I mean, how you gonna rap about 'girl, keep ya head and up' and then sodomize some girl in a nightclub? Is that what he fuckin' meant by 'keep ya head up'?" Tenille scoffed and threw her hands up in the air.

"Wait, wait, wait, you got it all twisted, T. First, he was never convicted of sodomizing anyone," said Esperanza. "The worst thing he did was, like, put his hand on her butt, and that wasn't in the nightclub. What happened is—"

"So it's OK for some guy you barely know to grab your behind?"

"No, Tenille, I'm not saying that, and that's not even my point."

"The guy was a hypocrite, plain and simple. Talking about all this political stuff here and living thug life over there. He hated being poor, and he was gonna work whatever hustle that kept him paid."

"Tupac was not a hypocrite! He had his contradictions just like anyone else." Tenille tried to respond, but Esperanza raised her voice to speak over her. "Look at yourself, Tenille. You're all into these movies about women who fight back and kick ass or whatever, but you still let that guy in the restaurant get away with what he did to you. You criticized your own mother but went and did the same thing she did."

The look on Tenille's face made Esperanza wish she could take back every single word. She meant what she said, but she never meant to hurt her friend. Tenille's expression made Esperanza feel like she had thrown another milkshake into her face. "I'm not judging you, Tenille. I mean, I'm the last one to judge anyone, right? I'm just sayin' that . . ."

Before Esperanza could finish stumbling through her apology, Tenille took her bag and rose to her feet. "I need to get home."

Esperanza said, "Stay, T, please." Ignoring her pleas, Tenille made her way to the apartment door as Esperanza followed. "I've got some other videos here that can explain it better than me."

Tenille unlocked the door. "I've had a long day, and I want it to end already."

"I feel you." Esperanza wanted to ask Tenille for her address and direction to her house, but she did not dare ask. Instead she watched Tenille as she made her way to the elevator. Not once did she look back, and she kept her back to Esperanza as she waited for the elevator to arrive. The elevator doors dinged as they opened, and she called out, "Call me later?"

Without looking at her, Tenille said, "Uh, huh." Then she was gone.

Esperanza closed the apartment door and locked it behind her. As she leaned against the doorway, she imagined Tenille going home to her father to cry on his shoulder and receive his comfort. She would tell him about the nasty customer and the project chick she thought was her friend. Esperanza imagined Tenille's father encouraging her to quit that awful job, assuring her that he would take care of her until she found something better.

Esperanza sank to the floor and wrapped her arms around her knees as she had in solitary confinement. *Nobody's a hypocrite, T. We're just complicated. Pac. You. Me. Just hurt and complicated.* The words came too late to comfort Tenille, and their truth did little to console Esperanza.

She waited for a call from Tenille that never came. On the third of July, Experanza called her. But when a man picked up the telephone, she hung up on him.

Balancing the giant thermos on her hip, Esperanza eased through the partygoers as they bounced to the Terror Squad's summer hit. When she saw the deejay, she realized why he looked so familiar. Not only was he the same deejay Jesus had hired for her welcome-home party, he was the bartender at the restaurant the night Xavier tried to embarrass Dulce in front of Chago. Jesus obviously worked that dude, paying him for being an extra pair of eyes and ears at parties, lounges, and other places where alcohol made folks careless with their acts and deeds.

She followed the trail of cigar smoke and the smell of burgers until she spotted Jesus by the grill wearing a goofy paper chef's hat, a large pink stain already on his undershirt as he used tongs to flip a row of hot dogs. It touched Esperanza to see him like that, even when Priscilla appeared with two plates, each holding a hamburger bun. Esperanza watched as Jesus switched to a spatula, scooped up two burgers, and laid them over the open buns. She waited until Priscilla disappeared into the crowd before she approached him.

"Can I have one well-done?"

Jesus looked up and stepped back away from the grill. "Espe," he said as he put down the spatula and wiped his hands on his jeans. He seemed embarrassed that she found him such a mess. "I hoped you might drop by, but I never really thought . . ." Jesus snatched off the hat, crumpled it up, and tossed it in the giant trash bin near the grill.

"Sista gotta eat." She offered him the thermos. "And I brought this. I call it *sangría Dulce á là Esperanza.*"

Jesus laughed as he took the thermos. Then he said, "Look, do me a favor. Go find Chuck and tell him to come here. Then grab a seat, make yourself comfortable, and I'll be right with you."

Esperanza rolled her eyes. She hadn't been there two minutes and already he was telling her what to do. But then again, he was being so nice about it. She didn't feel like she had to fetch Chuck if she really didn't want to. "Do you know where I can find him?"

"You know Chuck and them. They probably by the cigar bar."

"Is Xavier with them?"

Jesus huffed. "Better not be. I just sent that muthafucka for a pack of Newports. You know I was never into that shit."

Xavier's likely absence put Esperanza at ease. "OK." She started to leave. "Don't forget my burger."

"I got you, ma, I got you." He grabbed a raw patty and laid it over the grill. "That one right there, that's for you." He winked at her, and Esperanza's knees softened.

She navigated the crowd, keeping her eye out for Chuck, and as Jesus had predicted, he had pulled up a lawn chair to Natalia's table, his eyes shifting from her nimble fingers to her quivering cleavage as she rolled a vanilla cigar. Next to him sat Feli. "Hey, Feli, hi, Chuck."

"Espe!" Still gripping his forty, Chuck sprang to his feet and gave her one of his fluttery hugs. "Good to see you. How you been?"

"All right. You?"

Chuck slightly raised his bottle and said, "Chillin' like a villain that ain't been caught."

Feli sucked his teeth. "Stupid."

The possible slight to Esperanza went right over Chuck's head, so she let it slide. "Sus is looking for you."

Chuck scurried off, and Esperanza claimed his seat. Feli said, "I'm sorry about what he said."

"Ah, he always says that."

"Yeah, but considering what happened, what you did . . . it ain't right."

"He don't mean nothing by it," said Esperanza, and she meant it. Chuck tended to put his foot in his mouth, and most times she found it endearing. Maybe because Jesus and Xavier much preferred to put their feet in someone else's mouth. "So how're you?"

"I'm a'ight," said Feli. He took a big gulp of a aqua blue drink. "My *'buelita*'s pissed at me 'cause her church is having some big party today, and she wanted me to go with her. I ain't really wanna go, so we had a big fight." Feli tossed back another gulp. "Typical family drama. We'll get over it."

But Esperanza could see that Feli had doubts. "You know Doña Mili loves her little Feli."

Her words made Feli smile, but he said, "I hope you're right. She figured out it was Jesus's party. But you wanna know something, Espe? See that guy right there? And those two women over here? And that whole family back there? They all go to my grandmother's church. You think they don't know how Jesus pays for this shit? In the church they gonna talk about us like we the devil's spawn on earth, right. But then they gonna roll up in here, eat his food, drink his liquor, and try to win his raffle."

"People are complicated," said Esperanza. "That don't make 'em bad. You know what you do, though? When you get home, before she can start, you say, 'Oh, *Abuelita,* I saw Don So-and-So at Jesus's party and he said hi.'" Feli burst out in laughter. "For real. That way you can school her about her people without being disrespectful, you know."

"What's all the ha, ha, ha about?" Esperanza and Feli looked up to find Jesus hovering over them. He had changed into a burgundy silk shirt and put on his designer sunglasses. In one hand he held a plate with a hamburger, macaroni salad, and potato chips, while in the other he grasped a sweaty bottle of Corona.

"We were just talking about all the church people up in your party, eating your food while they talking shit about you," said Feli. "Tell their kids to stay away from us, but then later they want to send them to college on a Jesus Lara scholarship, word."

"That shit don't bother me none," Jesus said. "You know why I throw this joint on the Fourth of July? 'Cause ain't nothing more American than a thug. Ain't nothing more true to the American game than a gangsta. What'd your boy used to say, Espe? America's the biggest gang in the world, or some shit like that. Anyway, all these people who come here and eat my food and win my prizes 'cause they know for one day in the year, they can get theirs at my expense. I ain't mad at them for that. Yo, Feli?" Jesus jerked his head once to the side, directing Feli to make himself scarce.

Feli pulled himself out of the lounge chair. "I'll see you later, Espe."

"Later, Feli."

Jesus handed Esperanza the plate and beer and sat beside her. "Well-done, right?"

"Yeah." She took a huge bite. Jesus remembered just how she liked her burger—both mustard and ketchup, lettuce but no tomato. Esperanza liked onions, but Jesus never let her have them, complaining, *I'm the one who has to kiss you after you eat that shit.* Jesus watched her take another bite and snickered. "What?" she said through her mouthful.

"You'd think where you used to work, you'd be sick of eating hamburgers."

"I didn't eat the food all the time. I mean, ain't nothing like a homemade burger. Plus, it's not like the food's free or we were allowed to take home whatever's leftover at the end of the day."

"Word?"

"There are strict rules against that, and my boss—I mean, my ex-boss—ran the place by the book. And you know what? The employee discount ain't all that."

"Yo, that's jacked up."

Esperanza shrugged and took a swig of Corona. "It's business."

Jesus leaned forward and said, "Speaking of business, things are going really well for us, ma."

"Us?"

He shrugged. "Me. The fellas."

"Priscilla."

"She ain't no part of that."

Esperanza grabbed a few chips, then placed the plate with her unfinished burger on the ground. "You must really care about her after all." She placed a chip in her mouth and chewed furiously, refusing to look at Jesus as she waited for him to respond.

"You think I don't involve her 'cause she's all that to me?" She felt Jesus's finger hook gently under her chin and turn her face toward him. "Come with me to California next month."

Esperanza pulled away her head. "California?"

"Yeah, I'm ready to make some big moves, starting with a meeting with some cat in LA. I know you been working hard trying to do the right thing.

But doing the right thing doesn't necessarily come with a nice vacation, does it?"

Doing the right thing keeps me out of prison, Esperanza thought. Then she imagined Dulce running down the beach in the Dominican Republic, tanned and laughing, as Chago chased her into the crispy waves of the sea. Except for a family trip to Puerto Rico she was too young to remember, that trip to visit her mother, when she and Dulce saw nothing else but roads and runways, and her stint upstate, Esperanza never left New York City. She could not even imagine California in any way other than the slices she saw in her Pacumentaries. The vast luxury of Hollywood and its surrounding districts of wealth and the poverty of Marin City where Pac once said, "I left Baltimore to escape violence and get to Marin City . . ." She could not visualize the center of the extremes like the San Rafael of Chago's ex, with its friars and nuns. Esperanza could see, however, sitting across from her mother in her prison greens. Yet that image brought her full circle. "My ass is fired, remember. I'm already on vacation. Indefinitely."

"Take a long weekend with me in August. I'll take you to California and show you the kind of life I want to give you," Jesus said. Just as if she heard it from across the rooftop, Priscilla appeared before them with her fists parked on her bony hips and her head cocked. Jesus said, "What you want?"

"Chuck is messing up everything," she said, pouting. "He burned a whole package of hot dogs."

"So what the fuck you doing here? Go back there before he ruins my party. Just take over."

"You know he doesn't listen to me." For a moment Esperanza sympathized with her, but then Priscilla started to whine again. "I told him, 'Chuck, lemme do it,' and he was like, 'Just 'cause you a chicken don't mean you can barbecue one.' In front of everybody, J! They all started laughing at me. . . ."

"All right, I'll be there in a minute," Jesus said, inching out of the chair as if he had aged years since he sat down. "Go already. I'm right behind you." Priscilla hesitated long enough to glare at him, then spun around and fled into the crowd. Jesus reached into his pocket and said, "Now you see why I need you."

Then Feli reappeared. "Sus, you really gotta get back to the grill," he said between chortles. "One of the ol' church ladies is threatening to call the fire department and whatnot."

"Fuck!" Jesus kissed Esperanza on the cheek and said, "Think about what I said and let me know." Then he disappeared into the crowd, leaving Feli with Esperanza.

"Hey, Espe, a group of us are trying to get a Monopoly game going. You down?"

Esperanza had no love for Monopoly. Dominoes was her game. The only person she could not beat was Dulce, who had taught her how to play. She and Jesus used to play Xavier and Dulce every Fourth of July. Although they never beat them, she always had mad fun, even when Jesus and Xavier talked too much shit, as if they were playing for more than bragging rights. But Jesus was off overeacting to another one of Priscilla's dramas. "I wanna play dominoes."

"We kinda don't do that anymore. First Dulce quit, and then you left. You know how Xavier be. Once he didn't want to play . . ."

"We don't have to do a whole tournament. You only need two people. Play with me, Feli."

"Bet," he said, and they went off to find the dominoes.

FOURTEEN

Me and My Girlfriend

The night before Esperanza's science exam, Dulce gave Esperanza a timed practice test, allowing her eighty minutes to answer fifty questions. To her dismay, Esperanza correctly answered only thirty-seven of the questions.

"But you passed," said Dulce.

"By only two damned questions." Esperanza flipped to the first page of the exam with so much disgust, she almost tore a page. "Go over the wrong answers with me. Fuck it, let's go over the right ones, too. I don't want to be getting the right answers with the wrong thinking."

"OK, but after that you're going to sleep."

"*Que* sleep, *ni* sleep," Esperanza said, making Dulce laugh with her tribute to Chago, who had brought them dinner and then left to spend his Friday night with friends.

The morning of her exam, Esperanza arrived early, as Dulce suggested. She had turned in at a decent hour but slept in fits. Between bouts of insomnia, Esperanza dreamed of taking the exam. She neither passed nor failed; she neither found the test easy nor difficult. She just dreamed of sitting in the classroom by herself, taking the exam: pondering over questions, and scratching answers onto her answer sheet.

"What do you think it means?" Esperanza asked Dulce as she made her an omelet that morning. "Every time I fell back asleep, the same thing over again, without any feelings or consequences."

"It means you gonna do the damn thing. Now eat."

With a half hour to go before the official start of the examination, Esperanza sat at a desk in the back of the room, sharpening her pencils and shivering from the air-conditioning. Thank God Dulce insisted that she bring a sweater. Even though the radio predicted a ninety-plus-degree day, she explained, better for Esperanza to expect the room to be too cold. "It's OK to be a little cold; it keeps you alert. But if you're freezing, you're going to be too uncomfortable to concentrate," said Dulce. "And if your proctor's a dude and you don't have a sweater, *te jodistes,* 'cause all the other dudes in the room will complain it's too hot, to turn down the AC, and he's gonna side with them."

When Pete entered the classroom, her heart jumped. Ordinarily Esperanza could take him or leave him, but no one from her GED program was in her last two exams, so she found the sight of a familiar face comforting. "Hey, Pete!" She waved him over and patted the desk next to hers.

"Espe!" Pete bounded over to her and flopped into the adjacent seat. "You ready for the test?"

"No. You?"

"Hell, nah!" They both laughed. "Who you had for science?'

"Dupree. She was a'ight. You?"

"I don't even remember his name. I slept through the entire thing." Then Pete asked, "You had Hudlin for math, right?"

"Yeah, the bastard."

"It's true you wilded out on him in class once 'cause he read a love letter of yours?"

"That's old news." Esperanza grinned, hoping to mask her discomfort. Better not to talk about Hudlin. Let her pay for what she did that day some other time. But for the record, she said, "I tried to ignore him respectfully, and he couldn't hang and ODed, so I checked him."

"You a trip, Espe," Pete said. "If this is your test center, you must live around here. I'm on Morris Avenue, right across the street from Lincoln Hospital."

Esperanza leaned forward. "Yeah? I don't live too far from there. I'm in the Melrose Projects."

"For real? Maybe you know my friend—"

Pac's music blasted through the window from a car outside.

Pete grimaced with disgust. "Who the hell is playing that shit all loud?" He sauntered over to the window, and Esperanza rose to follow him. "That muthafucka better turn that down before the test starts."

When Esperanza joined him at the window, she recognized Jesus's Escalade parked at the curb in front of the school building. The music grew louder before Jesus finally stepped out of the car holding a large poster board. *All I need in this life of sin is me and my girlfriend.* Jesus walked around the car to the sidewalk and looked up the building.

"Dope ride," said Pete.

"Jesus, you didn't," Esperanza said.

And as if he were only inches away instead of four stories beneath her, Jesus spotted her in the window. He waved at her, then held up the sign, on which he had scrawled in thick block print:

GOOD LUCK, ESPE!
KICK THAT TEST ASS!
I LOVE YOU!

Pete asked, "That's your man?" He sounded disappointed.

Before Esperanza could answer, an authoritative voice behind them said, "Away from the window, please. The test is about to begin." She gave Jesus one last look, and he blew a kiss at her. Esperanza pulled away from the window and into her seat. As the examiner began to read the test instructions, Esperanza listened as Tupac's voice faded down the street.

"Pencils down," said the proctor. Some students groaned, while others sighed. Esperanza rushed to finish erasing a stray mark on her answer sheet. She had answered all the questions on the last section of the test with five minutes to spare, and Dulce had made her paranoid about filling in the bubbles perfectly.

"It's a science test, not an art test."

"Yeah, but if you've got a smudge between B and C, the machine can't tell which one you meant to give and might mark it wrong."

"Pencils down," the proctor repeated, and Esperanza dropped hers into her bag on the floor.

The proctor went from desk to desk collecting the answer sheets and then did the same for the examination booklets. He finally dismissed them, and the test takers wearily rose to their feet and commiserated over the experience. Esperanza jumped, yanking her sweater from behind her seat.

"So how do you think you did?" asked Pete.

"I don't know." She whipped on her jacket. "I kinda felt it was too easy sometimes."

"Too easy?" Pete gave a low whistle. "Damn, I should've studied with you."

Esperanza had enough of worrying over this exam. "I'm glad it's over. If I failed, I failed. Nothing I can do about it now."

They walked out of the classroom and into the corridor. "So what you gonna do now?"

She shrugged. These weeks before the science exam she took her books and studied in the park until her McDonald's shift ended. Then she went home, and sometimes Dulce was there and sometimes she wasn't, but either way Esperanza had to make herself something to eat and study some more. Now she wanted a break from all books but had no other plans. But perhaps Jesus would be outside waiting for her.

"I'm not sure," she said. She was sure, however, that Pete intended to ask her to hang out with him. Esperanza could not risk Jesus seeing her walk out of the building with him. As she veered toward the ladies' room she said, "I think my man might have something planned."

"Oh." Pete switched his knapsack from one shoulder to the other. "Well, maybe we can study together for the language arts test. We can call Kiki and the others, too."

"That'd be cool," Esperanza said as she opened the door to the bathroom. "See ya." She entered the bathroom and headed straight for the sink. She rummaged in her bag until she found her comb. As she ran the comb under the running water, then pulled it through her hair, Esperanza wondered how Jesus might have found out where she would be that morning. Maybe Feli realized it could never happen between them and decided to be a gentleman and step aside. Or maybe Jesus always had Feli keeping tabs on her. Yeah, that was more his steelo. Esperanza wasn't mad at Feli, though. She finished combing her hair, freshened her makeup, and buzzed out the door.

Esperanza bounded out of the school building and past the gate. Perspiration immediately bubbled on her neck and under her arms, so she pulled off Dulce's sweater and wrapped it around her waist. She looked up and down the street but no Escalade. Esperanza then glanced at her watch. The test had begun and ended on time. She waited until her test proctor exited the building and climbed into his own car and drove away. Accepting that Jesus would not come back, Esperanza finally headed toward the bus stop.

She spent the entire bus ride reviewing the test in her head again and again. Did she choose the right equation on that chemistry question? Why did she change that answer at the last minute? What if she accidentally skipped a question and all her answers were off? By the time Esperanza arrived at the empty apartment, she was more nervous than she had ever been before the exam.

She tried to rewatch *Tupac VS* so she could write back Isoke but could not focus. Then Esperanza dialed Dulce's number at work, but hung up when her supervisor answered. She thought about calling Tenille but decided against it. Then she remembered Maite and scoured her messenger bag until she found her number.

"Hello?"

"Hi, Maite? This is Espe Cepeda."

"Esperanza! It's so good to hear your voice. How are you?"

"I'm good. I just took my science test today."

"And how'd you find it?"

"I go back and forth, you know. It seemed kinda easy. Now I'm wondering if that's because I made a whole buncha stupid mistakes. Sometimes I sacrifice accuracy for speed." *Fuckin' Luciano.*

"Did you study?"

"Did I study? Maite, you don't know. I studied. My sister Dulce tutored me. We did practice tests and everything."

"Then I have no doubt that not only did you pass but that you did very well."

"Maite, can I ask you something?"

"Of course."

"That job as your teaching assistant? Is it still open?"

"I'm sorry, Espe. I filled that position about a month ago."

"Wow, that fast? I figured since school doesn't start for a while . . ."

"My assistant had to begin during the summer to get a jump start on the reading and research, help me organize myself to teach the class. . . ."

"Yeah, yeah." Esperanza preferred not to hear the details of a job she could have had and passed by. "I understand."

"I'd like to see you, Espe. Why don't you come by and visit my office one day?"

"Sure, when?"

"I'm teaching a political science course this summer that meets every day except Fridays from two to four, and I usually stay until about six or seven. What's your work schedule like?"

"I can come see you after class," said Esperanza. "How 'bout Monday?"

* * *

Esperanza knocked on the office door but no one answered. She sat on the bench beside the door and checked her watch. Maite still had fifteen more minutes of class. Esperanza hoped she impressed her by arriving early. And good thing she had spent the rest of her weekend doing laundry and fixing her hair. She even splurged on a new shirt—not too fancy for the street but not so plain to ignore. Esperanza had no doubt that her neat appearance got her past the guard in the lobby, who asked to see her student ID. In her best English, she told him she had a four-o'clock appointment with Professor Rodriguez, and he simply asked her to sign a book and allowed her to go upstairs. Had she been dressed in her usual 'hood gear, he might not have let her without making a call to Maite, who was still in class. That would have been embarrassing.

Esperanza noticed a bulletin board across the corridor and rose to read it. Some students sought work as typists. She had done well in her high school typing class. If she had a computer at home, this might have been a great way to earn money. Several psychology students wanted people for various experiments, and they paid, too, some as much as fifteen dollars per hour. Esperanza imagined Frankenstein movies and moved to the next posting. A call to audition for a play she had never heard of. A renter looking for a roommate. (These students paid eight hundred dollars to share an apartment in Manhattan when that same amount got a one-bedroom apartment in the Bronx, and they wouldn't let *her* into college?) An invitation to a meeting of women who had eating disorders and other "dysfunctional relationships with food."

The elevator dinged, and Maite stepped off with a young woman about Esperanza's age with blond hair and light green eyes. She looked distraught as she followed Maite and yapped at her like a stray puppy. "I didn't mean to offend him."

"I know you didn't, Allison, but you did."

"So how do I make it right?"

"You make it right by going to talk to Rodney yourself."

"But what do I say to him?"

Maite finally stopped, looked her in the eye, and said, "You don't say anything, Allison. You tell him what you told me and then you just listen. Don't try to explain or defend or justify. Just listen." They arrived at Maite's door. *"Hola, Esperanza."*

"Hi, Maite."

Maite reached into her pocket for a key while Esperanza stared at Allison. Why was this white girl still there? She already had her time with Maite.

"I don't know, Professor Rodriguez. I'm not the enemy just because I'm white," said Allison. "And I feel the harder I try to prove it, the more suspicious people of color become." Her eyes watered, and Esperanza began to feel sorry for her, even though she suspected that if she heard this Rodney's take on the matter, she'd probably side with him.

Maite placed a hand on Allison's shoulder and said, "You're not the enemy, Allison; racism is. The problem is that because you're white, you may benefit from racism whether or not you intend to, and whether you're aware of it or not. So like I said, the one thing you can do is listen to those who suffer. And it's also important that you not only try to have conversations about race with people of color, but also with other white people like yourself who genuinely want to fight racism." Allison clung to Maite's words like a devoted parishioner. "The way you feel right now is something to share with other white people who have been in the same situation. Maybe collectively you can get to the root of why you feel that way and what you can do about it. Believe it or not, part of what it means to be an ally is to be honest about your own self-interest. If racism were to disappear, what's in it for you? Before you can make someone like Rodney understand and have faith that there is something in it for you, you yourself have to gain clarity about what that something is." Maite inserted the key into the office door, then pushed it open. "I want you to go ahead in the assigned reading. Read the material scheduled for discussion the second week of August. Especially the Tim Wise and Peggy McIntosh articles."

Allison nodded. "You know what? I'm going to see if the other white students in the class want to read it and discuss it in a study group. Think that'd be a good idea?"

"That's an excellent idea, Allison. Now please excuse me. I have to meet with my other student."

Allison turned to Esperanza. She seemed so guilty for taking up so much of Maite's time. "Sorry."

"No worries." Allison left, and while Esperanza felt relieved to have Maite to herself, she thought that maybe Allison was all right. *Give her a chance, Rodney.*

"Esperanza, come in," said Maite as she held open the door.

She walked into Maite's office, which seemed half the size of her own bedroom, with one tiny window that overlooked a quiet residential street. On the other side of the window sat three rows of beige metal cabinets with two drawers apiece. Another wall consisted entirely of overflowing bookshelves that ran from the floor to the ceiling. Maite had a small desk filled with stacks of paper with sticker notes in various colors tagged throughout, and a computer with a thick monitor and wide keyboard. Right above the desk hung a bulletin board with a large calendar filled with handwritten notes and surrounded by photos and postcards. Sharing the wall with the bulletin board were posters of multiple colors and sizes. One had a cartoon of a Black woman with an Afro of twists shaking a fist and saying, "If you're dissin' the sistas, you're not fighting the power." Another featured the black outline of that bearded man with the beret against the red background that Esperanza frequently saw on T-shirts on dudes in the 'hood.

"Who's that guy anyway?"

"That's Ernesto 'Che' Guevara. You might say that he's the Latino Malcolm X."

Now Esperanza better understood his popularity. "You'd think he was a rapper or something like that."

Maite laughed. "In a way, I guess he was. As was Malcolm."

Esperanza's eyes moved across the bulletin board as she read the postcards Maite had tacked on it.

> *The most potent weapon in the hands of the oppressor is the mind of the oppressed.* —*Stephen Biko*

> *Women constitute half the world's population, perform nearly two-thirds of its work hours, receive one-tenth of the world's income, and own less than one-hundredths of the world's property.*
> —*United Nations Report*

> *When I dare to be powerful—to use my strength in the service of my vision—then it becomes less and less important whether I am afraid.* —*Audre Lorde*

"Isoke!" She turned around to face Maite even as she continued to point to the postcard. "She wrote the same thing to me in a letter and said she might know you. Isoke Oshodi."

Maite's eyes saddened even as her face glowed. "How do you know Isoke?"

Esperanza hesitated. "She was my cell mate. How do you know her?"

"Isoke told you that in the sixties she was a member of the Black Panther party here in New York, right?" Esperanza nodded, and Maite continued, "During that time I was involved in a similar group of Puerto Rican activists called the Young Lords. Have you ever heard of us?"

"Yeah, but I always thought you were . . ." Esperanza did not want to offend Maite.

"A gang? That's how the police and media tried to depict us to turn the people against us."

"Even if y'all were a gang, it's all good," said Esperanza. "Tupac said gangs could be positive. That this country was built on gangs and is still run by gangs, so what mattered was if the gangs were doing good instead of being self-destructive."

Maite pondered her words. "I never thought of it that way. I didn't want to demonize gang members, but I surely didn't want to be associated with them either. I'm going to have to think about that some more." She paused then asked, "How is Isoke, Espe? Is she OK? How do they treat her inside?"

"As OK as a woman in prison can be. And then Isoke's Isoke, you know. . . . It's hard to explain."

"You don't have to. I know exactly what you mean. If I had to do any more time than I did, I don't know if I would've survived."

Esperanza gasped at Maite's revelation. "You were in prison?"

"Nine years. From the age of twenty-one until the age of thirty. They convicted me and three comrades on several counts of conspiracy. But as was the case with many of us in the movement, we were really targeted for what we believed."

"Isoke says she was a prisoner of conscience."

"She is, and so was I. So are many others who remain incarcerated. All political prisoners."

Esperanza turned over the words in her mind. Prisoner of conscience. If conscience meant doing whatever you thought was right, then she was a prisoner of conscience, too. Because the code of the streets was that you didn't roll over on your crew. To give up your peeps to save yourself was wrong. The right thing to do was to go down alone, and that was what Esperanza had done. Meanwhile, the crew violated its own code when it dipped into her share of the loot. They should've held onto it for her or given it to her sister. In the past, they had deaded dudes for stealing like that. The crew's politics superseded the street's code. Crew politics dictated that they concoct bullshit excuses to cheat Esperanza out of her money. Those politics dictated that she got less money instead of more for her loyalty, for no other reason than that she was female.

"Me, too, Maite," said Esperanza. "I was a political prisoner, too." She expected Maite to argue with her. Women like her and Isoke and Pac's *titi* Assata and even his mom, Afeni, got locked up for defending their peeps, not holding them hostage in their own neighborhoods. Maybe you couldn't be a thug and a revolutionary at the same time, but they were opposite sides of the same coin. Esperanza remembered watching *Tupac 4Ever* and seeing an excerpt of Pac's interview while on lockdown at Clinton Correctional, when he said that if heads really wanted to be gangsta, they would start a revolution. Esperanza always liked that without ever understanding it until now.

Maite said, "You were." Esperanza searched her tone for sarcasm or condenscension but found neither. "And long before you went to prison."

"When my mother went to prison," Esperanza said, answering the question that Maite asked with her silence. "He kept beating on her and beating on her, and they would arrest him and let him go. They told her to leave him, but he said he would kill her if she did, and she had every reason to believe him. So *Mami* tried to get him to move out without breaking up with him. She begged him to leave. 'It's not good for my girls to see us fighting like this all the time.' And the *cabezón* . . . His name was Roland, but behind his back Dulce and I used to call him *el cabezón*, 'cause he had this big head in every sense of the word. *Mami* never even knew we called him that, 'cause she wanted us to show him respect. Anyway, at first Roland fronts like he agrees with *Mami*, and he starts packing. And little by little he loses it. He's ranting about all he's done for us, getting us off of welfare and buying us good food and pretty clothes. Roland's grabbing anything and everything he thinks he bought for the house, throwing things in his boxes. He storms into the kitchen and rips the radio out of the wall. *Mami*'s behind him. She's not trying to stop him from taking anything; she's just trying to calm him down. And then he reaches into the dish rack and grabs the knife. So, you see, *Mami* got lucky in that fight, because it was *el cabezón* who went into the kitchen and got the knife. I don't know how she got it from him, but if she hadn't, she'd be dead." Esperanza shook her head. "She'd be dead, and he'd be out by now beating on somebody else. But people in my neighborhood are, like, Brenda got lucky. She got the knife. She got lucky.' But *Mami* wasn't lucky. Three years of black eyes, loose teeth, and cracked ribs. But they called my mother a murderer."

"Do you see your mother often?"

"No. She's in California so it's been a long time since I've seen her." Esperanza gave voice to a longing she had long suppressed. "I want to, though."

FIFTEEN

Set It Off

"You know Ms. López?" The longer they talked, the more surprises Maite had for Esperanza.

"She helped me get this job."

Esperanza had no doubt that she spoke the truth, but she had difficulty understanding how a woman as young as Ms. López could help someone as powerful as Maite. "How'd she do that?"

"Elena was a campus leader while a student here at Barnard. She chaired an organization that once invited me to speak during Women's History Month." Maite slapped her hand over her heart at the memory. "Let's just say not everyone was pleased with the invitation."

Esperanza was eager to hear that story, too, but she had to take Maite's tales one at a time to keep them straight. "So then how'd you get a job here?" If someone with Maite's history could become a teacher, then why not she?

"Elena serves on the diversity committee of the alumni association. That means, she and other people who graduated from the college fight to get more women of color into the school. Both as students and as staff."

"That's dope!"

Then came Esperanza's turn. Maite's telephone rang, but she ignored it as she listened to Esperanza tell her about Brenda, Dulce, Isoke, and even Jesus. No one had done that for her before. Not caseworkers, the po, her public defender, Puente . . . no one. At about seven o'clock, Maite took Esperanza to dinner at a Chinese restaurant near the college, and the food seemed much different from the kind Esperanza got from the takeout down the street. Maite explained that different parts of China had their own cuisine, and the kind of Chinese food in any given neighborhood told from which part of China the people who owned the restaurant came. "That's why you find Cantonese food in place likes the Bronx, but Hunan or Szechuan in Manhattan," she said.

Then after dinner they went back to Maite's office and talked some more. Maite told her about coming from Puerto Rico to El Barrio as a little girl, growing up poor no matter how hard her parents worked, and becoming a Young Lord at the age of eighteen, when she took her little brother to get a TB test in a truck the young activists had stolen.

"We had an outbreak of tuberculosis in the community, and they were the ones who did something to stop it. The health officials expected these poor working people to go downtown to the free clinic or wait until the testing van just showed up in our neighborhood. So the Young Lords stole the truck and brought it to the neighborhood. The word got out, and I took my little brother so we could get tested. I turned on 111th Street and saw this van surrounded by about fifty people, and they're holding up signs that say, 'Health Care is a Right Not a Privilege' and 'Free Puerto Rico.' And flags, Esperanza! Puerto Rican flags everywhere. Then the police came. In cars and helicopters! But that didn't stop them from testing people, and I knew I wanted to be a part of that group."

Esperanza giggled. "You and Isoke, y'all are so gangsta!" Then she remembered. "Why did they call you La Pitirre?"

Maite groaned with amused embarrassment. "Isoke told you about that, too? *Una pitirre* is a little bird from Puerto Rico. Sort of like a sparrow. But the *pitirre* is known for attacking much larger birds. Sometimes in self-defense, sometimes in offense. Remember that women's studies group I told you about? Isoke and I were in it together, and sometimes our nationalism would get the better of us, and we'd butt heads."

"Y'all didn't like each other?" Esperanza found that hard to imagine. She had assumed they were good friends, if not pretty close, given all they had in common.

"Not in the beginning," Maite said, smiling as if even the memories of those tensions with Isoke brought her pleasure. "She felt that studying anything outside of an Afrocentric perspective was a waste of time and counterrevolutionary. If we studied Puerto Rico, and that was a big *if* with Isoke, we should focus only on its African heritage and history. Well, zealous *independista* that I was, I took great issue with that. Truth is, I had yet to embrace that heritage. That was part of why I resisted Isoke. I just knew I descended from Tainos, straight and pure." Maite paused to laugh at the memory. Then she became serious and said, "And after I convinced the group to allow me to do a small presentation on Puerto Rican culture and history, which included a passing reference to the *pitirre,* Isoke pulled me aside afterward and asked if I would go have coffee with her. She asked me so many questions—not to challenge me, but to really understand. And at one point she said to me, 'Sometimes I envy your people. I envy their language and their food and their music. Most of all, I envy your people's willingness to defend them.' And this shocked me. Look at this expansive and splendid place we know as Africa, with multiple languages, different kinds of food, all types of music. And I say this to Isoke, and she says, 'But I don't know which tribe is mine. I never had the chance to know. As much as I fight, I may never know.' And I say, 'Why not claim them all?'

"Then I confessed to her something I couldn't even admit to other Lords, which was that I was frustrated with Puerto Rican resistance, both in the past and the present. I knew we had moments in our history when we fought back, and we were fighting back then in the sixties. But I looked at the struggle of Black people in the United States, and I felt that as a people, Puerto Ricans were so far behind. Like we didn't have the same fight in us. And I was ashamed of that." Maite stopped as if the shame had returned, and Esperanza thought that she might even cry. But she collected herself and said, "So I admit this to Isoke, and she says, 'What's that Puerto Rican bird you mentioned in your presentation? That little warrior bird?' And I've been *La Pitirre* ever since. She called me that, and everyone else did, too. Even when I complained about machismo within the Lords, it was, *'Aquí viene la pitirre.'*" Esperanza laughed and laughed, and Maite joined her despite her confusion. "Is it that funny?"

Esperanza caught her breath. "Hell, yeah. A gangsta bird. That's what a *pitirre* is." Then she stopped laughing but held on to a twisted smile. "It's funny, Maite, 'cause they call women birds all the time, right? Or chickens. Pigeons."

"Sounds no different from 'bitch' to me," Maite said disapprovingly.

"Nobody ever calls you a chicken or a pigeon as a compliment. But now they just call us birds in general, right, and that's supposed to be the 'compliment,'" Esperanza explained as she squeezed quotation marks in the air. "'I'ma holla at that bird over here,' or 'So I was talking to this bird.'" She fell silent for a moment, then continued. "I guess it's not that different from 'bitch'. I mean, guys say things like 'That bitch is fine' or 'She a smart bitch', and it's all love. At least, it's supposed to be. Next time somebody calls me a bird, I'ma be like, 'What kind of bird. Get specific. 'Cause if you're calling me a chicken or a pigeon, it's on. But if you're calling me a *pitirre,* then we real cool.' "

Maite shook her head, smiling. "I suppose Isoke told you about my book, too."

"You wrote a book?"

Maite stood up and walked over to her bookshelf. From the row of thick hardcover texts, she pulled a sliver of a softcover from the stack and handed it to Esperanza. The once-red cover had paled with age into a grayish pink. At the center sat a hieroglyphic of what struck Esperanza as a woman with legs like a frog. Beneath her the title read *The Revolutionary Spirit: An Owner's Manual for the Warrior Womyn.*

Esperanza left Maite's office after ten P.M. and carrying a stack of books. Maite gave her money for a cab, and it pulled in front of her building within twenty minutes. While touched by Maite's generosity, Esperanza felt overwhelmed. Between Maite and Isoke, she had too many books and no time to read them. At least not until after she had taken all the GED examinations.

Esperanza lugged the books into the apartment and found Dulce alone, staring at the television.

"Where were you so late?" Dulce's voice crawled with suspicion, and Esperanza worried that she might have heard about her going to Jesus's barbecue.

"With my language arts teacher." Esperanza brought the books into the living room, set them on the coffee table, and flopped next to her sister on the couch. "You know, I would've called, but how am I supposed to know you were going to be here waiting and worrying?"

Dulce snapped, "I call you no matter where I'm at."

" 'Cause no matter where you at *I'm* always *here.*" Esperanza sprang to her feet and headed for the door. She didn't need this shit from Dulce. She probably had had some lovers' quarrel with Chago, which was why she was home alone with her bad attitude. Now that Esperanza arrived, she wanted to pick the fight with her that she should be having with her man? *I am not the one.*

"Oh, my God, where'd you get this?" Esperanza stopped and turned. Dulce flipped through Maite's book with amazement. "Your teacher gave you this?"

"My teacher wrote that." Esperanza could not have felt prouder than if she had written the monograph herself.

"Get the fuck out! Your language arts teacher is Maite Rodriguez? Do you know who she is?"

"Of course I know who she is." But Esperanza realized that despite all the things Maite had told her that night, she still did not know her. The more Maite told her, the more Esperanza needed to know. "How do you know her?"

"We talked about her in my women's studies class. Professor Daniels copied a section of her book for us to read and discuss, and everyone was fiending to read the whole thing. But they only published a few hundred copies back in the sixties, and they're mad hard to find. I looked everywhere. The library here doesn't have it, and the college library won't let you borrow it 'cause they're afraid someone will jack it."

Esperanza remembered her conversation with Feli at the library about the kind of books that got stolen. Although it contained essays and poems, Maite's book was not hip-hop, poetry, or even gangsta lit, but some straight-up political shit. She could not fathom how such a tiny book that looked homemade could be such a big deal. Then again, she remembered *The Prince.* That ran a little under two hundred pages, and that Italian dude wrote it centuries ago, and thousands of folks read it to this day. But she bet Maite had much more relevant things to say.

"Can I borrow it?" Dulce asked, hugging the book to her chest like a little girl would a doll. "I'll take good care of it, I promise."

"I don't know. . . ."

"Please, please, Espe, please. I won't take it out of the house or tell anybody I have it. I promise."

"But I wanted to read it."

"You're still studying for the GED. When you're through with your tests, I'll be finished with it. You know I read fast. Please, please, please!"

"OK, already." But for good measure Esperanza walked back into the living room and surveyed the books on the table. She grabbed *All About Love* because it was by that bell hooks woman. Then, on a whim, she grabbed *Sister Outsider,* too. Not only because Audre Lorde proved so important to both Maite and Isoke, but because she knew Dulce had her own copy.

Dulce smiled at Esperanza's choices. "Those are both really good." As Esperanza left for bed, her sister clicked off the television and began reading Maite's book.

* * *

The math GED left Esperanza with a pounding headache. The AC had broken down, and the room sweated in the August heat. Worse, she had underestimated that exam and left the building with no idea how she had fared on it. Jesus had not reappeared to wish her luck. He had not reached out to her at all. No calls, no letters, no messengers. Jesus had offered to take her to California this month, then disappeared.

And Feli barely spoke to her anymore. When Esperanza went to the library to study, he acknowledged her but went about his business. She suspected Feli's distance had more to do with Jesus than with Miss Henson. Maybe Feli stayed away because she bruised his heart, but wasn't he her friend? And a friend doesn't ice you just because you won't give him his way. *And when you love yourself the way you want others to love you,* Isoke had written, *those who cannot or will not love you simply will disappear.*

The thought of going home to an empty apartment aggravated Esperanza's headache. Except for Jesus's barbecue, she had had no kind of summer. She worked and she studied. Then when she lost her job, she studied some more, stared at the television, or just walked the street as if she were homeless. She was twenty-fuckin'-four years old. She deserved some fun, especially after all the hard work she had done to get herself on track. Any more of this legitimate hustling with no rest, and she just might do something ill to let off some steam.

When she arrived at her building, Esperanza saw Jesus's Escalade parked across the street. As she made her way toward the building, Jesus climbed out of the driver's side and headed toward her. "How was your test, ma?"

"Like you care."

"If I didn't care, I wouldn't be here asking." Esperanza skirted around him toward her building. "You wrong, Espe. You want a muthafucka to get straight, but you expect him to be up under you all the time. I'm a man, Espe, and I'm in this shit deep. I just can't quit like y'all did."

Esperanza saw Rosie and the twins standing in front of her building. She stopped and turned to walk back to Jesus. She did not want those little girls overhearing her business and running to report back to Priscilla.

"I just wish you were here this morning."

"I couldn't, ma. I had to do some running around to prepare for this trip to California. But I'm here now. Why don't you come back with me to my crib? Everyone's there, playing games, watching TV, and whatnot. It'll be fun—just like ol' times."

"I don't know. That test killed me. My head hurts."

" 'Cause you need to eat. We got some *chuletas* back at the apartment. Let's go." Jesus offered her his hand, and Esperanza took it.

When Jesus opened his door, the smell of frying pork chops and the bass of a movie playing too loudly engulfed them. "You like that, huh?" he said. Jesus stepped aside to hold the door open for her.

On the couch, riveted to *Scarface* for the umpteenth time, sat Chuck, Feli, and Xavier. By the window she spotted the abandoned Monopoly game sitting on a table surrounded by three chairs. Like a congregant during service, Chuck listened as Tony Montana drunkenly raged against the white-bread patrons in an upscale restaurant, hushing everyone as Feli snickered with glee. X took Chuck's irritation as his cue to jump to his feet and recite the dialogue along with Tony.

" 'Whattaya lookin' at? You're all a bunch of fucking assholes. You know why? 'Cause you don't have the guts to be what you wanna be.' "

Priscilla emerged from the kitchen, her hands greasy and her brow sweaty. "Did I hear J?" Her eyes fell on and burned into Esperanza. Then she muttered to herself and marched back into the kitchen. Esperanza heard the crash of pans and utensils as Priscilla threw her invisible fit.

"Cut out all that fuckin' noise," X yelled, making more noise than everyone, including Tony Montana.

"Make yourself at home," said Jesus. Esperanza considered turning around and walking out the door, but he stood in front of it, gesturing her toward the couch. Then he went into the kitchen.

Feli moved to make room for her. His eyes fixed on the television screen, Chuck did not budge. Feli nudged him. "Move down, man." Without blinking Chuck slid over, as did Feli, and Esperanza sat. Jesus returned with a bottle of Rémy, which he sipped from as he stood behind the sofa watching Tony's demise.

Long bored with *Scarface,* Esperanza always remained fascinated by its impact on the fellas. Ordinarily Jesus outdid Xavier in his rendition of each and every scene. He loved to sit next to Esperanza on the love seat and act out the scene between Manolo and Gina after Tony dismisses her from the nightclub. Esperanza smiled as she remembered the laughs she got saying in Gina's exaggerated Cuban accent, " 'I see the way you look at me, Manolo.' "

Then Feli would sandwich himself between them to reenact an earlier scene, when Manolo first sees Gina after all those years and remarks on how beautiful she is. " 'Hey!' " Feli barked in Jesus's face as Tony. " 'She no for you!' "

Jesus would clamp his palm onto Feli's face and shove him away from him. " 'Get the fuck outta here.' " And no matter how many times they had done that, everyone would fall into fits as if it were new.

But now Esperanza watched Jesus as his eyes bore into the television screen. She had never seen him like this, making eye contact with Tony Montana as if trying to communicate telepathically with this imaginary being. He used to revel in Tony's cunning and fearlessness. As well as Esperanza knew Jesus, she saw the tension rising in his green eyes and anticipated his explosion minutes before he broke.

" 'You need people like me so you can point your fucking fingers and say, "That's the bad guy." ' " said Xavier, mimicking Tony Montana's drunken shuffle and blocking the television. " 'So what dat make you? Good? You're not good. You just know how to hide. How to lie.' "

"Sit the fuck down, Xavier. I can't see," said Chuck.

"Leave 'im alone." Feli laughed. "Let 'im do his thing."

" 'Me, I don't have that problem. Me, I always tell the truth. Even when I lie.' "

"Yo, Sus, check your boy so I don't have to disrespect your crib."

Esperanza stared at Jesus as he glared at the screen. "Jesus, you all right?"

Xavier broke out of character. "Nigga hungry, that's what's wrong. Ay, Priscilla! What's up with the food? Been over an hour already."

A loud clang erupted from the kitchen. "It'll be ready when it's ready."

Jesus reached over the back of the sofa to where the remote sat on a cushion between Chuck and Feli. He grabbed it and clicked off the television. The guys groaned in protest. "Shut the hell up! As many times as you watch it, you niggas never really pay attention to that shit." He prowled around the couch and stood in front of the television. "This is all a fuckin' waste of time. We ain't never gonna roll like him, but we sure as hell gonna go out like he did. Don't get it twisted. We peaked right here."

"C'mon, now," said Xavier. "A little ambition never hurt a nigga."

"You don't fuckin' get it." Jesus stalked over to the Monopoly game and snatched the board, sending the game pieces around the room. "This game we in ain't no different than some corporate shit out there. Unless we invent crack squared, we'll never be that large."

"Sus, don't talk like that, man," said Chuck.

"Nigga drunk," said Xavier. "Ignore 'im,"

"Muthafucka, I ain't drunk. I'm real clear right here." Jesus stepped into Xavier's face. "Y'all are nothing but peons, and you know what that makes me? I'm not Tony Montana. I'm not John Gotti. I'm not Nicky muthafuckin' Barnes. I'm a goddamned middle manager. At best. Maybe not even."

"What you sayin', Sus?" said Chuck. "I mean, speaking for myself, I don't need to have all that to be happy. Look at Xavier. He loves this shit for its own sake, and it's all good."

"Damn straight," Xavier said as he munched on a toothpick. "This shit's to me like the army is to some white boy. It's not just a job. It's an adventure." He cackled, and Feli gave him a pound.

"And, Sus, if you in it for the clothes and the cars and the bling-bling, that's all good, too. Me, I just want to have the money to feed my seeds and the time to watch them grow. I'm giving 'em everything I never had, 'cause that's what good parents do. I do this shit so they won't have to. That's why I do this."

Esperanza had heard that before. Her scar began to itch, and she reached up to scratch it gently through her T-shirt. Jesus had said something similar to her that night, and later she had to rush to the emergency room.

Jesus stood eye-to-eye with Chuck. "How you figure, Chuck? If you don't want to rise up in the game, how you plan to give your kids a better life than you have?" He pointed to Tony's mansion on the television screen. "You think we can floss like that here? Ain't no cribs like that in the 'hood. Where do you keep a ride like that in the 'hood? When your son rolls through here with some fly gear, he's got a hundred eyes on his back looking for the right spot to stab him."

Chuck flustered. "Then I guess I stack my paper and move someplace nicer, like Pelham Bay or Riverdale."

"Stay in the fuckin' Bronx." Jesus laughed so hard he spit. "That's my point exactly, knucklehead."

"Yo, man, you don't have to go there."

"Chuck, if you want to play at this level, your ends are here. The better you do here, the more you gotta stay here. You either rise up or get out. What's the point of doin' this shit just to live in the middle of the goddamn PJs all our lives?"

"So we don't have to be flippin' burgers, like your girl over there," said Xavier.

"Food's ready," Priscilla said. Jesus looked at her as if she had just told them that their cab to Mars was waiting downstairs for them. He flung the Monopoly game board at the televison. "J, what's wrong?" Jesus stormed out of the living room down the hallway to his bedroom and slammed the door. "What the hell happened?"

"Your fault, bitch," said Xavier. "Nigga cranky 'cause he hungry. Drinking on an empty stomach and shit." With Jesus not there to check him, Priscilla shrank, and Esperanza felt a pang of empathy. Xavier hit the Eject button on the DVD player and popped the disk back into its box. "Fuck all this negativity," he said. "I'ma continue my research at my crib, 'cause not only am I gonna get paid, I'ma stay paid. In fact . . ." Xavier picked DVDs off Jesus's shelf and dropped them into his knapsack. *The Godfather. New Jack City. Empire.*

"Can I roll with you?" said Chuck.

"Whatever."

Priscilla said, "What about all the food I cooked?"

Xavier headed for the door, and Chuck and Feli followed him. "Bye, y'all," Feli said to the women, and then the guys left.

And Esperanza and Priscilla were alone. Each eyed the other with an understanding: The first to leave would lose Jesus. Esperanza moved to the center of the couch before the television, picked up the remote, and surfed the channels. Priscilla pivoted and marched into the kitchen. Esperanza landed on a recast of the Video Music Awards and dropped the remote in her lap. A few minutes later Priscilla sauntered into the room with a plate teeming with white rice, red kidney beans, and grilled pork chops smothered in steak sauce. In an obvious show of resolve, Priscilla planted herself next to Esperanza on the couch and began to watch the show. At most Priscilla was a size two, but she made a point to chew loudly and smack her lips. Esperanza rolled her eyes at her, but her stomach growled at the hearty aroma wafting from Priscilla's plate. In her own display of stubbornness, Esperanza waited until Priscilla got into the awards show, bobbing her head and singing along as Beyoncé strutted across the stage, just to click in the middle of her number.

Esperanza cycled through the channels as she sensed Priscilla attempting to hide her distaste or interest whenever she paused. She finally landed on Black STARZ playing *Set It Off.* A helicopter flew through the Los Angeles night, attempting to track Cleo, Frankie, and Stony as they sped into a tunnel in Cleo's '62 Chevy Impala. Esperanza put down the remote even as Priscilla lay her plate on the floor and leaned toward the television. She could like the movie all she wanted, because Esperanza had no intention of changing the channel just to spite her. Even though it always shattered her heart to watch the next scene, Cleo's sacrifice remained her favorite part. This surprised her after all she had been through in the past two years. *Set It Off* should have been a little too close to home in so many ways.

When Jesus wanted to expand, he decided they should hit a check-cashing joint. "That's hot," said Xavier. "But you can't pull off something like that without someone on the inside."

"I'm way ahead of you. I met this bird who works at one at 153rd Street off the Concourse. Name's Priscilla, and she's gutter. The girl's down for this. Not for a second did I have to play her to get what I needed."

"What do you need from me?" Esperanza asked.

"You just need to position yourself where I tell you and look out, that's all. I'm not trying to put you in harm's way. Prissy'll give us the signal; Xavier, Chuck, and I will make our move. Feli, you're driving."

"Sus, you know I'm down no matter what, but a check cashing joint?" said Feli. "Those places got mad security."

"That's why he had to get somebody on the inside," said Chuck.

"But Feli's got a point, *papi*."

"Fuck them vultures. Charging niggas to cash their checks and pay their bills."

"Well, they only do it 'cause the banks charge too damned much," she said. Between trying to open an account and taking a finance class at Lehman, Dulce had been ranting at Esperanza for weeks about the banking system. "I mean, they charge people to use their own money to make money that they don't give back. If we're gonna be all righteous about what to hit, let's go for a bank."

All the guys laughed at her, even Feli. Xavier said, "Bitch talks about us and *Scarface*, but she been watching too much *Set It Off*."

"Nah, man, she hasn't watched that shit enough," said Chuck. "Like the ending."

Jesus chucked her under the chin. "Yeah, ma, I think the bank's got a little more security than the checks-cashing place."

Esperanza joined them in their laughter. "OK, calm down, OK. But for real. Why not a liquor store or the OTB?"

"Oh, now I know this bitch is crazy," said Xavier. "We can't hit up no liquor store or OTB. Them's community services!"

"I want you to get out, and lean up against the wall," said Queen Latifah's Cleo, "and in sixty seconds I want you to run that way."

Esperanza leaned forward and brought her hand to her mouth. She never bought or even rented *Set It Off* because she could never imagine sitting through it once again. Yet whenever she discovered it on cable, Esperanza could not turn away from this scene no matter how hard it clenched at her insides. Her chest tightened as Cleo yelled, "You want it? Here we go. Me and you!" and shoots out of the tunnel with the police copters riding her fumes.

As Frankie and Stony expressed their love for each other, Esperanza stole a look at Priscilla. She had her head buried in her hands, her fists pressed tensely against her cheeks, and she looked even younger than her nineteen years. Tears rolled down Priscilla's knuckles as her eyes bore onto the screen when the LAPD cornered Cleo, aimed their rifles at her, and ordered her out of the Impala. Cleo dropped her low-rider, and the tense po reacted by cocking their guns. She lit her last cigarette, her mouth wrenched with tears she refused to let them see. As Lori Perri sang "Up Against the Wind," Cleo popped her hydraulics and rocketed forward as the police fired endless rounds into her Impala. Already shot multiple times, Cleo climbed out of the Impala, blasting her Uzi and convulsing in a barrage of police gunfire. Although Esperanza was crying, too, it took her by surprise when Priscilla let out a gasp and ran into the bathroom.

Esperanza waited but Priscilla did not return. She stood up and walked down the corridor to the bathroom. When she leaned her head against the door, she could hear Priscilla crying so hard she sometimes coughed. Esperanza checked the knob and found the door unlocked, so she let herself into the bathroom. Priscilla sat on the floor, slumped against the vinyl toilet seat.

"Priscilla, you OK?" Esperanza sat on the edge of the tub.

Without lifting her head, Priscilla cried, "I don't understand why sistas always gotta go out like that."

"Prissy, it's just a movie."

Priscilla's head shot up, her red eyes like laser beams. "Just a movie? Espe, it's practically *every* fuckin' movie."

"You know what I hate? When the guys flip out, giving Cleo daps by saying, 'Oh, she went out like a man. Latifah went out like a man.' It's supposed to be a big compliment, but it ain't. I'm like, 'Well, she's not a fuckin' man.' So what she had a girlfriend? She's still a woman, and when all those other muthafuckas were watching them on the news, she rode and died for her girls. Where were all those real men at?"

"Dre . . . Black Sam . . . whatever . . . didn't even want to give Cleo the guns after all the cars she jacked for him." Excited, Priscilla drew up on her haunches. "He even tried to get her to hook him up with Frankie for them!"

"Pimp her girl!"

They sat quietly for a moment. Priscilla shook her head. "Why it gotta be like that?"

Esperanza wished she had an answer to her question. She might have had she read any of the books that surrounded her these days. She at least knew one thing. "There are women trying to figure that kind of stuff out, 'cause they don't really believe it does have to be that way at all."

"Like who?"

"Well, one, her name's bell hooks. . . ."

Priscilla's face twisted with amusement. "She a rapper?"

Esperanza laughed. "No. Sounds like it, though, right? Anyway, she's got these books where—"

A harsh pounding on the door made them both jump. "What the hell y'all doing in there?" Before either could answer, Jesus banged the door open and eyeballed them. "Priscilla, you brought the wrong fuckin' soda. Go to the store." He reached into his pocket and pulled out several bills.

Priscilla crawled to her feet and took the money. "What kind you wanted again?"

"Caffeine-free Pepsi."

"I'm not going all over the freakin' Bronx looking for that."

"You'd best not come back without it."

Priscilla eased past him while Jesus and Esperanza stared at each other. When they heard Priscilla slam the door, Esperanza rose to her feet and approached Jesus. "You feelin' better?"

"No, but you can do something about that. Have you thought about going to California with me?"

"I'm not even supposed to be here with you."

"But you are."

"If my parole officer ever found out . . ."

"Who's gonna tell him? Your sister? Dulce ain't got nobody, so she wants you to be alone, too."

Esperanza almost told him about Chago but bit her tongue. Xavier must have thought his little show in the restaurant had put an end to Dulce's relationship with Chago, and bragged about it to his boys. So be it. She would never put Dulce on blast, least of all to this guy, who still had not admitted that her sister put a gat in his face to keep him away from her.

"You don't talk about my sister," she said. "She busted her ass to visit me in prison every weekend she could, which is a lot more than I can say for you, and you're the fuckin' reason I got locked up in the first place. When it comes to Dulce, you don't have a goddamn opinion."

"Espe . . ."

Jesus reached for her, but she dodged his hand, grabbed her bag, and fled his apartment.

Esperanza entered the lit apartment. Pleased to know Dulce was home, she hoped to find her alone. She needed her sister, even if only for a few minutes as she readied for a date with Chago. She peeked into the empty living room. "Dulce?" When she walked into the bedroom, she found her sister curled up on their bed, sobbing into her pillow.

"Dulce, what happened?"

"I think Chago's going to leave me."

"He's going back to his ex-wife?"

"No, I told him the truth. About me. About my past."

"Oh, Dulce, you didn't."

"I had to. If we were going to be together, Chago had to know the truth. And he had to hear it from me."

"Why?"

Dulce rolled over, and Esperanza sat on the bed. She brushed her sister's flattened curls away from her face. "I was reading Maite Rodriguez's book, and she's got this whole chapter in there about honesty, and she writes, 'There can be no love without truth.' Everything that's wrong with the world, from wars between countries to power struggles between people, is based on lies, and the biggest lies are those things we tell ourselves because we can't accept ourselves for who we truly are." Dulce sat up and hugged her knees. Like a child she rocked back and forth as she continued. "And I was thinking she's right, you know. 'Cause I love Chago, and one of the reasons why I love him is because he's been straight-up with me from day one. He could've lied to me about having an ex-wife and kids. He knew that if he told me that from jump that I might not go out with him, and he told me anyway. He could've waited until I fucked him or fell in love with him to tell me the truth."

Dulce buried her face in her knees, and Esperanza struggled to find consoling words. What could she say? That Chago might have told her the truth because he knew it eventually would come out? Only Dulce's guilt remained from her days as that *tigrita,* but Chago would always have an ex-wife and two children. Unlike Dulce, Chago most likely told the truth for no noble reasons. Under those circumstances, for him to leave Dulce for telling him something that no longer applied, he was a punk *jíbaro* who did not deserve her. But if Esperanza said that to her sister, would she really make her feel better about her choice and its consequences?

"You told Chago everything? About Jesus and Xavier . . . ? Even about LaVern?"

"Tonight over dinner he asks me about school, and eventually I tell him about Maite's book. I even pull it out and show him passages, translating here and there." For a moment Dulce seemed almost blissful as she spoke, but then her face fell. "We get to the chapter about honesty, and he says, 'Of course. Look how happy and strong we are. Neither of us is perfect, but we have no secrets.'" Dulce's voice cracked, and Esperanza reached over to the night table for several tissues and handed them to her sister. "So I tell him everything."

"And what did he say?"

"Nothing."

"He didn't ask any questions?"

"He couldn't even look me in the face. He gets up and goes to the men's room, and when he comes back he says he just got a call, and there's trouble—an emergency at the warehouse."

"And what'd you say?"

"What am I going to do? Call him a liar? Tell him he can't go? I just ask him if he's going to call me, and he says, 'Of course, of course.' But I haven't heard from him." Then Dulce punched her pillow, startling Esperanza. "Fuck it! If he can't accept me for everything about me, the way I accepted him, we weren't meant to be. Fuck him." The Cepeda sisters understood the profound difference between being a divorced father and almost bludgeoning another person over a catty remark, but they both remained silent. "Fuck him," Dulce said with forced conviction. "I don't need Chago's validation to know who I am and who I'm not. And maybe if I hadn't been the girl I was, I wouldn't be the woman I am today. If after all this time with me now, he can be so judgmental of me, then I'm better off without him."

She scampered out of the bed, headed to the bathroom, and slammed the door. Esperanza did not believe a word that Dulce had said. She knew that Dulce did not believe herself. For all of Dulce's newfound commitment to the truth, Esperanza understood that in order for her to get over Chago, some lies she still needed to believe.

SIXTEEN

Enough

Dulce grew colder with every day that passed without a call from Chago. At first she held fast to her fuck-him philosophy. After a week, Dulce swallowed her pride and called him.

When they were dating, she rarely missed Chago on his cellular phone. He programmed all her numbers into his phone and immediately responded whenever they flashed across his screen. But now Dulce could not avoid his voice mail. She called several times without leaving a message until one day she finally burst.

"*Mira,* Fernando, this is the last time I'm going to call you. If you want to break up with me, fine. But at least be a man about it, and tell me to my face." Esperanza overheard Dulce on her way to the bathroom and stopped to peek into the bedroom. She saw Dulce on the phone as she paced around their bedroom. "Don't just disappear and hope I eventually get the hint. No matter what you think of me now, I was good to you, and I deserve better than that."

Still Chago did not call, and Dulce went from cold to bitter. She spoke to Esperanza only to gripe about one thing or another. At first her complaints were general. Some jerk insisted he gave her a twenty when he only handed her a ten. She finally received her course catalog for the fall semester, and not a single class she wanted to take was being offered. It was too goddamned hot. But in a little time, she began to direct her complaints at Esperanza.

"Espe, you call that cleaning the bathtub?

"You better learn to cook for yourself.

"I can't believe you haven't gone deaf with that television on so loud."

Then Esperanza came home and found Dulce standing on the dresser and ripping the *Juice* poster off the wall. On the bed sat a cardboard box where she had already thrown in Esperanza's books, CDs, and the first few Tupac posters she had already torn down. As Dulce jumped off the dresser, Esperanza raced over to her and snatched the *Juice* poster from her. "What are you doing?"

"You want to be with Jesus? Go live with Jesus."

Where the fuck did that come from? "I don't want to be with him, Dulce, I just—"

"You quit your job, you sneak around—"

"Wait! I didn't quit my job. I was fired." Someone had used elements of the truth to lie about her. "Who told you I quit?"

"It doesn't matter who told me."

"Yes, it does, Dulce." Esperanza struggled to even her tone so as not to fuel Dulce's tirade by matching her agitation. With no place to go if Dulce put her on the streets, she could not afford to sound either too guilty or righteous. "You're going to throw me out because of something someone told you without telling me who it was and what they said? Whoever said I quit my job to be with Jesus is fuckin' lying."

"Priscilla."

Esperanza yanked her bag off her shoulder and flung it on the bed. "Priscilla? That little . . . You know why she said that, don't you, Dulce? Of all fuckin' people, Priscilla tells you that I quit my job, and you go believe her." Esperanza waited for Dulce to respond, but she merely glared at her with her arms locked across her chest. "Priscilla only told you that because she wants Jesus, and he still wants me."

"Apparently you want him, too."

"Hold up. One thing at a time. When did Priscilla say this to you?"

"She comes to my register and is all, 'Hey, D, long time, no see. How's Espe?' Then she says, 'So cute how her and Jesus got back together when she came home. It's like she never left.' I ask her if she saw y'all today, and she told me no, but that you were at Jesus's barbecue and even over his apartment a few times." Dulce slowed as if she had begun to recognize the motivation behind Priscilla's words. "Then she goes, 'That's love. First, Espe did . . . you know . . .' Her eyes-shifting all around. I'm hoping to God the freakin' person behind her in line isn't all in our conversation. And then she says, 'And now she quit her job at Mickey D's just to spend time with him.' "

"That is such a fuckin' lie! I didn't quit my job at all, let alone for his ass. He was the one bringing Priscilla to the restaurant to make some freakin' point."

"And what? You got into it with them, and you got fired behind that?"

"No, it had nothing to do with him, I swear." Now that Esperanza had Dulce's attention, she proceeded to tell her the circumstances of her firing. She did her best to stick to the facts and avoid exaggeration. Although Priscilla had lied to Dulce, the truth remained bad enough to warrant no embellishment.

Dulce said, "God, Espe, I of all people understand how fucked up these customers can be, but you can't wild out on people like that." Esperanza heard a bit of compassion lurking beneath her reprimand. Dulce had told her too many tales of checking strangers who believed good customer service entitled them to be abusive. More than once she herself had snapped at the assumption that she should swallow the insults, accusations, and even outright threats customers sometimes made. Still, Dulce had never attacked one physically. "I can't believe you did that," she said, sounding like she very much did believe and did not blame her.

But Esperanza knew her sister. Dulce could wild out. Yet she chose not to. Despite Dulce's hint of empathy, she had to own up to her crime and its cover-up. "I fucked up. Big-time. And I was gonna tell you, Dulce, I swear. I just wanted to find another job first so you could see I was sincere about making things right. When I told you what happened, I wanted to be able to say, 'But don't worry, Dulce, I already found something else over here.' And you were always with Chago. . . ."

"Don't you fuckin' put your lying on my being with Chago, OK? Any damned time you could've said, 'Dulce, come home. I have to talk to you.' For all you know, Chago might have been able to help you."

"I didn't want Chago to fuckin' help me! I didn't even want Chago to know. Just because you were with him doesn't mean he had to know all my business."

"You know what? Let's get the hell off Chago and talk about Jesus. I want you to tell me the truth. Are you or are you not back with Jesus?"

"I don't know."

"Dammit, Espe!"

"But that's the truth." When it came to Jesus, the truth could be whatever Esperanza wanted it to be. Jesus had made his desire for her known, and even Priscilla wove lies around that fact. But whether she and Jesus were a couple again depended on whether she wanted him or not, and Esperanza did not know that. All she knew was what being with Jesus could give her and what it could cost her.

"I'm going to make this easy for you. You cannot be with Jesus. Not if you're going to satisfy your parole. And I'll tell you something else right now, Espe: You cannot be with Jesus and live here."

"He's going to California, and I want to go with him."

Dulce paused. "Fine. Go with him to California. Stay with him in New York. I don't care. Just take all this Tupac shit with you."

"I don't want to go to California to be with Jesus. I want to go to see *Mami.*"

"Espe—"

"I admit, Dulce, OK, I hung out with Jesus a few times. Not to get back with him. I mean, everyone was there, so I was never alone with him."

"Everyone was there? Like Chuck and Feli? Fuckin' Xavier?"

"I only wanted to be around other people and have some fun, and then Jesus told me about this trip to California. Right away I was like, No, I can't go. But then I thought *I can see Mami*. But you know Sus, Dulce. He won't take me to see her if I don't front like he has a chance with me. And I really want to see her so bad. I need to see her. Don't you?"

Dulce sat on the bed and wrung her hands. "Of course I want to see *Mami*. When Chago started talking about moving there, she was the main reason I thought about it, not him. Like you said, we had just met, and he had all this . . . It doesn't matter. I can't go now. Because of school and work, I don't have the money. Between school and work, I don't even have the time."

Esperanza sat beside her and stroked her sister's hair. "If you want to go with us, Jesus can make it happen."

Dulce pushed her hand away. "No."

"He did it before, and he'll do it again for me."

"I don't want anything from him."

"Well, I do, Dulce. You want me to be truthful with you, so here it is. I do want something from Jesus. That muthafucka owes me so much. And the thing I want most of all is to see my mother, and he can take me to her."

"You want to be truthful?" said Dulce. "You can start by not lying to yourself. After all his bullshit, you still love him. No, I take that back. You still want to love him. Wanna know what's worse than that? You still think that Jesus loves you. You still need to believe that Jesus loves you. But the truth is, Espe, neither of you loves the other. That madness going on between the two of you isn't love any more than all that drama between Xavier and me. How're you gonna love Jesus or he love you when neither of you can barely stand yourselves?"

Esperanza gazed at her sister as she absorbed her words. "Whatever."

"Whatever? Is that all you have to say? Whatever?"

"What does it matter, Dulce? We can't be together, just like you said. But still, I want something for what I've been through. Put me out if you want to, 'cause I'm going to see my mother. Just remember that reason. If I can't find someplace else to go, and I end up at Jesus's crib, don't say it was because I was trying to be up under him. I may have lied to you about spending some time over there, but if I had wanted to be with him, you wouldn't be trying to put me out right now. I'd already be there."

Esperanza rose off the bed and walked toward the door.

"Espe, wait. I just realized something. Why are we waiting on these men to take us where we want to be?" Dulce stood up. "Let's just go ourselves. If we want to see Mami, why don't we just move to California? We don't need Chago or Jesus to do that. It'll take some time to get the money, but we can do it. I mean, I love New York, but what do we have keeping us here?"

"Nothing good."

"We can get away from all of them. Away from Jesus. From X. Chago. We can work anywhere, Espe. We can study anywhere. So why stay here? I can put in overtime and take off a semester."

"I can get another job, maybe two. Put off school just for a little while. Just until we save enough money."

"We save our money, pack our shit, and just bounce from here, Espe. We don't say shit to anybody."

"Ain't nobody here who needs to know."

"Then they can't stop us or get in our way. And we keep our plans to ourselves, Espe. He may have backed off me for now, but if X found out . . ."

"And Jesus . . ." The Cepeda sisters had no need to name the tragic capacity they shared. Each liked to believe she had a strength that enabled her to survive on her own. But when things grew desperate, neither was beyond returning to the very man who taught her all she knew about desperation. Each struggled to build her strength every day, but every day brought new challenges that slowed her growth. With Dulce losing Chago and Esperanza her job, as individuals and as a family they were extremely vulnerable. "Will you still put me out if I go to California in August with Jesus?"

"No. But I know Jesus, so you have to promise me—no hustling."

"No hustling, I promise."

"I mean it, Espe. Let me find out you got involved with some shit while you were over there with him, and I swear to God, it's over. And once you come home, no more Jesus. No more Jesus and no more lies."

Esperanza kissed two fingers and held them up. "I promise. No hustling, no Jesus, and no lies."

At least not to her sister.

Puente stared hard at Esperanza as she made her plea. "It's only for a long weekend. Between work and school I'm burning out. It'd be good for my relationship with my sister, too. She's big on the tough love, you know, and even though I'm busting my ass, she thinks I can be doing more with myself."

"You probably could be," Puente said. "You say you're going to California with your sister?"

"I don't want to go alone, and who else am I gonna go with?" She exhaled with relief when Puente did not recite the list of obvious suspects. "Kind of like a short family vacation."

"Your mother is incarcerated at Central California Women's Correctional Facility, isn't she?"

The muthafucka just loved to ask questions he already had the answers to. Esperanza fought the urge to acknowledge this annoying tendency and just nodded.

"I suspect you are going to make an attempt to visit her."

Damn right. "I'll report whenever or to whoever you want me to while I'm there."

"Esperanza, I don't appreciate your coming here presenting this trip to me as a vacation when you want to visit your mother."

"I'm sorry. I meant no disrespect."

"Ordinarily I like to encourage family contact. It tends to help keep ex-cons in line. But your mother herself happens to be a convicted felon who is still serving her sentence for a very serious crime."

She hated being called an ex-con, like a stereotype from an overwrought police drama on TV. But Puente was right in that the trip interested her only because it offered her an opportunity to visit her mother. But he also seemed to have no suspicion as to who was making her this offer and why. Esperanza had no idea what to say, and so she said nothing.

"You do realize that in addition to my permission, you have to get the written approval of the warden at Central California."

"No." Esperanza's chest tightened. "I mean, my mother put in all her paperwork the last time we visited, and my sister and I were both approved. I figured . . ."

"Well, you figured wrong. Things have changed, Esperanza. You're a convicted felon and a former inmate now. It's a felony for you to be on the grounds of any prison anywhere without the written permission from the warden of that institution."

"In other words, I can't go." She knew it took anywhere from two to six weeks just for the visiting officer to approve an inmate's visitors. If she had to go up the prison bureaucracy for the warden's approval in writing, it made no sense for Esperanza to go to California with Jesus. This invitation came on his schedule. If and when the warden came through, Jesus would have been gone and returned. "Can't you help me, Officer Puente?"

He leaned back in his seat and folded his arms across his chest. "There are three reasons why I'm even considering assisting you with this. One, if not for this ridiculous new law, you wouldn't even be in my caseload. Two, I doubt that you will reoffend while in Calfornia, since you have no real history or connection in the state. Three, despite the fact that your mother is serving twenty-five-to-life for first-degree murder, I'm thinking it might not be a bad idea to get you out of your neighborhood for a few days. Maybe you'll like California and decide to move there."

Esperanza's stomach burned. "Maybe."

"What's your itinerary?"

"Last time Dulce and I went to see Mami, we flew into Sacramento. Now we decided to fly to Los Angeles, rent a car, and drive to Chowchilla. This way we have a chance to see something different than we did last time. So, yeah, we're really only going to California to see Mami, but we didn't see why we couldn't get a little sightseeing in while we were at it."

"Where will you be staying?"

"We haven't figured all that out yet. Before we went to all that trouble, we wanted to be sure you'd let me go. I told Dulce that if I couldn't go, she should just go without me, but she's really hoping you'll approve of the trip. She's been waiting for this appointment before she goes and books the flights and hotels and whatever."

Puente pulled open a drawer under his desk and retrieved a form. As he wrote furiously across it, Esperanza attempted to peek. "Before you leave, I want to see the tickets. No e-tickets. Paper tickets for both you and your sister."

"Yes, Officer Puente." Jesus would not sweat buying an extra ticket in Dulce's name that would never be used. "Thank you. Anything else you need me to do?"

"Next time you want to do something like this, I want more notice."

Esperanza nodded. When she and Dulce made that permanent move to California, she would be sure to tell him. If by the time they were ready to go, her parole had come to an end, she just might tell Puente's ass some other things, too.

From the floor below his, Esperanza could hear Jesus and Priscilla yelling. If she did not need those tickets to show Puente, she would have turned back and gone home. She arrived at the door and waited until she overheard Priscilla refer to her as "that fuckin' Espe." Then Esperanza banged on the door, intent on getting her opportunity to set that little witch straight.

Jesus threw open the door. Even though he was expecting Esperanza, he flung his hands in the air at the sight of her. "I don't know which one of you got the crackerjack timing and shit," he said as he headed back into the living room. "You or her."

Esperanza followed him and saw Priscilla pouting, fists anchored to her hips. "Just give me the tickets and I'm out."

"I knew she was going with you," Priscilla yelled. "You fuckin' liar."

"You need to chill," said Jesus as he walked over to his desk, opened a drawer, and pulled out the airline tickets. When he offered them to Esperanza, Priscilla reached in and snatched them out of his hand.

"I'm telling you, Sus, check your girl."

"That's right, Jesus. I'm your girl. I'm the one who's having your back here, so why the hell does she get to go with you to meet the paperhanger in California?"

Jesus jabbed a finger in her face. "Yo, shut the fuck up, Priscilla."

An ugly feeling crept over Esperanza. "What paperhanger?"

Priscilla gave a sarcastic laugh. "Oh, she forgot already. See, you taking her instead of me, and she can't even keep track of—"

"I told you to shut the fuck up, and I'm not going to tell you one more time."

Esperanza said, "Then why don't you tell me what the hell's going on, Sus? What's this shit about meeting with some paperhanger?"

Wanting to exploit Esperanza's discomfort, Priscilla started to babble. "He finally got a meeting with No-No, so he's flying to Cali to meet with the—"

Jesus's backhand slammed into Priscilla's mouth. As she cowered in pain, he grabbed her by the throat with one hand and raised his other to strike her again. Priscilla shrieked, and Esperanza dove between them. "Jesus, stop it!"

"I told you I wasn't going to warn you no more, didn't I?" He still had his grip on Priscilla's throat, and the more she cried and wrangled to break free of him, the harder he clung to her. "That's why you're not fuckin' going to California with me. You talk too goddamn much." He attempted to reach around Esperanza to slap Priscilla again, but she planted herself in front of him to block his blow. "Sus, let 'er go."

"Fuck that whiny little bitch. I'm tired of her running off at the mouth."

"I said let go already." Although he kept swiping at Priscilla, Jesus eyed Esperanza suspiciously. "If you don't let her go, I'm gonna leave right now . . ."

"No, don't leave me alone with him!"

". . . and I won't go to California with you."

Jesus loosened his grip around Priscilla's neck, and she staggered toward the couch holding her throat and sobbing. Only then did Esperanza remember that for all her tough talk and grown clothes, the girl was barely nineteen years old. "Prissy, go home. Please."

"Yeah, get the fuck out of here. Now!" Jesus heaved, as if the drama had spent him most of all.

Priscilla grabbed her purse. "You don't have to tell me twice," she cried as she raced for the door.

"Gimme them fuckin' tickets."

Priscilla spun around and threw them at him. "I hate you!" She wrenched open the door. "I wish I never fuckin' met you!" Then she fled the apartement.

Jesus ran to the door and yelled after her, "That's what they all say." Then, laughing, he closed and locked the door behind her. When Jesus turned back to Esperanza, he looked down at the floor and then at her, surprised that she had not picked up the tickets. He scooped up the tickets himself, then extended them toward her.

Esperanza's gaze wandered between the tickets in his hand and his concerned face. "I thought you said this trip was about us."

"It is. It will be if you go with me. Take the tickets."

"What's this about No-No?"

"I'm not meeting him in California."

"And who's this paperhanger? Why're you going to meet with him?"

"You don't have to worry about none of that. The less you know, the better for you. I'm taking you to Cali to have a good time, not involve you in my affairs."

"Does this have anything to do with what you were telling me the night of the party?"

"Espe, when I told you that I wanted to show you the kind of life I'm working to give you, I meant it. It's gonna be candlelight and roses, ma. And you don't have to be involved with anything you don't want to. I know you ain't tryin' to be about that no more; I feel that. But you still paid your dues, so now let me give you the rewards. Take the tickets." Esperanza hesitated, and he added, "I'll handle my business, and you can chill in the hotel, go shopping or whatever. And if everything works out the way we planned, I'll take you to see your moms. Then our last night there it'll just be me and my girlfriend, like your boy said."

"I can go back to jail just for going with you, Jesus."

"I appreciate that, ma, and I'm taking all the precautions necessary so that doesn't happen. When I pull this off, I'ma have the means to make sure no one fucks with you. Not ever. Even if your PO finds out, he won't touch you. I promise. Take the tickets."

Esperanza eyed the tickets. She imagined candlelight and roses. She envisioned the palm trees and blue waters she missed all summer. She saw her mother. "And I can't get involved with nothing while I'm over there. Nothing, Sus. I mean it. I don't even want to know about it."

"Espe, take your tickets."

And just like old times, Esperanza did as Jesus told her.

Esperanza gave another pair of new jeans one last swipe of the iron. She folded them and added them to the stack in Brenda's suitcase. After she unplugged the iron and set it on the floor to cool, she folded the ironing board and carried it toward the closet. As she passed her night table, Esperanza caught sight of her borrowed books. She hung the board inside the closet door above the Tupac poster of him flipping two birds, then walked back to her night table. Esperanza picked up the books and reread the titles, wondering which, if any, she should pack in her carry-on bag. She had already tucked away her language arts study books, but the flights to and from California would be long, even if they showed a movie. But which title would not provoke the wrong side of Jesus's curiosity?

Before Esperanza decided, the intercom buzzed. She placed the books back on her night table, jogged into the kitchen, and pressed the talk button. "Who?" She hit listen, but only street sounds and static crackled over the speaker. "Who?"

"D," a muffled voice said.

Esperanza hit Talk. "Lost your key, huh?" Then she buzzed her sister in and unlocked the apartment door. She made it halfway down the hallway and had some soda when she heard the door creek. "Espe, can I talk to you?"

She whirled around. "What the fuck you doing here?" Esperanza bounded toward Priscilla, grabbed her by the shoulders, and tried to push her across the threshold. Priscilla clung to the door frame. "Please, Espe. I have to talk to you."

Esperanza let go of her and huffed into the living room. "I'm busy. Make it quick. What you want?" Her heart leaped when Priscilla reached into her pocketbook. Priscilla pulled out a DVD case, and Esperanza exhaled with relief. "I thought maybe you'd want to watch a movie with me or something."

"You give me all this drama, and now you want to hang out with me?"

It finally registered with Priscilla that Esperanza thought she had come to harm her. "You thought I had a gun or something?" She gave a little laugh. "I wish I could get down like that. That's why Jesus likes you more than me."

"I don't really get down like that either."

"You can if you want to," Priscilla said defensively. "If you had to." She dropped her gaze. "You didn't have to stop Jesus from hitting me the other day. Shit, you could've done it for him. Or joined in with him."

"Is that how he got you doing other females out there?" It felt strange to defend herself against Priscilla's bizarre praise. "I told you I don't get down like that."

Priscilla nodded, clearly just to appease Esperanza. "So have you ever seen this?" She held up the VHS. *Enough* screamed out in capital red letters above Jennifer Lopez as she looked over her shoulder in fear.

"Look, if you came here to thank me for stopping Jesus the other day, fine. You're welcome, *de nada,* whatever." It occurred to Esperanza that now that all her other tactics had failed, Priscilla wanted to make peace, then beg Esperanza not to go with Jesus to California. "Don't take it personal; I'm just tired of seeing shit like that."

"That don't mean you had to do anything about it. You coulda just said, 'I'm out,' and left me there alone with him to do whatever."

"You need to bounce, Priscilla. I got shit to do."

"I really want to be friends, Espe."

"We can't be friends." The rejected look on Priscilla's tiny face gave Esperanza a pang of doubt. "We're not enemies either, OK? But don't get it twisted. We ain't friends."

"I know you think I'm scheming, and I don't blame you, but tell me what I gotta do to prove I'm sincere, and I'll do it."

"Just leave me alone then." She grabbed Priscilla's arm and pulled her toward the door. "Get out of here and don't start any more shit with me. That's what you can do for me."

"I'm pregnant, Espe," Priscilla cried. "Jesus doesn't know. And I don't want him to know just yet, so why would I tell you that if I weren't for real?"

Esperanza let the suspicious news settle. "How do I know you're not lying?"

"Get me a test."

"That doesn't mean it's Jesus's."

"It is his, but it doesn't matter, right? Regardless, I'm telling you I don't want Jesus to know. So whether it's his or not, you got me either way."

"Why are you telling me this, Priscilla? Why's it so important that I know when you won't even tell him? You think that's gonna keep me away from him?"

"I don't care anymore if he's with you or not. But the other day when he hit me . . ." Priscilla broke into tears. "I don't know what he'll do. I don't know what I want. I just want him to stop. . . ."

She struggled to regain her composure, and Esperanza began to worry. "Wait here." She rushed into the kitchen and poured a glass of water. When Esperanza got back to the living room, Priscilla had collapsed onto the sofa, crying. "Drink this." Priscilla accepted the glass, and Esperanza took the VHS from her hand. She popped the tape into the player and clicked on the television. "So you've seen this before? It's good?"

Like an infant pacified with a bottle of milk, Priscilla nodded, rubbing her eyes and taking another sip of her water. As the opening titles played, Esperanza watched Priscilla relax, and remembered what Jesus had done when he learned that she herself was pregnant.

Esperanza had immediately decided what she wanted to do and never intended to tell Jesus a thing. She confided in Dulce, who helped her locate a Planned Parenthood in Brooklyn, even though the organization had a center in their own neighborhood, where Esperanza had always gone for her pills. "Before we make the appointment, take a home pregnancy test just to be sure."

That ordinarily wise suggestion proved almost fatal for both Cepeda sisters. The night Esperanza took the test, Xavier dropped by unannounced to treat Dulce to the movies. "Don't be saying I ain't spontaneous and romantic and shit," he said. He always had a knack for nosing out deceptive women, even when men like himself justified their secrecy, and he insisted on using the bathroom before they left for the Concourse. When he emerged from the bathroom he seemed normal, but no sooner did Xavier have Dulce in the car than he pulled the positive pregnancy test from his pocket and demanded to know if she was pregnant.

"What kinda shit is that, X, digging through women's garbage?" she said. He yanked her hair and she yelped. "It's not my test, OK?"

"Espe's pregnant? Why y'all being so secretive? It's not Sus's kid?"

"It's not even Espe's kid, 'cause it wasn't her test either."

"Don't lie to me, D. If you fuckin' lie to me, I swear to God—"

"It wasn't ours, I said. A friend of mine—"

"Who?"

"Why you need—Ouch! Xavier, stop it! Let go."

But Xavier never let go. He just drove around her block, one hand clamped on the steering wheel and the other on Dulce's hair.

"I'm telling you, you don't even fuckin' know this girl. She's new around here, and that's why she doesn't want anyone to know. She just got here from the Dominican Republic. Hasn't even been here three months, barely knows English. She laid up with the first nigga that looked at her and got caught out there. So she's scared, X. She's scared of getting shipped back to DR. She doesn't want anyone to know, 'cause she's gonna get rid of it. That's why she took the test at my house."

"She, she, she. Who the fuck is she, D?"

"I promised I wouldn't tell."

"I ain't gonna say nothing. Who am I gonna tell?" Then he pulled down on Dulce's hair until he almost forced her head to the car seat. "Bitch, I'm your man. You don't trust me?"

Dulce reached up and socked Xavier in the face. The car careened, and when he finally let go of her to regain control, she made for the door. The car jumped the curb and slammed into a parking sign, and Dulce managed to scramble out and run back home.

As Esperanza dressed her wounds in the bathroom, Dulce recounted what happened. "I didn't tell him, Espe," she said proudly. Then she began to tremble. "But I don't think he believed me." That had been the darkest of many such hours in Dulce's relationship with Xavier, until the night she broke up with him and he knew that she finally meant it.

Then came the worst day of Esperanza's life after her mother's conviction. Everyone knew about the car accident, but Xavier would have relayed his suspicions to Jesus even if it had never occurred. Jesus went about his business as if he knew nothing. Then one day as they were curled up in his bed, he asked Esperanza, "So tell me, boo. You pregnant?"

"Yeah." And before he could ask, she said, "And, yes, it's yours."

Jesus gave a reassuring laugh. "Oh, I don't doubt that. I never thought anything like that." Then in a wounded voice, he asked, "So when were you gonna tell me?"

"When I knew for sure." The safer she felt, the more quickly the lies flowed. "A woman's not supposed to say anything until she knows for sure, you know. 'Cause anything can happen."

"I feel that."

"I wasn't gonna even tell Dulce until I knew without a doubt, but she busted me with the home pregnancy test. I haven't even gone to the clinic yet."

"You got an appointment, though."

"Yeah, next Wednesday." That much had been true. The lie resided in allowing Jesus to believe the purpose of the appointment was to confirm the pregnancy rather than to end it.

"You don't sound too happy, ma."

Then Esperanza revealed nothing but her truth. "I'm scared, Sus." He began to rub her lower back, like he sometimes did when she had cramps. She never had to ask him. Somehow Jesus would know, and he would massage her, fix her a hot-water bottle, or make her a cup of tea, all without her asking. "I mean, the way we living. That's no way to raise a kid."

"We can give a kid a lot, though," said Jesus. "Much better than these muthafuckas out here on welfare or unemployment and whatnot."

"Yeah, but just like welfare, it can all be gone just like that. And we'll never know who's gonna take it from us. Or when or how. It could be the state; it could be the streets. We can't bring a baby into this, Sus."

"So you sayin' we shouldn't have this baby."

"Either we don't have this baby or we quit the game." Never had Esperanza suggested that Jesus do anything other than what he'd been doing since the age of fifteen. She had seen what happened to girlfriends who did that. But with a baby growing in her belly, maybe Jesus would understand where she was coming from and actually give her words some consideration. Only when she spelled out those choices could Esperanza imagine having his baby. Until then she had never even realized that she had wanted out of the game. But she loved Jesus enough to carry his baby, and she wanted him to love her enough to change his lifestyle. It warmed Esperanza that Jesus seemed so open to becoming a father, and took great pride in that she could influence him in a way no woman before her had.

But then Jesus said, "The game's gonna give this baby a good life. And I'm not just talking clothes and kicks and jewelry and shit. I'm talking a nice house. A good education. Some connections. We play the street game now so the world game can't play him later." Then Jesus laughed. "Our baby's gonna be the first Puerto Rican mayor of New York City, ma."

"Unless he wants to grow up to be just like Daddy."

Jesus stopped rubbing her back and lay quietly. Then he sat up and crawled out of the bed. "You right." He opened the door to the bedroom. "You're so fuckin' right." Then he left. Esperanza listened for him, first hearing some bustling in the kitchen and then the television blaring. She almost went to him but decided to give him some space. Awake with concern, Esperanza waited up for Jesus for almost an hour before she finally drifted to sleep.

Several hours later, a weight slammed across Esperanza's chest and jarred her awake. She snapped her eyes open, and they met Jesus's dilated pupils. He straddled her torso, his knees pinning the sheets against her arms. She felt the cold blade of the kitchen knife pressed against her throat. Only under the twilight seeping through his bedroom window did she see the trace of powder below his nose, and fear gripped her as it never had before, because Jesus never used his product. Esperanza struggled, her arms trapped under the blankets as Jesus screamed, "You don't want my baby? You tell me you love me, but you don't want my baby. You don't fuckin' love me. Think I'm gonna let a stranger shove a knife up your cunt and stab my baby? I'll cut it out of you my damned self." Jesus drew back, and Esperanza felt the blanket give. In a desperate attempt to free her hands and block the knife, she heaved herself upward. Her sudden movement jarred Jesus, and he jabbed her collarbone and slashed her down the middle of her bust. As Esperanza screamed in pain and her blood seeped through the sheets, Jesus fell back with shock at what he had just done.

Esperanza seized the opportunity to escape. She ran screaming from his apartment and down the Concourse. Dozens of gypsy cabs sailed by her until she suppressed her hysteria long enough to flag down an unsuspecting driver. When the cabbie saw Esperanza's bloody camisole, he raced to Lincoln Hospital and carried her into the emergency room.

She remembered the kind Black doctor who tended to her. As Dr. Neal stitched her wound, he gently asked her what happened. She ignored, lied, or otherwise resisted him, and he would nod his head, sew another stitch, and then politely repeat as if asking for the first time, "So, Esperanza, tell me who did this to you. Who did such a brutal thing to such a lovely girl?" She eventually broke down and revealed everything. Dr. Neal urged her to press charges, but Esperanza refused.

"Never has he touched that stuff," she said between sobs. "Not his or anybody's. It's a cardinal rule, and he never would've broken it if not for me. I upset him and drove him to it."

"You did nothing to make it right for him to do this to you."

"He didn't mean to do it. He loves me. Coke makes you paranoid and—"

"Violent," said Dr. Neal. "Are you saying he has never been violent toward you before now?" His voice remained calm and gentle. "Are you sure you don't want to speak to the police?"

"No. Please. Just call my sister."

"I have the nurse doing that as we speak." Dr. Neal made the final stitch and dressed the wound. He stepped back and whispered, "Do you want that abortion?"

Esperanza cried so hard, she could barely nod her permission.

"Fucked-up bitch!" Priscilla yelled at the television screen, cutting into Esperanza's memory and bringing her back to *Enough*. She had been quiet throughout the first half hour of the film while the abusive Mitch hid his true colors. Now Priscilla talked back at the screen at everyone who trivialized J. Lo–as-Slim's dilemma. The mother-in-law was a "fucked up bitch" for asking Slim what she had done to make Mitch hit her, and the cop at the precinct was a "dumb bastard" for being useless in Slim's quest for help. Esperanza found some parts of the movie dumb, but Priscilla's enthusiasm got her involved. By the time J. Lo's character began training in krav maga, they were commenting excitedly to each other over the action.

J. Lo's Slim bobbed and weaved throughout her training session, and Priscilla said, "She sets his ass up good."

"She sets him up?" Esperanza expected a final confrontation when Slim would triumph. But she assumed that her abusive husband would come after her as he always did, only for once Slim would see him coming and be ready. Slim would strike a lucky punch or reach the gun first. She was preparing herself for when he came for her, because experience taught her that he inevitably would. Other than for her to train in a martial art, it never crossed Esperanza's mind that Slim would get aggressive.

"He's gonna come after her, right?"

"No. That's what's hot. She goes after him." Priscilla wriggled in her seat with anticipation. "First she—"

Esperanza slapped her hands over her ears. "Don't tell me, don't tell me, don't tell me!" And they both laughed at her silliness.

Then Priscilla asked, "You think you could ever do that, Espe? I know I couldn't. If you really believed that somebody wanted to kill you, instead of waiting for him to come for you, could you, like, go on the offensive and get him first? I know plenty of dudes who could get down like that, but I don't think I know a single woman who could."

Esperanza thought of her sister. Dulce was the toughest woman she knew—much tougher than herself—and even she had not gone on the offensive with a man. Dulce liked to say, "I pulled a Tina," referring to the scene in *What's Love Got to Do with It?* when Tina Turner had her fill of Ike's beatings and fistfights him in the back of the limousine before finally fleeing him for good. Unlike Tina, however, Dulce knew exactly when the next time Xavier would put his hands on her was, and she decided to put her hands back on him. "I think on a subconscious level, I even instigated it," her sister said. It happened three weeks after the LaVern Bell tragedy. Even though Dulce and Xavier were in the middle of a rare honeymoon period, she had decided to quit him once and for all.

But Dulce had not plotted or trained for that moment. Xavier came for her, and for once she fought back. While he still managed to send her to the hospital, Dulce got him better than any man ever had, simply because he never expected her to stand up for herself. When the cops came for Xavier, they found him in Chucho's back room with a missing front tooth, two cracked ribs, and a busted blood vessel in his eye.

Meanwhile Dulce lay in the ICU, falling in and out of consciousness. For three days Esperanza sang in her ear the details of the damage Dulce had done to Xavier to the tune of "The Twelve Days of Christmas." "One missing toothus, two ribs a-crackin', *one busted eyyye."* On the third day of Esperanza's serenade, a smile cracked over Dulce's bloated face. *"Loca,"* she said, her eyes still swollen shut. "It's, like, September."

"Could you do that, Espe?" Priscilla asked her again, her voice weighted with conspiracy. "If he made it clear—kill or be killed . . ."

An obnoxious pounding at the front door interrupted her. Eager to evade Priscilla's question, Esperanza leaped to answer it without a second thought. Jesus and Xavier pushed their way past her. Chuck and Feli followed, each carrying two bags of groceries. "Put those away," Jesus directed them after planting a kiss on Esperanza's cheek. Then he and Xavier bounded into the living room. "I know how Dulce can be, so I thought better not to come empty-handed," he said, explaining the groceries.

If you care about Dulce, why'd you fuckin' bring X? "Thanks. But you can't stay long. You gotta be out before Dulce's home."

"I understand, ma."

Xavier walked into the living room and pointed at Priscilla. "What the fuck you doing here?" He looked at Jesus. "Yo, Sus, check this shit out." Jesus turned to Esperanza for an explanation.

"I saw her hanging outside with Rosie and the twins and invited her up here," she said. "So we could squash our beef once and for all."

Jesus asked, "And?'

"I think we both know our place now." Esperanza laced her voice with enough skepticism to convince him. If Jesus felt that she still did not fully trust Priscilla—and she fuckin' didn't—then he might buy her story.

He hesitated but then nodded. "A'ight."

Xavier snatched the remote from Priscilla. "You watching this shit?" With beers in hand for themselves and the other guys, Chuck and Feli entered the living room. "Lemme show you the scene I like." Xavier pressed the buttons on the remote until the VHS played the scene where Slim finally confronted Mitch over his ongoing infidelity. When he slapped her, Xavier yelped with glee. "Yo, that shit cracks me up. My man's like, 'Bitch!' Smack!"

"You stupid," said Jesus as he stretched across the sofa.

Despite the slap, Slim stood strong, so Mitch hit her again hard enough to send her crumpling to the kitchen floor. Xavier hollered, and even Chuck and Jesus laughed. "That's what you get for raisin' up," said Xavier. "Think 'cause you got that phat ass you can raise up on a nigga? Even J. Lo gotta know her place."

Xavier, Chuck, and Jesus laughed, while Esperanza and Priscilla shared glances of disgust. Feli snorted and said, "I don't know why y'all think that's so funny." The room fell silent as all eyes fell on him. "What's so fuckin' funny about watching some dude slap a woman around?"

"Aw, he just mad 'cause that's his girl getting beat down," said Jesus.

"It ain't got nothing to do with J. Lo. For real." The guys catcalled, and Esperanza saw Feli's back straighten with indignation. "What the fuck's so funny about that? Explain to me why that makes you laugh."

"Shut your bitch ass," Xavier said. "Little faggot. Just watch the fuckin' movie."

Esperanza had had enough of them and the movie. She went into the bedroom, closed the door, and returned to packing. Even though Dulce knew about the trip, Esperanza still felt the need to hide the new clothes she had bought herself with Jesus's money. For the first time since she had bought them, Esperanza could admire them as she lovingly folded them and placed them in Brenda's battered suitcase. The indigo Apple Bottoms with the fuchsia stitch. A black Baby Phat baseball jersey with lavender sleeves and print. A hot-pink Pelle Pelle camisole with matching thong. Esperanza realized that she had not bought herself a pretty dress for a night on the town, and searched everywhere for the blue one that Dulce gave her when Chago took them out to dinner after her promotion at Mickey D's. *Shit! I threw it out!* She could always shop for another one in LA while Jesus handled his business. Then Esperanza remembered that she needed an outfit to visit Brenda.

She leaned across the bed for the manila folder marked *CDC* and pulled out the information she needed to complete packing.

CALIFORNIA DEPARTMENT OF CORRECTIONS
VISITING RULES

Visitors must dress conservatively, and inappropriate attire will be reason to deny a visit. The following is prohibited attire:

- *Clothing which, in any combination of shades or types of material/fabric, resembles California State–issued inmate clothing; blue denim or chambray shirts and blue denim pants.*
- *Law enforcement or military-type forest green or camouflage-patterned articles of clothing, including rain gear.*

- *Hats, wigs, or hairpieces (except with prior written approval of the visiting sergeant).*
- *Clothing that exposes the breast/chest area, genital area, or buttocks.*
- *Dresses, skirts, pants, and shorts exposing more than two inches above the knee, including slits.*
- *Sheer or transparent garments.*
- *Strapless or "spaghetti" straps.*
- *Clothing exposing the midriff area.*
- *Clothing or accessories displaying obscene or offensive language or drawings.*
- *Brassieres with metal underwires or any other detectable metal are not permitted.*

Having only visited Brenda once, Esperanza had forgotten the bible of rules one had to follow. She never imagined what Dulce had to go through every morning she had dressed to visit her in Bedford Hills. Esperanza tumbled through the pile of clothes on her bed until she found a pair of loose-fitting black denim jeans and a plain black T-shirt. With her old sneakers, she was set. Not that long ago those jeans and kicks were the hottest gear to hit the streets. Then they fell out of fashion but were all Esperanza had to wear when she got sprung. Now even though she longed to trash them and finally could, they were the only appropriate clothes she had to visit her mother. Just like the orange jumpsuit that Esperanza left behind at Bedford Hills, that once-fashionable outfit was now and always would be prison gear. But when she and Dulce moved to California to be closer to Brenda, they would always have to own some kind of prison gear.

A knock at the bedroom door interrupted Esperanza's thoughts. Figuring that Priscilla, too, had had enough of the guys, or they had bogarded the remote in the middle of her movie, she said, "It's open, Prissy."

Jesus entered the room rolling a black luggage bag. Pleased to see her packing, he said, "I bought this for you, ma." Snickering at Brenda's worn case, he heaved the bag onto the bed. "Look," he said as he pointed to the emblem of the Prada triangle. Then he unzipped the bag and opened it. Inside sat a matching briefcase with two clip buckles. "I figured you'd bring your books so you can study for your tests or whatever."

"Sus, that's so sweet." Esperanza placed her papers on the bed, and immediately began transferring all she had packed in her mother's suitcase into her new luggage. Jesus picked up the papers and scanned them. " '*It is a crime to assist an inmate to escape,'* " he read aloud, " *'bring onto the grounds any weapon, firearm, ammunition, explosive device, tear gas, pepper spray, alcohol or controlled substance, cameras and/or recording devices . . .'* Damn, you can't bring a nigga a Walkman or something?"

If you had visited me more than once, you'd know that shit. Esperanza checked herself. Jesus had bought her a dope new wardrobe, designer luggage, and a trip to California. She had to let that shit go. "It can be a player," said Esperanza. "Just not a recorder."

"Got you." Jesus continued to read to himself. "Yo, ma, did you read this? It says here 'enter without the permission of the warden if you have previously been convicted of a felony.' "

"Don't worry about it. My PO took care of that for me."

"You sure about that?"

"He said he did."

"Sure that muthafucka's not setting you up?"

She was not sure. "Why would he do something like that?"

"Why not? Listen, you want me to look into this for you? I can make a few calls."

Esperanza placed a Marc Mattis red leather blazer in her new bag in case of a cool night. "Jesus, stop frontin'. You don't roll like that."

"You don't know. And you're not trying to know, remember." He eyed the leather blazer in her hand. "At least some of the time."

The tone in his voice made Esperanza nervous. Sometimes she liked him better when he ranted. When Jesus seemed calm . . . "Thanks, *papi,* I think everything's cool. Let's not take any chances on the wrong person getting a heads-up about this trip, OK?" She glanced at the clock on the night table. "Dulce's gonna be here soon, so you guys gotta bounce."

Jesus nodded. "No problem, ma. I wanna spend time with you, but I'm not trying to mess things up for you with your sister." Jesus opened the door and a boom of male laughter rolled in from the living room. "And just so you know, I didn't mean to bring X over here. He be doggin' Feli—calling him a devout Christian—but sometimes he be thinking he's my tail and shit. Anyway, when I stopped to buy the groceries, he paid for half of them. Whether you tell D that or not, I leave up to you."

Esperanza almost asked him to stay. But Dulce was on her way, and the last thing either of them needed was to find them all—especially Xavier squeezing his balls—lounging on her sofa. And if Jesus stayed, Xavier stayed.

"Y'all better go."

"OK." Jesus stroked Esperanza's cheek and pressed his lips against her temple. "I'll call you." He left the bedroom and gently closed the door.

Esperanza waited, then cracked open the bedroom door. As she listened to Jesus corral everyone in the living room out of the apartment, she still felt the slight moisture of his kiss tingling on her face. She turned back to her packing, removing her study guides from her messenger bag to the Prada briefcase. She reached across the bed to Dulce's night table and scoured the stack of books. She found Maite's monograph, *The Revolutionary Spirit: An Owner's Manual for the Warrior Womyn,* placed it into her briefcase, and snapped it shut.

SEVENTEEN

California Love

Jesus had bought a complete row of seats. He gave Esperanza the window and put himself on the aisle. Had Dulce come she would have sat between them, but Jesus eventually eased in next to Esperanza, leaving the aisle seat empty. He elbowed her, then gestured toward the man in the aisle seat in the row diagonally across from theirs. "Check that shit out, Espe." She looked up from her GED workbook. A white guy in his mid-twenties wearing a dress shirt and tie pressed his nose against his book: Sun Tsu's *The Art of War.* Jesus snickered. "Who that suit think he's fuckin' kidding?"

Esperanza shrugged. "I hear that businesspeople are into that stuff."

"Whatever."

"Weren't you the one who said there wasn't that much difference between street life and the corporate world?"

"I said that?"

"Yeah."

"I'm brilliant."

Esperanza giggled. "Did you bring anything to read?"

"¿Pa' qué?"

"It's a long flight."

"That's why they show movies." A curvy flight attendant walked past them, and Jesus gently tapped her arm. "Excuse me, miss. Y'all going to show a movie during the flight, right?"

The flight attendant batted her eyes at Jesus, and a pang of jealousy cut across Esperanza's gut. "Yes, sir, we certainly will." No matter what he said or how he said it, women were always checking for Jesus. Never mind he was with another woman. Sometimes they sweated him more because of that.

"Just one?"

"Yes, sir. About an hour or so into the flight."

"You don't have to call me sir, beautiful."

"Why, thank you. What should I call you?"

"Ah, see, how're you going to ask me that in front of my girlfriend? The skies are not supposed to be that friendly, boo."

The flight attendant feigned shock at his suggestion of impropriety, but she giggled as she moved on down the aisle.

Esperanza returned to her workbook. "Fuckin' player."

"Hate the game." Jesus lifted the armrest to his left and slumped into the seat that separated them. He leaned toward Esperanza until his head practically rested against her forearm. "Besides, we ain't official yet, are we?" Then Jesus peered over her arm and randomly read aloud a question off the open page.

> " 'I have included a copy of my résumé, which details my principal interests education, and past work experience.' "
>
> " 'Which correction should be made to this sentence? One, remove the comma after "résumé"; two, replace "principal" with "principle"; three, insert a comma after "interests"; four, replace "past" with "passed"; five, no correction is necessary.

Without a beat, Jesus said, "Three. Check it. Tell me I'm right."

Esperanza found the yellow sticker that marked the page with the answer key. She scanned the page. "You're right."

"Told you. I'm brilliant."

She looked at him and smiled. He stuck his tongue out at her like a schoolyard brat, and Esperanza laughed. "You should go back to school, Sus."

"Hell, nah."

"You be joking, but you're so smart. On the real. You always have been."

"No, I'm not. For certain things. Definitely not that shit."

"Yes, you are, and this stuff can help you with anything you want to do."

"I'm stacking my paper just fine without it."

"But you can be like that guy," Esperanza said, motioning to the passenger reading *The Art of War.*

"You mean a corporate clown?"

"I'm serious, Jesus."

"I'm serious, too. I ain't no school nigga, Espe, and you know it. Not no corporate nigga either. I'm a street nigga."

Hearing him use that word so many times made her uncomfortable. Then she thought of Isoke, and discomfort became shame. "You're not a nigga, period."

Jesus squinted those piercing green eyes at her. "A year ago you would've said, 'You *my* nigga.'" He straightened up in his seat. "You've changed a lot since going to Bedford Hills."

Esperanza missed his closeness. "Is that good or bad?"

"I don't know." Then Jesus shifted back to the aisle seat, propping up a long leg on the seat between them. "I'm still trying to figure that out."

You and me both. She tried to return to her studies but felt the weight of Jesus's stare. "You want something to read? I have another book in my bag." Esperanza leaned for the briefcase stowed beneath the middle seat in front of them.

"Nah, I'm straight," Jesus said as he pulled out his portable CD player. "Until the movie comes on, I'ma hang with Chingy right hurr, right hurr." He chuckled at his joke, then settled in his seat with his eyes closed.

An hour later, video monitors had descended from the plane's ceiling, but Jesus had fallen asleep. Esperanza considered waking him but changed her mind when Julia Roberts's name faded onto the screen. Wake him up for that shit, and he might cuss her out.

Having done well on her practice questions, Esperanza decided to take a break from studying. With Jesus asleep she could read whatever she wanted without inviting scrutiny. She laid her workbook on the seat beside her, then reached into her pocketbook on the floor and drew out Maite's book.

She opened to the table of contents and scanned her options. Maite told her that she wanted the book to be like an owner's manual, so that the reader could turn to whatever chapter she needed. Esperanza opened it with the intention of reading the chapter entitled "Truth," curious to read the powerful words that had compelled Dulce to reveal her ugliest secrets to Chago. Instead her eyes fell on another chapter called "Violence." Giving Jesus one last glance, Esperanza turned to that page and started to read:

> *There is a popular saying: If you love someone, let that person go. Yet the logic behind this statement is lost in the romantic relationship that becomes abusive. It is a fact that a woman with an abusive man is in the most danger when she leaves him. If he truly*

loved her, why would he insist that she stay when he knows he cannot or will not end his violence? If he truly loved her, he would want her to be safe and happy, even if it meant getting away from him. But the abusive man does not love himself, let alone his woman. If he truly loved her, he would let her go.

Esperanza dropped the book facedown on the serving tray in front of her. Maite's words contradicted everything she had ever heard or seen throughout her life. After *el cabezón* had busted her mother's lip for missing a few wrinkles when ironing his slacks, Esperanza asked her why Roland kept hitting her. "It's that he loves me so much, Espe," said Brenda. "When I make mistakes like that, he thinks it's because I don't love him as much as he loves me. I have to try harder not to disappoint him and make him angry." Then she burst into tears, but Esperanza knew that her mother was not crying because she had disappointed *el cabezón.*

Then Dulce got involved with Xavier, although she had initially set her sights on Jesus. Upon an invitation from Xavier, who had long had a thing for her, Dulce had gone to one of Jesus's barbecues and flirted with him. Jesus thought she was cute and funny but ultimately not his type. He liked his women younger. "And quieter," he confessed to Esperanza in bed after they first slept together. "Your sister's too damned loud for my taste." Still, Jesus kicked it with Dulce at the barbecue, probably thinking he could get into her pants, even if just for the night, and Dulce most likely believing that one night in her pants was all Jesus needed for Dulce to maintain his interest. And then Esperanza finally arrived—whom a frustrated Dulce had left at the beauty salon an hour earlier—and Jesus shifted his attention to her.

Later Jesus made his way to where Esperanza sat in a patio chair, bobbing her head to the music and holding an empty beer. With one of Natalia's cigars hanging from his lips, he stood before her and offered her a fresh bottle of Corona. Esperanza searched through the crowd to see Dulce eyeing them over Xavier's shoulder as they danced. With barely a glance at him, Esperanza shook her head to refuse the beer. She could not look into his face. Jesus was too fine. Dangerously fine, the way men like him always were.

Jesus sat next to her and said, "Don't fear me. Just love me."

Esperanza snickered. "I'm not scared of you." She accepted the beer and took a deep sip. "Don't love you neither."

"You will."

"I don't even know you."

"So get to know me. What do you want to know about me? Ask me anything."

"Is it true that your pop's a cop?"

"Damn, girl! No one's ever asked me that to my face. Let alone someone who just met me."

"I'm not going to ask you what I already know. I want to know what I don't know. Would you rather I talk about you behind your back?"

"Hell, yeah. Gossip about me, ma. Build my legend and shit." Esperanza laughed and took another sip of her beer. "You'd be helping me to stack my paper. That's what we call PR in this game."

"You're funny."

Jesus smiled at her. "Lemme show you something." He reached into his pocket to pull out his wallet. He opened it, found a card, and handed it to Esperanza.

POLICEMAN'S PRAYER TO SAINT MICHAEL

> Saint Michael, give us cool heads, stout hearts, hard punches, an uncanny flair for investigation, and wise judgment. Make us the terror of burglars, the friends of children and law-abiding citizens, kind to strangers, polite to bores, strict with lawbreakers, and impervious to temptation. And when we lay down our nightsticks, enroll us in your Heavenly Force, where we will be as proud to guard the throne of God as we have been to guard the city of men. Amen.

"Your father gave this to you?"

Jesus nodded. "I was about six, maybe seven when I realized that what he did for a living was mad dangerous. Those shows on Channel Thirteen be frontin' like all the po do is bring lost children home and direct traffic and shit, but I saw through that shit. So one night he tries to put me to bed and leave for work, and I start bawling 'cause I'm afraid he's gonna go and get himself killed. Pops takes this card out of his wallet, gives it to me, and says so long as I say this prayer and go to sleep, everything will be all right."

"Did he get killed in the line of duty?"

Jesus hissed. "That nigga bounced with some trick to Tampa somewhere. Left me and my moms just like that when I was eight. I don't give a fuck about him any more than he gives a shit about me."

Esperanza believed his story. The same thing had happened to her, and she had the same feelings. It seemed like the state of Florida existed to harbor faithless fathers and their unscrupulous mistresses. "So why you carry that card around?"

" 'Cause . . . read it. Might as well be a thug prayer. Like Tupac said, I wonder if heaven got a ghetto and shit."

"You like Tupac?"

When Jesus and Esperanza connected, Dulce defaulted to Xavier, who started to hit her almost immediately. After a week, "You real funny" became "You think you're so funny." A month later, "You think you're so funny" became "You think you funny?" followed by the back of his hand to Dulce's mouth. She convinced herself she deserved it. "Look how I did him, Espe," she said once as she dabbed her bottom lip with a cotton ball drenched with hydrogen peroxide. "I just got to prove to him that I'm not checking for Jesus anymore." One time Esperanza happened upon Xavier sitting on the floor in front of the bedroom door. Dulce had locked herself in the room, and from that point of safety, she shrieked, "You hate me so fuckin' much that you can't stop hittin' me, why don't you just fuckin' leave me already?"

"I don't hate you, D. You know I don't hate you. C'mon, now."

"Yes, you do. You wouldn't keep beating on me if you didn't hate me." Dulce stopped shrieking with rage and began to sob with desperation. "Do us both a favor. Just leave me. Leave me alone and don't come back."

"I can't do it," Xavier said. Unaware that Esperanza stood at the end of the hallway, he cried. It was the first and last time she had ever seen him cry. Muthafucka didn't even cry when he put Dulce in the hospital. Hell, that night he felt justified because Dulce seemed intent on fighting him to the death. According to Feli, the way Xavier spun it to the police, he was defending himself, and if they were going to arrest him on aggravated assault, they had to arrest Dulce, too, and charge her with the same. "Just because I'ma man, and I ain't let her get the best of me, don't mean she ain't try to vic me, yo."

Refusing to assume the victim role, however, Dulce corroborated Xavier's story when she gave her statement to the police. Wanting to see Xavier in jail for what he did to her sister, Esperanza protested. But Dulce said, "It's the truth, Espe. He came for me, and this time I went for mine. Besides, if he gets knocked, I get knocked. On top of everything that nigga put me through, I ain't going out like *Mami* over him. He's not worth it." So even though Esperanza let the po know that Xavier had hit Dulce many times in the past, they eventually released him. The trade-off was that they left Dulce alone, too. Dulce took her luck as an omen. "That's the second time I avoided lockup, Espe. My time's running out. I gotta get straight and stay that way, 'cause next time I'm gonna wind up dead from a beatdown or in jail for beating down somebody else. Next time's the last time."

Esperanza watched Jesus as he napped. He prided himself on not hitting her so much. Once she begged him to check Xavier, and he agreed to talk to him. She had eavesdropped on their man-to-man and heard Jesus say, "Yo, a real man shouldn't have to wild out on his woman like you be doing, man. It takes all that to control your woman? What kind of punk shit is that?"

"Espe don't be jawing at you, man. You tell her to shut the fuck up, and she shuts the fuck up," said Xavier. "And Espe would never think of raising up on you, but D? It's like she think she's a fuckin' man. She forgets her goddamn place and shit, and I gotta whup her ass back into it."

"Now you know why I ain't get with her," said Jesus.

Then they both started to laugh. Esperanza fumed behind Jesus's bedroom door, hearing them snicker and imagining them sharing a blunt and giving each other a pound. She almost barged into the room, but that would have made things worse for herself and her sister. Why give Jesus an opportunity to demonstrate to Xavier how to put your woman in check and then send him home to practice on Dulce?

His rare violence made Esperanza lucky, Jesus said. "Shit, I got the most cause to be wilding out like that. I'm the top dog of this shit right here. I got the most pressures, the most to lose. And I could do a bitch just like Xavier in order to maintain my shit, and still I'd never sleep alone. But not only do I choose you out of all the women I could have, Espe, I almost never do you like that. That's 'cause I know you love me, and I love you, too."

Esperanza tucked Maite's book into her purse and reached for her portable CD player. She opened it to remind herself which disk she had listened to last and found Tupac's greatest hits. Esperanza hit Play, and "Troublesome '96" began. "Tra, la, la, la, la, la, all you niggas die."

For the first time ever, she found herself put off by the harsh language and hit skip again. She skipped to the next song. Tupac's gravelly delivery made the foul words sharp enough to cut her ears. She skipped again, then again, and then one last time before she shut off the player and dropped it on the seat between Jesus and herself. Esperanza leaned her head against the window, closed her eyes, and willed herself to sleep.

In her dream, Esperanza saw herself like Jennifer Lopez's Slim in *Enough*. Crouched in a defensive stance, she stood with her hands wrapped in brass knuckles and cloth bandages. She wore a black unitard with boot-cut legs and steel-toed boots. Esperanza turned in her stance, waiting for someone to strike, but all she heard was a chorus of male voices. Over each other they shouted obscenities at her. They called her names and threatened her. Esperanza sensed a violent rush toward her head and dodged to the side. Before she could recover her balance, Esperanza felt an evil push behind her. The voices grow louder and uglier. She threw up her hands, ready to fight against her invisible attacker. Esperanza whirled around only to have a massive force smash her in the mouth and send her to the ground. As she lay like a child, curling her knees toward her throbbing jaw, all the male voices faded until all she heard was Tupac's boyish laugh.

Esperanza awoke from her nightmare with her mouth aching. She came to her surroundings and found herself lying across the seat with her head nestled in Jesus's lap. As he continued to sleep, his hand rested on her hip. Whether she had stretched across the seat between them and placed her head on his lap or he had pulled her toward him, Esperanza could not remember.

The plane landed in Los Angeles at half past two in the afternoon. Jesus rented a Honda S2000 GTS and drove them to the Château Marmont in West Hollywood. During the drive Jesus told Esperanza, "Know what they say about this place? That if you gotta get into trouble, do that shit here. This is where Jim Morrison jumped from the balcony and John Belushi ODed." After such a morbid introduction, the romantic surroundings surprised Esperanza as they drove up a hill through the thick greenery toward their cottage facing the ocean.

Esperanza unpacked her toiletries as Jesus called room service and ordered champagne and strawberries. His order both touched her and made her uneasy. Between jet lag and her nightmare, she had hoped that Jesus would go tend to his business and give her some time to herself.

"Isn't your meeting today?" She felt uncomfortable asking him about his plans. As he said himself, the less she knew, the better, and Esperanza did not need to spark Jesus's irritability by seeming to mind his business. But she had to know enough about his doings so she could make her own plans accordingly.

"Yeah, but not till later," Jesus said as he pulled out a suit from its travel bag and hung it behind the door. "I ain't trying to fuck with this LA traffic. You saw how it was starting to get when we were driving here from the airport."

Esperanza vaguely remembered Jesus complaining as she took in the view as they drove from LAX to the château. For her first and last trip to Cali, she and Dulce flew to Sacramento and drove two and half hours to visit Brenda. Before Esperanza could work up the courage to ask Jesus when he planned to drive her to Chowchilla, he popped a disk into the Honda's CD player and turned up the volume on maximum power. "California looooove," a robotic voice crooned over the speakers, followed by chunks of bass. Jesus bobbed his head and told Esperanza, "You like that."

Esperanza felt Jesus's arms encircle her waist; then his lips pressed against the crook of her neck. She expected him to woo her but hoped he would not come on too strong. Esperanza had to resist him even as she led him to believe they had a chance. At least until she got what she wanted. Then maybe she would have the courage to refuse on principle.

A knock on the door spared her. "Room service." Jesus pulled away from her to answer it. The waiter wheeled in a small cart holding a silver wine bucket and a matching platter. He reached for the champagne bottle, but Jesus stopped him. "I got that." He pulled out a roll of cash from his pocket and peeled off a generous tip. After the waiter left, Jesus popped open the wine. He poured two glasses and pulled the lid back off the tray of plump strawberries. Esperanza reached for one and sank her teeth into its juicy mass. Jesus handed her a glass, then lifted his own. "To California love."

Esperanza tapped her glass against his and took a large sip. She remembered Priscilla's condition. If she had come, would she have drunk the wine? Would she have taken a deep sip to hide the pregnancy she had not decided to see through birth? Or would she use this opportunity to confess to Jesus? Would he be happy? Would he think Priscilla a better woman because she wanted to have his child?

"What are you thinking?" Jesus asked her.

The question reminded her of one of Dulce's observations about men. "When a man asks you what you're thinking, he always cares. Dudes usually couldn't give two shits about what a woman's thinking enough to ask," she said. "But don't get it twisted. He could care 'cause he's really good, or because he's mad shady."

"What you sneering at?" Jesus said,

"What?"

"I asked you what you're thinking, and now you're all . . ." He imitated her cynical expression.

Esperanza took another sip of wine. "I was thinking about Priscilla." She sat on the corner of the bed.

Jesus exhaled. He picked up a strawberry and sat down next to her. He pulled Esperanza's glass from her hand and placed it on the cart. "Priscilla who?" Jesus brought the strawberry to her lips, but Esperanza slightly pulled away. Unfazed, he bit into it himself, and Esperanza watched as he licked traces of its juice from his lips. He always had the perfect lips.

He said, "You know why I brought you here, right?"

Esperanza nodded, but Jesus raised an eyebrow at her. He wanted to hear her say it. "You want to show me the kind of life you can give me."

"If I wanted Priscilla to be here, she'd be here instead of you." She nodded again. "We both came here to see what kind of future we can have together, and that future don't involve her. Why bring her up?"

" 'Cause . . . she's down with the crew."

"She ain't down with the crew. Not like that."

Jesus's adamant tone confused Esperanza. "Priscilla doesn't work for you?"

"She runs an errand now and then, but that don't make her part of the crew. Just 'cause I fuck her now and again don't make her part of the crew." Esperanza let his use of the present tense slide because the nonchalance in his tone bothered her much more. Was that how he rationalized cheating Esperanza out of her money after all she had done for the crew? Did sleeping with Jesus make her *less* valuable to him? Was that why no matter what she did—including losing a year of her life in prison and God knew how many more trying to rebuild it in the unforgiving world—she was no more or less part of the crew than Priscilla?

Jesus lifted himself off the bed. He tore off his shirt, balled it up, and chucked it toward his suitcase. The muscles in his arms and chest quivered as he unbuckled his belt and pulled it through the loops of his slacks. Esperanza felt the urge to place her palms against his pecs, then slide her hands down his etched torso. She began to reach out for him when Jesus turned around and headed toward the bathroom.

"Where you going?"

"I'ma shower, then take a nap."

"You practically slept through the entire flight."

"Barely." Jesus reached into his pocket again for his cash. He counted off a few bills and handed them to Esperanza. "Why don't you go do something with yourself?" Jesus dropped the money on the bed and disappeared into the bathroom.

Over a year ago, Esperanza would have seduced him into a deep sleep, skipped out the door to spend his cash, and, hot with gratitude for his generosity, returned to entice Jesus again. Now she hesitated to take the money. She eventually took the cash and stashed it in her purse. If Esperanza wanted to move with Dulce to California, she had to save every penny she could—take Jesus's money so she could leave him forever.

How did he do this to her? Only minutes ago Esperanza had hoped he would leave her alone for a while. Then he left her sitting on the bed yearning for him and feeling unwanted. If Jesus had gotten angry and stormed off into the bathroom or dismissed her from the room, she might have felt relieved not to have to avoid having sex with him. Instead he schooled her about Priscilla's place no differently than her science teacher reading a physics formula off the blackboard. Then he handed her a few hundreds and chose a second nap over her willing body. He did all of this without a hint of anger or hurt, and ironically this made Esperanza feel a bit of both. What the hell was going on with her?

"Espe," Jesus called from behind the closed bathroom door. She sprang to her feet, ready to get or give him whatever he asked. He poked his head through the door, and Esperanza glimpsed his thick arrow dangling between his cut thighs. "Call your sister and let 'er know you got here all right."

"OK. Sus, you all right in there? Got everything you need?"

But he had already closed the door and blasted the shower. Esperanza picked up the hotel telephone and read the instructions for dialing a long-distance call. Within seconds she heard the apartment telephone ring. Then the answering machine clicked, and Dulce's businesslike tone played into her ear.

"You have reached the Cepeda residence." This never failed to make Esperanza smile. At first because of the corniness of Dulce referring to their apartment in the PJs as a residence. But after a year of the occasionally incompleted collect call from Bedford Hills, Dulce's little effort to make their apartment sound like a home warmed her. "We are unable to take your call, so please leave a message, and we'll get back to you. Unless you're a telemarketer. In that case, get lost and have a nice day."

"Dulce, you there? Pick up. It's Espe." She waited, then proceeded. "Just wanted to let you know we got here OK." She recited the hotel and room numbers. "And remember. Be on the lookout for my PO. His name's Conrado Puente. He hasn't been sweatin' me much what with his more important parolees in his caseload and shit. But now that I'm here, he may start sniffing around. I left his number on the table, so if you see it pop up on the Caller ID, go 'bout your business, and watch your back on the streets. Love you; call you later."

Esperanza jumped on a random bus, noting the number so she could retrace her steps at the end of her jaunt. She sat in the back and peered out of the window as the bus rambled through the streets of western Los Angeles. When the white faces in suits rushing in and out of corporate buildings became brown bodies in jeans chilling in front of mom-'n'-pop shops, Esperanza hopped off the bus. She walked a few yards and entered the first salon she found. As the petite *mejicana* blew-dry her thick hair, Esperanza asked her where she might buy a pretty yet inexpensive dress, and the hairdresser recommended a boutique right across the street.

With her hair and nails complete, Esperanza headed to the boutique, surveying the clothing in the window as she jaywalked. An oncoming driver blasted his horn, but Esperanza ignored him, her eyes fixed on a cherry-red dress. When she arrived across the street, she stopped in front of the window to admire it. It had a low-cut cowl neck, a shirred waistline, and a handkerchief hem. Jesus, Dulce—even Xavier who horded compliments like a crackhead his last rock—everyone always told Esperanza she had nice legs. "Full where it matters, slim where it don't," Jesus said. Dulce told her, "You have *Mami*'s legs." And unlike Dulce, who had tomboy elbows and knees, Esperanza had no scars anywhere on her body save the ghastly one across her chest.

In the boutique's dressing room, Esperanza pulled off her Baby Phat jersey and prayed that the dress's collar hung so that its folds concealed her scar. But when she pulled on the dress and looked in the mirror, a line of raised flesh peeked through the opening. Esperanza tried to rearrange the folds to cover the scar, but as they were cut to do, they fell away to reveal the curve of her inner bosom, and with it the ugly reminder of the savagery that always lurked beneath Jesus's suave demeanor. No matter how much the skirt flattered her legs, the color complemented her face, and the neckline showed off her bust, Esperanza could not bring herself to buy the dress. Instead she opted for another red dress—a sleeveless mock turtleneck with a slit on each side of the ankle-length skirt. While not as sexy as her first choice, it had to suffice.

She returned to the cottage to find the room clean and empty and a message from Jesus on the bed. He had instructed her to meet him at Café La

Boheme on Santa Monica Boulevard in West Hollywood at eight. Esperanza quickly showered, rubbing cocoa butter into her scar even though her new dress would hide it. She spent another twenty minutes applying a full face of makeup. She brushed a few strokes through her straightened hair, then dashed out the door.

As Jesus discussed the specials with their waiter, Esperanza gazed at La Boheme's decor. It resembled a mansion with its wrought-iron chandeliers, burgundy drapes, and old paintings. Jesus asked for a table on the patio, which boasted two fountains with mosaic tiles and a beautiful garden of flowers. Despite the August warmth and the fact that she had never had one, the sight of the stone fireplace made Esperanza shiver and feel a bit homesick.

"OK, I'll have that," said Jesus. "Boo, what you having?"

Esperanza quickly scanned the menu. "I'll try the jidori chicken. . . ."

Jesus held up his hand to stop her. "Nah, ma, I ain't bring you here to eat no chicken. Order something else. Get some seafood."

She really wanted the chicken but reexamined the menu. "OK, bring me the lobster salad to start and then the wild salmon."

"That's what I'm talking about. What about dessert?"

"Later."

Jesus drank half his glass of wine and then poured himself more. "What'd you do with yourself this afternoon?"

"Just rode around on the bus. Did my hair and nails. Bought this dress."

"Only thing hotter than that dress is you in it."

"Thanks."

"Thanking me . . ." Jesus shook his head. "Girl, you know with that body you can make a recycling bag look like high fashion and shit. None of these pasty, flat-ass bitches out here can compete with you." He flailed his arms as he gestured to the Hollywood types seated around the restaurant.

"Sus, stop." She giggled. "Lower your voice."

"Finally you seem to be having some fun. A few seconds ago you were talking about your day like all you did was work. 'I bought groceries, washed the car, mowed the lawn. . . .' "

Esperanza quieted herself. Fingering the stem of her untouched wineglass, she said, "It's kinda hard for me to have a good time knowing my mom's so close."

Jesus eyed her. "You know, it really ain't all that close, Espe. It's over four hours from here."

He did not seem annoyed, so Esperanza chose not to remind him that he had promised to take her. Instead she said, "I know. Visiting hours are on the weekend from nine to three, so I thought I get up early tomorrow and go see her. You know, while you're out and about, doing your thing."

"And how're you going to get all the way out there in the boonies?"

"Well, I know you need the car, so I thought I'd rent another one for the day."

Without taking his eyes off of her, Jesus leaned back in his seat and drank his wine. The server came with Esperanza's lobster salad and Jesus's red-pepper soup. He left, and they ate a few bites in silence. Desperate for even mundane conversation, Esperanza said, "This salad's fantastic."

"I'll take you. I'll take you tomorrow to visit your moms."

Esperanza's heart quickened. "You don't have to if you don't want to. I can go on my own. I know you've got things to do."

"I did what I had to do today. And if anything comes up, I'll have tomorrow night to deal with it. You say visiting hours end at three o'clock?"

"Yeah, but we don't have to be there all day. . . ."

"Let's leave about six, seven. If we don't get there early, muthafuckas make you wait until it's too late, then send your ass home without seeing nobody. You know how COs can be."

"Yeah, I know." How Jesus knew Esperanza did not know, but this was not the time to test him.

"A'ight." Jesus took another spoonful of soup. He licked those perfect lips and said, "You do look great in that dress."

Suddenly famished, Esperanza dug into her lobster salad.

EIGHTEEN

Dear Mama

Esperanza became willing and eager to show Jesus her appreciation. Not only had he kept his word, he had made her feel beautiful all night. While in the bathroom readying for bed, she tore off her casual Pelle Pelle underwear and slipped into a black lacy merry widow with matching Brazilian panties. But when Esperanza came out of the bathroom, Jesus had already sprawled across the bed and fallen into a deep sleep. She crept under the sheets in the little space he left for her, careful to not disturb him.

Although frustration, excitement, and discomfort took turns keeping her up for a few more hours, Esperanza arose the next morning at five thirty. She showered and dressed in her black denim jeans and a black T-shirt, then headed toward the main cottage. To her disappointment, the gift shop would not open for another three hours. So Esperanza took to the street and hoped to find an open store.

She walked a few blocks and happened upon a twenty-four-hour drugstore, where she spent over a hundred dollars on the necessities she herself never had too much of in Bedford Hills. Checking the list she made against the list of allowable items she found in the manila folder marked *CDC,* Esperanza dropped things for Brenda into her shopping cart:

Coffee
Nuts (no shell!)
Cheez-Its
Newports (two cartons max!)

Plastic mirror
Notebook, ballpoint pens, colored markers
Jigsaw puzzle (must be more than five hundred pieces)
Playing cards
Makeup kit
Utensils (plastic only)
Slippers
Socks (white!)
Underwear

Esperanza double-checked her purchases to be sure none of them were prohibited in one way or the other—no alcohol, foil, metal, pressurized cans, logos. When she selected the clothing, she steered clear of the usual prison colors of blue, black, gray, and orange and made sure nothing exceeded the prohibited values in keeping with the rules meant to thwart escape attempts and inmate jealousy.

Esperanza returned to the hotel room an hour later to find Jesus still asleep, and she began to stress. They had to get on the road soon. If it took four hours to drive from Los Angeles to Chowchilla, they might not arrive until almost twelve, flirting dangerously close to the two-P.M. cutoff for visitor processing. If California was anything like New York, she might have to wait two hours before they allowed her to see Brenda. And God forbid they were to experience car trouble or get lost.

But Esperanza feared waking Jesus. In an angry fit he might decide to not take her. She tiptoed to his pants and rifled through his pockets until she found the car keys. Later she could say he needed his sleep and she did not want to disturb him. Esperanza started to write him a note but then stopped when she recognized that he was not beyond getting angry and leaving her stranded. The thought of Jesus checking out of the château and moving to another hotel without leaving behind word or her shit made Esperanza crumple up her note. Just as quickly as she dropped it into the wastebasket, she dove to her knees, fished it out, and shoved it into her pocketbook. Better to wake him up. If he got pissed off and decided not to take her, she might have the time to find out if and where she could catch a bus to Chowchilla.

Esperanza knelt on the bed and gently tapped his arm. "Sus? Jesus, honey, you gotta get up. It's gonna be too late to go."

Jesus groaned and rolled over. He glanced at the clock and groaned again. "Espe, it's seven in the freakin' morning." He turned his back on her again and slammed his head against the pillow.

"You said we should leave at six or seven." Esperanza resisted the urge to shake him or sound desperate. "*Papi,* visiting hours start at nine, and it's not like they just let you roll in once you get there.

"We could be waiting for hours before they let me see my mother." Anger started boiling in the pit of her belly. *He visited me once,* she thought sarcastically. *That should be enough for him to know how these fuckin' things work, but maybe his ass don't remember.* Esperanza eyed the car keys, where she had forgotten them on the desk. She was going to see her mother today. If he didn't get up, she would take the car keys and fuckin' go by herself, so help her God. God help her so she wouldn't have to do that.

Jesus groaned once more and lifted himself out of bed. "All right. I'm up. Quit whining. You know I hate that shit." He dragged himself toward the bathroom. "Don't think you driving either."

If it had not been for Jesus's mother, Esperanza thought, he might not have entered the game. Dulce always said, "How you get 'em is how you lose 'em," and his moms herself had been Officer Lara's mistress before getting pregnant with Jesus. His father left his then-wife and married Jesus's mother, but soon followed his wandering eye to another woman. Like Esperanza's own father, Jesus's pops was a stand-up guy in every other respect—an attentive father, a loyal friend, and a good neighbor—and just like Esperanza's father, he felt that entitled him to philander. And when, just like Esperanza's father, Officer Lara left with his mistress to Florida, Jesus's mother fell apart. But she did not attempt to replace him with a parade of losers the way Brenda or even Xavier's mother had. Instead she turned to Jesus, expecting him to fulfill her endless needs for financial security and emotional support. At first he tried to fill his father's shoes. Like No-No and Feli, he worked hard at legitimate work, but the more he gave the more insatiable his moms became. One day she complained that he worked too many long hours and left her home alone too much; the next she whined that he made too little money and caused her stress about the bills. Jesus claimed that he took to the streets to get away from her as much as to make more money in less time, but Esperanza believed he also did it to become the antithesis of Office Lara so his moms would stop expecting him to be the man of the house. At first she screamed and cried and otherwise carried on about Jesus's new lifestyle, but eventually she shut her mouth and took his money. Jesus finally convinced his mother to move to

Florida herself, buying her everything she needed, from the house in Tampa to the minivan for the eighteen-hour drive. After watching her car disappear down the Grand Concourse, Jesus turned to everyone where they sat in front of his building and said, "Now she can track down Pop's ass and become his fuckin' problem again," and they all laughed.

"Honey, you have to let go. They can make you go if you hold on too long." But Brenda herself made no attempt to pull away from her younger daughter.

The visit would end before it started. Thanks to Jesus's laziness and the prison bureaucracy, Esperanza had only a half hour with her mother. Despite the rule against excessive contact, she clung to Brenda in the visitation room. She knew from her own experience that if the CO wanted to cut them slack, she would allow it at the very beginning and end of the visit. "This isn't just from me. It's from Dulce, too. We each owe you six years' worth of hugs and kisses." Esperanza spotted the guard as she made a move toward them, so she finally let go of Brenda. They sat down on a bench and held hands, careful to keep them in plain view of the guards.

Brenda asked about her sister, and Esperanza related every little detail, incorporating colorful anecdotes Dulce told her about work. Esperanza praised Dulce's work ethic and academic achievements and expressed sympathy over her breakup with Chago as if she were the mother instead of the youngest. Esperanza wanted Brenda to feel as much as possible as if she still lived with them and had not missed a thing in her daughters' lives. That was what she had wanted when she was in prison.

"This Chago. He was a good man?" Esperanza sadly nodded. "Well, just because a man is good doesn't make him right. Dulcita will be OK. She's got a strong sense of self; she's a survivor." More than ever Esperanza could see her sister in Brenda's face, and in her mother's night-black eyes she also saw herself. *"¿Y tú, negrita?* You have a boyfriend?"

"Not really." Esperanza saw no purpose in being as transparent when talking about herself as she had about Dulce. Her mother had never approved of Jesus, seeing through the lies Esperanza told her about the well-paying government job he had through his father the police officer. During their last visit, Brenda spent fifteen minutes ranting about Jesus and Xavier with no appreciation that Dulce and Esperanza would not even be there if not for them. "*Negrita, ¿por que no salgas con el nieto de Doña Mili?* That Felix is a good boy."

"The guy who drove me here's just an old friend. You know if he were all that, I'da asked you to put him on the list so he could meet you." Actually, Jesus had refused when Esperanza suggested it, and when she offered him Maite's book to read as he waited in the parking lot, he snorted at the title and turned on the radio. As she shoved Maite's book back into her purse and made her way to the visitor processing center, Esperanza was so happy that she hadn't fucked Jesus last night, because right then she could barely stand him. "Mami, how's your case going?"

The light of hope on Brenda's face took Esperanza by surprise. "Just last week I had a visit from two lawyers. They heard about what I was doing here—"

"Ay, Mami, you still doing that?" The same shit got her transferred out of New York in the first place. Esperanza understood Brenda's desire to help others who could have the second chance she might never have. But becoming a jailhouse lawyer meant becoming a target for the system and even the helpless inmates, who lived by the credo, *Do your own time*. But like Isoke, Brenda felt she had no choice. Advocacy became her purpose in life, and it gave her a reason to live while behind bars.

"But let me tell you, Espe. These women came to see me 'cause they want to take up my case. They gonna argue that the system failed to protect me, so I had no choice but to protect myself. They got cases just like mine all around the country, and they're gonna do it pro bono."

"Pro bono is what got you here in the first place, Mami." She hated being so negative with Brenda, but no more than she hated Brenda's being naive.

"No, *negrita*, these are not your run-of-the-mill public defenders. They got a different idea about what's justice in my situation." Brenda placed her hand over her heart and patted her chest. "Every time they win, they get paid right here."

Esperanza finally saw her chance to ask what she had long wanted to know. "Mami, do you ever regret what you did?" She wondered this many nights as she lay on her bunk during her yearlong bid. Would she have preferred to die that night than to have caused his death? Did she miss Roland? If she had to do it all over again, what might she have done differently? Esperanza leaned toward Brenda so she could whisper with honesty, because as even Jesus knew though he had never done time, there were no secrets in the penitentiary.

Brenda squeezed her hand and said, "When anybody makes it clear it's you or him, *negrita*, you always choose you," says Brenda. "If I had done that from the start—the first time he called me a bitch, the first time he said

I was nothing without him, the first time he forbade me to do something that I knew was in the best interest of our family, the first time he hit me—I would've never had to kill him. He said and did many things warning me all along that eventually it would be him or me, but I didn't pay attention until much too late. That's my only regret." Then she repeated her initial advice. "Anybody whose words or action tells you it's you or him, *negrita,* always choose you."

The correction officers began to round up the visitors to leave, and Brenda tightened her grasp on Esperanza's hand. "Before you leave, sing me that song you used to when you were little." Although she felt desperate to do anything for her mother, Esperanza had no idea what Brenda meant. She never sang as a child. "Mami, that was Dulce who used to sing for you. . . ."

"No, *negrita,* it was you. That song where you're, like, writing me a letter. I would come home from work and tell you to turn down that godawful rap music. I guess you weren't that little, maybe like twelve or thirteen. But instead of getting mad, you'd come into the kitchen and hug me and sing me the words."

The memories rushed Esperanza. In an attempt to re-create them, Esperanza rose to her feet and pulled Brenda along with her. She stood behind her mother, wrapped her tightly in a bear hug, and started to rhyme.

A prison guard said, "Ma'am, visiting hours are over now. Please step away from the inmate and exit the visiting room." But Esperanza clung tighter to Brenda. "Ma'am, that constitutes excessive contact. Step away from the inmate and exit the visiting area." With nothing to lose and her heart crumbling in her chest, she continued "Dear Mama." Even with the obvious differences between Pac's lyrics and her life, the words were too right, and she could not let go. The CO stormed over and ripped Esperanza's arms off Brenda and dragged her toward the exit. "*Mami,* you can still hear me! Listen to me, *Mami!*" Brenda looked up, tears streaming down her face, and through the pain in her own throat caused by the trapped sobs, Esperanza finished rhyming the first verse. *A poor single mother on welfare, tell me how ya did it/ There's no way I can pay you back.*

"I love you, Espe!" Brenda called. "And tell Dulcita I love her, too."

Before Esperanza could echo her mother's words of love, the CO slammed the heavy door to the reception area between them. Esperanza tried to collect herself as she made her way down the corridor. With as much dignity as she could muster, she asked the CO, "Is it too late to leave something behind for my mother?"

The guard cut her a suspicious look. "Like what?"

"Just a book. I want to write her a little note on the inside cover and leave it with her. It's in my pocketbook." Esperanza only wanted to write, *We love you, Mami. Always and forever. Dulce and Espe.*

"If you haven't gone over the weight limit for packages, it shouldn't be a problem."

"Thank you."

As she crossed the parking lot toward the Honda, Esperanza toughened. If Jesus did not care enough to go in with her, she would not share a damned thing with him. Jesus had raised the roof and had fallen asleep at the wheel. She banged once on the hood, cracking a smile when he jumped. Jesus unlocked the door, and without a word she slipped into the passenger seat.

"So?"

Esperanza shrugged. Jesus stared at her for a moment. "It got hot as hell out here, so I put on the AC, but I can put the top down again if you want."

"I don't care either way."

Jesus unlatched the roof from the windshield, turned on the car, and hit a button on the dashboard. As the roof folded back, Chingy's Mound City drawl filled the air. Esperanza reached forward to turn it down. She didn't want to hear that party shit right now. Jesus glanced at her but said nothing. "What you want to listen to?" Esperanza just shook her head to let him know that she didn't care about that either.

They were on the road for just a few minutes when Jesus turned off the radio. A moment later he placed his hand on Esperanza's knee. "So how's Ma Dukes holding up?"

His uncharacteristic tenderness caused Esperanza's despair to explode, and she sobbed liked any child ripped from her mother's arms. Jesus immediately pulled off to the side of the road. Then he pulled Esperanza to him. Stroking her hair, Jesus whispered over and over again, "I got you, ma." And even as Esperanza clung to him, weeping, she hated herself for losing her resolve against his ever-unpredictable charms. The more he stroked her hair and whispered in her ear, the harder Esperanza cried and clung to him. "It's all right, ma. I got you."

When they arrived at the hotel, Esperanza curled onto the bed while Jesus called room service. Without asking Esperanza if she even wanted to eat, he ordered a steak for himself and chicken for her. He peeled off his shirt, then sat on the edge of the bed to untie his boots.

Esperanza hugged the large pillow as she watched the muscles in Jesus's back flex as he loosened his shoestrings. Her eyes traced the indentations in his shoulders. She remembered burying her fingertips in those curves of tense flesh as if they were made just for her to hold on to Jesus when he made love to her. She told him that once, and he surprised her when he smiled and said, "They were."

Esperanza crawled across the bed toward Jesus. She knelt behind him and softly kissed his left shoulder. Jesus just pulled off one boot and set to work on the other. She leaned forward to kiss his right shoulder, knowing that he wanted her despite his nonchalance. Jesus almost always wanted Esperanza, and when he did not, he let her know with a harsh word or a strong shove. Even those rare times, she always succeeded in seducing him, even if inspired by nothing more than the need to soothe her injured pride.

Jesus dropped his other boot and leaned forward, resting his elbows on his knees as if waiting for her to make another move. Esperanza sat back, parted her legs, and straddled his hips. She slipped her arms under his and wrapped them around his waist. She squeezed against him, pressing her face and chest against Jesus's back.

"You don't gotta do this," he said. Jesus remained still, and Esperanza closed her eyes and listened to his heartbeat. "I don't need this kind of thank-you. I said I was gonna do something for you, and I did it. You don't gotta do anything you don't really want to on some kind of thank-you."

"I want this."

"That's not what you told Priscilla at the party."

Esperanza tensed, and she knew Jesus felt it. She should have known that Priscilla would tell him that she said that. She searched for an explanation to offer him, but none sounded genuine. Besides, Jesus knew what Esperanza had said, and still he sweated her. He called her on Valentine's Day, wrote her that love letter, and brought her to California. Was Jesus sincerely hurt by her remark or was he just manipulating her? Probably both.

She sighed and wrapped her arms tighter around his waist. "I was mad at you then. For lots of reasons." Esperanza laid a hand over his crotch and squeezed gently. "And I had a right to be. Admit it. That's why you did all this for me."

He exhaled and placed his hand over hers. "So you still mad at me?" Esperanza hesitated. Jesus removed her hand from his crotch and stood to his feet. He turned around and looked down at her. "You gonna sleep with me now and then dis me when we get back to New York City? Don't play me like that, Espe. Any other nigga out there would just fuck you and act like nothing happened when you got back home, but you know how I feel about you, and I would never do you like that. Do this 'cause you feel the same way about me."

Esperanza did feel that way about Jesus, and that was her problem. She loved him. At least like this. If only he were like this all the time.

Jesus mistook her silence for indifference. "Never mind." He picked up his shirt and started to redress. "I'ma see if they can give me another room for the night."

Esperanza leaped to her feet. "No, don't go."

"I'm not some kid with a crush like Feli, Espe." He buttoned his shirt with a fury. "I'ma grown fuckin' man with a grown man's needs and a grown man's feelings." Before Esperanza could ask Jesus why he mentioned Feli, he said. "And all those needs and feelings I got are for you, so if you think I'ma lie in the same bed with you one more night and . . ." Jesus moved for the door.

Esperanza jumped in front of him. "How am I supposed to believe anything you've been saying to me all these months if you don't stay?" She looked into Jesus's face as his green eyes darted back and forth, searching for something behind her words. How many times had she looked at him the very same way? "You think if I asked Feli to stay, he would leave?"

Jesus laughed. "You a little smart-ass, you know that?"

"You're the one who brought him up, so answer the question."

"You're the one who brought up Priscilla, so answer me this." Jesus lowered his face so that his perfect lips hovered right above hers. "She may be young. She may be inexperienced. She may even be a little desparate. But that little girl loves me. So what do you think she would do if she were here?"

Esperanza's heart quickened. She ran her fingers up Jesus's chest and knotted them behind his neck. "Nothing better than me, *papi,* and you know it."

Jesus pulled Esperanza against him and buried her lips beneath his. She slipped her tongue into his warm mouth as his hands grazed down her back and over her ass, finally nestling in the tender folds at the top of her thighs. With one hand Esperanza ran her fingers through Jesus's hair, while the other wandered down his torso, past the waistband of his baggy jeans, and down into his boxers. He moaned as her hand gripped his hardening cock.

Esperanza tugged at him, and with every pull Jesus tightened his grip on her thighs.

While kissing and stroking him with increasing passion, Esperanza slowly backed Jesus toward the bed. As he lowered himself onto his back, she pulled her hand out of his jeans and knelt between his legs. Jesus folded his hands behind his head and watched as Esperanza unzipped his jeans, pulled out his shaft, and eased her wet mouth down it. As she now stroked him with her tongue, she felt Jesus run his fingers through her hair and heard him call her name.

Then Jesus grasped her by the shoulders and pulled her up on top of him. They kissed deeply as he eased his warm hands under her T-shirt. He unhooked her bra and ran his hands up and down her back, then over her belly, and finally on her hardened nipples. Jesus squeezed them and then grabbed Esperanza's shirt to whip it over her head. He drew her nipple into his mouth and sucked gently, and now she called out his name. And then Jesus stopped.

Esperanza looked down at him and realized that Jesus was staring at her scar. She did not want him to stop. Her other nipple ached for him to curl his tongue around it. She wanted Jesus to push her on her back, pull off her jeans and panties, and sink those perfect lips into her wet pussy. Esperanza needed him to slide himself into her and thrust and thrust until she was clutching at the sheets and yelling every dirty word she knew. But all Jesus could do was stare at her scar.

Jesus sat up and buried his face between Esperanza's breasts. His warm breath on her wet nipple sent a shiver up her spine. Fighting tears of both frustration and rejection, Esperanza looked over his head for her T-shirt. She spotted it on the bed behind him, but just when she reached for it she felt Jesus kissing her breast. He lay back down on the bed, pulling her on top of him. He continued to plant kisses up her breast until he reached the end of her scar. Esperanza braced herself for him to either yank off her clothes, roll over on top of her, and start fucking her or push her off of him in disgust and storm into the bathroom for a cold shower. He had never done either of those things, but he always had ignored her scar. Now Esperanza could not imagine Jesus doing anything else but one of those two things.

And then she felt Jesus's warm tongue gliding up and down her scar. Very slowly he licked his way up and then just as slowly he licked his way back down. It began to tickle, and Esperanza let out a soft giggle. But then the giggle gave way to tears, and in response to her cries, Jesus pressed his lips against her scar and sucked at the raised skin like a cane of sugar. He sat up, and Esperanza wrapped her arms around his head and her legs around his waist. She buried her teary face into his hair, and they rocked back and forth on the bed.

Esperanza knew it was over for her. She had avoided sleeping with him not because she did not want to lead him on. She did not want to sleep with him because she knew he would get under her skin in every way. She would enjoy him as she always had. And now whenever Jesus wanted her, he would not have to show up at her doorstep or blow up her phone. Esperanza would chase him. She would fight Priscilla. She would defy Dulce. Now that Jesus had shown her a tenderness she never knew he possessed, Esperanza would even risk going back to prison to experience whatever more love from him she could get him to spare.

Esperanza pulled herself off Jesus's lap and stood back to undo her jeans. While still sitting on the bed, Jesus worked his own jeans past his hips and down to his ankles. As she lowered her jeans and panties to the floor, stepped out of them, and walked toward Jesus, she admitted to herself that she had not gone to California just to visit her mother or explore where she and Dulce might settle when they moved there. When she straddled Jesus to engulf him with her soaking desire, she knew she went to California to get herself into trouble, and had gone to the Château Marmont to do it.

NINETEEN

R U Still Down?

Esperanza unlocked the door of the apartment. "Dulce, I'm home!" She began to lug her bag across the threshold when a masculine hand reached past her to grasp the handle.

"Déjalo, joven," said Chago. *"Yo la tengo."* He effortlessly picked up Esperanza's bag and started toward the bedroom. She followed him down the hallway with a mixture of happiness and dread.

They walked into the bedroom, where Dulce stood before the mirror reapplying plum lipstick. "Espe!" She ran to her sister and threw her arms around her. "You know as much shit as I give you, I hate it whenever you're gone." Dulce asked Chago in Spanish to wait for her in the living room.

When he left and Dulce closed the door, Esperanza asked, "Are you guys back together?"

"The other day he comes into the supermarket, stops by my register to say hi. I'm like, whatever. And he's hanging around long after he's done with his business with the manager, staring at me. I leave for lunch and he follows me. 'Let me treat you.' 'No.' 'Do you mind if I walk with you?' 'Free country.' Next thing I know he's going on and on about how wrong he was, how sorry he is, how much he misses me. . . ."

"Wow. Outta nowhere. So what'd you say?"

"I tell him, 'That's cool, Chago, but I'm not trying to get back with you.' And you know what, Espe? I meant it. No game. I was real with him in a way I had never been with anyone except fam, and he discarded me *como un trapo. Me dejó como basura en la calle.* I said to him, 'If you had tried to hang with me and later decided that you couldn't deal after all, fine. But you dropped me just like that *sin pensar*.' "

"But you took him back, right?"

Dulce grinned and shrugged. "You were so right, Espe. We were going too fast. So this time I'm going to take it slow, not seeing him every night and practically living at his place. 'Cause he's talking again about moving to California by Christmas, and he wants me to go with him. Says he wants me to work in his business and put me through school. I don't know about all that. . . ."

"Pues ¿nos vamos pa, comer o que?" a hungry Chago called from the living room.

Dulce said, "I said we'll see when the time comes."

At that moment, Esperanza watched Dulce leave her. By the glow in her eyes and the lift in her voice, her sister had already gone with Chago to California. "I didn't get to see that much, but I think you're gonna like it over there."

Dulce stopped and turned. "You gonna go to dinner like that?"

Ordinarily, Esperanza would have jumped to go, but she suddenly felt an overwhelming need to stay home alone. Maybe to learn to get used to it for good. "You go ahead without me. I'm mad tired. You know, jet lag."

"But I want to hear about your trip. I want to hear about Mami. Don't tell me fuckin' Jesus didn't take you to see her."

"No, I saw her, but I'll tell you everything when you get back." She understood Dulce's desire to remain truthful with Chago in every way possible. Until he proved she could trust him with Dulce's heart, however, she preferred that some things remain the private matters of the Cepeda women. "Have fun."

"¡Dulce!"

The Cepeda sisters laughed. Dulce said, "OK, I know this is going to sound corny, but I really missed the way Chago says my name." Then she gave Esperanza a strong hug. As she held her she said, "You know I'm not moving anywhere without you, right?"

Esperanza pulled away. "I want you to do what you have to do to be happy, Dulce. Please don't worry about me. Stay or go, I'll be OK."

Defying Dulce's nagging advice, Esperanza stayed awake past midnight studying the morning of her GED math exam. No matter how often she scored correctly on her practice questions, her confidence never improved because she still continued to miss questions for no other reason than rushing her calculations and making careless mistakes. With the test only hours away and in need of sleep, Esperanza decided to give it one more hour.

Sweaty and agitated, Esperanza raced into the classroom to find the math test under way. She forgot to set her alarm clock before crashing at three A.M. If Dulce had not awoken first, Esperanza might have missed the exam altogether.

The proctor rushed to help her settle. "Three more minutes, and I wouldn't have even let you into the room," he whispered to Esperanza as she took her seat. "Good luck." Then he placed the scratch paper on her desk and went back to his own.

Esperanza nodded her gratitude and set to work. Dulce told her to save herself time by skipping the instructions. "They never change or tell you anything you don't already know," she said while waiting for the dispatcher to confirm the cab she was calling for Esperanza. "And if a question seems hard, skip that shit. Do all the easy ones first. You don't want to miss out on correct answers because you ran out of time. If you have time left, then you go back and figure out the tough ones."

"I know, I know, I know."

Esperanza turned to the first page of her exam booklet. The first five questions she had done well on this part or Hudlin's class.

"Pencils down," said the proctor. Esperanza had three more tough questions left to answer. Her pencil still in the crook of her right hand, she hurried forward through the exam booklet, searching for the question she had skipped. "I said pencils down." She looked up and found the proctor glaring at her as if to say, *Don't take advantage of me.* Esperanza placed her pencil in the groove at the top of her desk and waited for him to collect her answer sheet.

Her head throbbing from so much mental exertion, Esperanza slowly walked out of the school building. As she passed through the gate, she heard a horn honk. Ignoring it, she started down the street toward the bus stop.

Another honk chased after her. "Yo, Espe!" She looked toward the street to see Jesus sidling up to her in his Escalade. "Get in. I'll give you a ride."

Esperanza thought about the long wait for the bus and the bumpy ride home and climbed into the SUV. Jesus leaned over to kiss her on the cheek, then switched the car into drive. "Damn, ma, you look busted."

"That's how I feel," she said. Esperanza pressed her head against the closed window, the coolness from the air-conditioning providing some relief.

"You want me to stop and get you some aspirin?"

"I've got aspirin at home. I just want to go home, take two pills, and go to bed."

"All right." He turned a corner. "How was the test?"

"I don't know. I have no idea. I think when I skipped the tough questions to save them for the end, I might have fucked up my whole alignment and shit."

"Alignment? What kind of fuckin' test was this?"

"Math." She really did not want to explain this to him. For once Esperanza wanted Jesus to ignore her, and he tracked her down craving chitchat. Still, he cared enough to remember the test and offer her a ride home. *Just because you've been fucking up all day, Espe, don't take it out on him.* "Like, let's say I skipped question number two to answer later. But when I figured out the answer to question three, I filled in the circle on the line where I was supposed to put the answer to question two. So all my answers from two on down—even if they're right—are actually wrong 'cause they're off by one line." Esperanza was unsure she actually did this, but oversleeping that morning and running out of time had given her a paranoia that only a long nap could cure.

Jesus smirked at her. "What you skipping questions for?"

"Huh?"

"Point of taking a test is to show you know shit, so why you skipping questions and fucking up your alignment or whatever?"

Something told her to let it go, but Esperanza found his sudden attitude too baffling to resist. "So what was I supposed to do, Sus?"

He looked at her as if she had broken into a foreign language. "Guess, goddammit. This one of those test where you, like, lose points if the answer is wrong?"

"No, but—"

"Fuckin' but nothing, Espe. This a multiple-choice test?"

"For the most part."

"What the fuck you mean, for the most part?"

"The majority of the questions give you five possible answers, but every once in a while you have to calculate the right answer and write it on the answer sheet."

"But for most of the questions you have to pick one answer out of five choices."

"Yeah."

"So you got a one-out-of-five chance of getting the shit right. If you guess wrong, you don't lose shit. You got zero points. Same as you were before you answered the question. But if you answer the question right, bam! You got a point you might not have had otherwise. On a test like that, you don't skip the freakin' question, Espe. You guess the muthafuckin' answer."

Esperanza wished she had let it go. She wished she had taken him up on that stop for aspirin. No, she wished she had never gotten into his fuckin' Escalade. The only thing worse than having Jesus screaming at her at a time like this was realizing that he was right. Not that Dulce was wrong. Esperanza could have combined both her sister's and Jesus's strategies and boosted her score. When she came across a tough question, she could have filled in a random circle on the answer sheet, marked the question in the booklet, and then moved on to the next one. If she had time left when she reached the end, she could have gone back to the questions she marked, tried to figure out the correct answers, and changed the marks on her answer sheet if necessary. This way, when the test ended Esperanza might have had a response for every question and, if nothing else, the reassurance that the answers to the easy questions were on the right lines.

"C'mon, ma, don't get so upset. I don't want you to sweat that fuckin' test for another second," said Jesus. "I know you did good. Better than good. And if by some crazy chance you fucked up, so what? We all do, and it don't mean shit anyway, 'cause I got your back." Jesus reached Third Avenue and turned left.

"Where we going?"

"Back to the crib."

"No, Sus, I want to go home."

"You can rest at my place. I'll get you aspirin, give you a massage, whatever you want."

"Jesus, please. I just want you to take me home so I can sleep in my own bed. I just need to be by myself."

Jesus stopped at a red light. Esperanza prayed that he would hear her pleas. She had no will, let alone energy, to fight him. The light changed, and Jesus made another left. "All right," he said. "I'll take you home."

* * *

Jesus pulled up in front of Esperanza's building. He watched her as she reached into the backseat for her messenger bag. When Esperanza reached for the door handle, he asked, "Do you really want to be alone?"

She stopped and turned to face him. "What do you mean?"

"You said you needed to be by yourself. You wanna be alone forever?"

"No, of course not." *Alone. Forever.* Each of those words by itself caused opposite feelings in Esperanza. She usually hated *alone* and always loved *forever.* Together in any order they terrified her. "When did I say I wanted to be alone forever?"

"Ever since we came back from Cali, I been thinking about all we've been through, you and me. Been thinking about a lot of things. About making some changes. Big changes. But big changes require big moves. If I'm gonna make these changes on accounta you, then you gotta have my back when I make those moves."

"What kind of changes?"

"I'm thinking of getting the fuck out of the Rotten Apple and moving to California, and I want you to come with me. But I can't just up and leave with what I got, Espe. That'd be like heading all the way over there and starting from scratch. So I got to go through with this deal I have planned for October, and I can't swing it without your help, ma. Once we close that deal, we can take our ends and go west. We can start over, but not start from scratch, know what I'm sayin'?"

The pounding in Esperanza's head intensified. She had started from scratch, too, and her life never became easier. The more she learned to want simpler things, the farther simple things drifted from her reach. Like she had busted her ass to prepare for that math exam, only to walk away from it feeling more stupid than ever.

But Esperanza also knew what Jesus meant by *deal.* In his life only certain activities qualified as *moves.* Esperanza understood, because deals and moves had been a large part of her life, too, and she had had her fill of them. Still, making deals and moves promised more than starting from scratch and going legit. Like moving to California. Saying, "Fuck off," to the GED, Mickey D's, and *alone forever*.

Catching herself before she put herself on the line, Esperanza unlocked the car door. "I need time to think about it." She climbed out of the SUV and slammed the door behind her. She jogged toward her building.

Instead of driving off, Jesus lowered the passenger window and called, "How much time, Espe? 'Cause I ain't got a whole lot to give you. I need to call a meeting with the crew ASAP." As Esperanza ran into the building, the last thing she heard him yell was, "Remember I love you."

Dulce went easy on Esperanza for the next few days, allowing her to sleep as much as she wanted, shuffle around the house in a sweat suit, and watch soap operas and talk shows during the day. She even babied her some. Dulce came home from work and cooked dinner and just sat with her, quietly reading to herself as Esperanza stared at the television. Sometimes she tried to get Esperanza to talk more about her visit to Brenda or assured her that she had succeeded on the math GED exam, but Esperanza would give her respectful nods and say nothing.

Esperanza knew the tough love would return soon, and Dulce would pressure her to find work and bring money into the house, especially now that she was attempting to maintain boundaries with Chago. She allowed him to pamper her on occasion with dinner and flowers, but she stopped short of letting him pay her tuition or buy her schoolbooks. Watching her sister as she argued playfully with him over the phone about refusing his money, Esperanza resisted the urge to tell her about Jesus's proposition.

One night Dulce finished reading her book as Esperanza flipped another channel. After putting the book down on the coffee table, Dulce exhaled and stretched as if she had just completed a strenuous workout. Esperanza glanced at the title. *Sister Outsider.* She picked it up and flipped through it. Had not Isoke recommended a chapter in this book in her last letter? "You read this again?"

"Sure, why not? It's dope. I should take it back to the school library though. Why hold on to it when somebody else could use it, you know?"

Esperanza missed Isoke and felt guilty that she had not written her for so long. She had wanted to write when she had something good to say. The woman was doing all day and a night—on the installment plan, no less. What person facing life without parole wanted to get Esperanza's depressing letters about her petty issues in the world? Esperanza had to finish reading the books Isoke had had her take home so she could return them to the prison library for other inmates to read. She would start with *Sister Outsider.*

"Listen, Espe, can I borrow Maite's book again? Chago and I were talking the other night, and he said he wanted to see it." Before Esperanza could protest, Dulce rushed to say, "I know you don't want me to lend it out. I just want to read parts of it to him, like the chapter that convinced me to tell him about my past. I'm gonna have to translate for him here and there."

"It's not that, Dulce. I don't have the book anymore. I gave it to Mami."

"Oh." At first Dulce seemed disappointed. Then she smiled as if it made perfect sense. "I bet she's loving it." Esperanza wondered if Brenda had ever received the book. If Assata and Afeni's biographies were considered contraband in New York State, chances were that Maite's book would be banned by the California Department of Corrections. She hoped that as a self-published book with poems scattered throughout the essays, it had made it past the prison censors and into Brenda's hands.

Esperanza grabbed the cordless telephone from the table. "You know what? I'ma call Maite. Maybe she's got another copy." As she dialed Maite's number, Esperanza felt more hope than she had in weeks.

"Maite Rodriguez."

"Maite, hi. It's Espe Cepeda."

"Espe, my love! How are you?"

"I'm OK."

"Just OK?" Before Esperanza could answer, Maite said, "When am I going to see you again?"

"Whenever."

"So come by my office next week."

"Cool!" They set a time and date, and Esperanza hung up. "I'm going to go see her next week. I'ma ask her for another copy of the book then. You know what? I'ma ask her for a job, too."

"Yeah, the college semester is going to be starting really soon."

"And if Maite can't give me a job, maybe she can at least help me find one."

"Word."

"Dulce?"

"What?"

"You should let Chago put you through school."

"No."

"Yeah! He's a good guy and he loves you. When you gotta good one, you gotta let him feel needed sometimes."

Dulce gave her a wicked smile. "Trust me, Chago feels very needed."

"Too much information!"

"What did I say?"

"Seriously. You want to finish college, and he's willing to pay for it. If you love him and he loves you, so what if you take his money from time to time? You both know you're not with him for it, and you're not wasting it on bling-bling or anything stupid like that. Go to school, get a better apartment, buy a car. . . ."

Dulce grew somber. "I'm not going to ask Chago to do anything for me that I can't do for myself."

"Even if it's mad hard to do on your own?"

"Especially if it's mad hard to do on my own. Espe, if Chago really loves me then he'll let me do my thing for a while. Now, if we get to that point where my thing is his thing, too? That he's just not giving me something now so I feel obligated to eat some bullshit later—like with his ex-wife or his business or whatever—well, then maybe I can accept his help."

Esperanza shook her head. Dulce had lost all sense of game, doing shit the hard way unnecessarily on principle in a world that punked the principled left and right. "I don't see why you can't let Chago pay your tuition. This way if he does turn out to be full of shit, you'll have something to show for it. Once you have your education, he can't take it away from you." Dulce lifted herself off the sofa. "You mad at me now?"

Her sister walked into the hallway and pulled her jacket off the hook. "I'm not mad at you, Espe. I'm scared for you. Just when you were making all this progress, one or two little setbacks, and you're starting to think like a hustler again."

Esperanza expected Dulce to spend the night at Chago's, but she came home in a few hours. She pretended to be asleep to avoid talking to her sister, but that did not stop Dulce from speaking to her. "I never should've let you go to California with Jesus. I did it not so you could see *Mami*. I just knew you would go anyway. If I said no, if I threatened to put you out for it, then you'd go to Jesus anyway. I figured, 'Let her go, hope she has been through enough to finally see him for the manipulative asshole he is, and she'll come home.' And you did come home, but he still got to you."

"He didn't get to me, Dulce. I'm just not that different from him."

"Don't say that. You're very different. You got a lot of good in you, Espe. But it's like you're not even trying to see it."

"How can you say I'm not trying?"

"You're doing it for all the wrong reasons, Espe. Good or bad, you do everything for everyone else. Sometimes doing the right thing for the wrong reasons is just as bad. Like if I don't take Chago's money to go to school so I can earn my own respect, that's good. If I don't take it 'cause I'm scared he may use it against me later, that's bad. That's still game, and I'm playing no one but myself. And I know this is gonna sound weird, but sometimes I wish you'd do the wrong thing for the right reason. I think that's why I didn't get that upset with you when you got fired. Yeah, you did something wrong, but you did it for the right reasons. You did it 'cause there's a lot of good in you, Espe. You just can't or won't see it, so it can only come out in crazy-ass ways. If you're gonna do some crazy-ass shit for the right reason, at least do it for your own sake."

Dulce laughed to herself and rolled onto her side with her back to her sister. Within minutes she fell asleep, but Esperanza lay awake with her words for most of the night. She remembered the story Maite had told her about joining the Young Lords because they stole a medical van to give free TB tests to the people of El Barrio. They had done some crazy-ass shit for the right reason, and in doing it for their neighbors, they did it for themselves.

Isoke insisted she had never shot that undercover cop who had infiltrated her organization to try to get them to do something that would really bring the heat, like bomb a state building or rob an amored car in the name of revolution. Other than that she happened to be in the same building when it happened, no evidence existed to connect her to the fatal shooting. Still, she refused to roll over on her colleagues, and the state hit her with enough charges to keep her in prison for life with one bid after another. When Esperanza compared her situation to Isoke's, the old woman told her not to get it twisted. "You're in here protecting some boys out there victimizing their own people. And no matter how tough you try to present yourself, I hear you in that bunk beneath me, tossing and turning all night. I'm in here protecting those who defended their people. My people. And although I miss my family and friends, I manage to sleep at night." Isoke had told her many stories about the Black Panthers taking over school buildings to teach the students about their history, chaining themselves to the doors of the police precinct when a cop killed someone under suspicious circumstances, and a bunch of other crazy-ass shit for all the right reasons. Things that they never felt they were doing for other people, but things they felt they had to do for themselves because they were the people. *We are one class. One team. One community.*

So Maite had her Young Lords and Isoke her Black Panthers. Martin Luther King, Jr. had his church, and Malcolm X his mosque. They did crazy-ass shit for all the right reasons because they had a people. Hell, even

Jesus—doing crazy-ass shit for the all the wrong reasons to benefit no one but himself—had his crew.

Who did Esperanza have?

The knock on the front door thundered through the apartment. Dulce looked at the alarm clock. "Who the fuck is that at six in the morning?"

"I want to know how they got upstairs."

Dulce crawled out of the bed and pulled on a robe. "Girl, they broke the damned security door again."

Esperanza followed Dulce to the door, her stomach twisting into knots even though she knew it could not be Jesus. He never got up this early. Dulce squinted through the peephole, then gasped. She turned around and mouthed to Espe, *Five-oh*. Immediately Esperanza thought that something terrible must have happened to someone they knew. Or worse—and more likely—someone they knew had done something terrible to someone else.

Dulce unlocked the door and opened it. Still holding his badge in the air, Conrado Puente marched into the apartment. "He's not five-oh," Esperanza said. "This is my parole officer. Officer Puente, what're you doing here so early in the morning?"

Puente stormed into the living room and began to investigate. "I'll ask the questions." He picked up a photograph of Esperanza and Dulce as children. "No, I don't have to ask questions. Why ask questions? You'll just lie to me again." Puente pulled back the lapel of his jacket to reveal his handcuffs.

"Just say what you know already."

"Espe!"

"I know that you lost your job for attacking a customer. I know you haven't been gainfully employed since. And I know you went to Los Angeles with Jesus Lara and not your sister." Puente unlatched the handcuffs from his hip. "All grounds to violate your parole."

Esperanza chucked her pride. "Officer Puente, please don't violate me. It's not like I lied about everything or haven't been doing other things. Good things."

Dulce stepped in front of Esperanza to shield her from him. "She's been studying day and night for her GED exams. She only needs to take one more."

Desperate, Esperanza said, "And I have a new job."

"Where?"

"With a professor at Barnard College."

Puente scoffed. "You work for a Barnard College professor? Barnard College of Columbia University?" He laughed and laughed.

Fuck you, asshole! Esperanza said, "I'm an assistant to Maite Rodriguez. In the political science department."

Puente stopped laughing. He believed her now. "Maite Rodriguez? How did you meet this Maite Rodriguez?"

"She was my language arts teacher at the GED program."

"She's been mentoring her," Dulce said.

Puente said, "Maite Rodriguez is an unapologetic radical who has caused the people of New York State millions in law enforcement costs. She's a convicted felon, and as such associating with her is no different from fraternizing with Jesus Lara. You can never see her again, let alone work for her."

Esperanza felt as if Puente had thrust a knife in her chest. He had just asked her to cut off the only person outside of her family who gave a damn about her. Maite had done more for Esperanza—believed more in her—than this son of a bitch ever had. Meanwhile, this public whose money he felt compelled to mind paid him to do things he never did. Had Puente been on his job, she might not have ever met Maite. But Esperanza refused to be sorry about that.

"But Maite's been mad good to me, Officer Puente. . . ."

"Espe, please don't fight with the man."

"He needs to know, Dulce. Maite got me through that GED program. If not for her, I might've gotten thrown out or quit. She pushed me to do better than just enough to get by. You may not like what she did thirty years ago, Officer Puente, but no way can you put her in the same category as Jesus Lara."

At first it seemed that Esperanza had touched Puente, if only a little, with her defense of Maite, but mentioning Jesus brought him back to task. "Did Maite Rodriguez advise you to accompany Jesus Lara on this trip to California?"

"No, she never did. She never even knew. And I know I was wrong to go with him, but damn, Officer Puente, he gave me the chance to see my mother. Can't you understand that?"

"No, he doesn't, Espe," Dulce said. "To him she's nobody's mother. She's just another convicted felon."

"That's where you're wrong, Miss Cepeda. If I wanted to stop your sister from seeing your mother, all I had to do was make one telephone call and your request to visit would have been denied."

"So why didn't you?"

"You may not believe this, and I actually couldn't care less if you don't, but I've reviewed your mother's case, and I don't believe she belongs in prison. But had I known you were traveling with Jesus Lara, I obviously never would have allowed you to leave the county, let alone the state." For the first time since he had barged into the apartment, Puente broke his intense glare. He walked away from them toward the window. Then he exhaled and said, "Ironic, isn't it? The same man who allowed you to go to prison was the only one who could take you to see your mother, herself in prison for killing an abusive boyfriend. Esperanza, don't you see the irony in that?"

"Look, Officer Puente, Dulce and I, we're planning to move from here, like you've been saying all along. We want to save our money and move to California before the year's out. You have to give me one more chance. Please."

Puente stared at them, searching their demeanor for more lies. Dulce said, "Let's be real with each other. I may not have done any time, but I know you know that I don't exactly have the cleanest past. I also know that you know that I've been on point for the past three years. I have a full-time job, and I take college classes at night. And I certainly don't run with my old crew. I know you know all this, because you never would've allowed Espe to move back in with me if I hadn't changed. So I'm begging you, Officer Puente, to give me another chance to help my sister get on the same track."

"Yes, Miss Cepeda, I do know all these things, and I don't question that your desire to save your sister is sincere. Or that you truly believe you can help her. But I'm going to be as honest with you as you have been with me." Puente continued to speak to Dulce, yet shifted his eyes to Esperanza. "I think Esperanza is a lost cause. She's a smart girl. She's warm. She's loyal. Esperanza's many good things, but she needs to hear that from all the wrong people. I don't mean to be hurtful, but I've supervised hundreds of young women like her. The damage is done and irrevocable. It's only a matter of time before Esperanza tries to make the wrong people happy and winds up back in prison or dead."

Esperanza ran from the room and locked herself into the bathroom. Like Priscilla that night at Jesus's apartment, she fell to the floor and collapsed against the toilet. No matter how many times she had been called a bitch or a trick, it had never wounded her like being called lost or damaged. As she leaned against the cold porcelain, sobbing, Esperanza thought she would die. A gentle knock on the door triggered an explosion. "Fuck you,

you useless piece of shit! Take me back to fuckin' prison! Or just fuckin' shoot me!"

"Espe, it's me. Puente's gone. Unlock the door."

Esperanza climbed back to her feet, dizzy from wailing. She unlocked the door, and Dulce rushed in to hug her tightly. "We convinced him, *negrita.* He's not going to violate your parole. He's gonna give you one more chance."

Esperanza clung to her sister, filled with relief and gratitude. "Thank you, Dulce. Thank you for defending me. Thank you, thank you, thank you." She squeezed and kissed her sister over and over.

Dulce then pulled back from Esperanza. She brushed her hair out of her teary eyes, then said, "But you've got to do three things. One, you've gotta get a legitimate job. And you've got to do it in two weeks."

Esperanza nodded like a recalcitrant child. "OK, OK, OK."

"Two, you gotta stay away from Jesus." Dulce grabbed Esperanza's shoulders and shook her. "Espe, this is serious. You've got to stay away from Jesus or you are going back to prison."

"OK." Esperanza hesitated, because she knew it would be so hard. He was seriously considering quitting the game for her. He needed her to stay on the right path. What could be worse than giving him up now that he finally was becoming everything she wanted him to be?

"Three . . . you can never see Maite again."

Esperanza waited until the last minute to call Maite. It took days to believe, then accept that she would no longer have her in her life. They were scheduled to meet at one that afternoon, and Esperanza called her office on the hour.

"Esperanza! Is everything OK? Are you running late?"

"No, Maite. I can't go. I . . ."

"Honey, what's wrong? Are you in trouble?"

"No. Yeah. Maite, my parole officer says I can't see you anymore." Esperanza heard Maite's breathing grow deeper. "He says if I see you, he'll violate me and send me back to prison."

"On what grounds?"

"Fraternizing with persons known to have a criminal record."

"I see." Maite's sigh sliced Esperanza's heart in two. "I'm going to miss you, Espe. You remind me so much of me when I was your age, and never got the opportunity to explain why that is."

Esperanza caught the sob in her throat. How could Maite see herself in someone like her? Maite went to college. She sacrificed herself for the community. She taught and wrote things that inspired people. Then Esperanza remembered. "Maite, can I ask you for one last favor?"

"Anything, my love."

"When I went to visit my mother, I left your book behind for her to read. Dulce loved it, and I never had a chance to finish it. If you don't have any more, I understand—"

"I'll put another copy in the mail to you today. And please keep and enjoy the others, too."

"Thank you."

"Will you do one last favor for me?"

"Yeah?"

"There's a speech by Audre Lorde in *Sister Outsider* that I want you to read. It's called 'The Transformation of Silence into Language and Action.'" As Maite spoke, Esperanza walked to her night table and found the prison library's copy in her stack of books. "Now, don't be intimidated by the title. It's actually short and accessible and . . . well . . . promise me that you will read it very soon."

"I promise, Maite. I'll read it right away. And I want you to know that . . ." The call-waiting tone interrupted her. "Maite, would you hold on for a sec?"

"Yes, of course."

Esperanza hit the receiver button. "Hello?"

"Espe."

"I'm on another call, Jesus."

"No worries, ma, I'ma make this real quick. I just need to know right now if you're down. 'Cause if you ain't, fine, I'll just put Priscilla on. Espe, you still there?"

"Yeah."

"So you down or what?"

She heard a click. Maite had hung up the telephone. Although Esperanza had no idea why she could no longer wait to wrap up her intruding call, she figured it really did not matter whether Maite took another call, had a student drop by, or just grew tired of waiting for Esperanza to return to their conversation. It just didn't matter.

"I'm down."

TWENTY

Your Silence Will Not Protect You

On her way to Jesus's place, Esperanza walked by her old McDonald's. She peeped into the window and saw Tenille at the register. She yearned to go inside and talk to her, but what if Luciano saw her and decided to call the police? *He'd be doing me a favor*. Esperanza walked a few paces before she heard someone call her name. She turned around to Tenille running toward her.

"Hey."

"Hi."

They stood there in silence, offering awkward smiles when not avoiding each other's gaze. Tenille finally said, "Seen any good movies lately?"

Esperanza smiled. "Yeah, but it's mad old. You probably saw it a long time ago. *Enough* with J. Lo?"

"Oh, yeah! I admit I liked it, even though it was so stupid." Tenille seemed relieved when Esperanza laughed and nodded.

"Some parts were mad unrealistic."

"Like a woman could really take out a dude like that."

Esperanza's laugh faded. Her problem with *Enough*'s realism had nothing to do with Slim defending herself against an abusive man. Her mother did it. Dulce did it. For whatever reasons not all women could or would do it, but the possibility was not as unreal as Tenille insisted. Esperanza's biggest problem with *Enough* was that J. Lo walked. No arrest, no trial, and certainly no prison. That shit was unreal. Women like her mother who defended themselves were called murderers. They got knocked. They did time. And certainly not because they first learned krav maga, broke into his crib wearing steel-toed boots, and beat his ass in the dark. The last thing any of these women did before killing their men was plot.

She started to explain this to Tenille but held her tongue. Although Tenille loved *Girlfight* and *Aliens* and *Terminator 2*, her view of *Enough*—the girl power film she personally could relate to the most—was not much different from that of Jesus and his boys. Esperanza's heart suddenly felt weighted like a hot-air balloon that had just been sandbagged. "Look, T, I'm mad sorry for the way I ODed that day at my place."

"Me, too, girl. I apologize for icing you." They hugged. Tenille fixed her Mickey D's cap and said, "I'd better go back. I snuck out to talk to you. Listen, let's stay in touch. I got your number. You got mine?"

"Yeah. OK."

As she watched Tenille walk back into the restaurant, Esperanza knew that if she never called Tenille, she would never hear from her again. They just were not meant to be. She was headed where she belonged.

When Esperanza arrived at Jesus's apartment, Feli and Xavier were already there playing a game of Monopoly and swigging forties. After opening the door for her, Jesus went back to smoking his blunt while staring out of the window. "We waiting on Chuck," he said. No hello, no kiss or any other kind of greeting. Esperanza sat on the couch and pulled *Sister Outsider* from her bag.

Xavier cackled like a warlock. "Nine fifty, nig-ga!" Esperanza broke from her book to see that Feli had landed on Tennessee Avenue on which Xavier had built a hotel.

Feli groaned as he counted out his payment. "Yo, why don't you give me Vermont and Oriental for Pennsylvania already?" He turned to Jesus and said, "I got Connecticut Avenue, he got North Carolina and Pacific, but muthafucka won't trade me so we can both have complete groups."

"Nigga, I ain't trying to help you stack your paper. Quit moaning and pay your rent, beeyotch!"

Jesus shook his head and laughed. "C'mon, X, why you holding on to them cheap streets?" He took another toke on the blunt, then passed it to Feli.

Esperanza said, " 'Cause he'd rather yoke a brother even if it keeps himself stooped over."

Xavier cut her a menacing glare. "Shut the fuck up, Espe. Ain't nobody ask your 'pinion." He noticed the book in Esperanza's hand. "Bitch think she Oprah now." He pushed back away from the table and stalked toward her. "What the fuck you readin'?"

Esperanza looked to Jesus to check Xavier, but he only laughed and turned back to the window. Xavier lunged for her book, and she yanked it out of reach. "Back the fuck up off me!"

He grabbed Esperanza's wrist, then grabbed the book from her. "Who this butchy-lookin' bitch? You got turned out by some dyke in lockdown, huh?"

"Leave 'er alone, man," said Feli, rising to his feet. "Come back to the game."

"Yo, Jesus, did you know your woman plays for the other team now?" Xavier read the back cover. "Women's studies? Oh, yeah, I bet you be studying women now. That's why her and Priscilla all buddy-buddy alla sudden." Esperanza leaped for her book, but Xavier pulled it out of her reach. "Sus, you one lucky nigga."

Then Jesus jumped off the windowsill. "Chuck's here." On his way to the front door, he bounded between them, snatching the book from Xavier and flinging it onto the couch. "Espe, just put that shit away." Esperanza picked up the book, hugged it to her chest, and flopped down on the sofa.

When Jesus opened the door, Chuck bopped in carrying a large grocery bag. Jesus gave him a brotherly hug and a pound. "Espe, get Chuck a forty."

"What?"

With an authoritative jab, Jesus pointed toward the kitchen. Still holding *Sister Outsider*, Esperanza obeyed. When she returned with the malt liquor, Chuck had joined Feli and Xavier at the table. She handed him the forty and waited for thanks that never came. "Espe, sit down," said Jesus as he stood at the table holding the grocery bag in the crook of his arm. "We're gonna get started."

Esperanza took a seat next to Feli and watched Jesus as he placed the grocery bag right on top of the Monopoly board. He pulled out a half gallon of soda, then a large bag of potato chips. Then Jesus grabbed the bag by the bottom and flipped it upside down. Bundles of fifty- and one-hundred dollar bills rained on the game board, and the guys swooped down on it like pigeons to bread crumbs.

"Just like the real thing, ain't it?" Jesus said.

"All this shit's fake?" asked Xavier.

"Counterfeit," said Chuck. "Every last bill."

Jesus finally sat down, leaning into the center of the table as if there were others in the room he did not want to overhear him. "No-No's asking five hundred grand for five kilos, but that nigga's only gettin' three." Xavier clapped his hands in approval. "We transport the product to my connection in Cali, and make ourselves a nice profit."

"We tryin' to gank No-No Knowles for two hundred Gs?" asked Feli.

Xavier yelled, "That's what's up!"

"Now check it," said Jesus. "No-No's got the worst mix of traits a cat in this business can have. He's smart and he's shady. So Chuck, you check the quality of the product, 'cause I ain't trying to get burned. No perp, no slack . . ."

"I never heard that No-No Knowles was a beat artist, man," said Feli. "I don't know about this."

Xavier growled with impatience. "Dead him, Sus. Muthafucka always whining and doubting and reneging and shit. I'm telling you, heart attack, my ass!"

"Yo, X, you do not want to be talkin' about my grandmother."

"Why don't you just admit it, Feli? At the last minute you bitched out. Ain't nothing happen to that holy-rollin' ho."

Feli got to his feet. "Disrespect my grandmother again."

Xavier howled as if impressed with Feli's heart. "It's like that, juggler?" Then he stood up.

"Step up, bitch."

It surprised Esperanza to see Feli so hostile. Esperanza had always wondered what Xavier would have to say to push Feli to his limit, and now she knew. But Xavier was not one to fuck with, so she tugged at Feli's cuff. "Let it go, pa."

Jesus jumped to his feet and planted a firm hand on both men. "Feli, sit yo' ass down. X, shut the fuck up. We need to ride together on this shit. No dissent, no doubt, no ego, no nothing." Xavier began to protest when Jesus said, "I. Said. Shut. Up." He turned to Feli. "While Chuck and I execute the hand-to-hand, I need you to have our back inside." Jesus gave Feli a reassuring slap on the back of his shoulder.

"Inside," Feli sighed, and Esperanza knew that he felt he owed it the crew to step up his role, given what had happened last time. "I got your back inside."

Xavier applauded. "That's what I'm talking about, kid. That's why you the devout Christian." He extended his fist toward Feli, who smiled and gave him a pound. Then he looked at Jesus. "And I got your back outside."

"No doubt." Then Jesus and Xavier exchanged pounds. "This time I want you driving, too."

"Holla, nigga."

When Jesus decided to try his hand at playing stickup kid, he had asked Esperanza to drive, against Xavier's advice. He supplied her with a gat and a walkie and told her all she had to do was rent the SUV and wait for them up the block. When the heat arrived, the guys scattered on foot, and no one attempted to contact Esperanza. With no help from any of them, Dulce bailed her out, and Jesus arrived at the apartment to convince her that their splitting up had been in her best interest. "All they have on you is the gun," he kept repeating. "Had we rolled with you, you might have been hit with everything. But all they have on you is the gun." And since they had minimized her culpability, Esperanza owed it to the crew not to roll over on any of them to save herself.

Jesus said, "Espe, you're more important than ever, ma. You'll be with Chuck, Feli, and me inside. If No-No gets too close to the money, I need you to distract him."

"Distract him?"

"Yeah, chickenhead," said Xavier. "Ho down."

"I thought I told you to shut up," said Jesus. "I don't be laying up with chickenheads, so you need to dead that shit before you piss me the fuck off."

Chuck finally spoke up. "Look, Sus, I know y'all on some Bonnie and Clyde type shit, but I really think Espe needs to sit this muthafucka out."

"Fuck you, I'm in this shit."

"Boo, calm down."

"Y'all muthafuckas owe me big-time."

"Espe, chill!"

"And I want to be strapped."

Chuck and Xavier groaned. "Why can't we do this without her, Jesus?" said Chuck.

"I say strap her, and let's keep it movin'," said Feli. "You said it yourself, Jesus. We need to ride together. No half-steppin' on anyone's part." Esperanza sent him an appreciative glance, but he avoided her gaze.

The guys argued over one another until Jesus raised his hands to quiet them down. He reached across the table and took Esperanza's hand. "I appreciate you wanting to have my back, ma, but if you get busted on another gun charge . . . Sorry, boo, I can't risk it."

Esperanza fought the urge to fall for the genuine concern on his face. She might have returned to the game for this last time, but she did not come back unchanged. "I'm strapped or I'm out."

Jesus grinned at her but only said, "We'll see." He pulled back and assumed his authoritative position. "So here's how it's gonna go down next Saturday."

Jesus lay on his stomach with his arm across Esperanza's torso. He reached up and began to stroke a tail of her hair that hung below her shoulders. "Why you so serious all of a sudden?" She stiffened. "Tell me. I'm not gonna get mad. Promise."

"I've got a test on Saturday morning. The last of my GED exams. The reading test." The one subject Esperanza never doubted she would ace.

"Oh." Jesus pulled himself up and reached for his cigarettes and lighter on the night table. "You know, it's good you're going to school. I'ma be real with you, Espe. He's my man and all, but Chucky's dumb. Xavier . . . I don't trust. Feli I can't trust 'cause he's dumb." He laughed as he pulled out a cigarette and lit it.

"You sayin' I should sit out this, too."

Jesus dragged on his cigarette. "Nah, I'm sayin' the exact opposite."

"Oh."

"We gonna put that money to good use, ma. When we get to Cali, I'ma start fresh. You noticed I ain't mention shit about moving to Cali during the meeting, right?"

She had not. "Yeah."

"That's 'cause none of 'em niggas is coming with us. Well, I haven't really decided about Chuck. I go back and forth on him. Like I said, what he lacks in smarts he's got in loyalty. And he got a family. But Xavier's a fuckin' liability through and through. And Feli? It'd be kinda cruel to bring him along with us, knowing how he be crushin' on you and whatnot. Anyway that's one kid that should be going to college, helping his grandma singing in the choir and all that shit. This ain't for him."

But it's for me. "By starting fresh you do mean quitting the game?"

Jesus hissed, releasing a stream of cigarette smoke between his lips. "That would be sweet." He tapped some ashes into the ashtray on the nightstand and put the cigarette back into his mouth. Then Jesus lowered himself under the sheets and propped his hands between his head and the pillow. "I know this whole GED thing means a lot to you, ma. I can push back the meeting with No-No on Saturday so you can take your test. How 'bout that?"

"OK." Esperanza chastised herself for entertaining the idea that everything—the plan to scam No-No, the move to California, and even the sudden support of her education—meant anything to Jesus outside the game. "Can I ask you something, Sus?"

"What?"

"What if No-No gets too close to the money?" She rolled over on her side to face him. "What if I can't distract him as you say?"

Jesus reached down to pull the cigarette out of his mouth. He gave her a crooked smile and said, "Ma, there's no such thing. And never mind the money. If he gets too close to you, I'ma have to buck him."

Once that kind of talk would have made Esperanza's heart pound and her thighs wet. Before Bedford Hills, she would have smothered Jesus with pledges of her undying love and offerings of boundless sex. While a small part of Esperanza needed to believe his words were true, it no longer was enough for her to encourage him to take as much possession of her as possible.

"Ma, can I ask you something now?"

"Sure." *Please ask me if I would still love you if you quit the game. Ask me to forgive you for all that you did and did not do to make me feel loved. Ask me if I really want to do this.* Esperanza crawled out of the bed and wrapped his shirt around her naked body like a robe.

"How come you never wear that little "two" pendant I got you when you came home? Don't you like it? I told you what it means, right?"

"Yeah, I know what it means. It's just that it bothers me to wear it. It aggravates my scar."

"You know what we're gonna do when we get to Cali? We gonna see a doctor about fixing that thing. You know LA's full of plastic surgeons, so somebody's gotta be able to take care of that for you."

Jesus flashed her a grin, and Esperanza forced herself to smile back at him. She walked out of the bedroom door and into the bathroom. When she looked in the mirror, Esperanza grimaced at the streaks of mascara in the beds of her eyes. She opened the medicine cabinet for something gentle to wash her face with, only to find a hodgepodge of metrosexual nonsense. She finally settled on the glycerin soap sitting at the edge of the sink. She patted her face dry and then reached for the cocoa butter. She dipped in two fingers and scooped out a healthy amount. Holding open Jesus's shirt by the lapel, Esperanza applied the butter all along her scar with the other. As she rubbed it into her raised skin, she remembered how she had done this every morning and night for months after Dr. Neal removed the stitches. Those first few days after the incident, she would rub and cry, knowing that it had little impact on reducing the long scar she would carry and conceal for the rest of her life.

Esperanza returned to the bedroom and found Jesus asleep with his cigarette butt still burning between his fingers. She reached over and slowly took the stub from his hand. After she snuffed the cigarette in the ashtray on the night table, she pulled the quilt over Jesus and left the bedroom.

Relieved to have a moment alone, Esperanza nestled into the sofa and picked up *Sister Outsider.* She flipped directly to the speech Maite had recommended and began to read. Audre's early identification as a "Black lesbian poet" first took Esperanza aback. Xavier had been right about this woman! Why did Maite ask her to read this? She had said that Audre Lorde inspired her own poetry, so was Maite a lesbian, too? Did she think Esperanza might be one? Esperanza put the down the book as if it were contaminated. She remembered her final conversation with Maite, and how painful it was to be forced to let her go. She remembered her promise to Maite and decided it didn't matter. Maite had been good to her. This Audre Lorde had inspired Maite—and Isoke, too, who had a husband and two grown sons on the outside—to become a woman who, in their brief time together, had become someone Esperanza quickly came to love and respect. Who showed Esperanza love and respect. So Black, lesbian, poet, whatever, this Audre had things to say that Esperanza had to know. With a new resolve, she picked up *Sister Outsider* again.

Soon after she identified herself as a Black lesbian poet, Audre revealed that only two months earlier she had been diagnosed with a tumor in her breast that was likely to be cancerous. Esperanza's pace quickened as Audre described the agony of the three weeks between her diagnosis and surgery, and she sighed with relief to learn that the tumor actually was benign. But Audre relayed all this in one swift paragraph, for the true focus of her essay proved to be the critical realization she made in that three-week period of excruciating uncertainty.

> *In becoming forcibly and essentially aware of mortality, and of what I wished and wanted for my life, however short it might be, priorities and omissions became strongly etched in a merciless light, and what I most regretted were my silences. Of what had I ever been afraid? To question or to speak as I believed could have meant*

> *pain, or death. But we all hurt in so many different ways, all the time, and pain will either change or end. Death, on the other hand, is the final silence. And that might be coming quickly, now, without regard for whether I have ever spoken what needed to be said, or had only betrayed myself into small silences, while I had planned someday to speak, or waited for someone else's words. And I began to recognize a source of power within myself that comes from the knowledge that while it is most desirable to not be afraid, learning to put fear into a perspective gave me great strength. I was going to die, if not sooner than later, whether or not I have ever spoken myself. My silences had not protected me. Your silence will not protect you.*

Esperanza put down the book. She took several deep breaths and forced herself to finish the essay. Although her eyes itched from reading in the dim light and her chest still ached from the power of Audre's truth, Esperanza had to reread the message she knew Audre—and Maite, Isoke, Brenda, Dulce, and even Tenille, in her own way—needed her to understand.

My silences had not protected me. Your silence will not protect you.

Esperanza hugged the book against her greasy bosom, curled up on the sofa like a baby, and cried herself to sleep.

TWENTY-ONE

Battle Cry

At three A.M. the morning of her last GED exam, Esperanza paced in her living room. Dulce had gone dancing with Chago the previous night and called at about ten. "We're gonna be out until after two, and I don't want to wake you up. I know you got your last test tomorrow," she said. "So I'm just going to stay with Chago tonight."

"OK."

"You sure?"

"Yeah."

"You sound nervous."

"I am. A little."

"Espe, you're gonna rock that test, I just know it. And don't make any plans for tonight. I'm gonna come straight home from work and make you a special dinner to celebrate. Just you and me."

"Cool."

"Oh, I almost forgot. There's a package for you on the table. I think it's Maite's book, 'cause the return address is Barnard College."

"OK."

"And Espe?"

"Yeah?"

"I'm mad proud of you, *negrita*. And there's nobody in this whole world that I love more than you. Believe that, 'cause it's true."

"I love you, too, Dulce."

"Now get your ass to bed!"

Dulce told her that anytime Esperanza needed her to come home, all she had to do was ask. But what would her sister say when she told her that not only had she hooked up with Jesus, she had also gotten herself involved in one more hustle? Not a hustle to end all hustles, but one to sink Esperanza deeper into the game. How much pride or love would Dulce have for her then? After all Dulce had done for her, the last thing Esperanza wanted to do was place her sister in jeopardy. The less Dulce knew, the safer she would be.

Esperanza found Maite's package on the kitchen table and took it into the bedroom. As wired as she was, she had no energy to read from her book, but Esperanza hoped to find a letter with some encouraging words. When she tore open the envelope she found not only another copy of *The Revolutionary Spirit: An Owner's Manual for the Warrior Womyn*, but also an audiotape. She thumbed through the monograph and scoured the envelope for a letter but found none. Hoping that Maite had recorded a message for her, Esperanza carried the tape to her stereo, slipped in the cassette, and pressed Play. Her heart inflated like a balloon when she heard the conga drums.

Raise your eyes, hermana . . .
For he cannot break you,
Pull up from the fall
You are your own strength
Heed your sister's call . . .
Stand to your full length.

For he is no warrior,
    For he is no king,
You gave him his power,
    Now take it back from him.

Stand tall, hermana . . .
For he is beneath you . . .
Your love is your own . . .
    Your passion from you,
A fight within, no man can undo . . .
Respect your fire and your glory you'll meet
Stand tall, hermana . . . stand on your feet.

For he is no warrior,
    For he is no king,

You gave him his power,
Now take it back from him.

Break free, hermana . . .
For you are not his . . .
Break free from the chains . . .
Resolve all your pains . . .
He cannot break you . . . He can never control . . .
You are your reasons, you own your own soul.

And he is no warrior,
And he is no king,
You gave him his power,
Now take it back from him.

To fight is to love, and to love is to fight,
Love is not blind, for your fury has sight . . .
The struggle is yours, the revolution as planned . . .
The promise of tomorrow is in your hand.

For you are a warrior,
For you are a queen . . .
You own your own destiny,
You own your own dream.

Raise your fist, hermana . . .
For the war not yet begun . . .
Though we have shed blood,
Our battle's not won . . .
But stand with the faithful
And stand with the proud
Scream out to the heavens,
Scream it out loud . . .

I am a warrior,
I am a queen,
I own my own destiny,
I own my own dream.

Esperanza rewound the tape and looked at her reflection in the mirror. " 'I am a warrior, I am a queen. I own my own destiny. I own my own dream.' " She took a step back and her eyes traveled upward. Tupac looked down at her through his wire-rimmed glasses. Thug life. Was that a look of betrayal? Concern? Understanding? Esperanza stopped the tape and walked over to her night table. She sat on the bed, pulled open the bottom drawer, and pulled out *The Killing of Tupac Shakur.* She cracked the book open to its center, to the promised photo evidence.

Tupac lay across a gurney, his head fallen to the side. Wide gashes by the coroner's scalpel cut across his collarbones toward his heart, almost like misplaced wings. Another deep gash ran from behind Tupac's ear to the back of his head. Although the photo had been printed in black and white, it left no doubt as to which areas once pumped bright pink with life, yet now sat brown and gray with murder.

Esperanza dropped the book and sobbed uncontrollably. At one time in Tupac's life, the criminals were the only ones who cared for him, so even when he escaped the poverty he loathed, he tried to speak for them. Tupac represented thug life, but he did not survive it. It seemed like he never believed he could. So many women had suffered more, contributed more, and even transgressed more than she, and still they found a way to believe that they could transcend their circumstances, including their own contradictions. Could she? Esperanza mourned Tupac and feared for herself.

She could bow out of this deal. She could come up with a story. Or maybe she could run. Esperanza could figure out the details after her exam, but for now she knew what she had to do, and that was what Feli had done. Just not show.

With that decision, sleep overcame her. She set her alarm clock for seven A.M. and crawled into bed. Within seconds she fell into a deep sleep with a smile on her face.

A hard rap at the door awoke her the next day. Esperanza moaned, rolled over, and looked at the alarm clock. Six thirty-eight. She hoped that Dulce had decided to come home and had forgotten her key at Chago's. And the housing authority needed to fix the fuckin' intercom.

When Esperanza opened the door, Jesus bounded inside holding a McDonald's bag. " 'Sus, what are you doing here so fuckin' early in the morning?"

"Good fuckin' morning to you, too." He walked into the kitchen and placed the bag on the table. "I came to bring you breakfast and take you to your exam." Jesus opened his arms. "Can I get some love for that?"

Esperanza stared at him. "Oh." She took a few unsure paces toward him, and Jesus swooped in to swallow her with his arms and kiss her on the head. Then he pulled back and leaned forward to kiss her on the lips, but Esperanza drew away from him. "You don't want to kiss me like that. I just woke up."

Jesus stepped back as if she were diseased. "Oh, damn. Well, go wash up, get dressed, eat your breakfast first."

"Sus, this is mad sweet of you, but you don't have to do all this."

"Don't sweat it, boo. I'll drive you to your test, wait for you outside, and then we'll roll from there."

"Wait for me outside? Sus, the test is over an hour long."

"I can wait an hour."

"You don't have to do that. Just drop me off and come back for me when it's over. I'll call . . ."

"No. I'll wait." Jesus's eyes bore into her face. "Now eat your breakfast and go get ready."

Esperanza stepped around him to walk into the kitchen. "OK." She sat down and stared at the greasy McDonald's breakfast while Jesus watched. Of all things to bring her to eat. He was clowning her. This wasn't love, just another one of his sorry jokes, like that "All About U" "serenade" at her so-called welcome-home party. "You want some of this?"

Jesus laughed. "If you cooked me some eggs or something, I might be able to get it down."

Esperanza sipped her coffee, washing away the nasty things she really wanted to say but could not afford to. "Can't. No time. Should've woken me up sooner." She offered Jesus her hash browns, but he refused it. "Thanks for working it out so that I could take my test this morning."

"No doubt."

" 'Cause I want to go all the way with my education. I want to at least go to college. I'm thinking of becoming a teacher."

"Gotta be plenty of colleges in Cali. When we get there, you can do your thing. I ain't got no problem with that."

"Then why do you have a problem with me packing today?"

"Ma, I already explained to you why that is."

"Yeah, but—"

"I don't want to hear it, Espe. This whole thing is gonna go down like a tired baby to sleep 'cause I planned this shit to the last detail. Ain't gonna be like last time, 'cause I accounted for everything."

"You said that you didn't want me strapped 'cause you didn't want to risk my getting caught out there on another gun charge. . . ."

"And I meant that. Why you questioning—"

". . . but if you got this shit planned to a T then there's really no reason why I shouldn't be strapped. I mean, if you—"

"Espe!" Jesus clamped his hand down on her wrist and began to squeeze. "Don't. Test. Me."

"You're hurting me."

Jesus let go. "I'm sorry, ma. But you're stressin' me, and I don't fuckin' need this right now. Not today."

"Well, I'm stressed, too. About this, my test, everything."

"If there's one person in this whole thing that ain't gotta stress, it's you," he said. Now he stroked the same hand that seconds before he had almost crushed. "I got your back."

Jesus silently watched Esperanza finish her breakfast. Then she stood up and said, "I'ma go shower."

"A'ight."

After she showered, she went into the bedroom to dress. Esperanza scoured her drawers until she found a catsuit she had not worn in years. As she expected, it fit tighter than ever, thanks to both Bedford Hills and Mickey D's. Still, Esperanza decided that if she could get into it she should wear it. Nothing else she owned seemed right for the task at hand. She completed the outfit with a pair of stiletto boots.

Then Esperanza applied a full face of makeup. Concealer under the eyes, more than she usually needed. Foundation and then powder. Then she gave her eyes the works—eyeliner and mascara and even false lashes and eye shadow, which Esperanza ordinarily saved for special nights on the town. She outlined her lips with pencil and then filled them in with a shiny reddish gloss. Esperanza streaked blush across her cheeks, then turned to her hair.

Although she had not adopted Dulce's wash-and-go look, Esperanza had bothered little with her hair lately. After showering she would at least pull it into a ponytail or braid so as to flatten her natural curl into sedate waves. Now she dug up her flatiron and slid it through sections of her hair to complete her look.

As Esperanza stiffened her hair with a pungent spray, she studied her face in the mirror. Not so long ago she had enjoyed the time it took to look this way. She thought of it as pampering herself. Without conducting this ritual each and every day, Esperanza could not feel beautiful. Now she looked at herself and felt like a clown. This mask made her ugly, hiding who she really was beneath inches of drugstore cosmetics. This concocted face, repressed hair, and desperate outfit all belonged to the girl she used to be. Not the woman that Maite and Isoke and her own sister believed she could be, and whom Esperanza herself wanted to be even when she doubted she could ever exist. But this was who Jesus wanted and who she had to let him believe she still was. If he could love anyone, this was she.

Then it became clear to her. He knew. The realization pumped anger through Esperanza's veins. Jesus knew that she might bail, and he would not allow it. He knew she did not want to go, and he could not have cared less. Jesus wanted her in on this hustle, and he would do whatever was necessary to make her behavior conform to his will. If at this very moment, Esperanza admitted to him that she wanted out, she would never make it to that test center.

Worst of all, Jesus wanted love for this selfish concession. Supposedly, he hooked everything up for Esperanza's sake, but what was best for her had not a damned thing to do with it. It was never about her, and it would never be. It was all about him, always was and always would be. Jesus had the nerve to play it off like love for Esperanza motivated his decisions and actions, and he expected love from her in return. Genuine love for his pretend love. Love and abuse cannot coexist.

She had none of that for him. All Esperanza felt toward Jesus was rage. And then she remembered the gun.

Grabbing her books, including Maite's monograph, Esperanza carefully opened the bedroom door and listened for him. He had gone into the living room and turned on the television. She stole into the kitchen and eased open every cabinet drawer until she found Dulce's Beretta. Esperanza tiptoed to her messenger bag sitting on the table and dropped it in. She packed her books.

Then she went to the hall closet for a jacket and found the leather jacket she had taken from Jesus's party. A jacket she never should have owned, taken from a place she should have never gone. Esperanza pulled it off the rack with the intention of giving it to Jesus to return to its rightful owner. She gave it a once over, hoping that she had not worn it out. When Esperanza discovered the pockets inside the lapels, she knew she had to wear the jacket one last time.

"Sus, I'm ready." As she walked into the living room to get him, her heart pounded against her chest. She did not know if and when she might need that gun. But Esperanza would be damned if Jesus insisted she be part of this hustle without some form of protection besides relying on him.

Only when Jesus pulled up his Escalade in front of the test center did Esperanza remember the metal detectors. No way could she take the gun into the school building. But did she dare leave her bag with Jesus? He just might search through her things.

"You ready, boo?"

"Yeah, I just want to review one last thing." Knowing that Jesus's eyes were fixed on her, she made a show of removing things from her bag one by one and placing them on her lap. A case of pencils. The workbook. A practice exam booklet. Saving Maite's book for last, Esperanza emptied her bag on her lap except for the gun. "Here it is." For good measure, she randomly opened the book and read a passage under a chapter Maite had titled "Love":

> *First and foremost, the warrior womyn loves herself. She knows that she cannot love anyone—not her family, her sister, her partner—if she does not first love herself. She loves and feeds her mind even as she accepts its limitations. She loves and defends her body even as she embraces its imperfections. She loves and demands her freedom even as she faces the barriers in front of her. Because our society does everything to make a womyn loathe herself, to love herself is perhaps the most revolutionary thing she can do.*

"If you're not ready for the test, maybe you should just skip it," Jesus said.

"No. I'm ready. I'm so fuckin' ready." Esperanza looked at Jesus and gave him a smile. "OK if I just take what I need and leave my bag with you?"

"No doubt, ma." He flashed her a smile, happy to have her trust. "Whatever you need."

Then Esperanza offered him Maite's book. "In case you want something to read while I'm taking my test."

Jesus took it from her. "Thanks. And good luck. Even though I know you don't need it." He leaned over and kissed her on the cheek.

Esperanza tossed her things back in her bag and placed it in the backseat. As she climbed out of the Escalade and walked toward the building, she knew that Jesus would not look through her bag and that she would ace her exam. Esperanza glanced over her shoulder in time to catch Jesus flipping through Maite's book and then tossing it into the backseat.

TWENTY-TWO

Some of Us Did Not Die

Esperanza skipped out of her exam. Never had she enjoyed taking a test! She loved reading the different passages of poetry and prose, and welcomed the challenge of having to prove her comprehension. Not even the lingering awareness that Jesus sat outside in his Escalade could undermine her focus. She bounded out of the high school building toward the SUV.

Jesus caught the big grin on her face. "Guess you did good, huh?"

Esperanza buckled her seat belt. "I rocked that shit." Although she loathed her itinerary for the rest of the day, she felt ready to deal with it. She would do what she had to do and be done with it. Meet with No-No and execute the transaction. Celebrate with the crew and make like a devout Christian. Play lovey-dovey to Jesus and get her money. Then Esperanza and Dulce would make moves of their own—tying up loose ends while lying low. They would leave for the West Coast as soon as possible. Hell, Chago would have to catch up to them.

"What's so funny?"

Esperanza did not realize that she had laughed out loud. "Just something on the test. They tried to snag me with a trick question, but I saw right through that bad boy." Even if she had had no hidden agenda, Esperanza had nothing more to say to Jesus. How did you explain to someone like him what hope felt like?

As Jesus turned the corner of his block on the Concourse, Esperanza spotted each of them one by one in front of his building. Chuck. Xavier. Feli. And then Priscilla. Wearing a skintight dress with no sleeves and high-heeled slingbacks, she wrapped her arms around her skinny torso and shivered in the October breeze. No way Priscilla insisted on being a part of this shit. Not this time. Not in her condition. When the Escalade drew closer, Priscilla's bloodshot eyes and frightened pout confirmed it.

"Sus, what the fuck is Priscilla doing here?"

"Espe, don't start."

"I told you I got this."

"I'm not dealing with this woman-scorned shit right now."

"What's she gonna do that I can't?"

"Think No-No ain't gonna roll deep? I know he's gonna have muthafuckas on the street outside the bar. While you're inside with me, she's gonna be outside."

"Is she strapped?"

"Yo, Espe, kill the bullshit jealousy." He sidled up to double-park, and the crew started toward the Escalade. "Y'all start jawin' at each other today, I swear on my mother, I'ma slap the shit outta both of you. Stay here." Jesus jumped out of the Escalade to say a few words to Chuck, and Esperanza took the opportunity to smuggle her gun out of her messenger bag and under the inside lapel of her leather jacket. She left the jacket unzipped to avoid suspicion and create easy access.

Everyone piled into the backseat of the SUV. Immediately Xavier said, "Espe, move the fuckin' seat up. I ain't got no room for my legs and shit."

"Well, I need legroom, too, so maybe Priscilla should sit up here."

"No, I should fuckin' sit up front."

She ignored him and caught Priscilla's eye. "Prissy, you wanna sit up front?"

"Yeah, X, let her sit up front," said Jesus. "Stop acting like a fuckin' little kid."

Xavier muttered as he climbed out of the Escalade. Priscilla stepped down after him, and Esperanza hopped out of the passenger seat. She hoped that Xavier would jump back into the car so she could have those critical seconds alone with Priscilla on the street, but instead he stood waiting for Esperanza to get into the backseat. "How you doin'?" she said to Priscilla. She ran her hand down the front of her catsuit as if to smooth out wrinkles and stopped with her hand over her belly. "What's new with you?"

Priscilla shook her head, then wrapped her arms around her waist. "Nothing."

Shit. Esperanza climbed into the backseat. Clueless, Xavier followed her. "Priscilla, move up the fuckin' seat." Esperanza looked forward and saw Jesus watching her in the rearview mirror. He winked at her, grateful that she had been so nice to the little girl who loved him. *Shit, shit, shit!*

Within forty minutes Jesus had driven them into Williamsburg. The Escalade crawled along the Brooklyn waterfront as he searched for the meeting place. He spotted a shabby bar beneath a huge banner that read UNDER RENOVATION—GRAND REOPENING HALLOWEEN NIGHT. "That's it," he said, and pulled the Escalade toward the curb.

Feli examined the raggedy establishment. "Halloween's right around the corner, and that place got a long way to go."

Jesus shrugged. "You know what time it is." Then up the block he spotted a Lexus right across the street from the bar and pounded his hand against the steering wheel. "What I tell y'all! How much you wanna bet those are No-No's niggas?" He hit a button that unlocked all the doors. "Let Priscilla out first."

Esperanza recognized the way Priscilla looked at him, her eyes pleading with him not to make her do this. In the beginning Esperanza had looked at Jesus the very same way at times, and quickly learned that she could not pick and choose when and how she wanted to be down. When she accepted this, Esperanza had turned her initial reluctance into unbridled enthusiasm until it led to the inevitable.

"Go," Jesus ordered Priscilla. "Everybody else wait right here until I say." Priscilla dropped out of the Escalade and walked up the street, trying to steady herself in her stilettos and fumbling through her purse until she found a cigarette and a lighter. Esperanza shook her head. Girl was still pregnant *and* smoking.

Priscilla hiked herself onto the hood of car parked in front of the bar and crossed her legs. Just as Jesus had hoped, No-No's men noticed her. One even hollered at Priscilla, asking her if he could bum a cigarette. She sauntered over to their car with a smirk on her face and a roll to her hips, playing disinterested yet attainable to the hilt. Esperanza could not have done better herself. Priscilla had to get out of this shit before she became too good at it and believed she could do nothing else.

"A'ight, Chuck, grab the shit. You walk ahead of me and Espe; Feli, you behind us. X, wait until we're inside. Give us about five minutes and then drive up and park in front of the bar."

While Xavier climbed over the front seat and plopped down into the passenger seat, Chuck reached behind him for a duffel bag, slung it over his shoulder, and bounced out of the Escalade. He bopped a few paces, and then Jesus and Esperanza climbed out, too. Esperanza instinctively waited for Jesus, and when he reached her he threw his arm around her and they walked toward the bar like a couple taking a romantic stroll along the waterfront on a crisp fall day. Jesus leaned over to whisper in her ear, "Next time we gonna be walking like this down Sunset Boulevard." Then he took her hand and started to walk a few paces ahead of her, eager to get to the transaction. Esperanza heard a door slam behind them and knew Feli had taken up the rear.

They walked inside the bar and found a mess. Sawdust and tarp covered everything, which was not much. Besides the dusty mirrors, a few outdated stools, and half-empty bottles, the bar was bare. The place had too little furniture for legitimate business, with secondhand tables overturned and a few chairs that looked half-eaten by termites. They headed toward the back, where they saw two of No-No's men standing guard, guns visible on their belts.

Esperanza swallowed a gasp when she saw Chuck step right up to one of No-No's men, place the duffel bag on the floor, and submit himself to a pat-down. Jesus lined up behind him and raised his arms, too. Were none of these muthafuckas strapped? If No-No got stupid, who would have their backs? Xavier? Priscilla?

Eager to put his hands on her, the second of No-No's men approached her. Esperanza grabbed the lapels of her jacket and spread them like wings, careful praying he would not notice the bulk of the Beretta. She jutted her hip, batted her eyes, and said, "Now, *papi,* where am I going to hide a piece in an outfit like this?"

No-No's goon licked his lips as he eyed her catsuit. "I can think of one place."

"And you ain't going near it," said Jesus.

"Jesus, come on in," a raspy voice called from the back room. "We're all friends here."

Jesus grabbed Esperanza's hand and yanked her into the room with him. At a faded poker table, No-No Knowles sat with another henchman at his right hand. Even though she had heard rumors to the contrary, Esperanza had still expected a ghetto gangster out of a B movie—a pimp in a loud suit with a jacket that swept the floor and a matching floppy hat, dripping in gold jewelry. But instead No-No sported an Italian navy suit in virgin wool with four buttons and flap hip pockets. He wore his Afro short and kept his accessories simple—a Citizen Skyhawk with a titanium bracelet, a platinum wedding band, and a twill navy necktie with orange satin stripes. No pomade or picks in his hair, metal on his teeth, or ice in his ears. No-No looked just like the Wall Street investment banker he pretended to be.

No-No rose to his feet to give Jesus a handshake hug. "No-No!" Jesus sang as he slapped him on the back.

No-No pulled away and examined Esperanza. "Who's the lovely lady?"

"This is my woman, Esperanza. Honey, this is No-No Knowles, one of the rising stars of the game."

No-No barked a laugh. "I don't know about all that." Before Jesus could protest his modesty, he added, "Everyone, sit. I'm sure we all have other business besides this to attend to today, so . . ." He motioned to his right hand, who reached under the table for a suitcase.

"No doubt." Following No-No's lead, Jesus gestured to Chuck, who sat down and placed the duffel bag on the table. Jesus took the seat next to Chuck and across from No-No while Feli stood by the door between No-No's two other lieutenants. Esperanza also stayed on her feet, standing between Jesus and No-No, and by the way No-No stared at her body, she knew he did not mind having her so close.

No-No's main man popped open the suitcase to reveal bundles of cocaine stacked against the burgundy lining. Chuck reached into the duffel bag and pulled out a suitcase, too. He unlatched it to display stacks of fifty-dollar bills. According to Jesus's plan, the top stack consisted of ten thousand's worth of bona fide Ulysses. Beneath those bundles of cash, however, lay forty thousand more in counterfeit Grants. Esperanza stared at the ten rows of bills she knew to be real and wondered if any of it had been her cash in the first place. She folded her arms across her chest, pressing the Beretta against her left breast, the handle against the raised skin of her scar beneath her catsuit.

Chuck and No-No's right hand exchanged cases, then investigated their contents. No-No's man picked up a stack of bills and thumbed through it. Then he stopped to rub a random bill between his fingers. He removed the rubber band and started to count. Across from him Chuck tore a tiny hole in one of the bags of cocaine. He dipped a sharply manicured pinkie into the hole, then brought it to his tongue. Satisfied with its authenticity, Chuck pulled a plastic bag out of the duffel, resealed the cocaine bundle with it, dropped it into the duffel bag, and then proceeded to the next one in the suitcase. Meanwhile, Jesus and No-No maintained a stream of chitchat about business.

"Yo, man, I heard the Colombians are getting slicker every day," said Jesus. "The purity level is, like, at an all-time low. Something like seventy-eight percent and shit."

"More like seventy-five," said No-No.

"Damn, that low?" Jesus gave a low whistle. "Yo, we need to forget about their asses and start fucking with the Saudis or some muthafuckas like that. Hook ourselves up with a prince and shit." Jesus laughed. Esperanza snickered, too, reminded of the argument among Tenille's father and her uncles about political parties. Thirty years from now, were Jesus and No-No going to be sitting at Jesus's annual barbecue, complaining about how both the Colombians and Saudis took their loyalty for granted? *Well, I'll never fuckin' know,* she thought, smiling to herself.

No-No gave Jesus an admiring grin. "What you know about Arabian princes, son?" Esperanza guessed that from his investment banker days, No-No had quite a few as clients who sought his expertise in offshore corporations.

Jesus grinned back. "I'm just trying to play at your level, bro."

No-No dipped his hand into the suitcase of cash and grabbed a fistful of bundles. "Gonna need a lot more than this to do that."

"Believe me, I know, but I'ma patient nigga. I ain't trying to grab too much too soon and get caught out there. All in due time."

No-No nodded. Then he began to thumb through the cash in his hand. Esperanza peeked at the suitcase, and her eye caught a sliver of burgundy where the bundle he had just picked once lay. She panicked as she realized that No-No had not only taken a layer of authentic cash but also the stack of counterfeits that hid beneath it. Esperanza looked to Jesus to see if he had seen, too. He had.

"That's why I always liked you, Jesus," No-No said as he rifled through the money like a deck of playing cards. "Always wanted to do business with you, but I had to wait until you matured some." He put the stack of money down and reached into the inner pocket of his suit. "We're here now because I think you're ready to arrive." No-No pulled out a pen. When he uncapped it, Esperanza recognized that it was a counterfeit-detector pen like they used at Mickey D's. No way No-No intended to check every bill. But he only needed to find one phony. She had to intervene.

"And when Jesus arrives, I want him to dress just like you, No-No." Esperanza reached out and stroked his lapel. "But until then I have a little somethin'-somethin' stashed away. Where can I buy my man a fly suit like this?"

No-No put down the cash and pen, hooked his arm around Esperanza's waist, and pulled him to her. "Ain't you a sweetheart?"

Jesus forced a smile. "Yeah, I'ma lucky man."

"Damn right, you a lucky man. How many bitches out here think about saving their ends or using them to buy anything for their man, let alone a nice suit? I'll tell you. Besides this Butta Rican right here, there're the Chance triplets—Slim, Fat, and No." Everyone in the room roared except for Jesus and Esperanza, who put on matching plastic smiles. "Jesus, let me give you some advice. If you want to be on my level, you can't have your woman parading around in gear like this while you try to break fly. What does that tell any potential associates about you?"

Jesus's smile tightened across his face. "So I'm supposed to walk around with holes in ten-year-old kicks to keep her up in Prada and shit?"

No-No did not even hear him. He stood up and pressed Esperanza to him. "She's beyond beautiful, this girl. All exotic-lookin' with that gorgeous body. But you got her in these fuck-me heels and cheap makeup. Girl, how many times have you washed that jumpsuit? Thinking about buying gear for him when a nigga like me can shower gifts on you?" His hand slid from her waist to her ass.

Esperanza tried to push away from No-No, but he just clung tighter to her. "Yo, respect," she said.

No-No tipped his head toward Jesus, who remained seated and fuming. "He's getting what he wants."

"I'm not talking about him." Esperanza looked to Jesus for help. Maybe from where he sat he could not see where No-No had dropped his hand. Still it had to have bothered him that No-No had made himself at home uninvited in her personal space, if for no other reason than that Jesus felt her personal space was his property.

Intense jealousy coursed through Jesus's eyes, but he only turned to Chuck and said, "Finish with that already."

From where he stood by the door between No-No's guards, Feli said, "Yeah, check that shit so we can bounce."

"Don't worry about him, Butta Rican," said No-No. "Jesus don't mind if we flirt a little." He pushed up against her so hard his belt buckle cut into her stomach. "If he's trying to rise in this game, he's got to know that business is business, and bitches are bitches." No-No and his men laughed, and then he ground into her. "Jesus, let me borrow your girlfriend for an hour, and I'll throw in another kilo."

"Don't get it twisted," said Esperanza. "I'm not for sale."

"You heard the lady," Jesus said. "She ain't for sale." *That's it?* He reached for the counterfeit detector pen. "Yo, No-No, what kinda pen is this?" Obviously, he hoped his interest would deflect suspicion. Jesus probably would have No-No demonstrate the pen for him—on a bill he knew was genuine, of course. *You claim to love me, and all you can do is say she's not for sale.*

Ignoring Jesus's question, No-No laughed like a howling wolf. "All women are for sale. Even you, Butta Rican." Pulling Esperanza toward him, No-No turned to Jesus and said, "Your woman could use a little retraining. I'm serious . . . an hour with her for me, another kilo for you. The men get what they want, and we teach Ms. Thang a lesson."

She had had enough of waiting for Jesus to have her back. "I said back the fuck up off me." Esperanza shoved No-No away from her, taking him aback with her assertiveness. "I'm not going to tell you again, I'm not for sale. And keep your fuckin' hands to yourself. For real, I'm not playing."

No-No shot Jesus an incredulous look, and Jesus jumped to his feet, "Yo, Espe, what the fuck you think you doing?"

"What you obviously won't, *pendejo*!"

"Jesus, if you can't control your woman then I don't know if we should be in business together."

"No-No, please, I got this."

"You ain't got shit," said Esperanza, her heart pounding into her chest. No-No's deputy and Chuck both rushed through their respective tasks. They were almost out of there, but things already had gone too far. "None of you . . ."

Before she could finish, No-No backslapped her, sending Esperanza reeling across the card table and slamming her face on a stack of bills. Behind her she heard Chuck mutter, and one of No-No's men laughing. Then No-No said, "I'm going to handle this, Jesus, and I want you to just watch and learn." Esperanza felt No-No's thick palm grab the scruff of her neck.

As he pulled her up, Esperanza reached for the Beretta inside the lapel of her jacket. No-No hauled back to hit her again so she pulled the gun, and squeezed the trigger. The shot punched through his stomach. While she had the element of surprise still in her favor, Esperanza shoved his body against his right-hand man. Lucky for them all, the turn in events registered immediately with Chuck. Just as No-No's body flopped on top of his lieutenant, he reached into the duffel bag for a Magnum and pumped two rounds into the lieutenant's head, then dropped to the floor. Feli rushed Jesus, knocking him out of his chair and onto the sawdust-covered floor, out of the line of fire.

Esperanza spun around and fired at one of No-No's guards just as his bullet ricocheted past her shoulder. With only a second's realization that she had hit her target, she ran for cover behind the bar. Her heart pounded blood into her head as she leaped behind the bar, waiting to feel the burn of rocketing steel puncturing her back. She flattened along the wooden floor with a booming thud. Ignoring the pain that shot through her entire body, Esperanza rolled onto her butt, scampered backward into a corner, and trained her gun at the top of the bar over her head. Then she waited for the guard to come for her. But all she heard was the sound of splintering wood and groans of agony.

Esperanza slowly crawled along the floor to the bar. With the deliberateness of a cat stalking a mouse, she inched upward until she could peek. Feli had already crawled out from under the table and offered a hand to Jesus. When Jesus finally emerged, he held a Glock Esperanza had never seen. She walked around the bar, and the three of them stood in the center, spinning slowly in place to inspect the carnage.

Jesus snapped out of his astonishment to slap Feli on the back. "Good lookin' out." Then he walked over to where Chuck's body lay on the floor with two gaping red holes in his chest. "I got 'im for you, Chucky," he said as he glanced at the second bodyguard. He bent down and picked up Chuck's limp wrist. "I got that muthafucka for you." But when Jesus checked his best friend's pulse, his face twisted in anguish.

"Espe shot No-No, then took out one dude by the door," Feli said as he looked around the room and tried to reconstruct what happened. "And while I covered you, Chuck bucked No-No's man right there."

Jesus stood up. "I don't know what the fuck was going on while we were on the floor, 'cept I saw that muthafucka's gat in his waistband and took that shit. Then I came out from under the table to cap the dude Espe missed, 'cause he was after Chuck. But by that time I bucked him, he already got Chuck."

They stood there, taking in the drama that had just rained over them. Although the immediate madness had ended, Esperanza's heart continued to pound in her chest. She could feel their adrenaline fill the room and mingle in the air like wet smoke. The energy from Feli sank, heavy with residual fear, but with every second Jesus's rush grew into an excitement she knew no one would be able to predict or contain.

Jesus would never quit the game, and misery demanded company. And if he had to lie, manipulate and even abuse Esperanza to keep her by his side, he would. But they were not a team. Or a family. Or a community. So she had to separate herself from the men *and* the boys. With them—because of them—she had no land to free. But Esperanza did have her mind, her body and her soul. And she wanted them back. She had to dare to be powerful so she could stop being afraid. Esperanza lifted the Beretta and aimed it at his head, and when he turned to bark an order at her, he found the barrel pointed right at his neck.

"Espe, what the fuck . . . ?"

"How could you let him treat me like that? How could you let anyone treat me the way you do? As bad as you do, like it isn't enough."

Jesus made a step toward her. "Look, ma. . . ."

Esperanza cocked the Beretta. "Don't call me ma. And I'm not your boo. I'm not your bitch, your shorty, I'm not anything of yours, so don't call me shit. Just put the gun down on the floor."

"What's gotten into you? We gotta get the fuck outta here now. Take all the money and coke, anything of worth, anything they can trace, and be out now!"

"I'm not going anywhere with you. Now put the gun on the floor." Esperanza backed up a few paces so she could cover both Jesus and Feli. "Feli, take the money—just the real shit—and put it in the bag." Feli leaped to her command.

"You want the coke, too, ma?"

"No, just the cash."

"It's like that?" said Jesus as he watched Feli dump the cocaine from the duffel bag. "You and Feli . . ." Feli paused at the way Jesus said his name, but then continued to replace stacks of cocaine with bundles of cash.

"He almost took a bullet in the back so you wouldn't, so shut the fuck up and put the fuckin' gun down. I'm not gonna tell you again."

"You not gonna tell me again?" Jesus lifted his arm, pointed his gun at Feli, and shot him in the gut. Esperanza screamed but kept her gun on Jesus. Feli tumbled to the floor, dropping the duffel bag and spilling its contents across the floor. Jesus took a step toward her. "Say the word, ma, and I'll dead Xavier, too." Feli clutched his stomach and moaned as he rolled along the floor in agony. "Then we can head to California by ourselves and start fresh."

It occurred to Esperanza that Jesus did not believe she had it in her to shoot him. A clump of tears and mascara flicked into her eye, but she resisted the urge to rub her face against her sleeve. Instead Esperanza steadied her gun and fired at his feet. Jesus sprang into the air, and the Glock went crashing to the floor, firing off a round into the wall. Jesus threw his hands in the air.

"Bitch, you've gone crazy!"

"Back up some more. Against the wall." When Jesus made enough distance between himself and the bag, Esperanza rushed to the floor. With her gun on Jesus in one hand, she gathered the stacks of money and threw them into the duffel. She grabbed a stray brick of cocaine and flung it at Jesus. "Y'all can keep that shit," she said as Jesus ducked. "I don't want shit from you anymore, Jesus. I only want back all I gave you that you had no business taking."

"That's why you're taking the money."

"Figures you'd only think about the money. Yeah, I'm taking the shit, 'cause you owe it to me anyway. And I'm taking back my dignity. My peace of mind. And my independence."

"What's up with all this? What about California?" Esperanza ignored him, backing toward the front door, careful to not trip in her stilettos over the lifeless bodies on the floor.

"How you're gonna leave me now after all we've been through together? After all that struggle." Jesus took a step toward her. "Now that the struggle's almost over."

Esperanza refused to say anything more to him. She let her feet do the talking as she continued to back up toward the door, the gun pointed at Jesus and her hand quivering with rage. She made it through the threshold of the door to the back room.

She sidestepped across the main floor, one eye on the back room, the other on the front door. The stillness behind her made her nervous.

"Espe, look out!"

Although Feli called her name, Esperanza did not need his warning. *If Jesus loves me, he'll let me go. But he doesn't love me. He's not going to let me go.* She finally understood that Jesus loved no one—not even himself. Esperanza did not have to see him to know that Jesus had the Glock in his hand and was coming for her.

So she waited until Jesus appeared in the threshold of the back room door, his hands concealed by the frame. He weaved as if drunk with the shock that Esperanza would turn on him. "Dammit, Esperanza, I love you."

But finally Esperanza had learned that love and abuse could not coexist. Jesus could not love Esperanza the way she wanted to be loved, and that meant one day or another, he would disappear. But he only believed there were only two ways out of the game, and she refused to disappear with him. She loved herself, or at least she was learning to, and so she had no reason—Esperanza did not deserve—to disappear.

Jesus crossed the threshold, and the Glock came in plain view. "I said I love you." But all she saw in his piercing green eyes was hatred. "And I know you love me."

So much that you'll shoot me in the back if I try to leave now, right? "You don't love me, Jesus," said Esperanza, and it surprised her how much it hurt to say that aloud. "You never have. It's okay though 'cause I don't love you either." Just as Jesus aimed the Glock toward her head, Esperanza raised the Beretta and fired.

TWENTY-THREE

Keep Ya Head Up

With as much composure as she could muster, Esperanza walked out of the bar. Priscilla flirted across the street with No-No's men. Catching sight of Esperanza approaching, they began to whistle and leer. "Hey, you didn't tell us you had a friend."

Esperanza shot them a smile over her shoulder. "Sorry, I got a man." *And his name is Beretta.* No-No's men hollered their disappointment, and Esperanza grabbed Priscilla and leaned into her ear. "We got to get to the car now, but play it cool, OK?"

Priscilla smiled at her admirers and waved good-bye. Pulling Priscilla behind her like a reluctant toddler, Esperanza double-timed to the Escalade. From behind the wheel of the car, Xavier spotted them. He revved the engine and pulled the Escalade toward them. She had not forgotten about Xavier, but had not yet determined what to do about him. She had to lose him and tear the hell out of there, all without arousing the suspicion of No-No's men and before the edge surprise had given her expired. "Prissy, take this and get in the backseat," she said as she handed her the duffel bag.

Xavier stopped, and Priscilla jogged around the front to the passenger side. He rolled down the window, and the stench of buddha wafted into Esperanza's face. "What's up?"

Esperanza said, "Slide over."

"What?"

"Slide!"

Xavier did as she told him but continued to run his mouth as she took over the driver's seat. "What the fuck is going on?" Esperanza reached for the gearshift and Xavier clamped his hand over hers. "Nah, we ain't going nowhere without Jesus and 'em. Where the fuck they at?"

"Get off me, Xavier."

"Where's Jesus and 'em?"

"Now that the exchange has been made, Jesus wants us to get the fuck out of sight. He'll meet us near the bridge."

"How's he gonna get there?"

"No-No's gonna drive him; I don't fuckin' know." Esperanza managed to wrench her hand from beneath his grip. She started the SUV. "Stop asking so many questions and do what you're fuckin' told for a change."

"I don't answer to you, chickenhead. We ain't leavin' with out Jesus and 'em." Xavier grabbed for the keys in the ignition, and Esperanza slapped away his hand. He decked her in the head, and Esperanza swung back, catching him in the jaw. "Bitch!" Before he could lunge for her, she sprang on him. For herself, for her sister, for every woman he had ever abused, Esperanza pounded on him.

When Xavier latched onto Esperanza's hair, Priscilla jumped in. "Get the fuck off of her, you bastard!" She dug her salon nails deep into his face. Xavier yelled and lashed out wildly, socking Priscilla in the mouth and sending her reeling to the floor of the backseat. Xavier reached behind his back for his own gat.

Esperanza yanked the Beretta out of her jacket and pumped a single shot into his chest. Xavier's torso crashed against the passenger door. "You wanna know where Jesus and 'em are at?" She cocked the gun, and Priscilla shrieked from the SUV floor. "That's where Jesus and 'em are at." Esperanza glanced in front of her and caught No-No's driver eyeing them through his side mirror while his partner looked over his shoulder through the back windshield. Blood started to bubble past Xavier's lips as he clutched his chest. Esperanza unlocked the passenger door and reached past him to unlatch it. The door swung open against the weight of Xavier's body. As his upper body dangled out of the passenger seat, Esperanza gathered his legs and pushed.

"Oh, my God!" Priscilla had climbed back onto the seat and looked out the front window. She pointed and yelled, "They shot Feli!" He had stumbled out of the bar with his bloody hands pressed against his stomach. No-No's men saw him and rushed out of the Lexus with their guns drawn.

Esperanza gave one final heave, and Xavier's body landed on the asphalt with a thud. She closed the door, then jammed her foot on the gas, and the

Escalade ricocheted down the street. No-No's men planted themselves in her path. "Priscilla, get back down!" Screaming, Priscilla dove to the floor of the SUV as Esperanza shielded her face behind the steering wheel. Seconds later three bullets tore through the windshield. Esperanza popped her head up in time to swerve the Escalade away from a row of parked cars. She peeked through the rearview mirror as she sped down the street. In it she saw No-No's driver roll off the parked car had he had flung himself over to get out of her way. Having recovered more quickly, his partner took a stance in the middle of the street with his gun aimed at the Escalade. She ducked as he squeezed off three shots that ripped into the body of the car. The last thing Esperanza saw before she careened around the corner was Feli collapsing to the ground from the loss of blood.

"We gotta get Feli," yelled Priscilla.

"We can't. We can't go back." The image of Feli staring into the barrel of a gun tore into Esperanza's gut as if she, too, had been shot in the stomach. If she had had any way to help him, she would not have thought twice, but Esperanza had no choice. "They'll kill us if we go back."

As Esperanza raced toward the Williamsburg Bridge, Priscilla lay on the floor, behind her, crying hysterically. "Everything's gonna be OK, Prissy. *Mamita,* calm down. We're going to be all right now." She dropped the gun on the passenger seat to better command the SUV.

"What are you going to do to me?"

"I'm not going to hurt you." Esperanza found the entrance to the bridge and zoomed into the fast lane. "And I promise you, Prissy, this ain't *Set It Off.* The sistas are not going out like that this time." With no more ideas on how to calm Priscilla down, Esperanza leaned forward and snapped on the radio, and Tupac appeared with all the right words. Tears streamed down Esperanza's face as she laughed at the irony. She joined Pac in his rhyme, but this time instead of imitating his delivery, she rapped in her own voice. *Why we rape our women? Do we hate our women?* Esperanza became so lost in Pac's rhythm, she had not noticed that Priscilla had nabbed the gun from the passenger seat until too late. Aiming the Beretta at Esperanza's head, Priscilla climbed to the front and settled into the passenger seat. "Take me over there," she said, motioning toward the right lane." Esperanza did as Priscilla directed but continued to rhyme. When they arrived at the right lane, Esperanza expected Priscilla to ask her to pull over as soon as they reached the edge of the bridge. Accepting that her fate had slipped out of her hands, Esperanza sang with the chorus.

Priscilla listened to Esperanza sing. Then she lowered the window and flung the Beretta out of the car and into the East River. She looked at Esperanza and sang with her. *Ooh, child, things are gonna get easier.*

Esperanza parked the Escalade in front of Dulce's supermarket. As she opened the door to get out of the SUV, she caught her reflection in the side-view mirror. Mascara had run down her face. She closed the door and asked Priscilla, "Do you have a tissue in your pocketbook?" Priscilla reached for her bag, looked through it, then shook her head. After maintaining her cool throughout their escape from Brooklyn, Esperanza felt something inside her unhinge. "I can't see Dulce like this. She'll know right away, and if someone sees me it'll bring heat on her. I can't go in like this." Esperanza looked into the rearview mirror and rubbed her cuff over her eyes, which only smeared more makeup across her face. "I can't. I can't. I can't let my sister see me like this. Oh, my God, I can't go in there like this."

Just when Esperanza thought she would fold, Priscilla said, "I'll go in for you."

Devastated, Esperanza realized there was no other way. She reached behind her for the duffel bag and shoved all the stacks of money but one into Priscilla's purse. "You take half of that, and you give the rest to my sister." Then Esperanza grabbed her messenger bag. When she opened it to shove in the cash she had taken for herself, she found Maite's book. She took it out and put it in Priscilla's pocketbook, too. "Promise me you'll read that and then pass it on to someone else. Someone you know who needs it and who'll read it."

Priscilla looked confused but said determinedly, "OK."

"And you tell Dulce that Espe said thank-you for everything and that no one in the world loves her more than me. And tell her that she shouldn't worry about me, 'cause I'm gonna be just fine now, because I really have changed, even though it may seem like I went from bad to worse. That I did change, just too little, too late, but even that's not true, 'cause if it were, I'd be dead in the street or alive in prison, but I'm not, so . . ." Esperanza stopped to relieve the sob in her throat.

Priscilla reached over and wiped the tears off her cheeks. "I got you, Espe. What else? What else you want me to tell Dulce?"

But there was too much to say in no time. Esperanza took in a deep breath and thought about how to say it all in just a few words. "Just tell Dulce Esperanza said, 'Picture me rollin.'" Priscilla then threw her arms around Esperanza, and the two friends hugged tightly. Esperanza waited as Priscilla bounded out of the Escalade and crossed the street into the supermarket. She kicked the car into drive and headed home. She would abandon the Escalade, throw her bare necessities into the duffel bag, and then grab a cab to the airport.

Epilogue

Esperanza closed *This Bridge Called My Back* and rubbed her belly as if she had just finished a satisfying meal. She took a sip of lemonade from her thermos and then placed the book in the cardboard box beside her. As always, a visiting student she had befriended from one of the travel brigades would take the package back to the States and then mail it to Bedford Hills for her. But first she wanted to add a letter to Isoke.

As if he read her mind, Luisito came running over to her, waving an envelope. "*¡Esperanza! Una carta vino para ti.*" He handed her an envelope. "*¿Cuándo vamos a comer bizcocho?*" Luisito asked.

"Check you out! You'd think it was your birthday," she said. "*Ahorita*, OK. *Dáme un besito.*" The little boy leaned down and kissed her on the cheek. Then he ran back up the beach toward the house. Esperanza watched him, loving him every step of the way as if he were her own.

She looked at the envelope, and her heart skipped with joy. After all these months, Dulce had gotten another letter to her from California to Cuba. Esperanza tore open the envelope and found a card commemorating her twenty-fifth birthday, along with photographs of Dulce and Chago's wedding. She smiled and put the card and photos aside to read the letter Dulce had included.

Dear Espe,

As you'll see from the pictures, the wedding was small but beautiful. Perfect in every way, except that you and Mami could not be there. I couldn't stop crying, and everyone thought it was wedding jitters or tears of joy, but Chago really knew. He promises that we'll find a way to Havana for our honeymoon, even if we have to defy this stupid blockade to do it.

Priscilla visited me before I moved to say good-bye. She's huge (and happy!). She said Feli turned state's evidence, so they're going to give him a reduced sentence. He told them that you and Priscilla were there against your will, and that everything you did was in self-defense. Jesus's lawyer pressured the police, and they harassed Priscilla for a long while, but she corroborated Feli's story and stuck with it.

You're not going to believe what I'm going to write next, but eventually Jesus fired his lawyer and backed up everything Feli and Priscilla said! For the longest time he refused to cop a plea, then he had this change of heart. He even told the police that you spared him. He said that if you had wanted him dead, he would be. I was shocked to hear that. We know Jesus is not the kind of guy to admit that a woman got the best of him.

And you know what? I truly don't believe Jesus buys that Priscilla's baby is Feli's. Chago's theory is that when he lost his ability to walk, he regained his ability to see right from wrong. I say that he needs to believe you spared him because you love him. Guess anything is possible.

Puente says he doesn't think all this makes it safe for you to come home yet, though. There are still other charges and unanswered questions. But we cross our fingers and pray real hard. And like I said, I will find a way to come to you soon.

Anyway, Priscilla's thinking about moving to Puerto Rico once the baby's born. Did I tell you? It's a girl, and she wants to name her Maite. She read the book you gave her and found out that the name Maite means love. And Prissy says she doesn't care where in the world you are, that as far as she's concerned you're little Maite's godmother. By the way, Priscilla gave me Maite's book, which I sent to Bedford Hills. I thought you would like me to do that.

I have to get back to this paper I'm writing. Just wanted to let you know what was going on here, and that I love you so much and miss you really bad.

Love always,
Dulce

P.S. Congratulations are in order! Your GED test scores came in the mail, and you are now a high school graduate. I'm so proud of you.

Esperanza folded the letter and tucked it into her notebook. She reflected on all the news she wanted to share with Isoke before she started her letter. Surely Isoke would laugh when she read that Esperanza would not tell her how she made it to Cuba, remembering how Esperanza had complained about that very thing when she read Assata's biography. Isoke would be happy to know that she had found a new family in the Posadas, who worked at a hotel and discovered her on the beach. They took her in and treated her like a daughter, as well as helped her find her job as a teacher's aide. How this summer she was going to help organize a hip-hop concert in Havana and hoped to make new friends in the States who would send her more books and CDs.

Brushing her dark curls out of her eyes, Esperanza gazed at the rolling water with a bittersweet sense of freedom. The breeze tickled her freshly scrubbed skin, and she took off her blouse so the sun could kiss her scar. Only on days like this did she even wear such a thing, preferring to walk the hot Havana streets in her sarongs, tank tops, and *chancletas*, and feeling beautiful.

A man wading in the ocean caught her eye. His bald head gleamed in the sunlight as he splashed water over his ebony torso. Then he turned to face the beach, and Esperanza saw his tattoos. She rose to her feet.

Tupac?

The Black man in the water noticed her and waved. Then he motioned for her to join him. Esperanza took a few steps toward the water. Then she stopped, shook her head, and blew him a kiss. He responded with a boyish laugh and then dove under the water. Esperanza walked back to her blanket and began her letter to Isoke.

READERS GUIDE

Picture Me Rollin'

BLACK ARTEMIS

READERS GUIDE

A CONVERSATION WITH BLACK ARTEMIS

❖

Q. What inspired you to write Picture Me Rollin'*?*

A. Picture Me Rollin' began as a screenplay for a short film. I had seen so many—maybe too many!—films about convicted felons who upon release from prison return home to negotiate the same conditions that lead them down the criminal path and wanted to take a fresh approach to this genre. What if the felon were a woman? What if she were Latina? But I also wanted to do more than just change the race and gender of the protagonist. I hoped to explore other themes that are important to young women of the hip-hop generation, especially young women of color who are growing up poor in urban environments and facing the same obstacles as their male counterparts with the additional challenge of being female. I also had been reading all of bell hooks' books about love and wanted to write a story about a young women's quest for self-love. And being a conflicted fan of Tupac Shakur who still finds his lasting impact and political contradictions, I wanted to make sense of that for myself. What does it mean to be a woman who loves hip-hop when often times it increasingly seems like hip-hop has nothing but hate for me? Trying to weave many ambitious ideas into one story, *Picture Me Rollin'* became too large for a short film, and I decided that as novel I could explore and combine them much more effectively. Then through the course of writing the novel, other themes and objectives arose as well.

Q. What do you hope the impact of Picture Me Rollin' *will be?*

A. So many things! I couldn't possibly list them all, but let's say I can have five consequences as a result of this novel. They would be: (1) many young women in abusive relationships and/or the criminal lifestyle becoming inspired to find the self-love, courage and support to leave; (2) less tension and greater appreciation between the hip-hop generation and the Civil Rights generation; (3) a meaningful debate among hip-hop fans on the notion that one can be "revolutionary but gangsta"; (4) more people across ages, race and gender discovering the works of feminists like Audre Lorde and bell hooks; (5) a critical reexamination of our criminal justice system and the huge discrepancies between its stated objectives and the way it actually operates.

Q. So in what ways has writing this book changed you?

A. Writing *Picture Me Rollin'* has changed me in profound ways. It was such a challenge to write on so many levels. I found myself raising questions on issues on which I had yet to formulate my own opinion. It was in the process of writing this book that I grappled with my own views and feelings about some things. There was a point where I had lost compassion for people engaged in street life, because I felt that in hip-hop circles our social and political understanding of what crime is and why people participate in it gradually turned into excuses for self-destructive behavior. Then it went as far as saying that selling drugs or pimping women was some kind of political act of resistance! I became so outraged by this that I eventually adopted a "we vs. them" stance, sounding just like other pundits who slam hip hop unilaterally when their "understanding" of it is one of selective ignorance. Through the process of writing *Picture Me Rollin',* I rediscovered my compassion especially when I had to write male characters like Jesus, Xavier and even Officer Puente. In fact, I learned that I can maintain compassion for others who make choices I would not even as I stay true to my own values and beliefs. *Picture Me Rollin'* is about—among other things—transcending one's contradictions.

Q. You invent a book—Maite's monograph The Revolutionary Spirit: An Owner's Manual for the Warrior Womyn—*in the novel. Why did you do that?*

A. I continue to draw inspiration from the writings of women of color activists involved of the movements of the sixties and seventies. The majority of these women, however, were African American or Chicana. Even though Puerto Rican women were vital to these movements, very few of them have documented their experience or have had their work achieve the classic status of women such Audre Lorde, June Jordan, Cherrie Moraga or Gloria Anzaldua. The character Maite is my tribute to these Puerto Rican women—some of whom I know and have the honor to call mentor.

Q. Given the significance of Tupac Shakur and his work in the story, how come there are only snippets of his lyrics in the book?

A. That's such great a question because it's an opportunity to educate folks about both the publishing and music industry, especially from the unique perspective of hip-hop! The law only allows you to reprint a few lines of someone else's copywritten work without permission. I attempted to get permission to use more of Tupac's lyrics, but the prevalence of sampling in rap music makes the process of acquiring those permissions costs a great deal of time and money. As the writer who wanted to use the material, it was my responsibility to get the permissions. I just think I waited too long to start that process given how many people's permission I had to seek. I'd like to think that if I had started this much earlier—had clarified my vision for which songs I wanted to use sooner—I would have received most of the permissions I sought. My hope is that readers of the novel will seek out the entire lyrics of the songs referenced to gain a better understanding of their relevance to the story. Maybe even play these songs as they read the scenes to accompany the movie in their minds! Especially for chapters 17 and 22.

Q. Do you believe Tupac Shakur is still alive in Cuba?

A. Tupac's body rests in peace, but his spirit lives and continues to evolve through people like Esperanza and me.

QUESTIONS FOR DISCUSSION

1. Some members of previous generations have a disdain for hip-hop culture and harbor some resentments toward the generation that grew up under its influence. Others appreciate and even participate in hip-hop culture. How does the novel use hip-hop to draw links between the two generations? How does it give voice to each position? What are your thoughts on the relationship between the Civil Rights/Black Power and Hip-Hop generations?

2. How would you describe Esperanza's role in her crew? What happens to her when she does not fulfill that role? How does her experience compare to your observations about other young women you may have encountered like her?

3. What are the contradictory messages that Esperanza receives through Tupac's music? What contradictions, if any, do you observe?

4. At first Esperanza resists *Sister Outsider* because the vocabulary of Audre Lorde frustrates her, but later not only does she understand her, she is moved by her experience. What are other examples in the book where Esperanza goes from resisting to understanding?

5. Were you aware of women like Audre Lorde and Fannie Lou Hamer, etc. before you read *Picture Me Rollin'*? If so, how did you learn about them? Why do we readily know who are Malcolm X and Martin Luther King yet cannot name female leaders for civil rights with similar ease?

6. What did you think of the various relationships between the women in the story? What things caused them to compete with one another? What things encouraged them to support one another? How did they relate to each other across differences such as age, education or race?

7. How did the relationships among the men differ from the relationships among the women? To what do you contribute this difference?

8. What meaning did you find in the poetry Maite wrote as a young woman during the sixties? How is the content of her poetry similar or different from that of the rap music you have heard?

9. In what ways does Esperanza seek to be loved by others? What does love look like to her? How does her concept of love change throughout the novel? What contributes to this changing perception? Has witnessing Esperanza's journey changed or reinforced how you define love?

10. How does Jesus wield power over the women in his life especially Esperanza? What tactics does he use and how do they work? From where does he get his power?

11. Did learning about the abuse and abandonment experienced by Jesus and Xavier make you feel more or less compassionate toward them you might have for characters like Esperanza, Dulce or Tenille? Why or why not? How did you feel about the fate of each of the men in Jesus's crew?